QUEEN
of FLOWERS
and PEARLS

Global African Voices

DOMINIC THOMAS, EDITOR

Indiana University Press
BLOOMINGTON & INDIANAPOLIS

QUEEN
of FLOWERS
and PEARLS

a novel

GABRIELLA GHERMANDI

Translated by Giovanna Bellesia-Contuzzi
and Victoria Offredi Poletto

This book is a publication of

INDIANA UNIVERSITY PRESS
Office of Scholarly Publishing
Herman B Wells Library 350, 1320 East 10th Street
Bloomington, Indiana 47405 USA

iupress.indiana.edu

This book was originally published in Italy by Donzelli Editore under the title
Regina di fiori e di perle
©2007 Donzelli Editore

Manufactured in the United States of America

Library of Congress Cataloging-in-Publication Data

Ghermandi, Gabriella, [date]-
[Regina di fiori e perle. English]
Queen of flowers and pearls : a novel / Gabriella Ghermandi;
translated by Giovanna Bellesia-Contuzzi and Victoria Offredi Poletto.
pages cm — (Global African voices)
Includes bibliographical references.
ISBN 978-0-253-01546-4 (cloth : alk. paper) — ISBN 978-0-253-01547-1 (pbk. : alk.
paper) — ISBN 978-0-253-01548-8 (ebook) 1. Ethiopia—History—1889–1974—Fiction.
2. Italy—Colonies—Africa—History—Fiction. 3. Italians—Ethiopia—History—
20th century—Fiction. I. Bellesia, Giovanna, translator. II. Poletto,
Victoria Offredi, translator. III. Title.
PQ4907.H48R4413 2015
853'.92—dc23
2014044313

1 2 3 4 5 20 19 18 17 16 15

I gather flowers and pearls.
Flowers of all kinds: large, small, invisible, anonymous.
Flowers brightly colored like the imperious sun,
and others, with subdued colors, like a spring breeze.
Fragrant flowers and flowers whose secret scent
tells stories to the soul.
I gather pearls and flowers.
Pearls of all kinds: shiny, perfect, imperfect, white, pink, and black.
Hidden pearls and visible pearls.
I gather flowers and pearls from the enchanted garden of my land.

CONTENTS

TRANSLATORS' NOTE

IN *QUEEN OF FLOWERS AND PEARLS* THE ITALIAN-ETHIOPIAN author, Gabriella Ghermandi, has presented us, the translators, with a dual challenge: we are translating from Italian into English, but often the culture behind the words—at times even the phrasing—is purely Amharic. As Cristina Lombardi-Diop says in the afterword to the Italian edition, Ghermandi has invented "a new Italian, a language based on the oral culture of Ethiopia." We have endeavored to transmit the flavor of this duality.

Throughout we have retained the Amharic honorifics (*Abba, Woizero, Ras,* etc.) and also the Italian ones (*Signor* and *Signora*) to give the reader a clearer sense of place. Wherever possible, we have paraphrased the words in Amharic that appear in both the Italian and the English versions, to avoid interruption of the storyline. Others are defined in footnotes and in the list below. Still others are self-explanatory and create a delightful leitmotif to the story, such as *"Woine!,"* a recurrent Amharic expression of dismay. In a few instances where the Amharic is loosely rendered into Italian, we have chosen to rephrase the meaning, rather than try to find a specific equivalent expression in English that the readers might find both jarring and distracting.

Finally, Gabriella Ghermandi's original intent in writing this captivating story was to educate Italians about their own colonial history, largely ignored and rewritten to hide the brutality of the occupation. We hope that this translation will help a much larger audience understand the far-reaching consequences, both past and present, of the Italian colonization of the Horn of Africa.

—*Giovanna Bellesia-Contuzzi and Victoria Offredi Poletto*
SMITH COLLEGE, NORTHAMPTON, MASSACHUSETTS

NOTE ON AMHARIC PRONUNCIATION

THE FOLLOWING IS A LIST OF THE MAIN RECURRING sounds, transcribed from Amharic, of proper and common nouns found in this book. The spelling of certain place names has been changed to reflect the accepted English spelling.

Ch as in _ch_ild
Ci as in _ki_n
Gh as in _g_in
Gi as in _gi_ggle
Ge as in _gue_st
J as in _j_am
Sh as in _sh_e
Ts as in _Ts_etse Fly
W as in l_oo_p

Proper nouns are often preceded by forms of address. These are the main ones, each followed by an explanation:

Abba = father, in a respectful way, reserved for older men; _Ato_ = mister, in an informal way; _Etie_ = madam, in an informal way; _Immebet_ = madam, in a very polite way; _Gash_ = mister, in a respectful way; _Woizero_ = madam, in a respectful way; _Atse_ = honorary term used for past emperors.

The Ethiopian calendar follows the Julian calendar and has thirteen months. Twelve months have thirty days and one month five. This calendar is eight years behind ours. The year begins with the first day of Meskerem, approximately September 11 or 12, and it continues with the months of Tikmt, Hedar, Tahsas, Tir, Yekatit, Megabit, Meyazeya, Genbot, Senay, Hamlay, Nahasey, and Pagume, the month that only has five days.

AMHARIC WORDS
AND EXPRESSIONS

aja A cereal similar to barley.

amba A flat-topped mountain.

arbegna Ethiopian Resistance fighter(s).

areke Distilled corn liquor.

Ascari Indigenous soldiers from Eritrea and Ethiopia who were part of the Royal Corps of Colonial Troops of the Italian Army during the period 1889–1941.

azmari Storyteller and poet, the equivalent of the East African *griot*.

banda Scouts.

berbere Mixture of spices and hot chili peppers that is the base of most Ethiopian dishes.

Danakil An ethnic group in the Horn of Africa, also known as the Afar.

dirkosh Pieces of dried *injera*.

doro wot Spicy sauce with chicken.

fir fir Traditional dry bread, broken into pieces, used to soak up sauces.

fukera Traditional war chants.

gabi A piece of cloth similar to the *shemma*, but a little heavier.

gebi Palace.

genfo Porridge made from different flours, served with a hole in the middle for melted butter, spices, hot pepper, and yogurt.

getoch Master, boss.

gibir Feast.

Habesha Term Ethiopians sometimes use to define themselves.

injera Traditional bread, made from *teff* flour.

kallicha Fortune tellers or people able to communicate with spirits.

karia A hot green chili pepper.

kebele Neighborhood committee.

kolo A common Ethiopian snack. Crunchy roasted barley grains, peppered with chickpeas, dusted in a light salty seasoning.

korkoralleo A peddler.

masinko A traditional single-string violin.

Meskel The feast of the Holy Cross, one of the principal religious celebrations in the Ethiopian Orthodox Church.

Meskerem Approximately September 11 or 12. The beginning of the year in Ethiopia.

mezmur Church hymns or songs.

mitmitta A very spicy small chili pepper.

nech White.

negarit A kind of bass drum.

netela Thin, white cotton shawl, spun and woven by hand with a brightly colored border, used only by women.

qene Ethiopian style of speech, in which one says one thing while implying a different meaning at the same time and in the same sentence.

quanta Spiced dried meat.

Ras Noble feudal chief of a region and the head of a regional army, subordinate to the Emperor.

sefer Neighborhood.

Selam "Peace be with you." Used as a greeting.

shemma Thick, white cotton cloth, spun and woven by hand, used for wrapping around the body, especially by men.

shiro Sauce made from chickpea flour and spices.

sigawot A spicy beef stew.

sistrum An Ethiopian metal musical instrument.

sollato From the Italian "soldato" (soldier).

Tabot Wooden or marble tablets, forty-four in all; replicas of the Tablets of the Law as given to Moses; each one dedicated to a saint, to an Archangel, or to Our Lady, and used in the practices of the Ethiopian Orthodox Church.

talian From the Italian "italiano" (Italian).

teff Whole-grain flour made from an ancient cereal grass.

tej Fermented Ethiopian mead or honey wine.

tella Fermented barley beer.

tibs Meat sautéed with onions and hot green chili peppers.

Timket The Ethiopian Orthodox celebration of Epiphany. It is celebrated on January 19 (or January 20 in a leap year).

tri A communal dish.

tukul A hut.

woi gud! My goodness!

woine! Amharic exclamation of dismay.

wst arbegna An Ethiopian infiltrator in the Italian colonial system who worked as a messenger and go-between to supply weapons and food to the Resistance.

Zapatie Native squads of policemen on horseback.

QUEEN
of FLOWERS
and PEARLS

Part One

THE PROMISE

CHAPTER ONE

W HEN I WAS A LITTLE GIRL, I WAS CONSTANTLY BEING
told by the three venerable elders of our household, "You are
the one who is going to tell our stories."

Round the coffee pot warming on the brazier sat the women. The
elders, slightly off in a corner, wrapped up in their white *shemma* and
looking distinctly like protective birds, blessed the coffee for the
women and took note of everything around them.

"She's very curious," whispered old Selemon with an air of satisfaction. The others agreed, slowly nodding their heads. They were
well aware of that irresistible bait that hooked my soul whenever
the adults used to tell stories and anecdotes about other people, and
especially when they spoke about the secrets of Ato Mulugheta. But
that is another story that I'll tell you some other time.

"So curious that she becomes patient!" whispered old Yohanes.
The other two continued to agree, slowly nodding their heads.

I was quite capable of waiting a long time for the beginning of
some tale born by chance on the lips of a woman, while she was putting down her empty cup after her first coffee.

"So curious that she becomes patient—and wily. Look at her!"
whispered old Yacob, and the three pairs of eyes converged on me.

Children were not allowed to listen to the conversations of grown-
ups and curiosity was considered bad manners, but I managed to
listen without their noticing me. I would sit in a corner and play
while the women chatted. I was able to split myself in two: on one
side my body was busily absorbed in play that, to the casual observer,
gave the impression that I was totally uninterested in what was going

on. On the other side, my mind was paying attention to every single word, every blink of an eye that came from the women.

I was able to blend in like a chameleon. Nobody had ever noticed anything, to the point that when one of the women had some spicy gossip to report to the others, she would glance at me and, just to be sure, said, "What about the little girl?"

My mother would answer, "Don't worry, when she is absorbed in her games she is totally unaware of the world around her—a war could break out and she wouldn't notice anything. Come on, sit down and tell us!" No one noticed the flash of amusement in the complicit glance of the three elders.

"So curious she becomes patient and wily," whispered old Yacob.

He was my favorite and every now and then he would stretch out his arm to scratch my head. I would look up and he would smile, his mouth wide open, with that solitary upper tooth dangling like a white rag hanging out of an open window.

I would return his smile. He would then bend down and, like a bird trying to peck at something, bring his face close to mine and whisper, "Hold on tight to that curiosity of yours and collect all the stories you can. One day you'll be the voice that will tell our stories. You will cross the same sea that Peter and Paul crossed, and you will take our stories to the land of the Italians. You will be the voice of our history that doesn't want to be forgotten."

Then I grew up and forgot all about the words and the glances of our three elders. I even forgot about the day that old Yacob had suddenly opened the kitchen door facing the rear courtyard and had gone outside. The cats, huddled on the landing, waiting for leftovers, had scuttled off in every direction, and he had smiled, satisfied with that trick that always worked; then he had stretched out his arm through the door and with his hand had gestured for me to follow him. Abba Yacob had gone down the stairs and, slipping along the wall of the house, had taken me to the other courtyard. The one by the main entrance with the garden full of flowers that was my mother's pride and joy. Passing under the arch of the purple bougainvillea that climbed up the wall to the second floor, up to my brothers' room, he had opened the door to his room and had invited me in.

It was the first time this had ever happened. We children were not allowed to cross the threshold of the rooms of the three elders. They were considered sacred. That was why they lived on the first floor, in single rooms of their own, in an area separated from the rest of the house.

I felt honored by the invitation and, stiffening my body into an almost military pose, I tried to assume the demeanor I deemed suitable for the occasion.

Old Yacob smiled. "Don't stand there all stiff," he said to me. "Watch out, I know you! You have my permission to take a look around!" Everything was flat inside of me; no feelings, no desire to look around came from my curious soul. Only that acute sense of the honor bestowed upon me that kept me frozen like a statue.

"So . . . show me what you can do."

In order to please him, but still not moving a muscle, I strained my eyes in every direction to observe as much as possible.

He laughed with that solitary tooth of his. "*Woi gud anchi lij*! My God, what a phenomenal child! You don't have to satisfy your curiosity just with your eyes—you have my permission to touch everything."

Intimidated by such extreme indulgence, I lowered my head.

"Come, sit on the bed. Here, next to me," he coaxed.

I joined him and sat down by his side.

The skirt of my dress rustled against the bed blankets. "I like your dress," he said. "Skirts are becoming to women. They make them even more beautiful. Remember that when you grow up." I kept my eyes lowered, fixed on my hands that I was wringing while waiting to get over my embarrassment.

"So?" he taunted me roguishly, "don't you want to give in to your curiosity?"

But what curiosity? In that moment it was as if it didn't exist. It was out of reach, buried deep in my soul to escape the spotlight of his attention trained on me.

With an enormous effort, just to please him, I began to explore, moving my head in every direction.

There wasn't much in the room. On the stone floor rested the feet of a bed frame with a mattress, and next to the bed frame were some empty shelves. In a corner there was a small table with some icons on it, including one of the Virgin Mary that stood out, making the others invisible; the stub of a candle, and then spiders. Spiders and cobwebs in every hole and in every corner of the room. Finally, at the foot of the bed frame, there was a trunk covered in green paint, peeling in some spots, and fastened with two huge brass-colored padlocks.

My mind lit up.

Who knew what could be in there! Perhaps the secrets of old Yacob's life. I didn't know much about him. While drinking coffee together, the women had never said anything about him. And how could they? The three elders were always present, and as often happens, people didn't talk about those who were present. Only a few times, in the evening, at home, when the three elders had retired to their rooms downstairs, I had heard a few comments. My mother and my Uncle Mesfin said that the three elders, especially old Yacob, had been valiant warriors, great *arbegna,* but, so my father said, old Yacob had only fought for two years, and then he had been forced to return because of the birth of Rosa, my mother's second cousin. My father's observation was like the signal from a conductor to his orchestra. Immediately, one of my uncles began to tell the story of my favorite elder. Unfortunately, after the first few comments, my mother said that it was getting late for us children and sent me to bed on "empty ears."

With my imagination captured by the trunk, my mind had started to spin, moving from one fantasy to the next. In the background I could hear the *fukera,* the war songs, coloring my imagination. Heroic deeds by the three elders paraded through my mind as if I were watching an Indian movie, like the ones they showed at the cinema in Debre Zeit. Those corny movies with heroes galore.

"Have you finished your reconnaissance?" asked old Yacob, bring-ing me back to reality. Biting my lip, I turned my head toward the trunk.

"Woi gud anchi lij!" he said with an air of satisfaction.

He put his hands under his shemma, rummaged in his pants pock-ets, pulled out a set of keys, and handed them to me. As if they were on fire, I instinctively hid my hands behind my back, and I began to shake my head in a sign of denial.

I wasn't going to take them.

Old Yacob got up, went toward the trunk, and opened it. "Come on, come over here," he said. I got off the bed, went up close to him, and sat on my heels, just like him. "If you want to know what's inside you'll have to stick your hands in."

"In your trunk?"

"Certainly!" he answered. I looked at him incredulously.

Something unbelievable was happening. An adult, an elder in fact, was encouraging me to openly break one of the most important rules my mother and father had taught me: don't put your nose in grown-ups' business, each person to his own place.

"Come on," he continued, "put your little girl's hands in the trunk and show me where your curiosity takes you."

I glanced at the trunk, tickled by my inner curiosity that wanted to know what was in there. I resisted the impulse.

Perhaps it was a trick. If I gave in to my inner temptation someone would punish me: if not old Yacob, then certainly God, who was looking at me along with the saints from the icons on the table. He would punish me through the spiders. I had already been bitten on my foot by one of those little beasts. It hadn't been pleasant. My mother had to take me to the herbalist because it had swollen up and I wasn't able to walk.

"So? What's going on, you're not interested in my trunk?" teased old Yacob.

I was interested, and how! I perused the trunk and then locked eyes with him. "There aren't any spiders in the trunk, are there?"

He understood. "I swear by the Virgin Mary on my altar that nothing and no one will punish you, neither I, nor the spiders, not even God. This will remain a secret between us. Come on, show me what you can find."

I took a deep breath and focused on that inner itch that was beginning to fan into blazing flames of curiosity. Following their cue, I stretched out my arm and stuck a hand into the open trunk.

My fingers touched the soft fabric of a shemma. I ran my hand over the wavy folds, then slipped my hand into the next layer and explored every inch of it.

There was nothing there.

I moved on to the next layer.

Again, waves of soft cotton woven by the Dorze people from Chencha, and nothing else.

I sifted through all the layers of the first shemma, then of the second, and finally of the third. There was nothing there.

I pulled my hand out of the trunk, undecided whether to continue or not, and I turned toward old Yacob. "Go on! Go on!" he said.

I took a breath.

"Go on! Keep looking!" he repeated.

Once again I stretched out my arm and put my hand in the trunk under the third shemma. I found a coarser fabric, cotton used for shirts. I fingered collars, pockets, buttons, the thin thread of the stitching, the patching, and nothing else. I pushed my hand further in and found some pants, two with belts, others without, and again side pockets, back pockets closed with a button, stitching, mending . . . and under the pants in a corner a small rectangular cardboard box. I opened it and pulled out the contents. It was a box of candles. One was missing, probably the stump that was on the altar.

That was it for the contents of the trunk.

"Abba Yacob, your trunk is empty."

"Empty? But it's full of clothes and shemma!"

"All the same, it's still empty."

"What do you mean?" His eyes were shining.

"I mean that in your locked trunk there is nothing but your clothes!"

"And what did you expect to find in there?"

With a whisper, as if someone else could hear and scold me, I went up close to him and said, "Stories . . ."

"What kind of stories?"

I was so flustered that the words couldn't come out of my mouth.

"Go on, try harder and explain to me what kind of stories you expected to find in my trunk."

"Stories that . . ."

"That?"

"That talked about you. About your secrets," I said all at once.

"But perhaps I have no secrets."

"That's not true! All adults have secrets! And I know that you must have some as well!" I said, thinking of those fleeting comments I had heard every now and then, at night.

"Woi gud anchi lij! Here's what we'll do: I'll tell you one little secret. My trunk holds something that you haven't been able to find yet."

His words sounded like a challenge. Without saying anything I turned toward the trunk and stuck my hand back in. I went through it carefully, inch by inch: shemma, shirts, and pants. Back and forth, over and under.

There didn't seem to be anything there.

I started all over again; if something was there I was going to find it. The third time, I heard a crinkly sound coming from one of the shirt pockets. I undid the button, put my hand in, and deep down, rolled up, I found an envelope.

I felt triumphant. I pulled it out and, laughing, I waved it under old Yacob's nose.

"Woi gud anchi lij!" He was satisfied. "Come, let's sit on the bed; I'll show you what's inside."

Old Yacob took the envelope, opened it, and pulled out a small yellowish sheet of paper with ragged edges. He shook it and the little sheet unrolled, filling the air with dust that tickled our noses, making both of us sneeze. Stretching forward, I craned my neck to get a peek at the contents. It was full of stamps and writings, not in Amharic.

"It's written in Italian," old Yacob told me, and he flattened it out with his hands and laid it down on my dress. The stamps and the writings danced before my eyes. I lifted the sheet and sniffed it. I sneezed again. I turned it over in my hands. "What is it?" I asked.

"It's called a Submission Paper: when our country was occupied by the Italians you always had to have it with you. You had to show it to the Italian soldiers whenever they asked you for it. If you did not have it you could even be killed. We used to go around carrying a very long cane with the paper stuck through the point so that the soldiers could see it." While he was speaking he jumped off the bed to act out the scene. He stretched his arm out in front of him with the sheet between his fingers. "We used to hold it this way! You see, like this," he said, "and when they passed by we used to do this . . ." He lowered his head and started speaking in that strange language that sounded funny.

I burst into laughter and he continued to hop up and down on those little bird legs that stuck out of his shemma, speaking that strange language. I kept on laughing and he looked at me with satisfaction.

After a while he sat back down and laid the form back on my dress. "I did not get this form right away—at first I was a rebel, an arbegna, I fought against them, you know?"

"I know, sometimes at night, when you are asleep, Mama and Papa talk about you . . ."

"They do? That's why earlier you were so sure I was harboring secrets." I remained silent and he went on, almost chuckling. "And what do they say?"

"Mama says that you were a valiant warrior and Papa says you only fought for two years, and then you returned. Because Rosa was born."

"Your mother is right, and so is your father, but I had no other choice," he said, talking more to himself than to me. "And then, what else do they say?"

"I don't know—when they start telling your story, a little after that, Mama sends me to bed!"

"If you want to hear it, I'll tell you."

I wanted to hear it, and how! I nodded.

"But it is a long story—are you sure you want to hear it?"

I certainly did. I nodded again.

"Okay, I'll tell you, but you must listen very carefully because one day you will have to tell it."

"Me?" I asked surprisedly, opening my eyes wide.

He chuckled, making his bony shoulders shake. "Woi gud anchi lij! Yes, you!"

"But Mama and Papa do not want me to tell things about grown-ups." I lowered my gaze. "Actually, they don't even want me to listen to the adults' conversations."

He laughed again, shaking his bird-like shoulders. "Don't worry, the story I am going to tell you today will remain a secret between us, and as far as telling it is concerned, you won't have to do that now. Later, when you are a grown-up."

"So, if that's how it is, then it's all right," I said, continuing to lower my eyes. "When I am grown up no one will be able to scold me because I talk about adults' business!"

He laughed again, and this time I laughed a little too.

"Now, my dear child, make yourself comfortable. Do you want to lean against the wall? I'll give you my pillow. Take it!" I took the pillow, propped it against the wall, and slid back to lean against it. I fixed my dress and turned my head toward old Yacob.

"Are you ready?" he asked me. I nodded.

"So, dear child, open up your heart. This all happened a long time ago. I was only twenty years old. We had lost the war against the Italians and I, like many others, had joined the Resistance. We had been hiding for some time in a place called Mengesha. A forest with huge, ancient trees, over four hundred years old. It was almost a magic forest that protected us. The trees had been planted by our great Zeri Yacob. The rays of sunshine played among their emerald green leaves, and on their branches sat little groups of *gurezas,* the great black-and-white flying monkeys. It was a safe hideout. We had been taken there by our leader Haile Teklai, after our hideout near the source of the Awash River had been discovered. He had grown up on land near the forest and as a child he used to play there. He knew every hole, every secret of the forest. There were many of us—men, women, even children, sons and daughters of the rebels, some donkeys, some mules, and a herd of sheep. In the forest there was a rock face with two caves. That's where we slept. They were like houses; we had put everything we needed in there and at night they sheltered us from the cold mountain wind."

While old Yacob was speaking, I began to feel a bit restless. I tried to ignore this feeling, but it had already spread to the muscles of my legs, which began to twitch. Old Yacob interrupted his story. "What's the matter, child? Are you uncomfortable?"

"No, Abba. It's my legs that don't want to stay still," I said.

"Then try to rest your feet on the floor—perhaps that will relax your legs." I slid forward on the bed. I rested my feet on the floor; I fixed my dress and motioned to old Yacob to go on.

"As I told you, we had created real homes in the caves where at night we found shelter from the cold mountain wind, even though we men spent many nights away from the hideout, because it was when darkness fell that we attacked the Italian soldiers. They didn't know how to orient themselves at night, like guests who cannot move around in the dark in a house they don't know. So we proceeded, and as quick as leopards we attacked them and then ran back to the forest."

I became increasingly uncomfortable.

There was something in the way old Yacob was telling his story that I didn't like and that made the story totally uninteresting. My whole body was twitching in discomfort. To calm myself down I began to let my eyes roam round the room. He became aware of it and immediately stopped recounting his story. "What's the matter, child?" he asked me.

"Nothing," I answered, a little embarrassed.

"Perhaps you don't like my story?" As if bitten by an ant, I jumped to my feet. "So? You don't like my story?" he asked again. I did not answer. "Come on child. Speak up!"

"It's not because of the story."

"So? What's wrong, child?"

I didn't know how to tell him. "Abba . . ."

"Tell me!"

"It's just that . . ."

"Come on, speak up!" he urged me.

"I no longer listen to Abbaba Igirsa Salo's stories on television," I said.

"What does that have to do with it?" he asked me. It certainly had a lot to do with it, but if he hadn't asked me that precise question I would never have told him. I was embarrassed enough as it was. He understood. "Okay, tell me, why do you no longer listen to Abbaba Igirsa Salo's stories on television?"

"Because he tells them using words for children."

"What do you mean?" he asked. I did not answer. "Come on, child, be brave, you can tell me what you think without feeling worried. I promise it will remain a secret between us."

I stared at him to figure out if he really meant it. His eyes were clear. Filled with sweetness. A sweetness that was directed at me. I could trust him. "When the women gather to drink coffee I listen to the stories they tell each other, grown-ups to grown-ups," I said in a low voice, my eyes staring at the floor.

He began to laugh heartily. "Woi gud anchi lij! You do?" I nodded my head vigorously. "And what if you don't understand?" he asked me.

"I understand everything; I've grown accustomed to the way they talk." I stared at him and in a whisper I confessed, "Sometimes Mama Eleny suspects that I am not really playing—she is the only one who sometimes has doubts—and she begins to tell the story of Ato Mulugheta using difficult words, but I understand everything all the same."

Old Yacob laughed one more time. "You really surprise me. All right, may your wish be granted! Make yourself comfortable, I'll tell you the story of the Submission Paper. One grown-up to another." I sat on the bed with my feet resting on the floor, my elbows on my legs, and my face cupped in my fists. "Are you ready?" he asked. I nodded.

Yacob's Story

I was about twenty years old. We had lost the war against the Italians and I, like many others, had joined the Resistance. After fighting in the North we had retreated. Ras Imiru's army, under orders from the emperor, had headed for Gore, to try and form a government far from the capital but still on Ethiopian soil. I, along with others, had decided not to follow them. Instead, we had headed for Holeta and joined the Resistance that was already on the move.

For about ten months we had been hiding in the Menagesha Forest, that ancient forest of trees planted by Zera Yacob hundreds of years before. We had been living there ever since we had abandoned our previous hideout near the source of the Awash River. After a series of attacks on the railroad, the Italians had put the area to the sword and had forced us to flee. The place had been chosen by our leader, Haile Teklai. That was where he was from. He had spent his childhood in that part of the forest and he knew every hole, every nook, every cranny. It was a secure hiding place that would save us from constantly having to move from one place to another. From the paved road up to the great olive tree the path was invisible to those who did not know about it. It consisted of rocky crags and patches of grass. Without the help of local spies the *talian sollato,* their *banda,* and the *Zapatie* would not be able to find us, unless they stumbled upon us by mistake.

That day we were awaiting the arrival of a messenger from Ras Abebe Aregay, the great, revered leader of the Showa Resistance. You must remember this name: Ras Abebe Aregay. It is the name of a man so great that merely uttering it causes the celestial forces to tremble.

Usually the messengers arrived between the final hours of the night and the early hours of the morning, when the sun had not yet warmed the air.

One of our young men was on the lookout in a field at the edge of the trees. Disguised as a shepherd, surrounded by our little flock of sheep, he was keeping a constant watch over the valley beneath us, known as the Hollow of the Virgin Mary. A valley encircled by two treeless mountain ridges which descended sharply, leaving barely enough room for the path that passed between them. Dawn had just broken, the sun was beginning its ascent into the clear sky, melting away the night mist, but a thick fog still enveloped the valley, concealing from our eyes the path that crossed it, as it wound its way up to where we were located. Only one point was visible, but barely. A slight elevation in the terrain, right in the middle of the valley, broke through the fog, parting it on either side. The path passed along that elevated terrain, and the eyes of the lookout were constantly fixed on that spot. Our safety was in his hands. From that elevation it only took a few minutes to reach us, just enough time for us to prepare for any eventuality.

Suddenly the lookout alerted us with a first whistle. Some shadows were passing along the spot he was observing, a group of people. Perhaps it was the messenger with some followers. Maybe they were Italian soldiers who were looking for us, or maybe they were simply people passing through.

We prepared ourselves. Each man took up his position, while the women stayed back, spreading out toward the caves. Two whistles pierced the air. It was not the messenger. Haile Teklai, our leader, signaled to us. We had to be ready to shoot. A shout from the lookout stopped us: "Stop! These are women!"

Deadened by the dense fog, snatches of voices reached us from below: "We are looking for Yacob Haile Mariam Shifferaw!" It was my younger sister, Amarech. A chorus of voices shouted, "We are his sisters!" Barely able to distinguish each voice I counted them: Helen,

Seble, Selam, Dagma. Four plus one. They were all my sisters. I was stunned. What were they doing here?

Haile Teklai nudged me with the butt of his rifle. "So? What are you doing? Why don't you run toward them?"

I went down the hill. They welcomed me with smiles. "Good," I thought. "They haven't come to bring me bad news."

We greeted each other. *Endemin adderachihu*? . . .[1]

I embraced and kissed each one of them and only later did I realize that they had traveled with two mules, one loaded with supplies and the other with a saddle. Without asking any questions I led the way up to my fellow rebels. We would have a chance to talk later.

I left them with some of our women, who took them to the cave area so that they could freshen up and rest. We were not used to these kinds of visits. Their arrival had livened things up. Our women began to talk about what foods they might cook, which quickly turned into a heated argument, and at some point Alemtsehay, Emebet, and Meron decided to put an end to it. There was not much to discuss and not much time to waste. It was the right day to kill a couple of our rams.

And that is what we did. Some men butchered the rams and the women cut up the meat and prepared the *tibs* for everyone. The sound of knives chopping, of pots and voices, went on for several hours, and then a woman summoned all the men. The food was ready.

I went to call my sisters. Amarech was sleeping in the large cave, on my pallet. I stopped to gaze at her for a few moments. Her face reflected a world of enchantment. With eyelids closed and a peaceful expression, she still had that look of an angelic little girl which she had always exploited to get into all kinds of mischief.

I wondered why they had come. I roused her gently; she awoke out of her dreams. She smiled at me, her eyes still half closed. "The food is ready," I said. She got up without saying a word and followed me into the thicket where our women had already placed the pots in the middle of small groups. We ate.

To liven up the meal for our guests, Aron, our *azmari*, took out his *masinko* and started to tune it. As soon as he moved to take hold of

---

1. "How did you spend the night?" (a common greeting in Amharic upon waking in the morning).

the masinko the air began to vibrate, like the body of a young bride in front of her groom. Music, along with Aron's songs and improvised verses, made for one of our few happy moments. Aron waited for the air to be filled with expectation and when the tension matched that of the stretched skin of a drum, he began to recite his verses, accompanying himself with the music.

They were verses in my honor:

> *Afer tekelelachew iellum behiwot*
> *af keftew motu Yacobn siaiut*
> Dust envelops them, they are no longer alive,
> they have died with their mouths wide open at the sight
> of the great Yacob

The shrill sound of the single-string violin opened up the dance to the words. Every verse referred to an event of which I was the protagonist. Worku, Nuguse, and Haile Teklai recounted the details of these events. Aron would begin, and then they elaborated on them. Stories and more stories about me. About my heroic acts to be preserved for future memory, and everyday facts, those silly facts that bring laughter to the lips of the listeners.

Anecdotes about those long months with the Resistance followed one another like unraveling rolls of yarn. Looking at my sisters I thought that it was nice to have someone to tell these stories to. Someone who was not part of our everyday life. Someone whom we had left behind in our past, in the world of before, when the war against the Italians had not yet begun. To me, they seemed like a ray of light brightening our objective. After more than two years spent fighting and organizing the Resistance, our objective had receded in the face of the emergencies created by our day-to-day existence shaped by weapons and blood. Just by being there, they restored color and vigor to our objective, bringing it back to the forefront: we were fighting for a dream, in order to return to our families, and to taste the normality of sharing food and talk around the domestic hearth, in a country that was both free and ours. As it had always been.

In front of me, Alemtsehay, busy fanning the coals under the coffee pots, smiled at me. She seemed to perceive my thoughts. Her eyes were shining with encouragement: "Soon, very soon, that is the way it will be," they said. Those big eyes of Alemtsehay, serene as a mountain lake. There existed a special bond between us. We had been together during the battles in the North. She was following her father, one of the leaders of Ras Imiru's army. And fleeing south, we had traveled together to Holeta to join her brother Haile Teklai. And she had become the coordinator of our women, of our warrior women who shared everything with us. Even death.

When I was still a child, my father often said to me, "Women are the solid pillars on which humanity rests." For us they were like the wooden structures of our cottages called *gojjo,* and among them, Alemtsehay was the great central pillar that gave stability to the house and on which rested the roof. She was the one in charge of organizing the supply of ammunitions, along with Meron and Emebet, her seconds-in-command.

Alemtsehay had managed to befriend Ato Kebede, a farmer who sold his produce at the Saturday market in Holeta. A man known as someone who kept to himself, who had never wanted to get involved in the government business between us and the Italians. He had always said he was only interested in his own work, the selling of the fruits of his land, but Alemtsehay had managed to make him cross the boundaries of neutrality, to come over to our side. His help was invaluable and had been won thanks to her. Earlier when he wasn't yet on our side, our ammunition supply had been irregular, characterized by messages, counter-messages, waits, interceptions, ambushes of the Italian garrisons, and flights from hideouts. Often it had come at the cost of someone's life, especially of the women, who went to pick it up disguised as beggars, dressed in ragged, stinking clothes. After Ato Kebede joined the Resistance, the supply of arms had become more regular. The messengers from Ras Abebe Aregay left the ammunition at his stall, especially the bullets and hand grenades, and Alemtsehay and the other women picked it up and took it to the hideout, inside sacks of agave, among onions, potatoes, and carrots. No one had ever suspected anything since Ato Kebede's neutrality had always been very evident to everybody. Even to the *Ascari* and to their Italian commanders who had tried in vain to befriend him. Even after the events of Yekatit 12, those violent events that soaked our land with blood, causing it to moan and scream, those events that made our Resistance more united and focused all over the country, Ato Kebede's little stall continued to be our point of reference. One of Alemtsehay's cousins, Mesfin, had infiltrated, signing up to be an Ascari in the fort at Holeta, and had managed to get close to an Italian who worked in the telegraph office. He came from southern Italy and didn't consider himself very Italian—he recounted how the Italians had colonized his people as well, and said that he was willing to sell information about the movements of the Italian battalions, and about the movements of the small consignments of weapons that we could attack. The exchange of information for money took place at Ato Kebede's little stall. Ato Kebede took the money from Ras Abebe Aregay's messengers and gave it to the Italian in exchange for the information that he then passed on to Alemtsehay.

After the meal I went off with my sisters to a small clearing among the trees, a few yards from the place where we had eaten. The time had come to talk amongst ourselves, to find out why they had undertaken such a long journey.

We sat in a circle on tree stumps and rocks. Next to me was my older sister Helen, while furthest away, almost opposite me, sat Amarech, and spread out were Seble, Selam, and Dagma.

We had all grown up together. We had slept in the same beds, and yet that day they looked at me as if I were a stranger. A swirling vortex of looks passed between them. The air was filling with complicit giggles but they didn't utter a word. I seized the opportunity to feast my eyes on their presence. I hadn't seen them for over two

years. In spite of the trip they appeared fresh and rested, and that
game of complicity lent a special luminosity to their faces. They were
beautiful in their white dresses with embroidered borders. They reminded me of flowers offering themselves up, all aquiver, stretching
toward the sun of life. I observed Amarech, my little one. In reality
she wasn't much younger than me, we were only two years apart, but
"my little one" was what I had always called her. We had grown up
sharing the same bed. I knew every variation of the fragrance of her
body. The perfume of her dreams, the smell of her sweat, the drops
that collected on her forehead when she feared being scolded, the
dew that dampened her body after her long runs, her skin after bath-
ing. That mix of soap and wild flowers. Wild like her.

My beautiful Amarech. She was a terror. She had an incredibly
strong character.

When we were children in our shared bed, we slept with one head
facing the top, the other facing the bottom. Since I was the older
one, I got to choose first. After all, the bed was really mine. Had
she never been born, I would not have had to share it with anybody.
Neither of us liked sleeping with our head at the bottom of the bed,
but since it was I who decided, Amarech was forced to sleep in that
position which, as she complained with a whine, made her feel all
crooked, with no part of her body in the right place. But that terrible
child, exploiting the fact that I slept very heavily, was able to turn me
around during the night. In the morning, I would find her sleeping
with a triumphant expression on her face, her head exactly where
she wanted it to be.

Time was passing by and I thought I needed to start talking about
something. I understood that I could not go straight to the heart
of the matter so I ventured onto neutral ground: "I'm curious to
know how you found me!" There was no indication that their gig-
gling was going to stop. The words that reached my ears were jagged

like mountaintops, eroded by their warbling, a mixture of sounds, white teeth, and exchanged looks.

"You know how it is," said Helen. "News finds its own way. Every so often some of Ras Abebe Aregay's fellow combatants come to visit us. We found out from them where and how to reach you. They advised us to go as far as Addis by asking for a ride with a convoy; once there, we were to hire mules and continue on for Holeta, spend the night at the house of the local priest, and with his help find a peasant for the following morning who could accompany us for the first part of the path. As far as a giant olive tree whose spreading branches gave shade to a large field. After that we could continue on our own. They even advised us to tell whoever asked us that we were going to Melkam Petros, beyond the valley called the Hollow of the Virgin Mary, to visit a family. Relatives. Peasants who work the land belonging to Commander Zerihun Yetimgheta. But no one ever asked us anything."

"Well done, well done! And at home?"

"Everything's fine. Mother sends you her blessing," said Helen, without dwelling on the subject. We had reached the end of the neutral ground and I didn't know how to go on.

I looked at Amarech. A few rebellious braids of hair peeped out from under the *netela* which covered her head. I would have liked to go over to her, hug her and tease her a little, but something in the air forced me to restrain myself.

And yet, what in the world could it be? There was no indication of bad news; on the contrary, the feeling was festive. I tried to find another subject for conversation: "I noticed that you came with two mules, one loaded with provisions, the other with a saddle. How come? Who traveled on the mule?" My words had unexpectedly hit the right spot and suddenly there was silence. "Goodness," I thought. "Bullseye!"

Our roles were now reversed. This time, it was my turn to have some fun. I felt as if I were a boy again, almost an adolescent, taking part in those shared skirmishes of long ago in which they, the girls, had a secret and I, the only male in the family, tried to crack open the shell in which they were hiding it. I wanted to play with them like old times.

"Have I come too close to the reason for your visit?" I asked.

Amarech could not contain herself; her face brightened, and the others sent her furious looks. "Ah, girls!" I said. "You're making the game too easy. Is she the one who has the news that you have come to give me?"

The air became as tense as a masinko string, like the skin of the imperial *negarit* announcing war. A feeling of irritation upset my nerves. "Come on, why all this game of hide and seek? I understand that Amarech rode up on the mule, and that this is tied to the reason for your visit. Now, are you going to tell me what it is or not?"

The eyes of Sebele and Selam rested on my little Amarech's abdomen. "What?" I said, half in astonishment, half in joy.

"Your Amarech is expecting a child," confirmed Helen.

"I'm going to be an uncle! I'm going to be an uncle to my little Amarech!" I rejoiced, close to tears. "And who is the father? Do I know him? And will you get married? When? Have you come to tell me of the wedding?" The string of questions coming out of my mouth rendered the air more still, almost motionless. Cautious. My voice dropped until it died before their silent faces. What was wrong? One by one they had lowered their eyes, except for Amarech. She kept her head erect, her eyes challenging mine. "Yacob, I love the father of this child. He is an Italian soldier."

At those words, there was an explosion inside of me. Like the bombs on a battlefield, but louder. Everything was happening inside instead of outside. A blinding white light was gradually becoming stained with red foam. Evil-smelling, spewing rage, a mad rage. I could taste it in my mouth. It made me spring to my feet with a sole desire which could not be restrained: I wanted to kill my sister with my own hands. I began to yell. "An Italian? An Italian?"

She in turn began to scream: "*Woine! Woine! Woine!*" Haile Teklai and four of my companions ran over to restrain me.

"An Italian! She's pregnant by a filthy Italian soldier. Possibly someone in the air force, one of those who sprayed gas on us, who killed our father." I was shouting, trying to escape from their grasp. Meanwhile all the other fighters had come closer, putting themselves between her and me.

Now that she was safe, protected by a line of men, Amarech shouted, jumping up so that her voice could reach me better: "He's a simple soldier. He was recruited and he has never shot anyone. During the war, he fired his gun in the air. He was even wounded. Yacob, he's a good person." I could have stripped her flesh from her body with my bare teeth. "Good person! The Italians become good people only after they have surrendered their souls to God and He has cleansed them."

We spent that first night apart. They slept in the large cave and I outside further off, on a pallet that Alemtsehay prepared for me. Haile Teklai, Aron the azmari, Nuguse, and Worku were to sleep with me. Together, they were to watch over me to protect Amarech from my rage.

Before lying down to sleep, Haile Teklai went to see her and they spoke for a long time. Then he came over to where we were going to sleep. He sat next to me and allowed silence to fill the space between us. He gave himself time to assess whether I would be open to listening to him. After a few moments it was I who started the conversation. "So? Why are you gazing at the fire in that way? If you want to speak to me, do so!"

"Yacob, she says he's a good person. I believe her. Surely not all the Italians are devils. At least some of them must be worthy of admiration, respect. . . . Let me remind you that much of the work we are doing is thanks to that Italian soldier who works with Mesfin."

"And let me remind you of one thing, actually two things. First, he expects to get paid, and second, he doesn't feel Italian."

"Maybe it's the same thing with this one. What do you know? Listen, Yacob, try to trust your sister." He stood up, moved over a few feet to where his pallet was, and lay down.

The next day, my sisters made sure to keep out of my sight and I asked Haile Teklai if I could be the lookout for that day, with the herd of sheep. I would spend the morning in the clearing at the edge of the forest, keeping my eyes fixed on the Hollow of the Virgin Mary. When the morning mist had lifted toward the sky, Mama Worknesh appeared out of the field behind me. The oldest of our women and the mother of one of our fighters, she was carrying a wooden bowl containing some *fir fir* of *quanta*. "Eat up, son! An empty stomach doesn't help your thinking," she said, sitting down next to me.

"Mother, there's nothing I have to think about."

"Son, don't say that—listen to the words of an old mother. Eat up." So as not to offend her, I thrust my fingers into the bowl and ate a few mouthfuls. "Good! Son, do you want me to sort out your dreams from last night?"

"Mother, my night did not speak to me. I did not have any dreams last night."

"That must be why my night spoke for you. I had a dream last night and you were in it! Would you like me to tell you about it?"

"As you wish, mother!" I said, totally unconvinced.

"It was nighttime. You were immersed in that darkness typical of moonless nights. You were climbing up a hill. In the sky there was only one star. While you were climbing, the pale light of dawn began to appear. By the time you reached the top, day was already breaking."

"Mother, I do not think that day is about to break within me."

"Hmm! So you want to let rage dry out your heart, do you? But your heart isn't that weak. You'll see you will find the way. Your rage against your sister won't last beyond tomorrow. If your dreams haven't spoken, mine told me this: that the time of your darkness will soon come to an end." She spent the rest of the time sitting next to me in silence. When I put the half-empty bowl down on the ground, she took it, stood up, and left.

How could Mama Worknesh say that day would soon break within me? That the darkness of these events could be dissipated?

My gaze stretched out toward the mountain ridges that encircled the Hollow of the Virgin Mary. Ridges devoid of all the thickness of forest trees. Only half-dried grass, aloe plants with their red flowers, and the occasional thorny bush. It was just like the vegetation of another place. Of the high plains in the Tigray region, of the northern plateaus. Never more than on that day had they seemed so similar to me. And the ridges, they could be those same mountainous ones surrounding the small valleys that climbed and then descended to the Tekeze River. Valleys, clearings, ravines, rocks, forests, and crevices. Everything around me could have been another place in another time. My mind was whirling like a merry-go-round and was dragging me backward. It wanted to drag me to that place, and I didn't want to go. I didn't want to see it again, but my mind won. Suddenly I found myself there, on that first day. The first battle. The Tekeze River.

From behind a spur the gun barrel of a tank had appeared. My feet were nailed to the ground in surprise. Still as a rock. I couldn't imagine what that thing was. Behind the gun the rest of the tank had appeared. Then the gun had fired a single shot. A flash that had ploughed through the air and had landed with a loud bang, sending dirt flying in every direction. After the flash had died down, there was a hole in the ground. An uncontrollable sense of fear took possession of me and forced me to flee. Yes! I had fled, filled with terror. We had all fled, a disorderly scramble up the rocks, looking for shelter: the fighters with Shiferraw, leader of the advance party, those with Tesemma, I and the small group of men that my father had assigned to me. Those white men and their devils. They certainly spewed forth countless infernal inventions. While we were running off shouting, "*Ere! Seitan, Seitan,* the devil, the devil!" Tesemma, the leader, climbed up onto the tank, blew his horn to call us back, and began to shout: "What are you, women? Look at me, I am not afraid. They the devil, we God!" And with the handle of his round sword he began to bang on the lid of the turret: "Open up! Open up!" he kept yelling. And the Italian soldiers had opened up. I don't know whether they had opened out of surprise at such an unexpected action or in order to shoot him from the opening. Brandishing his sword, as fast as a diving hawk, he had sliced the air and the heads of the Italians inside the tank. One head had bounced out like a ball and had spun around in the air before ending up on the ground. Tesemma had raised his sword dripping with blood. "See, they die, like everyone else!" he said. We had turned in his direction again, a screaming horde, ready to fight. From the Italian fort up on the pass other tanks had descended, eight of them, and a platoon on horseback. Tesemma had sounded the attack on his horn. I, along with my father's men, had attacked and had surrounded a tank that had gotten stuck on an incline. One of the belted wheels was off the ground. The tank was revving its engine without moving forward. The three soldiers had opened the turret from inside. My father's men had killed them, one after the other. We had annihilated all their iron monsters and had surrounded the fort. The Italian soldiers had fled; Tesemma had shouted, "Don't let those dogs escape!" We had chased them in order not to let a single one escape.

On that first day, singing about our victory and enshrouded in a cloud of dust, we had caught up with the rest of our army that had stayed to the left of the Tekeze. They had greeted us shouting with joy. We were convinced this was only the beginning of our long triumph against the enemy who had come to take our land from us.

I had found my father in the middle of the rejoicing, he had praised me, we had won, and the men he had assigned to me were all alive. That night he honored me with a *gibir,* with all his men. His only son's first battle.

That evening, while we were celebrating our victory, we had no idea that the diabolical inventions of the *talian sollato* were not limited to planes and tanks. Never would I have imagined that less than fifteen days later I would see all our leaders disoriented, sitting on the ground among the dead, and Ras Imiru shaking his head and lamenting, "This is not a war among men. They are cowards."

In the early afternoon Nuguse came to relieve me. He shook me out of my thoughts. I had slowly slipped down on the grass, and I was stretched out with my eyes closed. The sheep had wandered off, and Nuguse did not hide his irritation: "And now, who is going to bring them back?"

I looked at him as if dazed. I was coming from another place, another time. "What?" I asked him.

"The sheep!" he repeated. "Come on, help me." But looking at my eyes he thought better of it. "Don't worry," he said, "I'll do it myself." The sheep had gathered together almost at the edge of one of the mountain ridges. He went to rescue them, on his hands and knees the whole way. It took him over an hour and when he came back he sat down next to me. "What were you doing before with your eyes closed?" he asked me.

"Nothing, I felt sleepy!" I replied.

"Don't lie to me! You never get sleepy when you are the lookout!" I began to angrily twist some blades of grass. "Yacob, you were thinking about the North, right?" he asked me in a scolding tone.

"Right, I was thinking about the North!" I raised my head, my gaze stretching to the horizon.

"Why? Why do you want to torment yourself?" he asked me.

"This is the first time I've thought about it this way."

"What way?"

"As if everything were happening here, now. There were the same plants near the Dembeguina Pass, in the small clearings among the rocks, aloe plants with red flowers. Perhaps because it was the month of Tahsas, just like it is here now."

"Yacob, don't let your mind take over. You must resist it if you want to continue fighting."

"All right, I'll stop now," I reassured him. He wanted me to stay with him, but I wanted to be by myself. I let him take over and, without going by the camp, I headed off among the trees. I went to the springs to bathe, in the hope that the cold water would release me from my dark thoughts.

When darkness fell, I went back, but I didn't go near the caves. I settled down again where Alemtsehay had prepared my pallet the night before. She arrived, just like the night before, she laid out the five pallets, and waited until Haile Teklai joined us. They nodded to each other. To avoid any kind of conversation, I lay down, and Alemtsehay, going off, blessed my sleep: "May the God of Ethiopia watch over your night, shed light on your darkness, and bring you peace!" After a few hours of sleep I woke up screaming. I had had a bad dream. About the bombing, the poisonous gas, the hissing of the bombs falling onto the ground, exploding and releasing that cloud that burnt inside the lungs. Our men were screaming, tearing at the skin of their throats with their fingernails. Ras Imiru yelled amid the rumbling of the planes: "To the hills, run to the hills!"

I was gasping for air; Haile Teklai, Worku, and Nuguse ran over to me. "Yacob! Yacob what's wrong?"

"The poisonous gas, the gas!" I kept repeating.

"Calm down. There is no gas now. We are here, in the Menagesha forest. Calm down." Haile Teklai tried to soothe me.

Aron ran over to the large cave and had returned with Alemtsehay and Mama Worknesh. I was agitated, still immersed in my hallucinations caused by the nightmare. Aron, Mama Worknesh, and Alemtsehay came closer, and I started to wave my arms violently. "Get away, get away, I need air."

"Yacob, there is no gas," Haile Teklai kept repeating.

Alemtsehay put her hand on my shoulder. She was the only one among them that I would allow to touch me. "Yacob, look at me, it's me! It was a dream, only a bad dream." I felt better, and I managed to shake off my nightmare. Mama Worknesh said that with the arrival of my sisters, the spirits of those who had died in war had made their presence felt. They had knocked on my soul and it had let them in. She gave me some herbs to chew.

"I don't want them."

"Son, you must take them. They will help free you from the spirits. They come from the *kallicha* of Addis Alem, they are healing herbs mixed with fresh grass burnt by a bolt of lightning." Alemtsehay, Aron, Nuguse, Worku, and Haile Teklai fixed their eyes on me as if they were snipers and I their target. I had no choice, I took a handful and put it in my mouth. I chewed slowly while they were watching me. I forced myself to swallow only after the two women left and Aron, Haile Teklai, Nuguse, and Worku lay down. I fell asleep and I dreamed I was throwing up something black. I awoke and I vomited my dream. Then I felt better. I fell asleep again and in the morning I woke up empty. I remained lying still, listening to my inner peace. I hadn't felt this way for a long time. With a steady soul, without that frantic galloping that never left me time to rein in my thoughts. Without that uncontrollable headlong rush of those who cannot stop.

I turned my head and I saw Alemtsehay making her way through the trees. She was smiling at me with her usual calm. I smiled too. When she reached me she sat down on one of the pallets. Her mere presence lessened my pain. She could read my heart, and I hers. Our fathers had died together, in the North, two days before Timket, killed by the gas. They had died in our arms, first one, then the other. We had not had time to mourn them. When my father died, Abba Yousef, the priest who was with us, had torn his body from my hands: "My son," he had said, "concentrate on continuing the fight, take over the command of your father's men—I will take care of his soul." In the evening, counting the victims, we realized that on that day Abba Yousef had died as well.

Before being hit, Abba Yousef had drained my father's blood into a clay jar. The jar had remained intact, in the hands of Melak Settegn, the faithful servant who, during the war, had followed my father, carrying his rifle.

Entrusting it to Melak Settegn and four of our fighters, I had sent the clay jar home so that they could bury his blood and mourn him with full honors. I had also sent his horse, Abba Mebrek, back with them. The great white warrior with his gray mane decorated with the trappings of war. On his saddle were tied my father's sword and his shield made from hippopotamus skin. My father, the great warrior who was no more.

"How are you feeling today?" Alemtsehay asked me, putting one of her hands on my shoulder.

"Better!"

"Then you can talk to your sisters."

"Not yet. Tomorrow, maybe."

"Today I will pray for you," she said. I didn't answer and she left.

I spent the day in the forest. In the evening I went back to the place of our makeshift beds. Mama Worknesh and Alemtsehay were waiting for me with dinner. I ate, then they told me that they would spend the night next to me praying to God so that He would bring about the dawn of Mama Worknesh's dream.

I believe God took pity on me and truly shed light on my darkness. The sky was sparkling clear in the morning, an intense blue. I could see some patches among the trees, crisscrossed by black kites and swallows. The air was cold and clean. And so was my soul. Without any effort on my part the blinding rage had left me, swept away by the light, just as Mama Worknesh's dreams had predicted. My delusional state of the previous day was gone as well. The only feeling left was sadness, as cold as the morning air, but that would stay with me for a long time. I thought of Amarech. I felt relieved that I was no longer outraged; on the contrary, I was almost willing to listen to her. I asked Alemtsehay to go look for her. Some time went by without anything happening. I was thinking of what to do, whether to get up and go look for her myself, or whether to wait for something to move toward me, but I didn't have the time to make up my mind.

I heard a noise behind me. I turned around and through the leaves I saw Amarech come toward me with her gazelle-like gait. She was carrying a pot with some freshly cooked *genfo*. "You used to love genfo when you were home!" she said, handing me the pot.

"Sit down here and eat some too," I answered back. "Mama always recommends it for pregnant women—she says it makes their backs stronger." But she wasn't listening to me.

"Yacob, I swear. He is a good person."

I wanted to get upset, at least a little bit, but I couldn't. To my surprise the dreams and prayers of Alemtsehay and Mama Worknesh had washed everything away. I surrendered almost completely. "All right, tell me about him; let's pretend he is a *Habesha*."

She laughed. "Yacob, that's impossible!"

"Why?"

"He's very different from us. Too much so. All of his colors are different from ours. You know, he has a piece of sky in his eyes. The sky at the end of Meskerem, when the swallows come back. It is as if God has given him those eyes to make us see the sky from up close. And his hair . . . that too . . . you know what it is like? Golden, the color of ripe *teff* announcing the time of the harvest. When the houses are emptied of men, and in the fields, together with the flashing of sickles, there is the sound of thanksgiving songs. All of his colors are the colors of the season of fruit and harvests. Can a man who bears the signs of the bounty and generosity of nature be a bad person? Yacob, he is my man." Her voice floated in the air, then came back down, more intimate, closer. "He speaks Amharic very well!"

"Hmm!" I mumbled. She knew. Something that morning had touched my heart and she was taking advantage of it. On her face there was a triumphant look of satisfaction, just the way there was when I was a child and I would wake up in the morning to find her sleeping with her head toward the headboard.

"Okay, let's hear what you want from me! You have everything you desire, right? You have a man you love, you are with child, what else do you want?"

"What I am about to ask you comes not only from me. It comes from our sisters and our mother as well. This is her message: 'Son, come back, this is your mother asking you this. Give up being an arbegna, come back home! Enough of this war against the Italians. Now, one of them is part of our family. We must live in peace.'"

"What? What?" I began to yell and bawl. The calm of the morning within me was overtaken by dense, dark clouds, heavy with rain and wind.

Haile Teklai, from the small cave, hearing my shouts, ran over to protect her. The blinding rage had left, but I was still a fighter, whose blood, for the last two years, had been constantly on fire, like the air of the sunken desert of Dancalia. Blood ready to strike. This is what my leader had thought. Amarech, however, had not become alarmed. Haile Teklai may have known the fighter, but she knew my inner man's soul, she knew the anger might come back, but it was not going to be the dangerous rage of that first day. She had managed to find the chink in my armor that would forestall my belligerence. She had come with a request not just from her, but also and above all from our mother. How could I ignore it? Could I perhaps set it aside without weighing those words and let my rage return? "Son, come back, this is your mother asking you." Could I suppress the echo of those words inside of me? She knew the answer and had remained seated next to me. With the quiet elegance of a princess she had lifted her hand to accompany her voice with a gesture: "Helen, come here. Why don't you explain things to this hard-headed mule!"

Helen joined us and sat on my other side.

Amarech invited Haile Teklai to stay and take part in our discussion, keenly aware that she had acquired a precious ally.

"Yacob," said Helen. "We are tired of having all of our men away fighting the war. All of our husbands are at war, you are at war, our family is at war. Enough! We want you all back home."

"So tell me, who has already agreed to come back?"

"You are the first we have been able to reach."

"It seems I am blessed by fortune!" I answered wryly. Then I took a deep breath—I wanted to put all of my strength in what I was about to say. The strength of an age-old tree, deeply rooted and unmovable, in order to counteract the weapon used by Amarech. I took my two sisters' hands and said, "I cannot, I cannot come back. I made a promise to our father, on his deathbed. That I will not return until the Italians are gone from our land."

"And your mother is begging you to come back," replied Amarech.

I jumped to my feet. I was enraged by that wiliness of hers that knew how to touch me to the quick. My mother . . .

I began to walk nervously. Back and forth, forth and back.

My comrades, pretending to be absorbed in other things, were sharing my dilemma. I was ready to snap. I had no thoughts in my mind, only a kind of endless mantra: "I won't go, I won't go."

I headed toward the edge of the forest to look out over the Hollow of the Virgin Mary. I wanted to be alone to try to think. From behind, I heard Alemtsehay and Haile Teklai yelling at me: "Be careful not to stray onto the commander's lands. Yesterday there were some Ascari down there. Don't go too far down the path, it's daylight, it could be dangerous." They kept shouting out all the possible dangers I had to avoid, just like a mother reminding a child where the hyenas are hiding when he goes out to play. I did not answer. I didn't have words to alleviate the fear they felt for me in that moment.

Once I reached that natural overlook I sat down, then I got up, then I sat down, then I got up again. It was my inner restlessness. I didn't know which way to go. Toward my mother or toward my father. Without reaching a decision, I let the day pass until it blended into evening and then turned completely into dusk. I ate nothing all day. Only toward evening did I accept a little *shiro* and then I prepared my pallet. I wanted to seek refuge in sleep, to stop myself from being torn apart by the contrasting feelings that were confronting each other inside me. I went to bed without seeing my sisters again after our morning discussion. I was almost asleep when Haile Teklai came to lie down next to me. I was half awake, half asleep, but his words reached my ears: "Goodnight Yacob. May the God of Ethiopia watch over your sleep."

The following morning I woke up in the same bad mood as the night before. I tried, unsuccessfully, to fall back to sleep again. An obsessive inner dialogue took possession of me: "Father, when I was little, you always used to tell me that I had to learn. That I had to learn what it meant to be a male, grow up, and have a family. Being a male, you said, means to be conscious of certain things.

"'For instance,' you told me, 'the children you will have. If you disagree with your wife about them, remember that your wife must have the last word. If God didn't want it to be so, He would not have made life begin in her womb. There will be other instances in which you will have the last word. Even with your mother, the last word about you and your siblings is always hers. Even if I do not agree about certain things at first, I later understand that it was better to follow her ideas. You know, women have a unique instinct about children. An umbilical cord through which heaven channels the right information.'

"Father, how I wish you were here in this very moment, so I could find out if you would say the same thing now. Should I listen to my mother or to what you asked me to do? Should I listen to my mother or keep faith with your dying words: '*Son, our land, fight!*'? I just don't know what to do."

Haile Teklai came toward me out of the small cave. "Yacob, are you awake?" I didn't answer. "You must be awake. Your eyes were open a few minutes ago." I continued to remain silent, focusing on not moving my eyelids, which would have let on that I was awake. I was hoping that he would go away. Nothing doing. He was not going to give up. "Yacob, stop acting like this. This is an order: open your eyes and listen to me."

Looking for a fight, I shouted out, "What is this? Is the whole world on my back? Even God the Creator? I'm not taking orders from anyone today, got it? Get out of here and leave me alone!"

"All right. Then, I beg you, in the name of everything we have fought for up to now, I beg you as your old comrade-in-arms, listen to me."

I realized that he was not going to let me off the hook. In that situation, I was the one who was really wavering, worn down as I was by my dilemma. I gave in and raised myself up on my elbows. "Go on, speak up but be quick. I have things to do," I said to him, almost snarling. He gazed into the middle distance, far off over the trees, and I lost my patience. "Do you want me to listen to you or do you want me to keep you company while you let your mind wander? Let me remind you that I have things to do, I have concerns that I need to deal with."

Ignoring my provocative words, he began to speak. "I still carry with me the image of our first attack, the one on the small truck transporting arms. Do you remember?"

How could I not remember? If nothing else but for that band of Ascari who retreated under a hail of scorn and insults from the people. "What kind of question is that? Do I look like someone who's lost his memory?"

"Yacob, I know that every moment, every second of that day is etched in your memory, but let me recall it. Only a few months have gone by since then, but it seems like ages. Do you remember? Mesfin had left a message from Ato Kebede: the following Saturday a small truck loaded with arms would be passing through on its way to the fort at Addis Alem. They were taking advantage of the road filled with people going to the market. A clever move to protect themselves against a possible attack. Besides the fact that we never attacked by day, they also knew that never in a million years would we have done so and endangered all those people's lives. So certain were they in their presumption that, like the stupid lion in the story of the monkey, they hadn't even provided the convoy with the necessary escort. The escort from Addis Ababa had stayed in the barracks and the one from Addis Alem was going to meet them on the road. There were only three platoons of Ascari, half in front, half behind, and an Italian junior officer with the group in the front. You were the one who came up with a solution: make up a song, simple lines that would announce the attack. You and Aron, dressed as shepherds, were going to jump into the road and sing the song. The people would understand and would scatter and we would launch the attack. You were going to start singing as soon as the convoy was past you, making it harder for the junior officer to understand what was happening. The rest of us, crouching by the side of the road, half in front, half behind, would surround them and subdue them by force. So many arms fell into our hands that day thanks to that ambush! Machine guns, ammunitions, rifles. The people themselves helped us carry them. Some lent us their donkeys, others their mules, some their hands, their backs. Remember?"

Sure, I remembered every single moment of it, but I said nothing. Haile Teklai continued.

"We distributed the arms to the group in Addis Alem and in Birbirsa. Our fellow soldiers in those areas held a gibir in your honor. Remember?" This time I nodded. "Listen, that day I thought that you had led us a good stretch down the road of resistance. But then there were other attacks, like the one on the tank stopped by Alemtsehay, and then the one at the mouth of the Awash River when you saved my life. Each time, after every action in which you were the determining factor, I thought that if ever you were to leave us, you would have already paid your dues."

"But I'm not going." I repeated, shouting, "I am not going! Not going! Till the very last day. Either the Italians go or I will die. Only these two reasons can make me take my leave of you all."

"Amarech is right. You're a stubborn mule."

"Don't let yourself be taken in by her. She is just like the woman who fed the lion."

He laughed. "The woman who pulled out the hairs from the lion's mane?"

"Perhaps you find it funny, but I don't. Amarech is trying to manipulate you, but I know her and even if she manages to convince you, you can forget about convincing me!"

"Listen, Yacob, go home, stay for a few months and then come back. You don't have to spend the rest of your life at home. Think of it as a bit of well-deserved rest."

"You don't get it. I am not going anywhere until that lot has gone back to where they came from."

"That's enough, Yacob. I've finished talking to you as a friend. Now I shall talk to you as your commander. This is an order. And should you choose to disobey me, I shall order everyone to kick you out and not consider you one of us. And I shall spread the word to our groups near and far. Not one of them will take you on because you do not know how to obey your leader."

Three days later I left. With my sisters, who were ecstatic while I was a useless rag. A condemned man with the noose already around his neck, waiting only for the stool under his feet to be kicked away.

I set off along the path of the Hollow of the Virgin Mary with the shouts of farewell from my companions echoing in my ears, eighty of them in all, men and women, with whom I had shared dreams, battles, rain, sun, songs, and words.

I didn't raise my head to acknowledge them, nor did I turn round.

Nothing but my eyes fixed on my feet moving forward in spite of everything.

I hadn't seen my mother since the beginning of the war. Since the moment when, during Meskerem over two years ago, my father, his men, and I, followed by wives, children, servants, mules, and loaded donkeys, had departed with Ras Imiru's army and she had not wanted to come along. She had stayed behind with my sisters to look after our house and our lands. Our big house with its modern roof, the corrugated tin roof like that of the *Gebi,* the imperial palace of the Ras, and our lands at Woha Petros and Melkam Woha. Fields of red earth, our generous, arable land that we had in part left to nature, to the tropical forest and to its animals.

Seeing her again did not lift my spirits. As is customary with us, my mother embraced me and kissed my cheeks, while I kissed her shoulders. Our embrace did not last long because even love, so say our elders, must have a certain decorum. The depth of her longing, of her love, was expressed in those sweet eyes of hers that never left me for an instant during those first few days. During the first three days the household greeted me with the lament for my father's death, to give me the chance to participate in the collective mourning and to receive the condolences that I had missed. The following three days were celebrated with songs, dances, and food for my return. During all those days, I moved about as if sleepwalking. I greeted the guests and I talked with the people I had not seen for a long time. It was as if, inside, there were two of me: the one who had received a rigorous education and who knew how to conceal his suffering because when there are guests, everything has to take second place to the welcome, and the one who was wandering around, trying to keep his mind focused on the mountains where the oppressor was being fought.

After the celebration, my days felt empty. Bare cliffs of hostile rock, down which the hours rolled away only to fall into nothingness tinged with bewilderment. My mother came up with the idea of sending me into the fields to work with our farmers. "A bit of hard work is what's needed for the spirit to regain some peace," she said.

Strangely enough, we still had our land. I didn't ask her how she had managed to keep it; it didn't interest me. Perhaps it was those endless prayers of hers asking God to protect her that had helped. I had heard her recite them since I was a child. *Be kegn awlegn asa- deregn kifu neger saiwutagns awtag.* "Keep me at Your right side, give me rest beside You so that nothing evil will swallow me up." There had been a time when I had recited them too. But from the time we had lost the war, I had stopped. Now, whenever I turned to God, it was only to flood him with my anger.

My mother, without waiting for the questions that I would never have asked her, briefly explained everything to me. When the Italian soldiers had arrived, she and my sisters had gone to speak to their commanders. Not with the blackshirts, with the others. That was the time that Amarech had met her man. "A good man," emphasized my mother. He and his sergeant had spoken to their junior officer, and then all three with the senior officer. In the end it was decided that for the moment the lands were to remain in our family's hands. A kind of stewardship. In return, our family was to give over a part of the animals and the grains for the battalions of the Ascari.

Without resisting or accepting, I let my mother send me like a small parcel a few miles from Debre Markos to the farmers at Woha Petros, with two mules and our trusted servant Old Alemu, who had raised me and my sisters. Before we set out, I overheard her telling the old servant what to do: "Make him work hard, he must tire himself out, and make sure that he eats. Genfo, heals the back, you need a good back to heal the torments of the soul." My mother's voice sounded worried.

Alemu was a man of few words, someone who was used to living and expressing himself through popular sayings and proverbs. "God did not create the world in one day. To each thing, its own time," were the words he used to reassure her.

I don't have a clear recollection of what happened in the ensuing days. Only a vague sense of the earth in my hands and in my nostrils, of moving around like a sleepwalker. That dense fog that each morning I used to see descending on the Hollow of the Virgin Mary now seemed to have invaded the emptiness inside of me, rising up to my head, to my inner eyes that lay inert and glazed over.

I followed the farmers with mechanical gestures, and in the evening I had trouble recalling even just one image of what had happened during the day. As soon as dusk fell, Alemu began bustling between the house and the open fire. He prepared steaming dishes of food and soups that he then brought to me, ordering me to eat while taking up a position in front of me like a guard with an unchained prisoner.

I had enormous respect for him. He had raised me. I did not dare contradict him. This was why my mother had put him on my heels. But the two years I had spent fighting in the war and in the resistance had left an indelible mark on me. It was as if a branch of a different species from the tree I belonged to had grown inside me and was preparing to sprout. Alongside the respect and the education I had been raised with, I experienced a torment that aggressively repelled all annoyances and bothersome facts.

One evening, with an insolent gesture, I overturned the bowl that he was handing to me. His little, watery eyes narrowed just like they did when I was small and he was about to hit me for some trouble I had gotten into. But this time, with the empty bowl in his hands and his white gown stained with splotches of butter and chili pepper sauce, he turned on his heels and left. I heard him moving around and slamming the door. Soon after came the echo of the mule's hoofs as he trotted alongside the dwelling. Alemu was returning home, mortally offended.

The next day, my mother, accompanied by Melak Settegn, my father's faithful servant, came to see me. She was angry. "Alemu traveled by mule all night, in these times when, if the wild animals don't kill you, then the Ascari or their white commanders will." Her eyes were flashing with fury. "You cannot put the lives of other people in danger just because you don't want to snap out of this state of yours. If your father were still around, he would whip you, I would beg him to stop, you would ask Alemu to forgive you, and everything would be settled. But your father is dead, and nobody can take his place. I have nobody who will whip you till I beg him to stop and it's clear that I will not beg you to come out of this darkness of yours. A mother does not beg her children. She commands them. If you do not agree to heal your pain, I shall find another way to punish you. I swear I will."

She packed up my things and the next morning she took me back home.

We went back along the same road we had taken with old Alemu, climbing up the gentle slopes of the same hills we had come down a few days previously, at times passing through dense forest growth.

I could have gone along that road with my eyes closed. How many times, as a child or as an adolescent, had I taken it, riding my mule next to my father, to Melak Settegn, and to a few of his men. We used to go to help with the sowing of the teff, during Meskerem, immediately after the feast of Meskel, and then we would return to check on the growth of the blades of wheat and my eyes would feast on the sight of that sea of green that swayed in the wind. Finally, we would return for the harvest, when the fields that stretched as far as the eye could see were as golden and as glowing as the sun, and for days the farmers would cut the blades with their scythes. Every evening there would be a great feast. "Father, where are you now?" I thought, wracked with a profound feeling of solitude.

We reached Debre Markos by the end of the day, just before sunset. When we arrived at the entrance to the house, the door opened. Behind it was old Alemu. He did not greet me. Quickly he came to meet my mother, gave her mule to Melak Settegn, and entered the house with her, without deigning to look at me. With the air of a sisterly accomplice, Amarech told me that I had really messed up this time. I pushed her aside. There were far bigger problems out there.

Several days later, clearly at my mother's request, our family's spiritual father, Abba Gebre, came to see me. Contrary to what I might have expected, he didn't lecture me, but only said, "At times even prayer becomes a kind of battle, a kind of resistance. My son, we must resist in hope," and then he began, *Egzio Meharene Kristos, Egzio Meharene Kristos, Egzio Meharene Kristos,* and I recited with him.[2] I followed him as you would follow someone who asks you to go along with him and although you don't know where he is going, you agree because, after all, you have nothing else to do. He prayed in my room, all day long, and I with him, and by the time he left, the prayers had calmed my breath. They had relaxed and lengthened it. How much time had passed since I had felt that sensation that is born of prayer?

Egzio Meharene Kristos, I continued even after he had gone.

That ancient prayer, the chant that came from the past. From the time of Zera Yacob, even before that. All my people had recited it.

Egzio Meharene Kristos, I repeated, and it seemed as though I could hear a chorus behind me that joined in with my voice. Warrior men,

---

2. A prayer in Ge'ez, the ancient Ethiopian language, that expresses a request for forgiveness.

monks, warrior women, women hermits . . . a whole crowd that grew behind me, reaching to infinity.

Egzio Meharene Kristos. They were all my ancestors and they were there next to me, liberating me from my loneliness.

Egzio Meharene Kristos. I began to pray even in my sleep. Over the following days, the fog began to lift, to rise toward the sky with the prayers, and the pain began to emerge like the bare earth.

Egzio Meharene Kristos. I was beginning to live again, clutching at hope. On my lips, the name of God was born again.

More than a month had gone by since my return. I was gradually embracing life again and certain things took on their old rhythm. The comings and goings of home, the emptiness on market days, the women rocking babies, the smell of food coming from the kitchens. . . . My mother asked me to take my father's role with the farmers who came to ask our advice, and who then stayed for the evening and exhausted our reserves of *tej* and *areke.* Now that my father was no more, I had to accept the role of leader. Or at least try to do so.

My older sisters, the married ones, had returned to their husbands' families to wait for news of their men, and little Amarech's belly had begun to show a slight roundness. A small *amba* concealed by her clothes, visible only to those who were very familiar with the shape of her slim body.

She was happy, in spite of everything. A happiness that seemed selfish in my eyes. She chirped all the time, like small birds when trees are blooming. I had not yet met her Italian soldier. My mother had wisely ordered her to keep him at a safe distance, and I was relieved, but I was aware that my meeting with that unwelcome man was getting closer all the time. One morning I heard Amarech singing more than usual and there was a voice behind hers. Words in Amharic, full of excruciating mistakes and in a strange accent. "This is it," I said to myself, and immediately I had a ridiculous thought, a kind of mean satisfaction: "So this is the Amharic that he speaks so well?"

My mother came to call me.

Words cannot describe the feelings I had in that moment. I felt defeated: the enemy had occupied and taken possession of our country even to the point of worming himself into our families.

They introduced him to me. "Daniel."

In a gesture of respect that imitated our customs, he bowed forward and stretched out his hand, the palm of the other hand holding the forearm of the outstretched hand. I, in a gesture of disrespect that was meant to imitate Italian customs, remained standing upright, my hand barely touching his in a swift, halfhearted gesture. My sister froze and stopped singing. He gave an understanding smile.

I never spoke to him, and when he was in our house, which was often, I shut myself up in hostile silence. He pretended not to notice.

Every so often my mother told me that I should stop it—she reminded me of our culture, of our tradition of hospitality. "I do not welcome devils," I replied.

"If you could only let yourself get to know him, you would realize that he is a good person," she said.

I cut her short. "Mama, he is a presumptuous devil. Only a presumptuous devil can go around with the color of God's sky in his eyes. We are the color of the earth and, like the earth, humble and welcoming. Between us and him there can be no meeting points." I was determined not to let that being, who in my eyes was as filthy as the foulest beast, get close to me.

But at home they often spoke about Daniel's upcoming demobilization. I caught snippets of conversation. I never heard any talk about Italy or Ethiopia, of their occupation. It was a dangerous subject that they had decided not to touch upon, but Daniel's demobilization was discussed every day.

The request had already been sent to his battalion commander, who in turn had sent it on to the governor of Gondar. Once demobbed, he and Amarech were going to live at Woha Petros. Daniel knew how to work the land. They were going to oversee a small part of our property, together with the farmers. Abba Ghebre was going to bless their union and baptize their child.

These were subjects that kept on coming up over and over again. Once the last sentence had been uttered, a few hours later, people in the house would start the discussion all over again. And although I wanted to stay out of the whole business, in the end I had not been able to remain completely deaf.

Another month went by, and Amarech's belly began to be unmistakably in evidence and her singing increased. She was getting impatient. She wanted her man all to herself. She no longer wanted just to see him for a few hours each day and then have to think of him for the rest of the time as he worked on the other side of the wall of the fort.

One Tuesday evening Daniel rushed into the house, excited. The previous day a telegram had arrived from Gondar; the sergeant had told him that a unit was due to arrive at Debre Markos the following morning and with it the orders for demobilization. The sergeant was certain that Daniel's would also be among them. "Let's go together to pick the order up," he said to Amarech, embracing her in front of everyone. My mother bowed her head, embarrassed by that bold gesture of affection in her presence, and I turned away in a show of displeasure. The two of them were going off, free, while I had to stay home, far from my post. I had trouble falling asleep that night, and the following morning I did not notice the bustle when Daniel came to get Amarech and they went off chirping like two little birds in springtime busily preparing to build their nest. When I got up the house was empty. I was relieved. I didn't feel like seeing anybody.

Halfway through the morning the front door flew open, banging against the wall. At first I thought it hadn't been closed properly and that a gust of wind had violently thrown it open, but immediately after that disruptive bang, shouts could be heard. It was Daniel. He seemed out of his mind. He was shouting wildly in Italian, repeating himself without stopping to take a breath: "Royal Decree 880, Royal Decree 880! What, didn't you know that there existed Royal Decree 880? Sure, Royal Decree 880, 880." He was in a state and was throwing things around the room. Behind him came Amarech, sniffling and begging him to stop and explain everything to her, but he just went on repeating "Royal Decree 880." I thought he had completely lost his mind. Amarech began looking for me. I heard her hurried steps around the house as she went from one room to the next. I went toward her. There were drops of sweat on her face, her netela had fallen from her head and revealed a mass of untidy braids, her clothes were torn in places.

"Yacob! Yacob. Help me. I don't know what has happened, but I am afraid." She knelt before me and stretched out her hands. "I beg you. I beg you in the name of our God. I beg you in the name of our father. I beg you in the name of Christ. Go to him. Speak to him."

I went to him and asked my sister to leave us alone.

He was surrounded by broken pieces of the objects he had thrown to the ground. He was gazing around with glassy eyes, wide open like those of the crazy people who used to make me take to my heels as fast as I could when I was a child.

A shudder made the hairs on my skin stand on end.

As soon as he saw me he stopped looking for things to throw around and he began yelling again—"Royal Decree 880, Royal Decree 880"—and, continuing to shout, he came up to me. "What," he said with his face almost touching mine, "what, they said to me, but don't you know about Royal Decree 880? Royal Decree 880, you understand, Royal Decree 880. You do know that Royal Decree 880 exists, don't you? Eh! Yacob! Yacob, Yacob, you have to help us. We have to run away. We have to leave here. You will help us reach your friends, right? The fighters? Yacob, we have to run away. You will help us, right? You're the only one who can help us, what do you say, I beg you, say yes. I beg you, brother of my Amarech."

"Calm down, Daniel."

"Yacob, you'll help us, right? We'll go to your fighter friends, what do you say?"

"Calm down, Daniel."

"Yacob, they want to put me in jail, you understand, in jail. But I haven't done anything. I haven't done anything."

I took him by the shoulders and began to shake him. "Daniel, calm down!" I felt the tension in his body dissipate in my hands. He began to weep, at first slowly, his tears falling and furrowing his face, and then his weeping increased until he was sobbing uncontrollably.

"I knew," he began to say between one sob and the next, "I knew that damn decree existed, but I didn't think it would really be enforced. I have seen so many soldiers going with the women from here and everyone in the fort knew about it. I thought they had proclaimed it to keep the Fascists at home happy. Not so. You can go with the women from here but you have to treat them like prostitutes. You cannot love them, have children with them, dream about having a family. If you do something like that, they enforce the decree. Got it, Yacob? There is an Italian law that condemns me because I love your sister and I will have a child by her. Italy, that great promoter of civilization. This is her real face. Today they should have given me my demobilization papers. I thought I could finally come back here to your house a free man; instead the sergeant told me that an order is on its way sending me back home and condemning me to five years inside because I broke Royal Decree 880.

"I have known the sergeant since I did my training in Italy. When we embarked at Leghorn, his wife and five-year-old daughter, Lucia, came to see him off. While he was embracing his wife, his daughter was trying to open his suitcase. She seemed to be more interested in that than saddened by the upcoming separation. Every now and then she would tug her father by the sleeve of his jacket and ask, 'But if it's such a big thing, how come it can all fit into your suitcase?' He smiled at her without answering.

"Once on board, he explained it to me. He told her he was going to Africa to take civilization there, and she wanted to see civilization, this thing that was so important that it was the cause of their separation. She thought he had it in his suitcase.

"As soon as his wife's letters arrived he would come to read them to me. She told him that in the evening Lucia would scribble on the kitchen floor with a piece of chalk, saying that she was writing to Daddy; she wanted to know if this darn civilization had been delivered and if he could finally come back home. This morning, informing me of the order to return to Italy, he said, 'I have to tell Lucia that it is not true. We did not come to deliver civilization but to destroy one, just like the barbarians did in the past. You must never lie to children. Daniel, you were betrayed by a Fascist centurion who noticed Amarech's belly getting bigger.'

"On my way here, I met those bastards and they began to make jokes: 'So, you filled the belly of your little black girl, eh? What's it like putting it into a pregnant black woman?' they taunted me.

"'Ah, but he isn't fucking. No, he's making love.'

"'Right, because this peasant from around Venice is a dumb ass and he can't read. He doesn't know that Royal Decree 880 exists,' said another. A real coward, short and lily-livered, who as soon as he hears shooting outside the fort, pees in his pants. A useless blackshirt scum. He only feels strong when he's with others. A real prick." Now Daniel had stopped weeping. "I am not going back to Italy. I want to live here with Amarech and our child. I have the right to live with them. Yacob, you must help us escape. Take us to your friends, to the fighters. I swear, I shall fight with them against the Fascists."

For a second, but only for a split second, his pain made me feel that he was one of us, that he was suffering too, because of the Fascists. But then, immediately after, he became an Italian again, the sollato, the one who arrived in our midst wearing the uniform of the enemy. But in that second of empathy I made a promise, with my whole being. A promise that I could not break. "I will help you. I will help you escape with Amarech. I will take you to my companions."

There followed days of frantic preparations. We had to act quickly, since the order to return to Italy could arrive from Gondar any day. Even Daniel's sergeant, to whom we said that Daniel and Amarech were going to stay with some relatives in the south, helped us by donating some tinned food for the trip, while Daniel, shut up in the barracks, pretended he was fearful of the forthcoming return to Italy.

It was going to be a long journey. We could not ask, as we had done two months previously, for a ride from one of the convoys of

trucks between Debre Markos and Addis Ababa. We were going to
have to do it all on foot. Over 120 miles—along rough paths, cutting
down by Malka Kalo where we would ford the Abay River, and then
straight down to the paved road to Addis Alem. And all this with
Amarech who was five months pregnant.

Within a week, before the order to repatriate came from Gondar
where the seat of the Italian government for North Ethiopia was
located, we were ready.

On the morning of our departure, long before dawn, Alemu came
knocking at my door: "*Getoch!*"

I opened the door and he came in. "Since when have you called
me getoch?"

"When you were born I was given a task: that of raising you. And
that's what I'm doing, right at this very moment. I call you getoch,
so that you become aware of your role. Now that your father is no
more, you are the getoch, the master of the house. Having made that
clear, let me add this: getoch, you cannot accompany Amarech and
Daniel." He paused. "Ask me why not."

"Let's hear it."

"Since when does the one who has just been born say to the
mother, 'I am the wise one here'?"

"What do you mean?"

"You are a young buck. You know nothing about women and children. How can you think of accompanying your sister in her condition? What's needed is someone like me who has experience." My
muscles tensed up and I leaned forward as if to protest. He narrowed
his eyes. "This time I shall not turn around and go away as I did at
Woha Petros. If you show me disrespect, I will kick you as I did
when you were small. So, first listen, think about it, and after, speak.
There's something else. Ask me what."

"Let's hear it."

"You cannot leave the house empty."

"But the house is not empty. There's my mother, there are all of you."

"A house without its master is empty. Every master is like the great
sycamore tree that protects the farmer's animals from the sun. The

woman is like the farmer who keeps the grass under the tree clean and the man is the tree. And have you ever seen a tree move? And here's the last thing."

"Let's hear it."

"The sollato know that you are here! They haven't asked where you came from, because the sergeant took care of things, but if you go away they'll come and question and torment us in the certainty that Amarech and Daniel are with you. Think about it," he concluded, and off he went.

Soon after, Abba Gebre knocked on the door. I let him in. He extended the cross to me and I kissed it. "My son," he said, "I don't think it is a good idea for you to leave. For everybody. When the sollato realize that Daniel has escaped, they will come here. I cannot even begin to imagine what would happen if you were not here. Someone might talk out of fear. The sollato might find out that you were a fighter and that you have never taken the Oath of Submission. The consequences would be endless. You must stay and face them when they come." Once again, as before with Alemu, I wanted to protest, but Abba Gebre didn't give me time. "My son, I will go with them as far as Malka Kalo. I will help them ford the river and I will hand them into the care of the priest of the Medania Alem Church. He is a friend of mine. We studied together in Waldibba. I will ask him to accompany them to the next church and to entrust them to the priest of that church. They will continue in this way, accompanied from church to church, up to the paved road at Addis Alem. There they will go to the priest at the Bete Mariam Church who will find someone trustworthy to escort them to the great olive tree on the path. From there Amarech knows the way. Ah! I know that Alemu wants to go with them. It would be a good idea. He is an Oromo and much of the territory they will be crossing belongs to the Oromo people. He will guarantee their safe passage."

Dawn broke. Among the colors in the sky, the last star was still shining. The little caravan was ready. My mother, my two unmarried sisters, and I accompanied Daniel and Amarech to the Yesus Church. My mother had given my sisters orders not to shed any tears. Amarech and her man needed to feel support, not despair. We said goodbye to each other as if they were going off on a joyful pilgrimage. My mother embraced little Amarech. "Don't worry," she said. "God will be with all of you and also with us. We shall follow you with our prayers. My daughter, I shall be here in body, but every moment, every instant, my spirit will be with you, in prayer." They mounted the mules. My mother blessed them. "May the Virgin Mary be with you! May she help you when in difficulty. May she keep your path free of danger. May the light follow you." As one, they answered "Amen." The mules moved forward. The last one to pass by was Alemu. A veil of sadness descended on my mother's eyes—she was parting from her youngest daughter. She nodded to the old servant. He answered in the same way, then, passing near her, he whispered, "I shall protect her."

We lingered until they were out of sight; then my mother, my sisters, and I headed toward the house, our hearts as heavy as stone.

All that day and evening we didn't have any visitors. None of the military came to ask where Daniel was. It was the sergeant who had played for time. "He must be at his little black girl's to say goodbye forever," he had joked with a blackshirt who had asked about Daniel. The next morning the Italians came. They banged on the front door, kicking it. I went to open it. There was a group of them, and among them was a short squirt who was hopping back and forth aggressively, probably the coward Daniel had told me about. One of them pushed an Ascari forward. "Where's your sister?" the Ascari asked me.

"She has disappeared with the Italian soldier!" I replied.

The Ascari turned toward the blackshirts and translated into Italian. Their faces darkened in anger. I suppressed a smile. By now Amarech and Daniel were far away and the sollato would not have been able to find them. One of them who seemed to be their leader raised his voice and barked out. The Ascari translated it into Amharic. "Where have they gone?"

"What do I know? They went off without our permission."

"What do you mean?" asked the Ascari.

"We were against my sister's relationship with the sollato," I answered.

The Ascari turned toward the blackshirt leader and translated into Italian. The leader came up to me and grabbed me by my clothes. He spoke, and in his anger saliva sprayed out of his mouth. "You, little black face, here we are the ones who decide and judge relationships," he yelled. "Here, we are the ones who do not want our race dirtied by yours."[3] The Ascari translated, and when he had finished speaking, the blackshirt leader kneed me in the belly. I doubled up in pain. The short squirt chuckled with satisfaction. "One day," I thought, "we will turn your grin into a howl of misery." They left.

Five days later Abba Gebre returned. The soldiers paid him a visit too. He got rid of them without much trouble, saying that he knew nothing about an Italian soldier and Amarech. He had gone to pray at the Betenugus Mariam Church. The priest of the church there could confirm it.

It took Daniel, Amarech, and Alemu almost fifteen days to cover the 120 miles to my old hideout where they met up with my companions. I followed them in my mind all along the way. Each night I lay down with them and in the morning I awoke with them. I followed them as they prepared breakfast and as they loaded the mules, and when all was ready, we traveled along together. I, too, went down the steep path toward the Abay River, carefully so that Amarech's mule would not slip on the stone steps; I suffered and sweated in the heat of the canyons; I forded the river at Malka Kalo and, once past the ford, I wound upward, reached Abuie, crossed the valleys of the Guder River and the plains of Abebe and Birbisa, until I was within sight of the Awash River, by now on the paved road to Addis Alem. I counted every house, every village, every church. I scrutinized the face of each priest to whom, from time to time, they were entrusted. I followed them right up to when Amarech got off her mule to embrace my leader, Haile Teklai. After that, I fell into a long, deep sleep that lasted for a whole day and night. When I awoke,

3. "Little Black Face" (*Faccetta nera*) is the title of a very well-known Fascist marching song.

I went to see Abba Gebre. Together we spent the night in prayer. To give thanks.

A month and a half after they had left, an unexpected guest, a messenger who had passed through Holeta, brought us news. They were well, all of them. Daniel, old Alemu, and Amarech, who, in spite of the rigors of the journey, had not had any problems. When the guest left, my mother rushed off to the fort to give the sergeant the good news. After that first messenger, at regular intervals we received guests and news about Amarech's pregnancy, about old Alemu and about a particular development: a strong bond, a brotherly bond, had formed between Haile Teklai and Daniel. Daniel had entered into the Resistance movement, keeping the promise he made to me the day he asked me to help them flee. That he would fight the Fascists. Those words, that phrase, had not been dictated by the anger of the moment, as I had thought that fateful day. Daniel had taught the group everything about the weapons that the Italians used, about the military organization, the patrols, the platoons, the companies, the battalions. He had even taught them how to taunt the Italians in their own language in order to force them to leave the protective walls of the fort. "Your wives are having it off with the Fascist higher-ups." "You are a bunch of girls, your mothers can only bear girls." He had taken my place within the group. Some of the messengers told me that sooner or later Aron was going to teach him to sing the fukera, and soon, very soon, Haile Teklai was going to have him take part in the attacks against the military and the Italian militias.

Despite hearing through the messages about how Daniel had become one of "ours," I continued to feel a persistent mistrust in his regard, which, at each message, was mixed with envy: here I was, near the fort, and there he was, among my companions. And if that weren't enough, I had ended up here because of him.

A week after each visit from one of the messengers, my mother would begin to examine the signs that presaged the next. She would sift through nighttime dreams, and she checked the movement of the wind, the flight of birds at dawn when she opened the door to sniff the air. She could announce with precision the day when someone would stop by to bring her the embrace of her little one, Alemu's greeting, and the stories of my Italian brother-in-law who was fighting on our side. In perfect synchrony, perhaps also following some strange sign himself, when the messenger left, the sergeant would appear. We had a debt with the Italian army. They had left us our lands, and in exchange we paid in produce. And the sergeant would come to us using this excuse. He came to claim their credit. In fact, he used to sit with us, eat, and get the news about his dear friend and Amarech. I think he guessed that I had been with the rebels, but he never said so openly. Each time, at the end of the meal, he would ask me to accompany him to the door, and before going out, he would say, "Yacob, sooner or later you must come to request a Declaration of Submission paper and to hand over your weapons, if you have any. It's what you must do; you are a leader. As long as you stay closed up at home, it isn't a problem if you don't have the form, but if you ever needed to move around, it could be very dangerous."

Opening the door, I would say to him, "I have no need to go out. At home I have everything I need, and I do have a rifle, but I am not going to hand it over. In our culture, men, in order to be considered as such, must have a weapon. A rifle, a spear, or a sword!" He would begin to walk away, shaking his head. I think I know what he wanted to say: "I won't be able to protect you forever."

In that period of transition, when the dry season still prevailed but the wind, the boom of distant thunder, and the brief, scattered showers announced the arrival of the great rains, Amarech gave birth. A little girl.

Two weeks later, when the sky had already initiated the dance of the first big storms, a messenger brought the news of the happy event, together with the words of old Alemu: "Mother, everything has its time in life, and when one's own comes around, each person cries, laughs, or speaks too much. Today it's my turn to speak too much. I'm sending you news that I am holding in my arms the child of our Amarech. It is a happiness too great to bear." That was the last message. Then the rainy season took over with its usual fury and the life of us all, as happened every year at that time, retreated inside. There wasn't anybody in the fields, or animals grazing, or traders or traveling merchants. Not even the trucks and the buses of the Italians dared move. Life went on inside, within the walls of the house. Outside, there was nothing but water and mud.

Aside from the occasional necessity, we spent the rainy season closed up at home. Almost two months huddled around the fire, telling stories, sharing events, and drinking the three ritual cups of coffee. Abba Gebre spent the entire season with us, right up to New Year's Eve.

The rains beat down rhythmically on the corrugated tin roof of our house. Between one story and another, we followed its course.

First the beginning, the sharp sounds of the first drops. Then increasing, the rhythm getting faster and more intense. Then the explosion, with noisy bursts and water that beat down on the roof, gusts of wind that displaced the rain, creating a lull of a few seconds in the violent hammering. Then, again, water, more water, and gusts, the deafening sound of thunder, and sudden shafts of light that lit up the dark rooms. Occasionally within the explosion there was a double rhythm: together with the water there also came hail, balls as big as peanuts. And then the gradually decreasing sound. The storm was coming to an end. A gentle, light rain tapped on the roof.

Between one storm and the next, under a sky that showed little promise of clearing, the rainwater formed pools, dripping from the plants, from the houses, from the hills . . . from every which way. It created rivulets that flowed one into the other, increasing little by little until they became a river of water and mud that forced its way down toward one of the tributaries of the Abay River. When the river began to subside, the wind brought another storm and the water started up again, beating down on the metal roof.

The rains continued without interruption until the end of the month of Pagume. On the first day of the year, suddenly they stopped. In just a few days the imperious sun dried the roads and my mother began to search in vain for signs of forthcoming news. The sergeant, who during the rains had rarely come to see us, now stopped by every day, only to leave soon after, disappointed that there was no news.

For the feast of Meskel, fifteen days after the new year, the yellow flowers that were used every year to decorate the houses for important celebrations inundated fields, gardens, road sides, meadows . . . their yellow stretched everywhere, as far as the eye could see. Only the return of the swallows was needed in order for us to know that the dry season had begun. But the swallows did not return. Days went by and instead of festive twittering, unseasonable clouds appeared. The sky turned leaden, a layer of persistent, stagnant grayness that showed no sign either of clearing up or of rain. Then, one evening, came the rain. For an infinite number of hours there fell a strange rain, slow, silent, that produced no sound on the metal roof, no rivers of water and mud that swept down to the valley. Only water that disappeared into the cracks of the earth, leaving no visible trace.

The following morning my mother came to wake me. "Last night's rain is a sign. It is announcing news that will bring well-being and flowers, or stifled lament. May God keep us from pain." After a few hours somebody knocked at the door. It was Abba Gebre. He, too, had read the same message in the rain and had come to receive the news that would arrive. He was not going to leave us alone. Together we would celebrate or face the suffering.

At lunchtime there was another knock at the door. My mother, the priest, and I rushed to open it. It was the sergeant. My mother invited him in. "Today we will receive news!" she announced to him, and then she asked him, "Is anyone expected today?"

"A convoy that left Addis Ababa on its way to Gondar. It will stop here for the night."

"There you are. You'll see, Sergeant, someone for us will come with the convoy!" she stated with certainty. At about five o'clock, the evening breeze carried the sound of the convoy of heavy-duty vehicles entering the city. From that moment on, our waiting grew more and more tense.

An hour and a half went by, and it was already dark when there was a knock at the door. We all rushed toward it. I was the one who opened it. The surprise hit me like a hard punch straight to the stomach. I was left speechless. Before me stood my companion-in-arms, Alemtsehay. "Welcome," I said to her. The words came out of my mouth spontaneously while I stood before her, completely confused.

"*Selam*, Yacob," she said. I wanted to step aside to let her in, but the slowness of my movements was too much for my mother, who pushed me away from the doorway. Without following the ritual greetings, she went up close to Alemtsehay and in a worried voice she asked her, "Daughter, do you come bearing good news?"

Alemtsehay did not answer her question. "Mother," she said, "first let me in."

My mother was deaf to her words. She was not prepared to listen to anything except the answer to her question. "Daughter, tell me, do you come bearing good news?"

"Mother, don't worry, I will tell you everything, but first let me in. I am tired—"

My mother interrupted her. "I beg you, daughter, tell me, have you come bearing good news?"

"Wait, mother, just a moment, let me in, close the door behind me, and I will tell you everything."

"I beg you, daughter, in the name of God, tell me, have you come bearing good news?"

Alemtsehay, overcome by my mother's insistence, gave in. She lowered her face with an eloquent gesture. No, she had not come bearing good news. My mother collapsed on the ground and began to scream, beating her chest with closed fists. Abba Gebre dragged her inside.

The night rain did not presage well-being and flowering, but stifled lament. A mourning that we would have to bear in silence and solitude, without erecting the mourning tent and calling people to come to weep by our side. In order not to show the military authorities that we had always known where Daniel and Amarech had fled and that we were in touch with them.

I remained on the threshold, stunned. Alemtsehay asked me if she could come in. "Certainly!" I said. "Forgive me." The sergeant came toward us. In the bewildering confusion created by the events, I had forgotten about his presence. The anguish in his eyes was palpable. He began to ask Alemtsehay questions, he wanted to know what had happened, but Alemtsehay did not answer him. She wanted us to remain alone, just the two of us. She wanted to tell me, her companion-in-arms, what had happened. I asked the sergeant to go into the kitchen and get them to give him a plate of food for Alemtsehay. She and I sat in a corner of the sitting room in the glow of the oil lamp. One in front of the other. She took my hands, placed them on her knees, and began to recount what had happened.

"In the beginning we were all wary of Daniel—one or two people asked themselves how you could have even thought of sending a white man to be with us, and only Haile Teklai had welcomed him without hesitation, out of respect for your name. Then it was Daniel who showed us the way, not just because of the fact that he had entered the Resistance but also because of his character. He was a simple soul, without malice and without secrets. Always ready to undertake any kind of work. He said he was the son of farmers from northern Italy. The son of poor folk, he was used to working and to being ordered about. Your sister, when she spoke of his origins, used to joke, 'Woi gud, I've ended up with a poor peasant, me, the daughter of a commander.' Alemu called him 'Ato.' He used to say that God had created him a gentleman in his ways and in his soul. A man to be respected and to be imitated." Alemtsehay gave a deep sigh as she paused to give herself a chance to steel herself to continue. "They captured them on the path to the hideout, near the paved road. A group of Zapatie on horseback. Alemu and Amarech did not have their Submission Papers and Alemu was carrying an old rifle—you know how our men are, never without a gun. It was an old piece of iron that did not even fire.

"Daniel tried to resolve the matter by saying that he would guarantee for them that Alemu and Amarech were his servants. But when they asked him where he lived, he did not know what to say. He didn't know the area well, and he couldn't recall the name of any of the villages. They knew that among the rebels there was an ex–Italian soldier. Two weeks previously Daniel had taken part in an attack and someone had seen him. The Zapatie became suspicious. In a few seconds the situation deteriorated. They tried to escape but the Zapatie blocked them. There was no way out. Alemu raised his rifle and threw himself against them, yelling that he wanted to die right away so as not to witness what they would do to his Amarech. They killed him instantly."

Alemtsehay stopped talking; she did not have the courage to go on. I squeezed her hand until I could feel my nails in her flesh. "For God's sake!" I said. "Go on!"

"They killed Daniel inside the fort. In a room. We found that out from one of our infiltrators: a shot to the head out of the sight of anyone. They did not want it known that an Italian was on our side. Amarech, they hanged. In the square in Holeta. They left her body swinging there all day, with a notice attached to her back: 'This is what happens to rebels.' The priest of the church in Holeta, after incessant begging, managed to have the body returned to him. He buried her himself, in the church cemetery. We were not able to take part."

A deep icy cold took hold of me. I did not know whether it came from outside or from inside of me. I tried to feel something, any kind of warmth to make me come out of it. But everything was still, frozen. I couldn't feel anything, not even my hands gripping Alemtsehay's. I couldn't feel any part of my body. Perhaps it was no longer part of me, nothing was part of me, except for my thoughts, words that floated around in my head, uselessly.

"My Amarech. My beautiful Amarech. Old Alemu, they even killed my old Alemu."

"Yacob! Yacob!" Alemtsehay squeezed my hands, just as I had done with hers. Her voice reached me from afar. "Yacob! Yacob!" I tried to answer her, but no words came out of my mouth. "You must pull yourself together! You cannot let yourself go! You have a duty." Through the cold air came a faint whimpering sound. Something so unexpected as to be able to crack the iciness and penetrate it to the point of arousing my attention. "Yacob, they are dead but your niece is alive. She stayed behind with me in the hideout. Yacob, you must shake yourself, get over it. For her. Every day Amarech used to say to me, 'If something happens to me, I want my daughter to be raised by Yacob.'"

In the darkness I had not noticed that Alemtsehay was carrying a bundle on her back. The whimpering started up again. It came from the bundle. Alemtsehay undid it and handed it to me. Something in her face softened. "Here," she said. "Let me introduce you to Rosa."

I held the bundle tightly. Something moved against my chest. A tiny, warm body that was whimpering gently, a life just budding. My iciness began to melt. I felt something wet on my face. I was weeping. Tears as silent as the night rain. Alemtsehay stood up to bring the oil lamp closer. "Yacob, look at her," she said. I moved her little body away from my chest and I opened up the blankets that were wrapped around her. A baby girl, an enchanted harmony that mixed the colors of the earth and of the sky, lifted her eyes to mine. At that very moment, any doubt or anger regarding that white man who had entered into and devastated our family vanished.

The sergeant came in with a plate in his hand. I told him to put down the plate and to come close. "Come, sergeant. Come here, close. Let me present Rosa to you. The daughter of your Daniel and my little Amarech." The following day I went to his office, I turned in my Mauser rifle and I requested the Submission Paper. I did not want to run any risks. Not now that there was her. Not now that there was Rosa.

CHAPTER TWO

"THERE IT IS," ABBA YACOB TOLD ME. "THAT'S MY STORY, the story of my Submission Paper, the story of my Amarech, your great-grandmother's sister." Then his eyes glazed over. He was lost in a faraway past where I could not reach him. It took him a while to return to the present. He shook his head slowly, as if he were chasing away bad thoughts, and picked up the paper that was still lying on my dress. He folded it and put it back in the envelope. He got up from the bed, put the envelope in the same spot where I had found it, then went and stood in front of the small table with the icons. He looked so sad to me that I couldn't stop myself from asking, "Abba Yacob, are you sad?"

"Yes, I am, my child, but in a little while, I'll be less sad. Come here."

I got off the bed and joined him. He embraced me and asked, "When you grow up, will you write my story?"

I would have done anything for old Yacob, so I nodded.

"Then make a solemn promise in front of the icon of the Virgin Mary. When you grow up you will write my story, the story of those years, and you will take it to Italy, so that the Italians won't be allowed to forget."

I promised as solemnly as a child could. Then a thought came into my mind: "Abba Yacob, how will I be able to go to the country where the Italians live?"

"You'll see—you promised in front of my Virgin Mary. She will find a way for you." Old Yacob scratched my head again and smiled, with his one-toothed smile. Now he seemed less sad. "Do you have any more questions?" he asked me.

"No, but I wanted to tell you something!"

"Tell me!"

"Abba Yacob, I am not sure I will be able to remember the names of all those battles."

"Then this is what we'll do: go get a notebook and we will write them down."

I left the room. I ran through the main courtyard and I started up the steps. I flew up the two flights of stairs, hoping I would not bump into my parents, but on the threshold of my home I ran into my mother. "Mahlet," she said, "where are you going?"

"To get a notebook."

"What do you need it for?" I bit my lip. "Mahlet, what do you need the notebook for?"

I answered hesitantly, "I must write some things down for Abba Yacob."

"Where is he?"

"Downstairs, in his room."

Her voice became stern. "You know you must not go into the rooms of the elders. You must not disturb them."

"He was the one who asked me to go in," I protested.

"I don't want you to get into bad habits."

"Mama, please," I implored. "I will bring him the notebook and I'll be right back, almost right away. I have to write one thing down and then I'll be back."

She gave me a halfhearted smile. "All right, but don't stay too long."

"Thank you, Mama!"

I ran to my room, pulled out the cardboard box from under the bed, and took out a notebook, a new one with a rough, aquamarine paper cover. I closed the box again, pushed it under the bed, and flew downstairs. I carefully opened the door to old Yacob's room and found him ready to tell me what to write. We smiled at each other, then I sat down on the bed, placed the open notebook on my knees, and looked at him.

"I'm ready," I said. But old Yacob didn't have the time to utter one word when the voice of my mother reached us: "Mahlet! Mahlet!"

"Coming!" I yelled.

"Come right now!" she said sternly.

"Abba, I cannot stay," I said dejectedly. "Mama doesn't want me to."

"It doesn't matter, my child, leave the notebook here. I will take care of writing things down."

The Passage

As if carried on a whisper from an invisible world, old Yacob's story continued to reverberate in my ears for almost two years. It was like a prayer that demanded to be committed to memory. Only once in those two years did he and I have occasion to speak about it again.

It was halfway through the morning on one of those days when it was my turn to go to school in the afternoon. Our school had few classrooms and we pupils had to alternate. I happened to be in the vegetable garden with old Yacob. He had called me to help him to free our vegetables from the weeds.

We had already been working for a while. Without even turning around, his back bent and his hands busy pulling weeds, he asked me, "Do you remember the promise you made in front of the icon of the Virgin Mary?"

"Yes I do, I haven't forgotten it," I replied. How on earth could I have forgotten it? After a few minutes of silence I called him to get his attention again: "Abba."

"Tell me, my child."

"And my notebook? I cannot keep my promise without my notebook." For a while I had been trying to find an opportunity to ask him to give it back to me.

"Don't worry about it; it's in my trunk, under the box of candles. For now it's better that I keep it. When the time comes for you to use it, you will get it back." And in a conspiratorial tone, he added, "I have written everything down. The names of the battles and other things that could be of use to you."

Our conversation could have ended there but there was something that I wanted to know. I let a few moments of silence go by and then, once again, I called him: "Abba."

"Tell me, my child."

"Abba, but Alemtsehay, Haile Teklai, Aron the azmari, Worku, Nuguse, Mesfin, Alemtsehay's cousin, Ato Kebede—are they still alive?"

"Yes, my child, thank God they are alive. We meet every year in Addis Ababa on the twenty-seventh of the month of Meyazeya, the day when those who fought for the liberation are remembered."

"Abba, is Meyazeya 27 the day when you go to Addis Ababa wearing that old uniform of yours?"

"Woi gud anchi lij! Nothing escapes those eyes of yours. Exactly, my child, that's the day." I would have liked to know more about the present life of his companions, but I didn't have the courage to ask him another question. Our brief conversation would have stopped there if he hadn't guessed my thoughts. "My child, isn't there perhaps something more you'd like to know to satisfy your curiosity?" he asked me, looking at me sideways, his hands continuing to move among the vegetables. I nodded in agreement. "So what else would you like to know?"

"Something about your old comrades-in-arms . . . ," I said timidly.

Old Yacob's single tooth appeared in a smile of satisfaction, and then he briefly explained. "Alemtsehay got married. She lived for years near Holeta, on her family's land. She had children and when her husband died she became a nun. Mesfin married too. After the end of the Italian occupation, he went to England to go to university. He graduated in law and now he is a judge. Just for a little longer. He'll soon retire. In fact, he should have already done so but he didn't want to because he loves his work so much. Ato Kebede still lives on his former land. He was best man at both Alemtsehay's and Mesfin's weddings, while Haile Teklai took the vows of a monk and withdrew to Debre Libanos once the war was over. But he always comes to the celebration of Meyazeya 27. Aron the azmari still sings the old stories in the church courtyards in Addis Ababa and at weddings. Worku and Nuguse are the only ones I don't see any more. They are abroad but I do know that they are still alive."

There was still one curiosity I wanted to satisfy. I would have liked to know why Rosa, his dear niece, had stayed behind to live at Debre Markos while he had come to Debre Zeit. But old Yacob had returned to work, his soul at peace, the soul of one who has nothing more to say, so I suppressed that single question inside me. Only years later would I find the answer, after discovering certain facts that I will not tell you about here because they are not part of this story.

Adolescence

After those two years, I entered the world of adolescence. Suddenly, in the blink of an eye, I stopped being interested in the world of the adults, in their stories and in their secrets. I was overwhelmed by new emotions that engulfed me and that were thrusting me forward just like a river in full flood.

Something unknown was exploding inside of me, making everything that had come before feel faded and fleeting. The warm womb of home where the life of the adults unfolded, those very people who, up to a moment before, I had regarded with adoration, had become like the womb for a nine-month-old fetus: I wanted to get out, take the first steps toward discovering and taking hold of what one day I would need in order to build my own life as an adult.

I was like the water in the bed of a river, racing toward the sea, incapable of looking back. Back toward its source. If the years of my childhood had been those of the heart, of inward-looking love, now there came the years of the senses and of a passion for the external. Deaf years, years of rebellion against all restraints that could hold me back from the impulse forward.

During that period, old Yacob's story, together with my solemn promise, vanished from my ears and from my consciousness. And if some vague trace of his story was kept alive by the evening chatter of my uncles and my parents, there remained no memory of that promise. Something in me had tossed it into the corner of the room of my memory. Well concealed. In an invisible and untraceable trunk buried under a pile of odds and ends.

The first wave of those strange impulses also marked the beginning of my disagreements with my mother, who could not fathom my disobedience. I took every opportunity to open the main gate and lose myself in the dust of Debre Zeit. All it took was for one of the women to express a need, the need to buy something, for me to immediately offer to go, even if it only involved a trip to the small store next door, just to buy matches, for example. I would go out, only to return hours later to find my mother behind the gate, her eyes flashing with anger. She berated me, yelling as she had never done before. Till then there had never been the need. Then she would go to her friends and sisters gathered in the kitchen. "Woi gud!" she complained to the others. "Even Mahlet has turned into an adolescent. I've just finished with the boys and now it's her. I thought it would be easier with her. She was always so obedient, polite, quiet. Do you remember how many hours she spent in silence, in a corner of the kitchen while we prepared the coffee? Now look at her."

"You're so naive!" the others said to her scornfully. "Don't you know that the more they seem like angels when they're small, the more terrible they are as adolescents? Ask anyone who has only had girls. You have to grin and bear it. After all, it only means waiting out the next three or four years." They laughed while my mother huffed and puffed.

I was the youngest of five children. Before me came Mikael, Fasil, Grum, and Mengesha. Mikael and Fasil were the two younger ones, sixteen and seventeen years old, respectively. Grum and Mengesha, the two older ones, were twenty-one and twenty-two.

I was my mother's only girl, but one of many in the household. Ours was an Ethiopian household with a large extended family. Under the same roof lived eighteen of us: in addition to us five chil-

dren, there were the three elders; my parents; my Uncle Mesfin, my
father's brother, with his wife Saba and their children Tomas and
Tesemma; my Aunt Abeba, my mother's unmarried sister; my Aunt
Fanus, my mother's sister, a widow and the mother of Alemitu and
Mulu, the two cousins with whom I shared a bedroom.

I had female cousins, many female cousins. Besides Alemitu and
Mulu, who lived with us, others lived in the houses close by, in the
same neighborhood. There was Little Fanus (Big Fanus was my
aunt); Negisty the Latecomer; Almaz, who had no nickname; Ruth
with the pale-skinned face, almost like a half-blood; Tsigereda with
the big nose; Worknesh the Sleepy, who was always sleeping, which
everyone made fun of her for; Fetle the Princess, who did not like
getting her fingers dirty with the *injera*; Tarakesh, who liked to go
to church; Aster . . .

With those girl cousins of my age, I shared that magical moment
when every limit could be challenged. We were like dogs that had
broken free from their chains. We roamed around the town, aim-
lessly, sniffing the air to drink in that intoxicating feeling of freedom
mixed with discovery.

My mother and my aunts shouted at us all the time, calling on
each other for support. We lowered our eyes, showing ourselves to
be submissive in front of them. After allowing just enough time for
them to be placated, we set off again. I think that at some point they
found themselves bereft of all resources. Although many girls had
been raised in that household, our mothers insisted that there had
never been a group as rebellious as ours. And my mother said it was
because of me. It was me, the angel who had grown up transforming
herself into a devil, capable of igniting that mischievous spark in the
other girls. My mother just could not get over it.

The Advice

By pure chance, one afternoon after the umpteenth telling-off, I
saw my mother talking furtively to old Yacob in the kitchen. Then
the two of them went out together, down the few steps, skirting the

wall to the arch covered in bougainvillea, going through it, and then entering old Yacob's room. I had never seen her go into his room before. My curiosity piqued, I followed them and crouched down under the window of the room, determined to eavesdrop through the broken glass.

For a while they did not speak. The silence was broken only by a gentle rustling sound. That must have been old Yacob moving around in his room. I tried to listen attentively to make sense of the movements beyond the window. I heard a match being struck against its box and a crackle as it caught alight. Perhaps old Yacob was lighting a candle in front of the icon of the Virgin Mary. Once more I heard the rustling from before and then silence, broken only by old Yacob's voice.

"So, my daughter, what do you want to talk to me about?"

"About Mahlet," said my mother, her voice full of concern. I felt my heart sink. Yikes—I had been worried that sooner or later she would speak to him about me, about how I was disappointing her with my disobedience, but I was hoping that it would be later rather than sooner.

"Mahlet?" he asked in a stunned voice.

"Yes. Lately I've been worried about her." Here we go, I thought; now she's going to tell him everything I do and that she thinks is wrong.

"And what's worrying you?"

"That she's growing up."

"But that's normal. I can't see the problem." And here I sighed with relief.

"She's growing up and I can't keep her in the house anymore, close to us." Once more I felt a shudder of fear. Yes, it was true. I was experiencing that uncontrollable urge, that desire to be out, and I felt I had the right to do so, but she would get angry and accuse me of being disobedient. Perhaps old Yacob would get angry too. I could handle my mother's yelling but I would not have been able to deal with a possible disapproving look from my favorite elder.

"My daughter, when a fruit is ripe, it doesn't remain attached to the tree," he said. A silent flash of joy filled my heart. Old Yacob was on my side.

My mother sighed. "Yes, I know, but—"

"You have already been there with your other four children," he observed gently.

"That's true, but they were boys," she pointed out.

"My daughter, what do you mean?" he asked her, feigning surprise.

My mother's voice dropped to a whisper. "I haven't had any experience with girls."

"If you wanted someone who had experience with girls, you should have gone to Mama Illeni who has raised nine daughters and many granddaughters."

My mother's voice dropped even lower. "But you are my family's elder and I want your advice."

"Well, if you put it that way, I want to begin by telling you that I see no difference between raising a boy or a girl."

Again, there was silence. I straightened my legs just enough to bring my eyes level with the broken window and peeked in. My mother was sitting on the bed, next to old Yacob, with an expression that was at once incredulous and questioning. "What do you mean, there is no difference?" she blurted out, her voice strong again.

I crouched back down under the window.

"Since I can't see any difference, why don't you tell me what it is," said old Yacob.

"Raising a girl is harder, because you have to teach her to hold sacred her 'inviolabilty'—her virginity—and concede it at the right time and in the right way."

"That's right, but in the same way you have to teach the boys to respect a girl's 'inviolability' and not force her to concede it."

"Abba, but life is not like that—a girl has to know how to protect herself, to be very aware that if she gets pregnant, it's all on her shoulders, that boys can refuse to be involved," she pointed out.

"My daughter, I'm surprised at you," said old Yacob with a note of reproof in his voice. "Do you perhaps mean to say that a mother can raise her boys by saying to them, 'Do whatever you want,' and say to the girls, 'Careful, even just one breath could complicate your future?' Certainly, there is a difference between male and female: God has chosen a woman's womb as the place to plant the seed of life. And a boy, if he has little or no conscience, might not concern himself with respecting a girl, but this difference often arises from having raised the boys the wrong way."

"What do you mean?"

"What I mean is that it is necessary to teach both of them how to be responsible for their own actions, even if the results of these actions appear only in the womb of one of them. What's more, we must teach each girl to think carefully and find the right moment to give herself, and teach the male to respect her choice."

There was another moment of silence. I straightened my legs again and peeked in. Now my mother had a more subdued look on her face and kept her eyes lowered.

"My daughter, has Mahlet already got her 'flower of the month,' as we call it?"

"No, Abba, she is still a child. She's just turned eleven."

"Woi gud! You're just like the woman who worried about giving birth even before getting pregnant." Old Yacob was almost chuckling, "Now, hold tight in your heart what I am about to tell you: even though our ways of thinking are different, and I ask you to reflect on them, I believe I can give you some advice. Your daughter must grow up. It is right that she do so. Your job is to allow her to do just that. You cannot keep her closed up in the house. This is no longer the time for that. Give her some free space. Decide when she can go out and where she can go. Give her a space of her own, which will allow her to try things out for herself. And while you are waiting for her 'flower of the month' to come, prepare her by talking to her about all those other things that are bothering you so much."

I straightened my legs one last time. My mother had a half smile on her face. A sweet, sweet half smile. It meant that she accepted old Yacob's advice. Without waiting to hear any more, I ran off.

The Flower of the Month

One evening soon after, instead of the usual command, "Mahlet, it's time, go to bed," my mother said, "I'll come with you to your room." Once we were in my room, she asked Mulu and Alemitu to leave us alone. I had already guessed. Since the day when I had overheard her conversation with old Yacob, I was waiting excitedly for this moment, just like an athlete waiting for the sound of the gun that signals the beginning of the race.

She slowly sat down on my bed. She settled herself and then began to speak to me. She began by saying that I was growing up and the time had come for me to explore the world beyond our house, but I could not roam around like a dog off its leash as I had attempted to do in the preceding months. Just as in my life up to that time, I had to follow certain rules in this matter too. I had my father's and her permission to spend part of the afternoon in my cousin Legesse's hairdressing shop, and on Saturday mornings I could go to the market. As for the rest of the time, I had to divide it up between my schoolwork and taking part in family life. She added that the same freedom had been conceded to my girl cousins of the same age.

Then she fell silent. I looked at her. She seemed uneasy. I had never seen her stumbling about in the dark struggling to find the right words to explain herself. She sat on the edge of the bed, her muscles tensed as if she were sitting on a prickly cactus plant. That was usually how I reacted when she spoke to me in that quiet, imperious voice that would countenance no answer. Now everything seemed to be reversed. She was navigating through the difficulties of someone who cannot find the initial words, the opening phrase to introduce what she wanted to say, while I sat there observing her, completely at ease. In any case, I already knew what she was going to talk to me about.

Finally something in her clicked. She cleared her voice, patted her hair, making sure her braids were in order, and began to speak again. "Soon," she said to me, "something important will happen to you, something that, in one single leap, will take you into the world of adult women and will change your whole life. Something beautiful . . ." Just as old Yacob had suggested to her, she was trying to explain about the 'flower of the month,' but I already knew everything. I had many girl cousins, of differing ages. Mulu and Alemitu were older than me, by six and seven years, respectively. Every month, with the regularity of the rhythm of the church drums, I saw them hang up their washed strips of cloth to dry.

Every first day of the 'flower of the month,' Mulu writhed in pain and her mother, my Aunt Fanus, gave her a soothing drink made with herbs and rue seeds, and in the evening she took a thermos to her room, filled with the semisweet concoction of *aja,* in case she had cramps during the night.

Besides these physical aspects, I also knew about the rest of it! About all those things as spicy as the *mitmitta.*

In the afternoon my older girl cousins would meet their friends behind the wall at the bus station, where the continuous coming and going of small vehicles made the dust fly. There was an old sycamore tree whose roots wove around the stones of the wall before going into the ground. Under its spreading branches that shaded in part a patch of the bus station courtyard and in part a wide stretch of rough ground, they exchanged secrets about love. Stories that took place over a brief period of time. Snippets of gossip like the beginning of the flight of the flamingoes on Lake Hora. A quick tap on the surface of the water, and off they went on wide, pink wings. A mere phrase or two, tossed out quickly in a whisper.

"Worknesh is pregnant by Milion."

Shock all around on the part of the girls. "Are they getting married?"

"No. She doesn't want to. When she found out she was pregnant, she had just broken up with him."

"So now what will she do?"

"Milion's mother has said she is willing to raise the baby."

"With all the children she has, she won't even notice that she has an extra one." Chuckles all around.

"Hi, Almaz," they shouted out in chorus to a friend who was joining them, dragging her feet in the dust sensually. "Your skin is glowing with the essence of well-being!" said one of them.

She gave a smirk of superiority. "What do you expect? I satiated myself till dawn." All eyes lit up with curiosity, so she, drawing nearer, revealed in one breath, "My parents have gone to a funeral in the village of Agi so Tesfaye stayed with me. All night!"

There was also discussion about those who wed as virgins, like Aster, who at barely nineteen had decided to marry Dawit, consecrating their union with the Eucharist. The more savvy cousins had commented, "Let's hope she likes the way he has sex with her."

Aside from this superficial gossip, I also knew about detailed aspects of sex from the conversations between Mulu and Alemitu. Mulu was still a virgin while Alemitu enjoyed the spicy joys of sex with Ghirma, a son of the Danakil. The boy with eyes of fire. In the evening after every meeting, tucked away in our room, far from the ears of the adults of our household, she would tell Mulu and me everything, sparing no detail. Once she had finished telling us about it, she ended with the usual phrase: "You should give it a try, Mulu. It would get rid of your 'flower-of-the-month' pains."

And Mulu would answer by saying, "I want to be a virgin when I marry, like Aster." Alemitu would then add, "What a waste of time!"

Then they would turn off the bedside lamp and the room was plunged into darkness.

"Mahlet, are you listening to me?" My mother called me back to the present.

"Sure, Mama!" I hadn't heard a single word. My thoughts had wandered elsewhere while she had used words in a roundabout way but never got to the heart of the matter. All it required was a single sentence—"You will get the 'flower of the month' and you will become a woman"—but as short as it was, it seemed that she could not get her tongue around it.

I wanted to save her from that embarrassing situation by saying, "Look, I know everything," but that would have meant telling her all about Alemitu and betraying her secrets.

I let her ramble on until she found her own way of getting out of the sticky situation. After all her agonizing she managed to blurt out in one breath, "Mahlet, soon you will get the 'flower of the month.' From that moment on you must consider yourself a woman. That will involve a whole series of precautions and behaviors that I will talk to you about in the next few days. Now, go to sleep and may God watch over your dreams." She patted my cheeks and went off without saying anything more, leaving to a future meeting the burden of going into the meaning of that phrase.

My cousins came back into the room. Alemitu jumped onto my bed and began to chant, from an old traditional song, "*Ieberet alga iaregergal.* Iron bedsteads make you bounce up and down," and she bounced up and down as she sang. My Aunt Fanus called her *iesat zer,* "daughter of fire."

She continued to sing and jump up and down for a while longer. "C'mon, Alemitu, that's enough," said Mulu, and turning to me she added, "I bet your mother tried to tell you about the 'flower of the month.'"

I nodded in assent and we all began to laugh. "Surely you didn't tell her you already knew all about it?" asked Alemitu.

"No, I let her talk."

"And what did she tell you?"

"Almost nothing—she talked for a long time without being able to explain anything," I said. "And while she was weaving circles around the subject I began to think of all those dirty things that you tell us about when you get back from your dates with Ghirma, the Danakil's son." Once again we fell about laughing.

"Good girl," said Alemitu. "Don't say anything, and let me take care of your sex education. Rule number one, don't follow Mulu's example, Mulu who wants to be a virgin when she gets married."

"Stop it, Alemitu," scolded Mulu. "You are always talking dirty." We continued to chat and laugh for half an hour until someone knocked on our door and called us to order.

We stopped immediately. We shot under the covers and I turned out the light.

In the darkness I felt my heart leap. "Starting tomorrow I am free and I have permission to go to the Saturday market," I thought, smiling at the spirits of the night.

The Saturday Market!

Of everything that they might have conceded to us, the Saturday market was the freedom that figured most prominently in our dreams. The first Friday night after the "concession," none of us was able to get a wink of sleep. That night we twisted and turned, each in her own bed, each in her own house. At times it was too hot and we threw off the covers, at times too cold and we wrapped ourselves in the blankets we had just thrown off. It seemed that I could almost see the other cousins, that there was an invisible thread that linked us to each other, across the houses, allowing all of us to share in the same restlessness. It was the thought of what we might see the next day. Not that we had never been to the market, but then it had been to run errands for our mothers, for our aunts, for the neighbors, for our fathers. "Mahlet! Mahlet! Run! Go and buy some coffee at Etie Ascalech's stall, the one on the corner of the street. And barter on the price. Don't pay more than five *birr* a kilo. If she's not there, go to Gash Selemon, that one near the onion store. Whatever you do, don't go to Etie Aregash—his coffee is old." We stepped on it, our heads down in order to take care of the errand and return home to get our reward: a velvety hand stroking our cheeks, a sweet look from eyes resting on our faces, a phrase, "*Gosh iene lij*! Good for you, my little child!" Some praise murmured among the women: "Mahlet is very helpful! She makes her mother's heart sing with satisfaction!"

When our desire to serve the adults had disappeared, blotted out by our adolescent yearning, and the errands had become the means to satisfy our curiosity, our mothers had called on us less frequently.

That first Saturday, when our households began to echo with the stirrings that announced the beginning of the day, we were ready to leave, waiting impatiently for permission to go out. We had agreed to meet in the courtyard of my house and there we all were, in front of the gate. We were just like young goats champing at the exit of the fenced-in yard.

Our mothers tried to remind us that it was still early, but it was no use. At that hour there were probably very few stalls open, but our frenetic excitement made us deaf to all reason. Tired of holding us back, around eight o'clock they gave us the signal to leave, with the order to return home before two o'clock. We tumbled out onto the street like spilled water from a bowl running over the earth in a tangle of rivulets.

They were right, there were only a few stalls set up in the market, but in a short time it filled up. It crackled, and was as unpredictable as a firecracker. Stalls appeared all over the place, as if the very earth were spewing them out like badly digested food.

Here was a shed in sheet metal revealing an interior full of sacks of pink onions, and another with little mountains of dried chili peppers whose pungent smell made passersby cough. Traders hung out lines of colored dresses on long metal rods, and women stretched out pieces of cloth on which to display small bags of spices: *kororima, kosserat, betsobilia, heel, kerefa*. . . . Other pieces of cloth bore sea incense: white from the Hamar people, black from Konso, Sendel, Korbe.... Farmers crossed the road with a swaying gait, carrying on their heads bamboo cages full of cockerels.

Stalls with pyramids of vegetables, and wheelbarrows piled high with pineapples and mangoes. The stall selling rope, the one selling tin containers, the one selling big and small plastic cans. The small store selling sacred vestments, the one selling secondhand articles, another selling mattresses, the blind sellers of lottery tickets who, in every corner of the market, chanted endlessly: "*Nege iemiwotà, nege iemiwotà, nege iemiwotà.* The draw is tomorrow, the draw is tomorrow, the draw is tomorrow!" The line of the Saturday tej stands: four planks of wood with two strips of tin on top and plastic cloths that served as walls. The tailor and the farmers waiting in line with the pieces of material they wanted sewn in one hand.

Small carriages with skinny drivers next to ladies plump in the flesh and in their rustling clothes. All customers whose passing was enough to raise the spirits of the vendors. Little girls who, like us not long before, had been sent on errands. And still more tej stands upon tej stands, the smell of fermented honey and the buzzing of bees, mixed in with the continuous sound of people wheeling and dealing, chatting, greeting each other with loud kisses on the cheeks and repeated salutations and bowing.

Just before two o'clock, trotting along and chatting, we went back to my house. My two cousins pushed open one of the sides of the gate and entered the courtyard. Our three elders were sitting in the garden, on the bench in the shade of the mango tree. Tossing off a quick greeting in their direction, my cousins continued to chatter excitedly, going toward the kitchen where our mothers were waiting for us. I instead slowed down. I stopped in front of the bench. Old Yacob looked at me. "Come here, child," he said. I went up to him. "Can I still hold you on my knees or are you too grown up for that?" I did not reply, instead settling myself on his bony knees. "Did you have fun at the market?" he asked me, and I nodded. "And what made it fun for you?" he asked again.

I could tell him and the other two elders what I liked about it. I lowered my head shyly and murmured, "Watching how grown-ups go about their lives."

The three elders laughed and then blessed me: "May God make you grow up and be worthy of a great injera. Now, off you go and have some lunch."

In the following months we observed the pulsating heart of the market with new eyes. With the eyes of those who have taken the first step beyond the protective circle of infancy. For a long time neither my cousins nor I became accustomed to the bustle. For a long time our Friday nights were heavy with excitement. And when finally we had taken in every aspect of it, every secret, it became the backdrop to our adolescent games.

We liked to discover the first drunk of the day. The game was even more hilarious if, hidden behind some hedge, we managed to witness the throwing out of the drunk from the tej or coffee stand and hear the accompanying insults of the tej blenders or coffee servers. Just thinking about those foul insults gave you goosebumps from the shame of it and made the scandalized passersby repeatedly cross themselves. Witnessing those scenes, hidden behind the hedges, we fell about laughing until we were discovered by the tej blenders and coffee servers who shooed us away, running after us with a broom.

Usually that first drunk of the day was poor Gasce Tlahun. Every Saturday, at the start of the market, he was already drunk. By eight o'clock the coffee servers had already had him thrown out and he spent the morning stretched out on the ground like an old rag waiting to come back to life, the complete opposite of the market all around him that was pulsating with life. Only toward the end of the morning, after buckets of ice-cold water had been repeatedly thrown over him, did he come around. Just when the vendors were getting ready to return home. Then you could see him with them, unsteady on his feet, looking for a last glass of tej or areke before everything definitively closed up.

Once the game of searching for drunks bored us, we began to take
an interest in the amorous encounters of our older cousins. That
first impassioned phase was the only time we were interested in our
cousin Legesse's shop, the other place we were allowed to go to. It
was a simple shop at the edge of the market, with a large room and a
second equally large room at the back of the shop. It was patronized
almost exclusively by farmers. They would arrive in town on Friday
afternoons. In the first big room they had their hair cut and in the
back room they stored the goods they would sell the following day
at the market, and they paid for both services. Nothing that could
arouse our interest. But then we invented that game. Our cousins
allowed us to eavesdrop on part of their amorous encounters if we
went to Legesse's shop to get "the makeup box," a precious box full of
cosmetics, some new, others already used, a box that Legesse had put
together over the years. He had bought or, more often, sponged the
cosmetics from the few relatives and acquaintances who lived abroad
and who, every now and then, came home to see their families.

In those years makeup, perfumes, nail polish, and other such
things were considered imperialist and consumerist, and you could
only buy them on the black market, at great expense and only with
American dollars. Legesse's box was a precious possession and people had to pay to use it. And for the ordinary girls and ladies of Debre
Zeit who used it for special occasions, the payment was in cash. We
cousins were permitted a deal: we could use the already opened
cosmetics in exchange for little jobs, like washing someone's hair.
Taking the inventory and overseeing the farmers' deposits in the
back room on Friday afternoons was traded for the use of unopened
products. And that was my job. After the first few times, Legesse had
begun to give out the box of unopened products only in exchange for
my afternoon help. According to him, I was the only one capable of
taking accurate inventories.

When even that game bored us, we began another and then another until we began to get bored, and then suddenly we stopped
that aimless roaming around. We separated, ceasing to be a single

unit, a busy swarm that moved compactly in unison, and each one of us resumed her old habits.

Just as I did in the old times, I stayed at home and took up my position in the corner of the kitchen, with the women drinking coffee and the elders perched in a corner, looking around and giving their blessing.

There was, however, an enormous difference from the past: I was no longer interested in listening to the chatter of the grown-ups. I sat there, surrounded by them, letting the empty hours roll by, waiting for evening. My mother, mistaking my apathy for reform and growth, told the others that finally I had returned to my old self. However, the three elders, who knew my soul intimately, kept their eyes on me during the coffee hour. They attempted to go beyond my outside shell and understand the reasons for that obscure behavior of mine. They did not give up until they felt they had understood. I never noticed anything and I had no inkling of it until old Yacob called me.

I was at home, munching on cookies and drinking tea, all wrapped up in that annoying boredom that wouldn't let me be. Suddenly, I heard his voice: "Mahlet! Mahlet!" He was calling up from the smaller courtyard. I looked out the kitchen door. "My child, come and give me a hand. The beets are full of bugs and weeds are growing up in between the carrots," he said to me, pointing to the vegetable garden.

I hesitated on the threshold of the half-open door.

"Child, if you're busy, you can help me another time," he said, giving me the chance to excuse myself from his request. It was a crafty way of freeing my spirit from possibly giving a response dictated by adolescent rebellion.

I stood still where I was and gave myself the time to observe him calmly. Against his dark skin you could see white: the white of his very short hair, of the short beard on the chin of his tiny face, of his shemma wrapped around his chest, of the pants that reached down to the leather laces of his sandals, and finally the white of his one remaining tooth that poked out from his lips.

He was standing there wearing the serene expression of someone who is not even expecting an answer. Almost without realizing it,

I went down the steps and joined him. Together we covered the few steps that took us into the rectangle of the vegetable patch. My plastic flip-flops sank into the wet earth that came up to the skin of my feet. Old Yacob turned around. "I watered yesterday evening, at sunset," he said, "but I waited for you to get rid of the weeds and the bugs from the beets. I was hoping you would help me. I like working with you in the garden."

It was morning. A gentle sun, just a notch above the roof of the house, was shining down on the courtyard. The chickens had sneaked into the vegetable patch behind us and were roaming around by our feet. It made me think of when I was smaller and of the grimaces old Yacob would make as he shooed them away. Deliberate grimaces to make me laugh. "I like working with you in the garden too," I said to him. We worked for almost half an hour in silence, a silence that was broken by me. There was something missing in the garden. "Abba, where did the rue bush end up?"

"I had to pull it out. The roots had all burned up."

"Really? I've only just realized that for days now we have been drinking coffee, milk too, without rue."

"I asked your Aunt Fanus if I could plant one of those plants of hers in our vegetable garden, the plants that she keeps in a pot, but she said she needs her rue for Mulu's 'flower of the month.'" He stopped talking abruptly and looked at me. "Your mother has spoken to you about the 'flower of the month,' right?" And without waiting for a reply, turning his attention toward the work in his hands, he continued: "Of course she has spoken to you about it. But then, you already knew all about it, didn't you? You've got so many girl cousins! Ah, mothers! When they have girls, they forget they were girls themselves and that they learned from the older ones. Anyway, coming back to the rue, there's nothing I can do but wait for someone to buy me a plant at the market." Once again he turned his head and fixed his gaze on me. I kept quiet.

"Perhaps you could buy one for me," he said.

"Hmm . . . ," I mumbled.

"This Saturday, when you and your cousins go and let loose."

"I don't go to the market on Saturdays anymore."

"Ah. How come?"

"I get bored."

"What?" he said, his eyes almost popping. "But I thought you enjoyed it so much!"

"True," I replied, adding in a whisper, "but now it bores me."

"The novelty has worn off, eh? You have explored every possible nook and cranny, right?"

This time it was I who turned toward him. He was on the verge of laughing. That darned old man was always able to read inside me. I felt like laughing too.

"Yep. I've seen everything that there was to see and now I get bored," I confessed, finding his laughter infectious.

"This is why you don't go out anymore?"

"Right!"

"You could go to your cousin Legesse's hairdressing shop."

"I don't like it," I said, making a face.

"What is it you don't like?"

"Abba Yacob, there's nothing there except the farmers who go to get their hair cut!" I answered scornfully.

"Perhaps you're making a mistake," he insisted.

"No, Abba. It's the most boring place I know," I said emphatically.

"Listen, child, I have to confess something to you. Abba Selemon, Abba Yohanes, and I have watched you carefully in these last weeks, so as to understand what was going on in your heart. It was clear that something was wrong. You gave off a bitter scent! We had sensed this boredom of yours, which you have just confirmed for me. If this is the reason for the gloom that we saw in your eyes, I am convinced I know the root cause of your discontent and the way to get rid of it. Actually, all three of us are convinced of it: Abba Selemon, Abba Yohanes, and I. If you're curious to know what we think, you only have to ask."

We spent the rest of the time working in silence. He, enveloped in his tranquility, I in my indecision. In the end I let myself be transported by that interior laughter that I had felt earlier, when I recognized his ability to throw light on my deepest, most hidden corners. I asked him to speak to me.

I saw no satisfaction register on his face, as I might have expected. But he was the wise one of our household who was able to see inside other people, but knew how to prevent people from seeing inside of him.

He simply said to me, "Come here, child. Let's go and sit on the bench under the mango tree. Soon it will get hot," and he walked toward the main courtyard.

Old Yacob sat down and adjusted his shemma on his shoulders, and when I too was settled next to him, he began to speak.

"Child, I know how you feel. Now you are older and you're no longer interested in the world you knew when you were small. And yet at the same time you don't find anything in the world of the adults that entices you forward. Your heart is stuck on a piece of land and sees, in front and behind, only deep chasms. It feels comfortable only when it moves sideways. Without going forward. But I'm telling you that in front of you there is a chasm that can be bridged in a single leap. After that comes a long plain." He paused. "You see, this year you and your cousins let loose, but only with your eyes and ears. You have observed the adult world just like someone looking in a restaurant with his face stuck against the window, without ever going in. And let me tell you, it's one thing to observe the adult world through a window, and another to go inside."

"And so?" I asked, as my adolescent impatience was beginning to make itself felt.

"So you have to enter into the adult world. Which means having to learn to carry out certain actions and see what the consequences are, and how, depending on the direction we take, that world comes toward us."

"Abba, you are speaking empty words to me. Nice thoughts with no substance," I said, irritated by the length of his preamble.

"In my opinion," he continued, weighing each word calmly, without paying any attention to my irritation, "or I should say, in our

opinion—on this I consulted Abba Yohanes and Abba Selemon—
you should begin to do some small jobs. Paid jobs. Like a real adult.
Assume responsibility for your work commitments and see what
happens."

That was easy for *him* to say . . . a job! "And, according to you," I
asked, my growing impatience spilling over into my voice, "how can
I find a job?"

It was the first time I had ever answered him rudely. He looked
askance at me, raising an eyebrow. "Calm down, my child, calm
down. If you want one, there is a job for you. Your cousin Legesse
would welcome you with open arms. He has often told me that when
you were in charge of doing the inventory in the shop on Friday afternoons, everything went smoothly with the farmers. You're good at
keeping accounts and at dealing with people. You could work for him
on Friday afternoons and on Saturday mornings. Think about it."

"And do you think he would pay me?" My previous impatience
had suddenly dissipated, transforming itself into a growing interest.

"Sure."

I had nothing to lose. Trying something new was better than being bored, and after all was said and done, the idea appealed to me:
"Abba . . ."

"Tell me, child."

"I've already thought about it. I think I would like to try it out."

Old Yacob smiled with satisfaction. "I'll speak to him about it tomorrow, after I have asked your father and your mother for their
permission."

The Consent

That Thursday evening following my conversation with old Yacob, my father and mother called me into the room known as the
conversation room: a small, old drawing room, used by my younger
brothers for studying and by the adults for important conversations.
It was only on special occasions that one was called to that room. It
had never happened to me before. I guessed it was about the work

in Legesse's shop, and the formal way in which they wanted to communicate their decision to me made me nervous. I entered the room apprehensively. My father and mother were sitting side by side on an old, sagging sofa, underneath the black-and-white photo of my father's family. Her slim face with the delicate features was serious. He, instead, wore a slight smile that accentuated his thin mustache, barely etched on his square face. My father asked me to approach him and to make a full turn. When I had completed the turn he had a strange expression in his eyes, a mixture of tenderness and regret. "So, here we are! Even my youngest chick has grown up," he commented.

My mother had remained seated, her expression serious and contained, like someone waiting to see how the quality of her work will be assessed. She was the one who would be praised or criticized for my eventual good or bad behavior. My father made me sit in front of them. "Mahlet," he said to me, "starting tomorrow you can go to work in your cousin Legesse's shop. You will work on Friday afternoons and Saturday mornings as Abba Yacob explained to you. You have our permission, but there is one condition that you must respect: you must never, for any reason whatsoever, take part in any discussion about the government. Whether it be for or against. And you must never, for any reason in the world, get mixed up in the affairs of the rebels. Is that clear?" I nodded in agreement. "Mahlet, Abba Yacob is convinced that you are capable of understanding the gravity of this condition." I nodded in agreement once again. "If it were not for his conviction, we would never have granted you this permission. You know this, right?"

My words came out, barely audible. "You and Mama mustn't be worried, Papa." My father smiled with relief and my mother nodded, signaling her approval.

The First Day of Work

The following afternoon I crossed the threshold of that non-descript shop on the edge of the market. I carried myself straight and proudly, like a person who has been given an important task. I climbed the three steps, deep in my adolescent turmoil, and entered the world of the adults for the first time. Legesse followed me with a smile. He was pleased to have his new helper. I immediately got to work as I had done on those Fridays when it was my turn to go and get the magic box of makeup. Back and forth from the back room, busily engaged between the baskets filled with teff and those with honey and with tej, among men and women farmers surrounded by swarms of children. Many of the farmers remembered me and welcomed me warmly. On the Fridays when it had been my turn to be with them, they had expressed their approval several times. I was good at taking the inventory of the merchandise that they were depositing and I wrote it down on a piece of paper. I listed the merchandise with a letter and, next to it, in Roman numerals, the quantities, which could be easily checked even by those who could not read but who were able to recognize Roman numerals. I did not write up untidy, indecipherable notes as my cousins did, driven by the desire to get away quickly. Notes that, at the end of the day, neither they nor Legesse were able to decipher.

That first day, when work was over, securing the door with two heavy locks, Legesse told me that the number of customers had increased. Now there were not just the farmers. A month before, a messenger had brought an announcement to the market. A public proclamation had made the rounds of the town; even I knew about it. There had been talk about it at home at the women's coffee hour. The town governing body was abolishing the crime of *ietsegur lewt,* literally meaning "changed hair"—that is, the crime, according to the regime, committed by women who styled their hair by copying the Afro-American fashion. On the Saturdays following the announcement, the number of women coming to his shop had increased. It had risen slowly and steadily, and it was still continuing to rise. On Saturday mornings women and young girls came to have their hair straightened with an old curling iron heated with alcohol that tamed the hair into marvelous corkscrew curls.

"Besides keeping the inventory of the deposited merchandise and washing the farmers' hair, you'll have to learn how to use the iron," Legesse said to me. I nodded in agreement without saying a word. By then it was late; it must have been around nine o'clock in the evening. I had never returned home at such an hour. I was born during the period of the military junta, the *Derg,* of the curfew that went from eleven in the evening to seven in the morning. Nobody used to go out after dinner. Legesse decided he would walk me home.

We set off across the darkened town, which was already empty. We were near the market but the area didn't seem familiar to me—on the contrary, it almost seemed as if I were in another world. In the dark I could hardly make out the contours of the houses. The silence was broken by the barking of some dog or by the shriek of the hyenas in search of food at the edge of the inhabited area. There was not even a moon to throw light on that darkness full of tension.

A few small groups of soldiers were beginning to move around the streets. Night animals just like the hyenas, out to hunt and scare those who had not yet locked themselves up in their homes. Two soldiers just a couple of years older than my younger brothers suddenly appeared out of an alley. They pointed their Kalashnikovs at Legesse and demanded to see his papers. Without saying a word he gave them his identity card and his card testifying that he belonged to the *kebele,* our neighborhood committee. They checked it with a flashlight and then they asked him what I was doing out with him at that hour. "She's my cousin, I'm taking her back home," he told them. They waved the flashlight to indicate that we could go on. The light traced a small arc in the darkness. As it traveled around, it lit up a stretch of the road and a pack of stray dogs digging through the garbage. Legesse put an arm around my shoulders to make me feel protected. "Starting next Friday I will not send you home so late. You must get home before dark. Seven o'clock at the very latest."

I found my mother and father waiting for us in front of the gate to my house. They invited Legesse to go in but he declined. "It's late. I better get home quickly. The soldiers are already out and about," he said, and my father froze as if an electric shock had made his muscles contract.

Trying to control himself, he said emphatically, "Well, hurry up then, my son—even if there are still two hours to go before the curfew, you can never be too sure with that lot." We went in, but my parents said nothing until we had crossed the threshold of our house. Once we were inside, my father put his hands on my shoulders. "Mahlet," he said, "remember what we told you?"

"Yes, Papa."

"We were worried all afternoon," said my mother. "If it were not for the trust we have in Abba Yacob, in such times as these we would never have given our permission for you to work at Legesse's." It was the second time that she had spoken to me as if she were sitting on a prickly cactus plant.

"Mama, don't worry. I will never get involved in the gossiping or in matters concerning the rebels or the government," I reassured her. I was determined to avoid any possible second thoughts about it.

"Tomorrow," added my father, "I shall tell Legesse that I don't want you to come home when the night patrols are already around. You must be home before then, as soon as it gets dark. Not later than seven."

I never told them, not even many years later, that the soldiers had stopped us that night, pointing their Kalashnikovs at Legesse. My father would have immediately withdrawn his permission for me to work in Legesse's shop. He feared for me, for my safety and that of all the family. How could I say he was wrong? When I think about it, considering the times we were living in, I'm still amazed at old Yacob's idea and that my parents gave their permission. Perhaps it was just my destiny playing out.

At Legesse's Shop

When I began to work in Legesse's shop, it was halfway through 1982 (in the Ethiopian calendar—the beginning of 1990 in the Western calendar). By then the Derg had been in power for sixteen years.

It had achieved power by taking advantage of the wave of demon-
strations led by students and by the small parties that wanted a new,
democratic Ethiopia, different from the old feudal system of the
monarchy. They had marched all together to the slogan of "The land
to the farmers! Fair wages for the military!" Then, once in power, the
Derg had done away with all student organizations and all opposition parties. And not just metaphorically speaking. In those sixteen
years all opposition had been swept away by force. In order to keep
a firm hold on his power, the leader of the Derg (the Ethiopian Red
Terror), Mengistu Haile Mariam, together with his military junta,
had ordered sweeping arrests, cruel torture, and mass killings. All it
took was to be suspected, to have said, in error, a word that might be
interpreted as against the politics of the Derg, and you were tortured,
slaughtered, and killed. During the first years of his government,
when I was not yet born, not a single night went by without shoot-
ings, and every morning the bodies of young students were strewn
in the streets of the town, ripped apart by machine-gun fire. In three
years they had eliminated all the groups that had publicly opposed
them. After that period, our people had acquiesced to wearing the
mask of resignation, but below the surface they were seething. Everywhere armed groups had formed that fought against the regime. In
the North, side by side with the Eritrean People's Liberation Front,
the Tigrayan Front was born; in the central Highlands there was the
Amharic Front; and in the South, the Oromo Front. As a result, the
regular Mengistu army was fighting on several fronts. The toughest
one was in the North, against the Eritreans and the Tigrayans.

In my family, there had always been little talk of all this. Only the
occasional half-muttered phrase. We children were not allowed to
talk about the dictatorship, about the rebels, about political ideology.
Any questions were silenced by a recurring answer: "This is not the
time to talk of certain things. There will come a day when we will
tell you everything. Today it is too dangerous." It was their way of
protecting us. I found things out at school, from my friends with
whom we exchanged the little political information we had, from the

by-now-familiar sounds of the nightly raids. The sound of the weapons, of the shooting, of the armored trucks that moved around the dark streets after curfew. But in fact we knew very little. These were not things we had experienced firsthand. Everyone in Debre Zeit lived like this. Either you ran off and joined the rebels in the forests, or you learned to carve out a space for yourself within the fabric of the dictatorship. And we who remained behind had learned. We had gotten used to their arrogant behavior and we knew how to avoid it. We accepted submitting ourselves to the rules imposed on us by the kebele and in exchange we could go on living undisturbed, continuing our traditions. We could meet; drink the three long, ceremonial cups of coffee; fill our houses with our humor, with one smart remark after another, all with double meanings; enjoy ourselves at weddings with singers who accompanied us in our dance for as late as the curfew allowed.

Together we all put up the tents for weddings and baptisms, lightening the task with loud laughter and bantering. Guests would come, even from afar, and after the festivities were over, they would stay and sleep at the houses of people in the neighborhood. On the day of the celebration, we filled the tents wearing our white clothes edged with embroidery in a thousand colors, and when the singers gave the signal to begin, our shoulders would move to the rhythm of the dance, the *iskista*. The end of the wedding feasts was marked by the *kurt*, enormous pieces of raw meat served with a mustard and hot chili sauce. For the entire day the women from the bride's or the groom's family, together with those in their neighborhood association, ran from one end of the tent to the other, approaching the tables and asking the guests, "Is there anything missing? What can I bring you? *Tej, tella*? A portion of injera?" We rejoiced at every birth and we ate the genfo in honor of the newborn, dipping our fingers in the hole in the middle in order to soak some pieces of it in the spiced butter and in the *berbere*. We grieved together at every death and we spent at least the first three days with the dead person's family, up until the burial. We observed the recurrence of the saints' holy days, both the monthly ones and the annual ones, with the grand procession of the *Tabot* outside the church and through the town, with the big drums beating out the rhythm of our singing. There were neighborhood associations and farmers' associations and we met every month to keep our ties strong. We took part in the sowing and in the harvests, and when we were closed up in our houses during the rainy season, the children were told stories of olden times, of Atse Yohanes, Atse Tewodros, of the Queen of Sheba. . . . We girls liked to roam around the market and the boys liked to spend the afternoon playing soccer with a ball made from rags that they kicked from one area to another, churning up the dust and shouts from the women who had just hung out the freshly laundered clothes on the wooden fences. People fell in love, girls and boys got engaged, got married, there were lovers . . . and the elders who settled arguments. Everything ran the same course as before except for our being more limited in our movements.

In a kind of way we had succeeded in separating our reality as ordinary citizens from that other reality, that of the Derg and of the rebels who were fighting them. There was only one point in the year in which the second reality erupted with violence in our homes, like streams in full flood during the rains, the devastating downpours from which you could only save yourself by finding shelter beforehand.

It was during those few days of the year when the Derg recruited for the military service. They passed through each house in order to take away the boys and send them off to fight the rebels, after a short training period. During those days, by tacit agreement, all the families passed the word around. They alerted each other, and then each person took care of his own, hiding the boys or, if they had money, bribing the soldiers who were in charge of the raids. In those days, my father and my uncles hid my brothers and my cousins as best they could. In the homes of the farmers living just outside of town, in the caves near the lakes, in the Abbo Monastery, among the priests of the church of Kecema Giorgis. After those few days, our lives returned to normal. In those years when my cousins and my brothers were eligible for military service, only my cousin Tesemma was caught. He returned home wounded in the leg after spending a year on the Eritrean front. My family gave thanks to God for having restored him to us. He never wanted to speak about that year in which he had to fight against his own people.

It was only in Legesse's shop that I experienced something of the reality of the regime that was usually separate from our everyday life.

The first Fridays that I worked, the farmers made me move their merchandise and count it. Dozens of colored baskets. Sacks upon sacks of onions and shallots. Eggs and squawking chickens. Clay pots full of honey, others with tej. All of the work was carried out in silence, broken only by the rustling of their robes, dusty from the journey on foot, and of the sacks made from agave, and by the chickens and the braying of the pack mules tied up outside to a wooden bar near the back room.

The farmers did not say a word, except for what was strictly necessary for the work and for greetings when they arrived and when they left. Not even their children spoke. If they needed to say something they opened their eyes wide and tugged at their mother's skirt until she put her ear next to their mouths. Quite a few Fridays went by before the farmers told Legesse that I was a person of few words. "Oh, yes!" he had agreed. "She's not one for talking much. My mother and her aunts say the same thing. That's the way she is. She listens without meddling in other people's business and speaks even less. She was brought up properly!" From that moment on, the farmers gradually began to speak without worrying about my presence. For some weeks I focused on my promise: I would never, for any reason whatsoever, take part in conversations about the Derg. Either for or against. And I would never, for whatever reason, get mixed up in the affairs of the rebels. To avoid reneging on my promise, I forced myself to remain deaf to all their conversations. I trained my mind on my work, and their chatter was like an indistinct buzzing in the background that saturated the air in the room. A promise is a matter of importance and one cannot retract it. Keeping a promise renders us trustworthy. Reflecting in this way, I was able to rein in my curiosity and subject it to the commitment I had undertaken as an adult.

But one Friday afternoon a *korkoralleo* arrived in the back room. He must have already done the rounds of the town looking for jars and metal cans to buy. His jute bag was as full as the belly of a pregnant mare. Appearing in the doorway, he asked the farmers if they wanted to buy any jars and asked me if we had any in the shop to sell. One of the farmers knew him: "Hi, Kebede," he said. "How was your day?"

The korkoralleo waved his hand, took the sack that he was carrying on his right shoulder, and put it under the eyes of the farmer who had greeted him. "As you can see, Gash Tariku, I spent it working."

"Come inside and drink a glass of areke."

"No, thanks, I'm going to try and see if I can sell something before I go home."

"Kebede, surely you too haven't turned into a lazybones? You prefer to sell now to avoid having to walk to our villages, eh? Ah, the good old days when one never turned down the company of a friend!"

The korkoralleo laughed, lowered his head, and then came in. "All right," he said, "I'll take a break for a moment in your company."

They began to chat. I didn't listen. When the korkoralleo got up to leave, "a moment" had turned into two long hours in which his glass had been replenished several times with the killer brew. The korkoralleo stumbled, trying to lift his sack to go on his way again, but it fell to the ground with ruinous consequences. The sound of breaking glass made me jump.

From that moment on I could not focus anymore, as if the noise had shattered my ability to distance myself from everything. I raised my head from my accounts. In front of me was the korkoralleo, who put his hands in his hair and began to wail: "Woine! Woine! Woine! All my work! Woine! Tonight my wife will murder me! Woine! Now what am I going to do?"

Gash Tariku put a hand in his pocket and took out some money which he offered to the korkoralleo. After all, it was his fault if the korkoralleo had gotten drunk and had broken all the jars. The korkoralleo took the money without showing the reticence that politeness demanded in such circumstances. He really must have been very afraid of his wife not to have cared about common politeness to that extent. He was in a state, but suddenly he didn't seem to be drunk anymore. "Now," he muttered, "I'll have to get rid of the glass. I'm going out to empty the sack and throw away the broken glass." He was about to leave without saying goodbye, when another farmer called out to him: "Korkoralleo, did your glass jars have lids on them?"

"Sure! They were jars of the best quality."

"Well then, I'll buy your lids."

In the back room silence had fallen. The farmer bargained on the cost of the lids and bought the lot. The korkoralleo went off relieved, and the farmer began to count and check the lids, laying them out on the ground and arranging them by size. "My son will be able to use them!" he said to the others. Some nodded. "They learned that from the Eritrean rebels. They brew the coffee and then they drink it out of the lids. Cups break from the vibration of the mortar fire. Those poor boys, at least coffee!" I absorbed his words as I stood there, my eyes as wide open as doors which anything can go through. Someone began to talk about Ghinda, in Eritrea, the trench warfare that had lasted for almost an entire year. It was there that the Eritrean rebels had taught the Tigray, Amara, and Oromo rebels about the trick with the coffee lids. The conversation continued and I didn't miss a word. The son of the farmer who had bought the lids had undergone some training in the Tigray and in Eritrea, then had moved south and joined a group of rebels in the area of Bale Goba. From there they used to go down to attack the soldiers.

That evening I went home weighed down with a sense of guilt. I had betrayed my parents. I went to bed without looking anybody in the eye.

Fortunately, when I got home at seven o'clock, the three elders had retired to their rooms and so nobody investigated further to

see if something was hidden behind my "Excuse me, but I'm tired,"
said with my eyes lowered. In the following weeks I tried to patch
up the crack in my ability to distance myself from everything. I felt
I had to recover and maintain my promise, but I wasn't able to do
so completely. Every now and then, on a Friday afternoon, I caught
snippets of sentences: "Ato Muddin's son has been captured. He was
carrying a message to Butajira."

"Any news?"

"No, only that he's still alive."

"Ato Abraham's grandson has escaped from the military camp.
He's joined up with the Oromo rebels from Herana."

"May God spare him!"

After a time, due to all these half sentences, the crack grew wider
and longer, shattering my self-imposed isolation. I spent a long sleep-
less night trying to assuage my guilt: It wasn't my fault if they were
talking about those things and my ears heard their conversations.
After all, I was not to get involved by participating in them or by repeating their discussions, but I could listen. I did not promise not to
listen. After that interior monologue, witnessed only by the spirits of
the dark while Mulu and Alemitu slept at my side, I stopped fighting
it. Starting the following Friday, while I was counting and moving
sacks of grain, onions, dried chili pepper, jars of honey and of butter
. . . I let myself follow their conversations, allowing my ears to receive
stories from that world that had always been separate from mine.

The farmers all came from different areas, and Legesse's shop was
a place where they all met, a place where they could hear the latest
news and exchange information. Even at the very entrance to the
back room, after greeting each other, they inquired about the various fronts of the rebellion. "So, Gash Mesfin, what news from the
North?"

"Last week the government ordered the burning of entire fields
of teff, near Adwa. They found out that some families were giving

half of the harvest to the rebels to feed them, so they set fire to the crops in the entire area." At that point Gash Mesfin paused to allow everyone who was seething at his every word to give a collective sigh. "They think they can stop the rebels with these strategies, they think they can scare the farmers who help them. But by now the North is entirely on the rebels' side. Right after the burning of the crops, that very same day, some couriers had already left to go to the west of the Tigray to get the reserves of grain hidden in the forests."

"Ah! Blood of my blood," said Gash Muddin, the one who had sons in the Oromo rebel forces in Herana. "We are flesh of the same flesh, and yet we are forced to kill each other. You should have seen it! The night before last, more than forty soldiers died. So young, too! They can't have been more than sixteen or seventeen years old at the most. Unfortunately, our rebels had to shoot them. I saw everything from my house. They arrived in the middle of the night. A couple of trucks with about fifty young recruits and some officers, two jeeps with machine guns, and two searchlights that they trained on the forest, on the hill in front of my house, where our men were hiding. The officers got down from the trucks, so confident. They thought they had the advantage. They ordered the recruits to advance and as they were nearing the hill, a band of rebels surprised them from behind. What can you expect—the soldiers are almost always young and inexperienced, while ours are almost all men who have grown up with the rebels. Those poor young recruits! Gun fodder! Not more than ten escaped the massacre. Ah! What terrible times, fighting for freedom by killing our own sons. I always tell my two: if you can, only shoot the leaders—those are our real enemies. Let the boys go!"

"You're right, Gash Muddin, we must tell our men not to shoot the young soldiers whenever they can," said some women.

Among the farmers there was one, Ato Worku, who had been nicknamed "Mr. Fanfare" because he boasted that he knew about the most astonishing events: "They entered there, came down here. There were four of them and they killed four hundred . . ." Many of his stories truly were pure inventions. From a tiny seed he created a great sycamore tree. But some of his stories were confirmed by others, like the one about the women in a small village in the Tigray.

One Friday there arrived some rumors: a group of women in a small village in the Tigray had defended themselves by chasing away the soldiers. The following Friday, Ato Worku came into the shop saying again and again, "Incredible, incredible! I've found out how it all played out in the village of May Abbo." He had arrived late, after the farmers had exchanged important information coming from trusted sources, after they had already consigned the messages to be delivered to Muddin's sons in the forest in Harenna, and after Muddin himself had informed everyone of the future movements of the rebels and of the soldiers. This latest news had been passed on by infiltrators in Mengistu's army. There was nothing important left to do, so it was fine to lend an ear to Ato Worku's chatter.

"Let's hear it, then, tell us!" said one woman, urging him on.

He immediately sat down on a sack of teff, adjusted his shemma, and placed his hat on his knee. "Well," he began, "you have to know that for some time the women of May Abbo had been accused of passing on their extra reserves of teff to the rebels."

"Go on, Ato Worku, we already know all that," Gash Tariku added, in order to stir up Ato Worku's usual touchiness.

Ato Worku answered brusquely, "I can't tell the story by stripping it down to the bare facts. Gash Tariku, let me tell it my own way. So, everything happened on a Wednesday morning. A woman, going to the well to get water, sees in the distance the dust raised by the military trucks on the paved road and runs off to warn the entire village. All the women arm themselves with sticks and bags of ground chili pepper and wait in ambush. Hidden in between the houses, through the gaps in the stones they see the trucks climbing up the hill toward their village. When the soldiers arrive, the village appears empty. They begin to go around the houses, convinced that the women have already run off somewhere. At a certain point, one of the women gives a shout and they all jump out.

"Just imagine, those men had come to beat them and arrest them, and instead after a couple of hours they had to retreat, their eyes on fire from the chili pepper powder and their backs broken by the sticks. That evening they returned with reinforcements, but of the women there was not a single trace. They had packed up their few possessions and joined their husbands and brothers in the forest," he concluded with satisfaction, putting his hat back on his head. And that was a true story.

The farmers' stories came out one after the other, and each Friday I left Legesse's shop with my head full of images of the rebels. And after hearing all those stories I began to imagine the rebels as invincible giants who were fighting for our liberation.

But in Legesse's shop there were not only stories about our revolutionaries. Along with the tales about them on Fridays, there were the stories on the lips of the ladies on Saturdays, when they came to have their hair straightened with the curling iron.

I used to wash their hair and prepare the iron. They had to wait awhile and they spent the time gossiping. There was one, Woizero Almaz, a woman of the impoverished bourgeoisie. Tall, with elegant facial features—thin nose and well-defined lips—she was dressed in the European style and on her right hand she wore a ring with a large diamond, a sign of past wealth. She came every Saturday and if she wasn't going to have her hair straightened, she came along with her friends and kept them company. The conversation always began with her words, with the usual observation: "One of these days that son of a slave will go"—it was said that Mengistu Haile Mariam was the son of a slave—"and when Ethiopia is free once more, all our boys will come home again. All those who have gone to study in Europe will return to rebuild our country." And from there began the stories of those who had left. "Oh yes, the son of Dr. Samuel Ighigu, the one who ran off at night with help from the farmers. He went as far as Sudan on foot, poor boy. Then from Khartoum he left for London, but only after having spent the three hottest months of the year there. And do you know what people do in those three months in Khartoum? Dr. Samuel Ighigu told me and he heard it from his son: in that heat people pull their beds out of the house and sleep in the streets in the hope of catching the slightest breeze. As if that were not bad enough, they take their television sets outside. In Khartoum it's not like here. They have two television channels! Imagine the chaos." Once he reached London, Dr. Ighigu's son had received a scholarship, "in economics," said Woizero Almaz, accompanying the words with dramatic movements of her hands and lips in order to emphasize the boy's prestigious undertaking. "Now he works for the United Nations, but when that son of the slave removes his backside from the seat of power, he will return."

Then there was Ashenafi, the son of the owner of the Hotel Hora. His very name, which meant "victor," alluded to what was to be his destiny, and as a victor he would return to Ethiopia. Ashenafi had become a professor in Sweden. He had left the same way as Ighigu's son: he escaped, not to Sudan, but toward Kenya. First Moyale, then Nairobi, and finally London, where he had received a scholarship. After getting his undergraduate degree and his doctorate he became a professor in Sweden. He taught in an MA program in African studies. "A course on the culture, the resources, and the life in African countries, because we," said Woizero Almaz, "we are not just a problem to be resolved, as many would have us believe . . ." Ashenafi, too, would return, after that famous day on which the dictator . . . and he would institute an MA program here too, and he would teach us to be mindful again of our riches . . .

And then Woizero Almaz and her friends would go on about Mekonnen Taffere's daughter, and Antonio Kunchir's son, and then Estefanos, that very thin, tall boy, who had escaped when he was doing his military training, and who else? . . . The pharmacist's two girls, and the farmer's boy near the Zuquala Monastery, Gash Ashagre, and Meseret's son, the one in the coffee shop near the station. All of them had ended up in the United States, in Canada, in England, in Sweden . . . to study. Finally, there were some, a few, who had

gone to Italy on scholarships which they had received directly in
Ethiopia. The scholarships for Italy were only given out before the
students left.

The West

At that time, Mekonnen, a classmate of my cousin Mulu's, won a
scholarship to go and study in Italy. The evening before he left there
were a lot of people coming and going in front of his house. Everyone had come to say their last goodbyes. I, too, with my parents, the
elders, all the cousins, and the uncles and aunts, went to say goodbye
to him. All of Debre Zeit was there. That farewell gesture took the
place of all the goodbyes they had not been able to say to the many
children, friends, and brothers who had fled by night, dodging the
trucks of the military patrols. Mekonnen assured each person that
he would return. He was only going away to study, to create a font of
knowledge to use one day for the good of Ethiopia. And each time he
repeated it, the women drowned him out with trills of joy. When it
was my turn, I said goodbye and stepped to one side.

If, in Legesse's shop, the farmers had fed my imagination regarding
the rebels, Woizero Almaz and her friends had left an indelible mark
on my future. That evening, watching the people and Mekonnen
in their midst, I, with that desire for glory typical of adolescents,
promised myself that I would go and study in Italy. I, too, like him,
would win a scholarship, and one day would return, like the boys and
girls that Woizero Almaz and her friends spoke about. I would be
part of that band of heroes who would use the knowledge acquired
in Europe and in America to rebuild our country.

Announcement! Announcement!

During my first year of work the situation in the country became
more incendiary. Each day the rebels became stronger. More and
more young people were running off to join their ranks. Mengistu
tried to preserve his power. He became more cruel and ruthless toward the rebels, although his orders were not always carried out

by his soldiers, who by then were exhausted. At the same time, he softened his behavior toward the people in an attempt to win them over to his side by bestowing concession after concession.

One Saturday morning the town criers for the regime sounded their horns in the market square. "Open the door, my child, let's hear what they're saying," Woizero Almaz said to me. I put down the curling iron that I was using on her hair and went toward the door.

"Don't bother, my child. Better to keep the door closed, otherwise the wind will blow the dust in," said Woizero Saba, one of her friends. I retraced my steps.

"Come on!" said Woizero Almaz. "Today there's no wind. Let's hear what he has conjured up this time, that son of a slave."

"Almaz, it is windy—look out the window. And then, what do you expect he might have conjured up . . . the usual schemes to trick us." The two women began to argue and I was left hanging about in the middle of the shop. Legesse decided to take the situation in hand and he went to open the door, but the town crier was sounding his horn to signal the end of the message. "Darn it!" grumbled Woizero Almaz.

To avoid further discussion, Legesse opened a window and shouted out to the woman in the coffee shop next door. "Sarah, what did the announcement say?"

"It said," she shouted back, leaning out of the porch of the coffee shop, "that they will return all confiscated houses to the people who are deemed trustworthy."

"See? What did I tell you?" said Woizero Saba. "Sure, I'll believe it when I see it. 'They will give back the houses they confiscated to the trustworthy.' It must be another one of his little schemes to win us over to his side." Right at that moment, a gust of wind blew open the door, bringing with it a cloud of dust and some withered bougainvillea petals. "I told you it was windy, see? You should listen to me more often, Almaz!" said Woizero Saba with a touch of irony.

Woizero Almaz did not respond to her friend's comments, but as I began to straighten her hair again, I had the distinct impression that I could detect the thoughts in her head, under her thick black hair: "It would be nice to own my houses again! I could rent them out and in that way not be dependent on the remittances from my relatives abroad. But my friend is right—what would I have to give in return? My loyalty to the dictator?"

In our house, as in all of Debre Zeit, the new announcement did not impress us. We had understood Mengistu's little game. Whoever chose to be on his side could get back his houses, and perhaps even something more. Since we understood what this involved, we soon forgot about the new announcement. We were not interested in possessions if we could not get back our freedom. And we were convinced that we would have regained our wealth, our houses, only by showing our support for the dictatorship and its leader.

But then one evening, about a month after the announcement, as it was getting dark, my father came home, calling loudly for my mother. You could hear his shouts well beyond our immediate neighborhood. He had come along the path from the intersection to our house shouting, "Sellas! Sellas! Sellas, come out here!" Those were times when such frantic shouts sent everyone into a state of panic. We were used to associating shouts of that kind with disasters that had been perpetrated by the military.

All the adults in our household and the relatives who lived next door rushed out to meet him. We children were behind, keeping a safe distance. All our hearts were beating furiously, like the sparrows that see the claws of the brown kites getting nearer and nearer. As I walked along I kept saying, "Lord, keep us free from suffering, Lord keep us free from suffering." Those few feet we crossed to the gate seemed like miles. My mother was the first through the gate and the first to go beyond it with the elders. I scrutinized their faces, trying to understand. And from a corner of the open gate I saw my mother's stricken face change expression, from frightened to surprised, and then change again to become almost angry. I, too, went out of the gate, and once outside, I did not find myself in front of a man in a state of panic, as everyone had thought. My father was drunk, and there he was, in front of us, his legs wide apart as he tried to keep his precarious balance, very precarious balance, and an idiotic grin on his face, beneath two glazed eyes.

My mother immediately addressed him with these words: "And since when did you start to drink?"

And my father: "Wife, don't ask yourself since when, but ask yourself why. Why did your husband who never gets drunk get drunk today? Do you know why? Ah! Do you know why? Because today is a great day!"

"Go on," she said, curling her lips in a grimace. "Let's hear what you have to tell us."

"Listen, you all, we must kill some chickens. Many chickens. Make a lot of *doro wot* and invite everyone over. Relatives and neighbors. We must celebrate!"

My mother could not take his words seriously. "Ah!" she continued, with that unpleasant grimace on her face and a tone in her voice, at once ironic and contemptuous. "And what, tell me, are we supposed to celebrate?"

My father took no notice of her tone or of the fact that she had used it in public, in front of the family, the relatives and the many neighbors who had rushed over in their evening shemma. Keeping his words to the bare essentials, he replied, "We are celebrating because they have given us back our old house in Addis Ababa!"

My Uncle Mesfin, turning to face the small crowd, said, "Take no notice of him! He's drunk." And a neighbor added, "Let's hope it is only the alcohol making him talk rubbish. You know, in these times it is easy to go crazy. Last week I saw one such case. One day he was sane, then the next he was going around chomping on a piece of glass from a neon sign, saying in English, 'Sweet, very sweet!'" My aunts crossed themselves to ward off the danger conjured up by the neighbor, while another added, "Let's hope it is only the alcohol—he's such a good person. It would be a pity. For the entire neighborhood!"

My father, lurching about, rummaged in his right pants pocket, then in the left one. For a moment he wrinkled his forehead in thought, then the line between his eyebrows relaxed and his face lit up again in that idiotic smile. Wearing the same expression, he pulled his hand out of his pants pocket, slipped it into the inside pocket of his jacket, and, delighted with himself, pulled out a crumpled sheet of paper. "If you think I'm talking rubbish and all that nonsense you're accusing me of," he said, "read this." And he handed the sheet to my Uncle Mesfin, who read it aloud.

"The government of the people . . . returns to the family of commander . . ." My Uncle Mesfin was stunned: "It's true, it really is true! It's written here: the house in Addis Ababa, situated in Arada Sefer, in kebele 13 of sector 2, number 1653. Our great grandfather's old house!" He began to shout and hug my father, who was still wearing that idiotic expression on his face.

My mother began to laugh, and laugh and laugh, and in all that joyful confusion the elders ordered my brothers to kill some chickens, lots of chickens. That evening we held a great feast, with all the relatives and area neighbors. We ate doro wot and drank the tella which had been put down to ferment for the feast of St. Michael the following Saturday. After the feast, everyone stayed on to sleep at our house. There were people lying everywhere. A carpet of bodies wrapped in their white *gabi* and in their shemma had taken over our house, inside and out.

When the sun came up at dawn, it warmed their bodies numbed by the cold night air and dispersed the fumes of alcohol. People woke up in groups, four or five at a time. My mother offered them fir fir of shiro to eat in order to lessen headaches from too much drinking.

Gradually, the carpet of bodies wrapped in white went off. Only those who had found refuge under the three elders' mango tree and under the coffee trees stayed until midday. These were the only places in the garden where the sun never shone.

When even the last guests had closed the gate behind them, my father called for me. As had happened a year before, he received me in the conversation room, seated next to my mother. That day he informed me that he would no longer allow me to go and work in Legesse's shop. It was too dangerous. The years of the dictatorship were quickly coming to an end, and we could not predict how it would play out. Therefore, it was better to wait, always opting for safe situations. Legesse's shop, besides being patronized by farmers who by then were considered an integral part of the rebel force, was not a safe place since it was near the market.

Arada Sefer

Our house in Addis Ababa was a big old house in the Indian style, built at the beginning of the twentieth century when Menelik had transferred the capital from Ankober to Addis Ababa and my great-grandfather had moved himself and his whole family to follow Negus Negest.

It was in the shape of a large rectangle with a wooden-floor veranda that ran all along the main side of the house. Small columns supported the roof of the veranda, those too in wood, and were inlaid with sandalwood. The house had many rooms, some of them communicating on the inside. Each room faced in two directions: toward the front of the house, the veranda side, and toward the rear, looking onto the courtyard around which were the bathrooms, the kitchen, a pantry, and the servants' quarters.

My father was born in that house in the year of the liberation from the Italians. It was the family home, and in the inner courtyard, under the largest and oldest tree, were buried the placentas of those born in that house.

The front courtyard was a very stony area that during the rainy season filled up with mud. Looking at it from that vantage point, it appeared immersed in a deep sleep. There was no sign of life.

It was only by crossing it from one side to the other, treading softly in the half shadow of the rooms, that one reached the inner courtyard, the very heart of the house that throbbed with life. Here the clothes were washed in great big metal tubs and hung out to dry; here the coffee was brewed and the dried chickpeas for the shiro were pounded in the big wooden mortars, as were the dried chili peppers to make the berbere. Here we gathered, and here the men always waited for the midwife to come out, the midwife who had been summoned to help a woman of the house to give birth. Here were the vegetable gardens, the chickens, the trees, the flowers, and all the people in the household. People often sitting in circles, working and telling stories, sometimes laughing, sometimes crying.

That was how my father talked about it with tears of nostalgia in his eyes. I had never lived in our house in Arada Sefer.

One year before the coup, my father, who by then was the only one living there with my mother and the three elders, was promoted to principal of the Comprehensive Secondary School in Debre Zeit. So my family, including the three elders, moved to the small town where most of my father's and my mother's families had been living for some time. They all went to live with my Uncle Mesfin's family in the house that the two of them had bought a few years previously.

The house in Arada Sefer had remained empty. My father and his brothers were undecided on whether to rent it out or keep it empty in the hope that the continuous transfers would result in some family member's going to live there again. While waiting to decide, they left the old caretaker, one of my grandfather's former warriors, to look after the house and our ancestors' old tree under which the placentas were buried.

Unfortunately, before they came to a decision, there was the coup whose waters in full flood swept over the country with devastating fury. Nothing was the same anymore.

The changes caught everyone by surprise, and when the new government began nationalizing everything, transforming Ethiopia's structure from that of a country based on private property to one based on shared property, the house in Arada Sefer was nationalized as well. Every family could own only one house and we already had the one in Debre Zeit, which belonged half to Uncle Mesfin, half to my father. A large house, big enough for two families and

more. . . . All my father's and his brothers' pleading served no end.
They tried to explain that the house symbolized a family that, together with the armies of Ras Mengesha, had fought against the
Italians at Adwa and then, from 1935 to 1941, against the Fascists in
the regions of Goggiam, Menz, and Minjar. When some members of
the kebele, our neighborhood committee, threatened to have them
thrown into prison if they continued to protest, my father and my
uncles finally gave up. If, in fact, it was true that my father's family
had fought against the Fascists, it was also true that they had been
part of a middle class that those in power wanted to eliminate from
the country. They sadly agreed that a new Ethiopia had been born,
an Ethiopia that corresponded not to the old laws handed down
through the ages, but to those of a regime that was modeled on the
Soviet one. A new Ethiopia that time would judge as being worse
than the preceding one.

The Move

A few months after the house in Arada Sefer was returned to us,
about twenty days before the celebration of Timket, my father and
Uncle Mesfin called the whole family together. We found them in
the conversation room, sitting between the elders. Announcing that
their idea had the blessing of the three venerables, they informed us
that the time was ripe. Soon the rebels would overthrow the dictatorship, and it was not safe for us to remain in Debre Zeit because
the Ethiopian Air Force had its base there. Everyone was predicting
a fight to the bitter end between the air force and the Oromo Rebel
Front that was preparing to break through from the south and meet
up with the other fronts in order to attack the capital. Therefore it
was necessary to move. We were to go to Addis Ababa, to our house
in Arada Sefer. My father's other brothers and their families would
come with us: Uncle Abebe, Uncle Iasu, Uncle Alemaiew, and Uncle
Dghemu, all of whom lived next door to us in Debre Zeit. Uncle
Abebe, Uncle Isu, and their families were going to come to live in

the house in Arada Sefer, while Uncle Alemaiew and Uncle Dghemu
were going to live with their wives' families.

In the ensuing fifteen days my father and Uncle Mesfin went back
and forth in their old cars between Debre Zeit and Addis Ababa,
moving people and belongings from one house to the other. Several
trips a day between the house in which I had been born and that in
which he and his brothers had been born. After each trip they told
us the house was big, but not big enough. In ordinary circumstances
they would have said that there was not enough room for everyone,
but since these were special circumstances, we would all squeeze in
so as to stay together. Mulu, Alemitu, and I, each accustomed to having her own bed, would sleep in one double bed; in the same room,
in another double bed, would sleep Aunt Fanus and Aunt Abeba.
My four brothers would share two single beds in a room with my
parents; Uncle Mesfin, his wife, and his children all in one room . . .
we would just have to put up with it. The only ones who each had
their own room were our three elders.

When the move was completed, we made one last trip from Debre
Zeit to Addis Ababa. A strange trip in my father's car. He was driv-
ing, old Yacob next to him and my mother and I in the back. My
father sweated the whole trip while my mother kept her hand on his
shoulder and old Yacob kept saying to him, "Don't worry, my son,
everything will go well. I know what to do, trust me. If I were not so
certain, do you really think I would have brought Mahlet with us?"
Before getting to the checkpoint at Addis Ababa my father stopped
the car. He got out of the car with old Yacob. They talked for a bit,
then they returned. My father had stopped sweating. At the checkpoint a soldier came up to the driver's window. Old Yacob stretched
over to speak to him: "My son, they're taking me to the hospital, to
the Menelik Hospital. I have an appointment for an eye examina-
tion, and we're late." The soldier let us pass without even checking
our papers. Once past the checkpoint my father began to laugh. An
almost liberating kind of laugh, and along with him, old Yacob and
my mother. I looked at them without understanding a thing.

The First Celebration of Timket in the Capital

That's the story of how we moved into that house which I had heard so much about. A few days later came our great feast of Timket. My first in the capital, my first far from Debre Zeit, and for my family, the first far from the town that by then they considered theirs. Even though there were many of us, we felt like orphans without our neighborhood association with whom we were used to sharing every part of the feast. We began with the preparations when, in the preceding days, at the market or from the farmers near the lake, we bought sheep, chickens, onions, potatoes, carrots... bargaining animatedly. Then there was the preparation of the food on the morning before the Tabot were brought out. The women crowded the courtyards and you could hear the rhythm of their knives on the boards that accompanied the chatter and laughter. Finally, there was the vigil spent in prayer the night before the ceremony... always all together.

Because of that sense of isolation, one or two adults in the family hazarded the suggestion that we not celebrate it. The three elders said that this was absolutely out of the question: Timket is the feast of special requests, of the renewal of one's faith; therefore it had to be honored. "We could go to St. George's and follow the procession with the Tabot," suggested old Yacob. "If we can't be with the members of our association, at least we shall be in the Church of Menelik, our Menelik, and may he together with his saints, help us topple that ... that son of a slave." His idea met with the approval of the other two elders and we, albeit some of us begrudgingly, went along with it.

As always, the grand celebration began in the early afternoon of Tir 10, which that year fell on a Friday, a day of fasting. After having spent the morning at home preparing the different foods for the following day, and in prayer, all my family and I went to St. George's Cathedral, the starting point for a part of the procession that ended at Janhoy Meda.

We arrived at around one o'clock. The courtyard of the church was empty. There were only a few groups of worshipers, including some monks and hermits distributing *zebel*, the holy water. After about an hour the courtyard of the church was filled with a sea of people dressed in white. Half an hour later the singers arrived with the drummers and they began to chant the *mezmur*. Then finally, at three o'clock on the dot, out came the Tabot and the garden of the church reverberated loudly with singing, with trills of joy, with the mesmerizing beat of the big drums and with the sound of the horns. My family and I participated in the singing without being really involved in the celebrations. That feeling of not belonging still clung to us. Looking this way and that, we could not find anything familiar that made us feel part of the celebration.

The Tabot was surrounded by lines of monks with colored umbrellas who began to walk toward the steep incline of Afincho Ber. My family and I followed behind with the singers and other worshipers. A third of the way down the incline, the head of the procession stopped to wait for the Tabot from St. Mark's that was descending the nearby hill, preceded by groups of Oromo and Gurage boys and girls, singing and dancing. When the two Tabot came together, a strange excitement suddenly rippled through the air, like an unexpected electric shock. I looked at Alemitu and Mulu next to me. We felt like laughing. We had all experienced the same sensation.

The procession from St. Mark's merged with ours and we set off again.

And so we slowly moved on, stopping at the designated points to be joined by other sacred altarpieces, more bowing, other processions, songs, singers, mesmerizing drums, and frenzied dancing. The procession was becoming more and more like a never-ending human serpent that wound its way along the wide road. And at each step, as each group joined the procession, the electricity increased, creating a vortex that gradually sucked even us in.

We reached Janhoy Meda. The emotional pull grew more powerful and I found myself keeping the beat with my hands, following the drums in a wild and mesmerizing rhythm. As did the rest of my family.

The sun began to set behind the Entoto Mountains when the procession, like a human river with the altarpieces at its head, poured into the immense open space of Janhoy Meda. The Tabot were placed in the center, in two rows, waiting for the arrival of the most important altarpiece.

And behold, after a short wait, the women crowded in at the entrance shouted out in joy, and accompanying their trills came the Tabot of the Virgin Mary followed by dozens of Oromo riders on bedecked horses. There was a roar of jubilation.

Following the general enthusiasm, I began to dance, lifting my hands toward the sky and then down, crouching, moving my hips, and then up again, my hands moving like a wave, stretched in front of my body, vibrating in the air, and then close to my breast, my hands rocking, and from my lips came the chant, "In the Jordan, Jesus was baptized in the Jordan." I suddenly looked at Alemitu and Mulu, then at the others, even at the elders. They, too, were dancing. All of Janhoy Meda was dancing. We were one body swept up in a cathartic dance.

That year, my first Timket in the capital was also the last year of the dictatorship.

My family and I spent the night of vigil in Janhoy Meda warming ourselves by the fires lit by the faithful and let ourselves be hypnotized by the swaying of the deacons, the sound of the *sistrums,* the rhythm of the church drums, and the mezmur, until we too experienced the magic of that Timket that had fused all the participants into one single body.

In that darkness brightened by the flames of the small fires, in that strange atmosphere that linked us together, we found ourselves all whispering the same prayer. A single invocation to Jesus. In that vigil in which the saints and the angels were also preparing to commemorate His sacred baptism in the Jordan, we begged Him to end the darkness of our Ethiopia's long night and make that Timket the last under the dictatorship.

The following day the Patriarch blessed the water in the great pool shaped like a cross. Then we all drank from it and sprinkled the holy water over ourselves to renew our vows and our bond with the Creator. Finally, we returned home to await the granting of our prayers.

Almost four months later in Addis Ababa, between Genbot 9 and 11, the air carried nothing but the noise and smell of war: shooting, machine-gun fire, smoke, fire, and exploding arms depots, including the one in the Kera quarter, where munitions continued to explode for three days. On Genbot 10, Mengistu left the country. For a week his prime minister took his place in a country descended into semi-anarchy.

The elders of our family ordered the gate closed and set up a guard-duty schedule so that our men would protect the house. We women barricaded ourselves in the house, and in the rooms around the inner courtyard. My father with old Yacob took apart the back seat of his car, revealing the motive for his strange behavior on that last trip from Debre Zeit. Tucked into the seat springs were some old rifles and a Kalashnikov, probably bought on the black market at Debre Zeit. They were weapons to be used to protect us from any possible sackings.

Fortunately, the city did not even remotely experience the dreaded sackings. Only a few settlings of accounts with some men, mainly officers and junior officers of the Derg who had ordered the killings of many young men. On Genbot 19, over the Addis Ababa radio, came the announcement of great news: the united Ethiopian People's Revolutionary Democratic Front was at the gates of Addis Ababa, with the Oromo at Debre Zeit together with the Tigrayan, and the Amhara in Ambo.

The day after, Addis Ababa awoke to the sound of the rebels from Ambo marching into the city.

Notwithstanding the general fear, the people in the capital poured into the streets, opening the main gates of the houses that had been locked shut for an entire week. Everybody wanted to see the rebel fighters.

Rumors went from mouth to mouth: "They're at Gulele." "They're at the gates of the Tekle Haimanot Monastery." "They're marching toward the Gebi." My family and I rushed over to the Churchill Road intersection. Our front, the invincible giants whom I had imagined through the stories I had heard, was about to appear before our very eyes.

"They'll come by here," said the people thronging the streets, tens upon tens, hundreds upon hundreds, all running to see them.

My cousins and I had managed to get into the front row, surrounded by our relatives.

At a certain point somebody, pointing to the street leading to the French cathedral, began to shout: "Here they come! Here they come!" I tried to look into the distance as far as I could. At first, there was only a shapeless, greenish mass that was moving toward us, but then they drew nearer and I was able to see them. The invincible fighters of my imagination were a band of people who aroused the deepest tenderness. As they marched with the smile of victory on their faces, their bodies were clothed in uniforms full of holes, darned and kept up at the waist by string; they were as thin as skeletons, bowing under the weight of their Kalashnikovs, of their cartridge belts, of the shoulder mortars. Each man's hair was a shapeless mass of dreadlocks as long as that of an old hermit; the women moved forward, driven by pride rather than by their muscles, their heads covered by scarves that hid masses of wild hair. These were people who had fought in secret for seventeen years in the forests, who had known hunger, thirst, cold, malaria; people who had seen their companions, their brothers, their sisters die.

The onlookers began to clap their hands, the women inundated them with trills of joy, someone began to sing, and others improvised verses in their honor.

The rebel fighters raised their Kalashnikovs in a sign of triumph and saluted the people who were hailing them as victors.

From the dense crowd, some people detached themselves to go forward and embrace them, to mix with them. The rebel fighters asked for water, and from the houses, buckets of drinking water were

passed forward. The older women went up close to the fighters, blessing them.

Then the fighters continued their march toward the seat of government. We followed them a little way until we decided to surrender
our places to all the other people who were arriving from other areas
of the city.

In the days that followed, the rebel fighters found whatever lodg-
ing they could, anywhere in the city, and when they had filled the
barracks and the government offices, they occupied the hotels. We
children continuously lined up to take a peek at their uniforms hanging from the balconies of the Wabi-Shebele Hotel.

Clothes full of holes and, people said, full of lice. Lice accumulated
during seventeen years of resistance, between forests and trenches
like the one at Ghinda.

The Chaos before the Calm

As if an explosion had thrown open the cages of animals cooped up
for a long time, after the liberation there came chaos, something the
country had not experienced before, not even during that dreaded
week when there was no real government.

It was like being immersed in a dusty cloud which eyes could not
penetrate, and in that cloud, a convulsed moving about of citizens,
armed rebels, merchants, petty thieves, farmers with their animals.
. . . People had been so inhibited for all those long years that now, all
brakes off, all caution thrown to the wind, they had come together
in a frenzied surge with no particular direction.

In my house, too, the adults had begun to move around franti-
cally, regarded with concern by the three elders who tried—but only
once—to warn them. "This is a dangerous moment!" they had said,
but nobody listened to them, and they did not repeat their warning
since they understood the situation. The adults in the household
could not be contained. After having been suffocated for years, each
one rushed around trying to realize dreams and to fulfill desires,

even those that had no real significance but which had been harbored for all those long years under the dictatorship. And they did so without taking the precautions they had taken in the preceding years.

Uncle Mesfin went back and forth between houses and . . . who knows where, to find out how he could get back his wife's properties that had been nationalized by the regime; Uncle Iasu wanted to set up a business of his own; my father wanted to repair the family tomb which had been desecrated at the beginning of the military dictatorship; Uncle Dghemu was trying to find out if he could return to teach at the university from which he had been thrown out at the beginning of the dictatorship. . . . Everyone went in and out of the house endlessly until nightfall.

Among all of them, the most driven was Aunt Fanus, perhaps because of her effervescent personality. For years we had heard her rant and rave against various deprivations "not befitting a woman," as she used to say. From the first weeks of the liberation, after the stores on the black market had all been emptied, it was rare to find her at home during the day. Until the first signs of dusk she would roam the city, slipping through the nooks and crannies of the market, to search for material, clothes, and cosmetics that she would buy only after exhaustive bargaining. In the evening she would torture the adults in the household by pressing them to express their approval and preferences.

After she had filled some cardboard boxes, in addition to the cupboard in the room in which we slept, she concluded that she had bought enough for herself and her two daughters. But still not satisfied, she began to purchase things for the other members of the family, dragging us all off on long pilgrimages from which only the elders of the house were spared.

Before all that confusion began to reveal its negative aspects, something that happened one evening to Aunt Fanus, Aunt Abeba, and me suddenly opened the eyes of all the adults in my family. From that day on, in my household that frantic moving around abated until it almost disappeared.

That day it was Aunt Abeba's and my turn to go wandering about with Aunt Fanus. Starting the previous evening, we had been forced to give in to her insistence and we hadn't been able to find an excuse to refuse her. Moreover, we all slept together, so not accepting meant that she would have tormented us all night with her relentless, petulant requests. Early that morning she had dragged us to the market and we had systematically gone through all the small shops that sold traditional clothes. She had conducted the bargaining, seated on a stool while the shopkeepers continuously ordered hot tea with spices "for our honored guest."

"Their honored guest," commented Aunt Abeba under her breath. "Sure, with all the money she spends!" In the afternoon, after lunch in one of the small restaurants in the market, we had moved on to the area behind the post office, to roam around the small shops that sold European-style clothes.

It was about seven o'clock in the evening when we ended our day of shopping. For those times it was very late. We walked along, looking for some form of transportation, and, thank heavens, in front of the post office a small van stopped that was going to the square. It was its last run of the day. Before letting us board the bus, the ticket collector, a young boy smaller than I was, asked us where we were going. "We're getting off at the Churchill traffic light," answered Aunt Fanus. The ticket collector made us pay in advance, then he took the bags from our hands, put them on the bus, and finally helped Aunt Fanus who, because of her size, had trouble getting on-board. Pulling her by the hand, the ticket collector could not stop himself from exclaiming, "Oh, Heavens!" and she laughed coquettishly, as if she had been paid a compliment. She climbed on, rustling the sensual clothes in which she cloaked her abundant flesh. The ticket collector waited until Aunt Abeba and I were on the bus, and then he said goodbye to the driver and got off. His workday was over.

The van was empty. Apart from us, there was only one other pas-
senger, curled up in a corner of the last seat in the back, enveloped in
the darkness that revealed only his profile glued to the window. The
van moved on, struggling up the steep incline of Churchill Road. Inside the bus you could hear the metallic sound of the worn pads that
turned, rubbing against each other, straining to move the vehicle
forward. The driver, accustomed to that struggle, without taking any
notice of that deafening noise, began to have a chat with Aunt Fanus.
He asked her what we were doing out and about at that time. Aunt
Fanus told him we lived in Arada Sefer and that we were on our way
home after a day of shopping. "After all these years of deprivation,
I want to celebrate the liberation by having some beautiful clothes
made for me and for all my family," she concluded with satisfaction.
The driver was about to ask her another question when, immediately
after the rotary, he interrupted the conversation abruptly and began
to swear: "Woi gud, Ah! A curse on these rebel fighters, these forest
dwellers, survivors, ridden with lice. These animals who have forgotten how to live. Ah!" Aunt Fanus asked him why he was speaking so
badly about the rebels. The driver didn't answer her but pointed to
something, saying, "Pray God that He will help us!"

On the road, a little way ahead, a rebel fighter in uniform was holding a pistol to the head of a boy dressed in tattered rags, and a second
rebel fighter in uniform was pointing a pistol in the direction of the
van to indicate that it should stop.

The driver stopped the van and they got on. The one who had
stopped us—whom we later nicknamed the Talker when we told the
story to our family—ordered him to drive on. The driver made the
sign of the cross and pressed his foot on the accelerator. The metallic sound of the pads started up again, the vehicle went forward, and
he, with an expression of relief on his face, raised his eyes to heaven
in gratitude.

As soon as the van began to move again, the Talker ordered him
to proceed to Gulele without stopping at the bus stops. "We want to
kill him there, like a dog, so the hyenas can eat his corpse," he said,

and turning to the ragged boy he added, "We don't want the stink of your dead body in our city."

The ragged boy began to beg him: "I made a mistake, sir, I made a mistake. I have never stolen in my whole life before. It was the first time. I beg forgiveness, sir, I beg forgiveness." The Talker began to insult him, wildly gesticulating with the hand that held the pistol. Suddenly, from the back of the bus came the voice of the man curled up on the seat: "Brother, be careful with that weapon—I have returned to my country after nine years of exile in Sweden and I do not want to die because of some stupid stray bullet."

Aunt Fanus instinctively turned around. "Oh God, poor thing! He's right, my son, be careful with that pistol!" she exclaimed, deeply concerned.

The Talker, without taking any notice of my aunt, turned toward the back of the bus and asked the man, with a certain arrogance, "How come you were in exile in Sweden?"

"During the first years of the Derg," he replied, "I was a student at the agricultural faculty in Harar. I fled to escape the constant raids at the university."

"Well done! So while we were dying in order to liberate this country you were leading the good life in Sweden."

"Brother, a country is freed with guns, as you have done, but it is built by other means. I prepared myself for this second phase."

Aunt Fanus, her head still facing toward the back, continued sympathetically. "Poor man! What a good person. Thinking of the reconstruction of our country."

At that point the Talker turned toward her: "Shut up, fatty," he ordered her.

Aunt Abeba, paralyzed with terror, fixed her eyes on Aunt Fanus in supplication, but Aunt Fanus, not at all intimidated, turned to the Talker. "My son," she said to him, "you may well have fought to liberate our country, but it will have served very little if we find ourselves in a country with young people like you who have eradicated the roots of our traditions. Since when, in Ethiopia, does a young man not respect a person ahead of him on the path of life?"

The silent rebel fighter, the one who was holding the pistol to the head of the petty thief, spoke up for the first time. "She's right. Apologize to the mother."

The Talker snarled a bit but then submitted to the order of his companion. "Forgive me, Mother. I did not want to offend you! It just slipped out, but it's all the fault of this scum and of all those like him," he stated, giving the ragged boy a punch.

The boy started to snivel. "Mother, help me! This is the first time I stole. I have never stolen before, never in my whole life. I beg for pity!"

The Talker replied, "Eh! Louse, we are the ones who are in command here. If you want to beg somebody, you must beg us."

Aunt Fanus, unconcerned about the danger, added, "What's wrong with forgiving him? God himself forgives those who ask for mercy. Who are you not to do so? I don't mean let him go. Turn him over to the police and they will take care of it. That way you would also respect the orders of your leaders. Did you not receive the order to turn in your arms and to avoid acts of summary justice like the one you are about to commit? Your leaders make these appeals every day on the radio." In the second when Aunt Fanus fell silent I looked at the Talker. Blazing flames of anger flashed through his eyes. "My God, help us," I thought. Something terrible was about to happen, that was clear. Aunt Abeba's body shrank back and Aunt Fanus tried to position herself between me and the rebel fighter to protect me from the shot that was about to be fired in the next second or two. I stiffened and waited for the explosion with my eyes closed, but fortunately for us the silent fighter froze the companion's action by ordering the driver, "Stop and let these people get off. Their stupid chatter has gotten on my nerves." We got out of the van and it went off with the two fighters, the ragged boy, and the driver.

Together with the stranger we walked home, Aunt Fanus and Aunt Abeba squabbling all the way. Aunt Abeba accused Aunt Fanus of being thoughtless and impulsive, a behavior that had taken us to the very edge of a precipice, and Aunt Fanus defended herself by saying that she had read in the silent fighter's eyes that nothing was going to happen. She added, "I cannot stand these young people who think they are the masters of the universe because they fought in the Resistance. How old might they be, perhaps twenty? And for how long do you think they fought? Maybe two or three years? And just because they waved around a Kalashnikov for such a short time they think they are exempt from showing respect to everybody? Fortunately, they are not all like them. There are the leaders, the older ones, who still have some sense. At least, let's hope so . . ."

A few days later, the driver of the bus came to our house. He found us by following the information he had picked up from the brief conversation he had had with Aunt Fanus. Aunt Fanus and Aunt Abeba welcomed him with joy. He spent the entire afternoon drinking coffee with us and eating fir fir of quanta. Before going away, he told us that the ragged boy had not been killed. Once he had gotten off the bus, in the place where he was to be shot, he had managed to run off. If the truth must be told, the driver was convinced that the two fighters had let him escape deliberately. Perhaps Aunt Fanus's words had dissipated their urge to kill.

When the driver of the bus had gone, the three elders said that unfortunately all this was the result of the poison that had remained in the rebel fighters' bodies. After having lived at war for so long, they had grown accustomed to violence, to extreme sensations and to actions dictated by the instinct for survival. The poison of that war would remain in the bodies of our fighters for a long time before it left them free to return to us.

It would take two years before the country began to fully breathe in the air of peace. Before the many refugees from the Tigray, where the fighting had been fiercest, and the hundred thousand men from the dictator's army would find the right course of their new lives. Before the rebel fighters would mix with civilians, turning over their arms to their leaders. Before the economic revival, before the various fronts would reach an agreement to form a new government, before

. . . two whole years. And still, after all that time, there remained traces of that barbaric behavior that followed the liberation. In the forests, near the main roads, some of Mengistu's soldiers continued to attack cars in order to rob the passengers, and at the edge of Churchill Godana, so many refugees from the Tigray continued to live in makeshift plastic tents.

Return to Debre Zeit

Anyway, 1991—that is, 1984 in the Ethiopian calendar—marked the beginning of a new era in the history of Ethiopia, and for our young people it signaled the start of the exodus.

We were no longer the property of the state, as we were when Menghi (that's what we good-naturedly called Mengistu) was around, so we, too, could join that flood that was engulfing the southern part of the world: we could dream of the West, and do whatever it took to realize that dream.

As for me, since I had very clear memories of the ladies' stories in Legesse's shop and of Mekonnen's triumphant departure, I still dreamed of winning a scholarship to study in Italy. To go to the university and to return, as Mekonnen had promised to do, in order to put the fruits of my study to work for my country.

At the end of the rainy season, in the month of Meskerem, five months after the liberation, all my family returned to live in Debre Zeit once again.

The old house in Arada Sefer was left in the care of my Uncle Iasu who had decided to remain in the capital. Now that private business initiatives of every kind were finally permitted, he wanted to try his luck at a travel agency. The rest of us returned to the South, life in our household started up again, and we settled into our normal routine, accompanied by the usual blessings of our three elders during the women's coffee time.

Without letting anyone know of my secret dream, for four years I channeled all my energy into my studies, with excellent results.

Once the third year of high school was over, with still one more year to go, I told myself—and not without some dread—that the time had come to tell my extended family of my wish. My greatest fear was telling my parents, who regarded Italy as a thorn in their side. The absurd thing was that my father was the person I needed most. Since he was the principal of the high school in Debre Zeit, where I happened to be studying, he had access to the information on the scholarships that was indispensable to me.

Not really knowing how to proceed in the matter, I thought of asking old Yacob for help: I needed his advice, and possibly I might need him to intercede for me.

For the very first time it was not he who called for me after having scrutinized my soul for days, together with the other two elders.

I was the one to go and look for him under the mango tree. "Abba Yacob, would you help me pull weeds in the vegetable garden?" I asked him. The other two elders stood up and went off. How simple, how clear-cut everything was with them!

Abba Yacob bent his head to one side and he scrutinized me for several minutes. I stood in front of him waiting for an answer. After what seemed to me an eternity he said, "Woi gud anchi lij! Do you perhaps need to talk to me?" I nodded and he said, "Well, there's no need to go into the vegetable garden. Taking you into the vegetable garden was my tactic when I wanted to get you to talk when you were a child and during your adolescent years that were as prickly as the thorns of the umbrella acacia tree. Now that you are older, and especially since it was you that expressed the wish to talk to me, I find it pointless to go and sweat in the vegetable patch. What's more, I am old and my back aches. Let's stay here, in the shade of the mango tree. What do you say?"

I nodded again.

"Go on, begin," he urged me. "Speak up."

"Abba, I've been studying a lot," I began hesitantly.

"I know. Your success at school is often talked about in the house."

"I study a lot because I have a goal," I continued, trying to overcome my hesitation.

"Let's hear it, then. What is this goal of yours?"

"I'd like to win a scholarship," I said, and stopped. Now came the tough part. How was I going to tell old Yacob that the scholarship I hoped to win was for an Italian university? I screwed up my courage. It was certainly better to talk to him first rather than to my father. If he did not approve at least he would not scold me. He would graciously use his powers of persuasion, like the wise old man that he was.

"Abba, I would like to go to Italy to study economics," I blurted out. His eyes lit up, contrary to everything I had imagined.

"You want to go to the land where Peter and Paul died!"

I felt a shiver run up my spine. "Excuse me?"

"Yes, my child, the land in which Peter and Paul died! It seems like an excellent idea!" The shiver became more intense. I think that was the first time that my mind registered something: to my great consternation, from the depths of my memory I vaguely recalled a promise that was escaping me. I tried to calm myself and suppress my mind's attempt to recall it. In that moment, the only important thing was to grasp the crux of his reply: I had his approval. I looked at him and he repeated, "I think it's an excellent idea."

I hadn't quite finished. Now I needed to ask for his help. I stretched out my hand and took hold of his, nothing but nerves and delicate bones. "Abba, please help me to get my parents' consent and my father's help. He knows everything about scholarships for abroad! I don't expect him to do anything for me, just tell me when the official announcements come out."

He smiled at me calmly, exposing that solitary tooth of his. "My child! I shall speak to your father and to your mother and, placing my trust in God's blessing and in your abilities, I assure you that you will leave for Italy." Floating on happiness, I left the bench under the mango tree.

Old Yacob called together old Yohanes and old Selemon to tell them what we had discussed and to ask for their opinions. A few minutes later, I heard them giving thanks to God for having set me on the path that they had hoped for for me.

Old Yacob talked to my mother and my father three evenings in a row, in the conversation room. Not once was I able to eavesdrop. I was too scared of being discovered. I entrusted my dream and my future to God and to my beloved elder. Only at a certain point during the first evening did a voice carry beyond the door. It was my father shouting, "I don't want her to go there. She would become like the stupid lion in the story with the monkey. She will only learn to say me, me, me, forgetting that there also exist you, they, you all, we . . ." When they came out of the conversation room my father was ready to explode—his face was like a teakettle from which the boiling water spews out, blazing steam from beneath the half-closed lid. I didn't go near him for fear of getting scorched.

As for my mother, well, she threw me a look that, when I was small, would have meant, "Afterward, I'm going to give you a pinch that will hurt for a week."

The second evening they came out looking a little less tense.

The third evening they summoned me into the room. They were standing and old Yacob was sitting with an empty seat by his side. "Sit down here, my child, next to me," he said firmly. In his eyes shone the light of victory. My father and my mother came and stood in front of us. Their faces were serene. Old Yacob spoke up: "My child, if you, on your own, without any help and with the intelligence that God has given you, are able to win a scholarship, you can go to Italy. Your father will keep you informed of all those scholarships you can apply for. All this, but under one condition: once you have finished university, you will return home. To live here with us and to work in your own country."

I lowered my eyes to conceal the happiness flooding over me and in a small voice I assured them, "That has always been my intention."

The Departure

A year and a half later, halfway through Meskerem, immediately after the feast of Meskel, I left for Italy. I was going to spend a year in Perugia to learn Italian and then I was going to Bologna to study at the Faculty of Business and Economics.

The morning of my departure, before leaving my house in Debre Zeit, the three venerable elders gave me their blessing. Each in turn placed a hand on my head and as I walked toward the gate I could hear their words: "May God unfold a path of peace at your feet, may He bring us together again in good health, may He grant you much good fortune and enable you to be worthy of a great injera. May your land call you back. Always."

I turned around one last time. They were smiling. Old Yacob with his solitary tooth. "My child, remember to observe the fasting days and to say your prayers. It will help you to keep faith with your spirit," were his final words, his final advice. By then I was outside, beyond the gate of our house. On my way to the airport in Addis Ababa.

There were leaves on the ground, in the streets when I arrived in Italy. Fall was just beginning, the rust-colored season, a season unknown to me. And which season is more suited to understanding how nostalgia can tear you apart? Fifteen days after my arrival, in mid-October, the migrating birds were preparing to leave. They practiced flying in the skies above the fields around Perugia. I saw them when I escaped from the historic center and went beyond the suffocating walls of the town, in search of green spaces that would allow my eyes to travel far to the horizon. Clouds of swishing wings stood out against the sky, came together, spread out, veered to the right and to the left. Looking at them made me realize I had never stopped to think that for them there were two places, each a place of arrival and of departure. An hourglass scanned out their time, and when the sand had run out on one side and the hourglass was turned over, the place of arrival became the place of departure.

I understood that they would soon depart when thick gray clouds settled in the sky. One evening while I was watching them, something about their flight made me realize that it was the last trial run. The next morning, at dawn, I hurried to watch them depart. The dark, swishing cloud came together and then spread out in the sky one last time, passing over. Then I was left alone with the fall.

That first year there was a line from a song by Mahmud Ahmed that was always playing in my head: "Nostalgia is a ship upon which dark thoughts travel." I took solace in the thought that it was only going to be for a few years, the time it took to complete my studies, but all the same it stirred up a well of nostalgia. Within those medieval walls, without the open spaces that were familiar to me, surrounded by stones the color of sand that took the place of the colors of our houses—of the greens, of the light blues, of the deep reds—and of the singing of the birds at dawn, of the early morning light that came through the windows without shutters . . . surrounded by those medieval stones, I lived, experiencing only the things that were absent. I missed my family, the neighbors, the chatter at home, the dust in Debre Zeit, my school friends, the sun, the storms, the smell of the pink pepper trees along the roads, the rhythmic sound of the two-wheeled carts. I missed the wide-open spaces, the lakes in Debre Zeit, the colors of the earth, my people. I missed everything.

I spent that first year studying Italian and I tried to lessen my nostalgia by mingling with the many foreign students who had come to learn Italian like I did. Sure, mixing with them did not mean that it filled my void, but it helped. They, too, experienced that estrangement brought about by changing countries, and they could understand me a little, but apart from that—our halting Italian and the need to keep each other company—we had little in common. Each one of us tried to create a niche in which we could feel less lost, and each of us did so by trying to recreate a piece of our own country of origin. In such situations, if there was someone else from your own country, it all became easier. Unfortunately for me, that year there was no other Ethiopian at the University of Perugia. . . . But I managed to survive and in some way they, the other foreigners, helped me to do so.

The following year I left for Bologna. And from the very first months of my university life there, where unlike in Perugia there were few foreigners, I had to resign myself to being subjected to the diseases of the West: loneliness and individualism. There was no way to avoid them. Even though I had not been contaminated by them, every single thing around me was. A thick cloak enveloped each person, keeping everyone isolated, the one from the other. A cloak that did not fall, not even when we were all together.

Two years later, while I was finishing my first year of university, old Yohanes died.

I wept, awash in that loneliness that was so alien to me. Nobody in Italy was erecting the mourning tent to receive relatives, friends, and all those who wanted to be near the members of the deceased's family, to share in their grieving and give them strength in their loss. My university friends thought it would be better to leave me alone. Even more alone. According to them, solitude would help me abandon myself to sorrow. It was their way of grieving. I wanted to tell them that for me it wasn't like that, that solitude would have made my sorrow more acute and unbearable. But they were Italian and I was Ethiopian. A deep, wide gulf divided our ways of living.

Another two years went by and old Selemon died. Once more I wept alone. Several of my university friends confessed that they found my attachment to those old men, who were only relatives from the second and third generations, very strange. I did not explain to them my relationship to the elders of our household, how I had been sustained by their wisdom as I was growing up, how they had taken care of my spirit, carefully watching over me at every moment. I did not even explain the meaning and the role of our elders, how they were the supporting columns of our household. Once again, they would not have understood.

I mourned for both of them without being able to go home, due to lack of money. Only the occasional phone call allowed me to dilute my grief with the encouragement of my parents, who urged me to go forward, and of old Yacob, who reminded me how life goes hand in hand with death. It was all part of the earthly nature of our existence.

I spent the fourth year at university terrified of losing old Yacob, too. Terrified of not being able to embrace him one last time, and to see his face with that smile, with the one solitary tooth, and that luminous look of his when he used to say "My child." That summer I found a job in a small restaurant in the hills around Bologna. I was going to work to save up enough money to return home for the feast of Meskel in the month of Meskerem, at the end of September in Italy. I had finished all my exams, only my thesis was left to do, and I could take my time and defend it in the spring session. Meanwhile, I would spend a couple of months at home.

Unfortunately, I did not make it in time. Old Yacob died on August 21, in our month of Nahasey, the day on which Ethiopia celebrates the assumption of the Virgin Mary into heaven.

His death came quietly. His life just came to an end. Like the stub of a candle that has lit up the night for a long time, keeping the dark shadows of the room at bay. Now it was dark.

I reached home after the celebrations of the fortieth day since his death, after his tomb had been blessed. My father, my mother, my brothers, Aunt Fanus, Aunt Abeba, Mulu, Alemitu . . . and many, many other people came to meet me at the airport. Perhaps even the entire neighborhood where we lived in Debre Zeit. I embraced them one by one, but without being able to fully enjoy the contact that I had dreamed of for so long. I felt confused. It did not seem normal to me that among all those people, they were not there. The three venerable elders.

We went toward the cars. I got in with my father and my mother. At Meskel Square my father did not turn left to take the road to Debre

Zeit. He went straight on and he took the long avenue that led to the old
Gebi. I looked at my mother questioningly, and she replied to my silent
question, saying that old Yacob had expressed the wish that they return
to Arada Sefer. "Everyone, including Uncle Mesfin, Aunt Saba, Aunt
Fanus, Aunt Abeba, your cousins Mulu and Alemitu who left behind
in Debre Zeit husbands, children, your cousins . . ." That had been his
wish: "You will spend the first eighty days following my death in the old
house in Arada Sefer." His wish anticipated my arrival, she added. Later,
perhaps the day after, she would explain in detail what this all meant.

Very early the next day I wanted to go to visit his tomb. My mother
came with me. We caught a bus at the short-trip bus station. During
the ride I was in such a state of torpor that I was not able to notice
anything. My mother tried to involve me in conversation: "Have
you noticed how spread out the city has become? It goes on forever.
Akaki has almost been absorbed by Addis Ababa. Did you see the
great circle highway? It's not finished yet, a piece of it is missing, the
part going to Gulele! All the same, it's beautiful. It's a pity it has so
few pedestrian crossovers . . ." She would have gone on forever to try
to distract me.

I turned to her, my eyes veiled in tears. "Every moment when I
was in Italy I dreamed of the day when I would return home. To my
land. Our land. I promised myself that I would gaze at each thing for
a long time with my eyes and with my heart. Each thing that always
seemed so normal while I was here, but then in Italy I understood
that they were uniquely ours, part of our culture, of our land. But
today, mother dear, I can't see anything. My eyes are blinded by
sadness. I feel defeated because I did not arrive in time, because I
did not see him one last time."

She squeezed my hand. "Take heart, my child." I turned my head
to the window. Hot tears ran down my face.

On his tomb, in the cemetery of the old Church of Kechene Giorgis, there was written *"Ye Itiopia arbegna"*—an Ethiopian patriot.
I wept until I could weep no more, but without being able to free
myself from the grief. My mother tried to console me. But who could
console me? I felt like a little bird that had fallen out of the nest.

I stood for a long, long time with my head on her shoulder, and when my eyes were finally dry, she spoke to me. "The evening before he died he asked me to go with him into his room. He was feeling well. He embraced me in front of his room. 'That daughter of yours that I love so much! Take care of her!' he said before he disappeared through the door. The following morning we would have celebrated the Ascension of the Virgin Mary and ended the sixteen days of fasting. At dawn I went to call him to go to mass. I found him deep in eternal sleep.

"He had a deep affection for you. He used to say that you had received a gift from God: you felt the ties to the past. Echoes of the great saints, soldiers, and warriors of Ethiopia resounded in you. You were not like other young people who have had their roots slashed by the ills of modern life and by Western consumerism.

"The evening he told us about your desire to go to Italy and of the approval of Abba Yohanes and Abba Selemon, your father objected with all his strength: 'Those who leave never come back and I do not want to lose my daughter to the very country that once wanted to crush us beneath its feet.'

"But Abba Yacob reassured him that it would not happen. 'Mahlet,' he said, 'has a very strong bond with her land and she will return when the time is right.' A few months before, he had told us of his particular wish: 'My children, I feel that my time in this earthly dwelling is about to end. Soon I shall go to the Heavenly Kingdom. When I die I ask that you spend the first eighty days in the old house in Arada Sefer. Mahlet will arrive before the end of that period.'

"He was convinced that you would arrive within the time frame he had established, as indeed you did. He left two requests for you: That you sleep in the room in which he slept during the months we spent in Addis Ababa at the end of the Derg regime. And for that reason he assigned us the task of putting his belongings in there after bringing them from his room in Debre Zeit. The second request is that you go to the Church of St. George in Addis Ababa. To pray for him."

Part Two
THE RETURN

CHAPTER THREE

WE RETURNED TO ADDIS ABABA, TO OUR HOME IN ARADA
Sefer. That very evening I took my stuff out of the room that
I had shared with my cousins, Aunt Fanus, and Aunt Abeba right
before and after the liberation, and I moved into the last room on the
left of the veranda, the one that had been old Yacob's room.

On the way out I cast a quick glance at the bed where I had spent
the previous night. There was a time when three of us shared it. And
on the first night of my return, three people shared that bed again:
Mulu, Alemitu, and me. "Just like old times," Alemitu had said. That
first night the nearness of their bodies kept me warm. In Italy I had
missed that physical contact, that natural way we had of sleeping
together.

Looking at the bed I felt a little sad about leaving the room, but
the following morning I woke up well-rested, and happy at not having had to spend the night fighting with overlapping arms and legs.
It was around eight-thirty in the morning, but the cold night air
still permeated the house. I braved the cold and jumped out of bed
shivering. Wrapped up in a gabi, holding my towel and clothes, I ran
through the courtyard to reach the bathroom. After washing and
getting dressed, I went to the kitchen, had breakfast, and, without
saying a word to anyone, went out. Anyway, everyone knew where
I was going.

I walked down our path and turned left at the bottom. I headed
downhill, and at the bridge I got on a small van that dropped me off
a little before the rotary near St. George's Cathedral.

In the months I had spent in the capital right before and after the liberation, I had come to love a particular aspect of the churches in Addis Ababa: that strange invisible barrier they created, a barrier capable of eliminating all noise.

Every church is just off a street constantly immersed in chaos, but as soon as you step through the gate, it is as if the church had the magical power to deflect sound. You find yourself immersed in total silence, a silence that is all-embracing and restful, like the shadow of a great sycamore tree in the hottest hours of the day. . . .

At St. George's this effect is even greater. The church overlooks a rotary that is always congested with cars, pedestrians, taxis, little vans, city buses, laden donkeys . . . not to mention the entry ramp where there is always a wall of beggars and peddlers ready to assault every member of the faithful.

While I was walking toward the rotary, observing the intense chaos and noise, it occurred to me that this was a most appropriate manifestation of my interior turmoil. The pain and confusion caused by the death of my old friend had created an inner noise, similar to a chattering crowd. "May God make the magic barrier of the church banish from its holy courtyard not only the sounds of the city, but also the sound of my inner turmoil," I said to myself.

There are two ways of entering the garden of St. George's Cathedral: the main entrance facing the rotary, and a secondary one on an avenue, almost hidden by the trees lining the sidewalk. From both entrances one can follow a short path leading to the garden that surrounds the church.

I crossed the rotary and reached the outside ramp of the main entrance. Once I had gotten beyond the barrier of beggars and peddlers I went in.

After passing through the gate I stopped, touched the ground with the tips of my fingers, raised my hand, and made the sign of the cross. I took a few deep breaths to absorb the silence, then, just as I was making up my mind to head for the garden, I froze in my tracks.

I had gone to St. George's not to breathe in its peace, but to fulfill old Yacob's request: to pray for him. Almost deliberately, ever
since my mother had told me about old Yacob's wishes, my mind
had blurred his main request and only focused on one part of it:
go to St. George's. Now that the moment to pray had arrived, and I
had to honor his request in its entirety, I found myself with my feet
nailed to the ground, in the middle of the path, unable take a single
step forward.

Ever since old Yacob had died I had been unable to pray. There was
nothing I could do about it. When I found out about his death I had
tried, but each time I was overcome by an unbearable wave of grief
ready to overwhelm me. I quickly gave up. I had found only one solution to soothe the pain: repress it as much as possible. That's when I
think that strange, inner noise had begun.

I mustered all my courage and took a few steps forward. I could
feel my heartbeat pulsating in my temples. I reached the garden and
continued slowly to the first courtyard. I walked across it, then went
up to the second courtyard and, following the other churchgoers,
knelt down in front of the sacred images hanging on the outside
walls of the cathedral.

But I did not pray; the only thing I did was ask, in a whisper, for old
Yacob's and for God's forgiveness. I was trying everything I possibly
could. To do more was beyond my capabilities. After spending over
an hour kneeling here and there and completing the ritual circle
around the church, I decided to leave. I could not take it any longer.
It was as if I had been sitting on a bunch of stinging nettles the whole
time. I could not spend another minute in the garden of the church.
I turned toward the exit.

I had just started along the small path toward the main exit when I
found myself in front of an old hermit. He was standing straight and
tall as a spear, his bearing majestic. He was wearing the customary
long, yellow tunic that reached all the way to his bare feet. On his
head was the traditional monastic headdress, on his serious face a
thin, scraggly beard. One of his hands was firmly holding the long

metal staff topped by the cross. Around his neck hung the bag holding his prayer book and many rosaries of different sizes, some with beads as big as walnuts, strung along a metal chain.

I acknowledged him with a slight, respectful bow and continued on my way. From behind I heard him shout, "You there . . . yes, I'm talking to you. I am Abba Chereka. I have never seen you around before, and I know everyone here."

I stopped and turned. "Abba, I am from Debre Zeit. I am here to fulfill the wish of one of the venerable elders of my family who died forty days ago."

"May you be blessed, dear child. Well done." I thought he had finished and I was just turning around when he called me again: "Dear child, you might be from Debre Zeit, but your clothes tell me that you're not from here."

"You are right Abba. I've just come back from Italy."

"Ah! Now I understand! You are one of the many who left our land in search of a better life! It's the right thing to do. You young people have a right to a better life. In Ethiopia—it is also written in the Sacred Scriptures—we will face many more dark years. Then a new emperor will arrive, sent by God, and our country will flourish once again."

"Abba, for me it is different. I did not go away to search to find a better life, but to study. Next year, after graduating, I am coming back, to live here for good!"

"My goodness! So, you are trying to surprise me. What is your name?"

"Mahlet."

"Mahlet?"

"Yes, Abba, Mahlet."

"My dear child, your name is almost a *qene*. If you remove the 'h' and shift the accent slightly, Malet means 'the significance,' while Ma'let stands for 'that time.' Therefore, their combined meaning is 'the significance of that time.' It is a name tied to the Annunciation of the Archangel Gabriel to the Virgin Mary. You are a special per-

son, my child. Make an offering, and I will pray for you." I slipped
my hand into my pants pocket and pulled out ten birr. He smiled as
he took the money and told me, "If you come back to pray for your
elder, wear a skirt. Skirts are becoming to women."

Hearing those words, a bell went off in my head.

Another voice, long ago, in a room, had told me those same words.
An image resurfaced in my mind: I was sitting on a bed wearing a
little white dress with ruffles. Next to me was old Yacob. For just a
moment, his voice had come to life again through the words of the
hermit: "Skirts are becoming to women," old Yacob had said, admir-
ing my dress.

I burst into tears. I was crying my eyes out. The old hermit put his
arm around my shoulders and led me to a quieter part of the garden.
I continued to sob and he stood silently by my side. I wanted to tell
him something, but I did not know how to explain that there was so
much inside of me. A whole universe. Old Yacob had died while I was
in a foreign land, a land that had made me understand the crucial
value of his presence, of my country, of my culture. These feelings
were all connected, intertwined in an indissoluble way, and I did
not know how to express them. I continued to cry until my tears
dried up. Then he asked me, "Dear child, have you been able to pray
for your elder?" I shook my head. "Then come back tomorrow and
we will pray together." He accompanied me to the exit, and before I
was sucked into the hustle and bustle of the city, he said once more,
"Don't forget, come! I will be waiting for you. If you pray with me,
you will feel much better." I nodded and he told me to meet him
under an old tree. "Go around the courtyard to the right, near where
the men enter the church. Don't worry, when you see it, you will
recognize it. It is the biggest tree in the whole churchyard." Then we
parted. He went back and I went off into the chaos of the city.

That day when I returned home, no one asked me anything. The
women were all in the inner courtyard, busy with their chores. My
mother came toward me. "Would you like to eat? I made a very good
shiro for you, with *karia,* the way you like it." I smiled at her, ate, and

then roamed through the house. I don't even remember the coming of the evening and night falling. Mulu brought me a lighted candle that she put on a small table in front of an icon of the Virgin Mary. "Would you like for me to sleep with you for a while?" she asked. "You're still grieving for old Yacob's death, aren't you? We have already cried, all together. You are the only one, left to cry alone. I feel so sorry for you."

"I hope, I really hope there is a reason, a meaning to all of this."

"I am sure there is. So, are you going to make room for me in the bed?"

"I believe it would be better for me to sleep by myself. Abba Yacob asked me to sleep in his room, alone. I believe there is a reason for this as well. Don't worry about me. Now off you go. Good night." She left and I remained in the company of the candlelight and the icon of the Virgin Mary.

The next morning, at the same time as the previous morning, without asking myself any questions, like a robot blindly obeying the words of the old hermit, I returned to St. George's, following the same route as the day before. Once again there was chaos in the street: cars, horns blaring, peddlers and beggars. Then the gate and, on the other side, the silence of the churchyard, and again my sign of the cross, my going around the first courtyard, then the second. . . . Everything just like the day before, without prayers . . . and, in the end, the tree where we would meet: an enormous old tree with a slab of stone under it for those who might want to sit there. I sat down and I immediately felt uncomfortable, so I got up again, removed my netela, took my sweater from my shoulders, and placed it on the stone to make the seat softer. I readjusted my netela on my head, took up my place again on the stone, and abandoned myself to gazing around in an attempt to quiet my inner turmoil.

At the church there was a slow procession of worshipers dressed in white—women wrapped in large white netela that reached to their hips and lower, and men wrapped in their shemma. They were going around and praying in front of the sacred images on the external wall of the church. Some worshipers were alone and others formed small groups of two or three people. Some with a silent bow greeted others sitting on stones under the trees. Still others, done with praying, went into the shade to chat with the people sitting there.

All this happened in hushed whispers and the comings and goings were having a hypnotic effect on me.

I had been waiting for over an hour, but Abba Chereka had not yet arrived. The previous day he had told me, "Come earlier if you can, earlier than you did today . . ." Anyway, the wait was not yet bothering me. The quiet awareness of people in prayer that left room for small sounds, for the gentle rustling of the breeze among the trees, for the song of small birds in the branches, had the power to calm me, to take me far from my inner tension.

Behind me a woman began calling "Eliye! Eliye!" and shaking the lower branches of some hedges. I turned to look. A medium-sized turtle came out of a corner. "So! You were here? Come over, I have some food for you." The woman started walking off, followed by the turtle.

About a half hour after the lady with the turtle had gone by, an old bishop appeared on my right. He was walking, his back bent, and he was holding onto the carved knob of his cane. He was wearing a black cap, his purple cape was wrapped around his black tunic, and an enormous cross was dangling from his neck. He was headed my way. He took a few more steps and I was able to make out his face more clearly. He had a triangular face and, notwithstanding his considerably advanced age, his skin was smooth, without a wrinkle. From his upper lip two long teeth stuck out, slightly bent toward the left side, like a pair of quotation marks. Those two teeth and the triangular face made him look like a mouse.

Slowly he arrived at where I was sitting. He wanted to sit on the slab. I jumped up in a sign of respect. "Stay, stay, my dear child," he said. I sat down and he joined me. An intense smell of incense emanating from his clothes made my nose itch.

The bishop had sat next to me with extreme simplicity, yet my muscles were slightly tensed. It was not common to have a bishop sitting next to you on a slab of stone under an old tree. I did not know if I was supposed to begin a conversation or if it was more appropriate for me to remain silent. Then I thought, I was tired of all that. I had spent five years reacting against my nature to please the people of the country that was hosting me. Now, the pain I had endured during my absence gave me permission to simply be myself.

I surrendered myself to silence, and after we had spent half an hour next to each other, he began chatting. "Are you waiting for Abba Chereka? Because this old tree is his office." I cracked a smile. "He is a great hermit. A man with a large belly, like that of our Lord. A belly that knows how to hold a lot." While he was speaking his lips moved around his mousy teeth and his face had a benevolent look that exuded a certain familiarity. I smiled more openly. "My child, you don't live here with us, do you?" he asked.

"Yes, Abba! You are right! I live abroad." I would have liked to add, "But not for much longer now. One more year and I will be back home." But I didn't bother.

"I understood it by the way you wear your clothes. There are stores with European clothes even in Ethiopia, but those of you who live abroad have a way of wearing them that makes you stand out. And where do you live, dear child?"

"In Italy, in Bologna."

"I visited Italy. Twice. I was in Rome, Loreto, Assisi, Padua, and La Verna. Ah! Italy. There was a time when we quarreled with that government of theirs that wanted to give orders in our own home. But we fought them, and that government, with all of its bosses, little bosses, and underbosses, was forced to move out. Our country regained its freedom and we lived in peace with the Italians who stayed behind—we mixed with them and we created many families, mixed families."

The old bishop, leaning on the knob of his cane, raised his body slightly from the stone, removed a corner of his cape from under his bottom, and, eliminating the few inches between our bodies, sat down right next to me. Looking as if he wanted to tell me a secret, he leaned his head next to mine. "The truth is, my dear, that their government, with all those bosses and underbosses, was like one of those faucets I found in certain hotels in Italy—I have never been to one here in Ethiopia. From those faucets, whether I turned them off tightly or turned them full on, the same small stream of water trickled out. 'The faucets are encrusted with limestone!' the staff would tell me, when I asked for an explanation. Well, the Italian government of those days was like those faucets, encrusted and stuck in a single position." The bishop raised one of his hands to his chest and tapped himself repeatedly with his fingertips. "They were always like this, with their hand pointing toward themselves and with a single word on their lips: 'Me.' They felt superior and were not willing to look at themselves from the outside, through other people's eyes. And, my dear child, only when you agree to look at your image reflected in other people's eyes can you see and take stock of yourself. But they were unable to do that, so they ended up like the stupid lion and the monkey."

"What lion?" I hadn't felt such a spark of curiosity for a long time.

"What? You don't know the story of the stupid lion and the monkey?"

"I'm not sure—there are so many stories with lions and monkeys! I might know it."

"But this one is special, and when people mention the stupid lion and the monkey they always mean this story. So you don't know it? Well! Here it is. Open your heart, my dear, and listen to this story."

The Story of the Stupid Lion and the Monkey

There was once a lion who considered himself invincible. Greater than everything else. Greater even than his own kind. One day he realized he did not have a single servant: "What!" he said to himself. "All the other lions have servants and I, the best of them all, who clearly should have some because of my inborn superiority, have none!" So he decided to get himself a slave. He went under a big sycamore tree and gave a mighty roar.

A Barbary ape who was eating, hidden up in the branches, hearing the roar, fainted from fright and fell from the tree right at the feet of the king of the forest. When she came around and opened her eyes, she met those of the lion, who was staring at her. Quickly she shut her eyes again. She was hoping he would think she had died and would go on his way. Instead, he shook her with his paw: "Stupid monkey, get up. Get up and follow me. Starting today, you are my slave." The monkey reluctantly opened her eyes, got up, followed him, and became his slave.

For many months she went along with his insolence, waiting on him hand and foot, but that was not all. In those months she learned not to fear him anymore and she began to notice his weak points. She realized that the king of the forest was rather stupid. Inflated by his unbearable arrogance, aside from his physical strength he amounted to very little. One morning while the monkey was still lost in her dreams, the lion entered her cave and woke her up. "I'm thirsty. Go to the river and get me some water!" he ordered, and went off, filling the cave with his pungent, unpleasant smell. The lion did not like washing; in fact he hated water, and since he was endowed with four armpits you could smell him even from afar.

The monkey thought to herself, "That's it, I've had it. Today is the day I am freeing myself from that stinky, arrogant beast." She took the bucket, went down to the river, and stayed there for over an hour. Then she went back, pretending to be very weary. Once in front of the lion, she placed the bucket on the ground. The lion lowered his head in order to drink, but found the bucket empty.

"Stupid monkey, why didn't you bring the water?" he shouted.

"Down by the river," she answered, "there is a large, scary, horrible beast that prevented me from getting the water."

"What do you mean? Did you tell him that it was for me?"

"Certainly!"

"So?"

"He said that you are a nobody, that the water is his and he can give it to whom he likes."

The lion gave an angry roar and grabbed the monkey by the paw. "Take me there, to the place where you met him. I'll show him who is in charge."

The monkey, smiling to herself in silence, led the lion to the river-bank and showed him a spot where there was a thicket of tall reeds. "There, that's where he appeared, behind those reeds."

The lion moved the reeds aside with his paw and went toward the water. "Monkey, I don't see anyone here."

"Lean over a bit further," she said, and he went closer toward the water.

"I tell you, I can't see anyone."

"Lean over more."

Once again, the lion leaned closer to the river, and he saw his own reflection in the water. Since he had never seen himself in his entire life, he thought he was facing his enemy. He roared as loudly as he could, "Now I'll show you who is in charge!" and, opening his mouth wide, he jumped forward to bite his reflection, but he fell into the water, and the river carried him away. He died, and the monkey was free once more.

CHAPTER FOUR

"Y OU SEE, MY CHILD, THAT'S HOW LIFE GOES. KNOWING
nothing cannot heal anything, as they say, and I would add:
knowing nothing about ourselves can bring about our own destruc-
tion." After finishing his story, without waiting for my reply, the
old bishop patted my shoulder and, wishing me good luck, got up.
Slowly, taking the necessary time for his old bones to change position, he started walking away, his back curved and his hand on the
knob of the cane. He crossed part of the second courtyard and, without forgetting to kneel in front of the main entrance to the church,
the one with the Tabot, he went toward the exit and disappeared.

Once alone, I again became entranced by the slow comings and
goings of the churchgoers.

I am not sure how much time had gone by when a loud, metallic
clanking next to me made me jump. It was Abba Chereka, who, as
he sat down next to me, made the beads of his many rosaries bang
against the chain around his neck. Without commenting on having
startled me, he turned his eyes toward where I had been looking before his arrival. "There was a time when I too used to sit here and let
myself be hypnotized by the churchgoers. It gave me solace. At the
time I had not become a monk yet and this tree wasn't as big as it is
now, but it already reminded me of another majestic tree that grew
along a path . . . an important path," he said, and then he let silence
fall between us.

Once again, I turned my eyes toward the comings and goings in
the church garden. He did the same. At one point I heard the rustling
of his clothes; I turned around and found him looking at me. "I see

you are wearing a skirt. Good!" he said, and then his eyes looked at my bare arms, half covered by my small, inadequate netela. "You are certainly wearing a skirt . . . and yet you continue to follow the customs of the country you're coming from. You're baring God's gifts, showing that you are no longer accustomed to the sun of your own country." Without saying a word, I took the sweater, lifted the netela without uncovering my head, put the sweater on, and sat down again. "Good, now you are dressed properly. Let's pray."

He took my hand, closed his eyes, and began moving his lips. I closed my eyes as well, but I could not find the words to pray; that inner noise that was tormenting me took over, thrusting me forward and making me lose my balance. In the darkness of my closed eyes I felt as if I were falling backward, into a bottomless vacuum. I abruptly opened my eyes, breathing quickly, just like after a nightmare. To calm down, I tried to focus on the peaceful courtyard. Abba Chereka sensed something and opened his eyes. "What are you doing, my child? Why aren't you praying?"

"I don't know how to. Ever since our venerable elder died I have been unable to pray. When I close my eyes I am overcome by a wave that sweeps over everything, a wave that overwhelms me, thrusting me down into endless darkness."

"What was the name of your elder, dear child?"

"Abba Yacob."

Through the thickness of his unkempt beard I saw the vague hint of a smile that immediately vanished. He squeezed my hand and said, "Then, my child, close your eyes again and try to recite this psalm in his honor: 'Bless the Lord, O my soul, and all that is within me; bless His holy name. Bless the Lord, O my soul, and forget not all His many benefits.' Repeat these words silently to yourself, without pausing. I will do the same."

I closed my eyes and began to recite the psalm. At first my temples were throbbing but after a while my heart calmed down; the psalm made me breathe more regularly. Little by little, images of my childhood and adolescent years began to form in my mind. The women's coffee hour, the first Saturday at the market, working in the garden, the romantic escapades of my older cousins, the celebration of the return of the home in Arada Sefer. Old Yacob was present in all these memories; he would pop up suddenly, with his solitary tooth. Once again I was overcome with grief. Once again, as on the previous day, a flood of tears started rolling down my cheeks. I wept for a long time, while Abba Chereka, with his hand resting on mine, kept moving his lips, keeping his eyes firmly shut.

That day I left St. George's a little more serene. For the first time since old Yacob's death, I felt as if my tears had diminished my grief, making it less overwhelming. At the main gate, the old hermit invited me to return the following day: "Early in the morning. If you can, even earlier than today. Mornings are the best time," he said, and once again he asked me for ten birr: "You'll see, dear child, you won't be sorry!" I fumbled in my bra where I had hidden my money, took out ten birr, and gave it to him. "Well done, child; you keep your money where our mothers and grandmothers did," he added.

We parted. He went back in and I merged into the chaos of the city, heading toward home.

As I had done the previous day, when I went into the inner courtyard of our home in Arada Sefer, I found all the women of my family there, busy with their many chores. My mother called me over: "Mahlet, come sit near me." I took a three-legged stool and sat next to her. "So," she said, "there is a glimmer of light in your eyes." I rested my head on her shoulder. "Tell me, my child."

"Mother, at St. George's I met an old hermit. His name is Abba Chereka." Suddenly, all the women stopped working. Aunt Fanus, who had been chopping an onion on a cutting board that rested on her knees, stopped with her knife in midair. She raised her head to meet my mother's eyes. Only for a split second. The air became heavy, then everything returned to normal.

That evening, Aunt Fanus came to bring me a lit candle that she put on the metal table, in front of the icon of the Virgin Mary. "It's for your prayers," she said, "so that they can rise to God on the candle's flame." I thought she would leave right away, but she remained standing in front of me, hesitantly.

"What is it, Aunt?"

"You've never heard of Abba Chereka before?"

"No, until yesterday I didn't even know he existed!"

"Ah! You met yesterday?"

"Yes!"

"And today?"

"Yes, we met again. Yesterday he invited me to come back and today he invited me to go back tomorrow."

"My dear child, you are lucky—he is a great hermit. He is over ninety years old, you know," she told me, and then she began laughing.

"What is it?" I asked.

"I will tell you because at this point you are old enough. Know that when I think about this, I still feel a bit ashamed, so be understanding with me. After the liberation I did not only buy clothes. I also wanted to find a husband. I had heard about Abba Chereka and about his great ability to see into the future.

"I went to see him. He gave me appointment after appointment, on many consecutive days. Every day I went, and after a long wait he would come and would tell me to come back the following day. One day I almost accosted him, so he invited me to join him under the big tree in the courtyard, the one they call his 'office among the branches.' He invited me to sit on a stone slab resting against the trunk of the tree and asked me, 'What do you want?'

"'I want to know if I will find a husband. A good one, well-mannered and with some money.'

"'A woman does not ask if a husband will come her way . . . she simply takes one. If a woman does not know how to do that, it means she doesn't really want one,' he said, and dismissed me, strongly advising me not to go back to see him for such foolish matters. For almost a year I thought he had told me those things to get rid of me, even punish me a little; then, with time, I understood what he meant—he had read inside of me and he had understood. I loved my dead husband too much and no one could ever have taken his place. There, now you know my secret." She stroked my cheek and headed toward the door. "May God watch over your sleep," she said, and left.

The following morning, my mother woke me up at seven, about an hour and a half earlier than I had woken up the previous two days. "If you have an appointment with Abba Chereka you must be there early. You are supposed to visit hermits a little after dawn," she said, shaking me awake. In her hands she had an airtight container. She opened the lid and the aroma of spiced butter and berbere immediately whetted my appetite. "You have always loved genfo. Do you still like it?" she asked. I nodded, still half asleep; I felt chilly, wearing only a tee shirt while my naked legs dangled over the bed. "Then go wash in the bathroom and come and eat. Hurry up, before the butter gets cold." I put on a track suit, put my bathrobe on over it, took a towel, and went out into the inner courtyard, heading toward the bathroom. It was early, the air was colder than on the previous morning, and it would take another couple of hours of sunshine to warm it up. And even after several hours of sunny skies, the breeze coming down from Mount Entoto and the hills around Addis would carry traces of the cold night air. The sun would be strong only between noon and three. We were entering the coldest months of the year, when the temperature does not go over eighty-two to eighty-four degrees Fahrenheit during the day and at night it gets close to freezing.

The house was still deep in sleep. There was no one in the inner courtyard, only the watchman, all bundled up, who asked me how I had slept. In the distance, one could hear the first sounds of the city. The first trucks of the morning with their cargo beds rattling over every pothole, the first vans struggling uphill . . .

I washed quickly and ate breakfast, contentedly dipping my fingers into the soft dough of the genfo. I broke off pieces and dipped them into the melted butter spiced with berbere, then I dipped them again into yogurt and all but tossed them in my mouth. My mother, sitting in front of me, was looking at me, pleased. "You're starting to feel better," she said. "This is the first time since your return that I see you enjoying your food."

"Perhaps," I teased her, "it's because you had not made genfo for me yet."

"You see," she continued, "you are even in a playful mood." I felt a sharp pang of nostalgia for old Yacob. I missed him. Death is such a drastic event. One moment a person is there, in the world, with his whole range of life experiences, and a few seconds later all that is left are the memories you have of that person. A sudden separation. Like a branch cut off by the blade of an axe. On one side the living, on the other the dead. It takes time to process such a dramatic break. At the beginning it almost seems possible to return to being a whole tree. It feels like only a momentary separation. Someone left, went to a home nearby, but will soon return.

My mother, sensing the darkening mood of my thoughts, drew my attention away by putting her hand on my shoulder. "My dear, it is time. You must go to see Abba Chereka!" I had never heard her sound like that. Gone were her sternness and restraint; in their place was old Yacob's sweetness, as if he had passed her the baton. I smiled at her and chased away the threatening cloud of my thoughts. I dressed quickly and left. Without any explanation, at the gate she handed me a netela larger than the one I was wearing. "May light follow you, my child," she said. Without a word, I took the netela, handed her mine, embraced her, and went through the gate.

I followed the path leading to the paved road, but instead of turning left and going downhill toward the bridge and the bus stop, I turned right and started climbing. I felt like walking and St. George's Cathedral wasn't that far. I would go there on foot.

Until I reached the little shops before Enrico's pastry store, the street was almost deserted, but starting from the first *suq*, the open-air marketplace on top of the hill, it began to come to life. In front of the old Italian bookstore the sidewalk was crowded with shoe-shiners and all their supplies, and with peddlers. Some had wooden crates filled with roasted peanuts and, scattered on top of them, some open packages of chewing gum. Others, with old measuring scales hanging from their necks, had crates filled with fruit. Just before the pastry shop, I turned right and continued walking uphill. When I reached the area of Piassa, the dynamic rhythm swirled all around me. I came out to the left of Piassa and to the right of the Ras Movie Theater. In front of the theater were lines of yellow-and-red buses picking up streams of people who were also standing in line. Some buses spewed out clouds of black smoke, darkening the air and the lungs of the passersby. Further ahead there was a bus stop with lines of white-and-blue vans. Some of the vans reached the stop by weaving through the other cars. They stopped in between the parked vans, while the ticket collector held the door open to jump out quickly. As each new van arrived, a concert of car horns started up. There were those who sounded their horns in protest because a van had passed too close to their car, and those who sounded their horns to greet the driver of the arriving van. In the middle of all of this randomly chaotic traffic there were other cars, pedestrians, laden donkeys . . .

The noise filled my head. I almost regretted having decided to walk, but I was nearly there. I could almost make out the rotary with the equestrian statue of Emperor Menelik. I entered the avenue with the tree-lined divider and continued on my way. I tried to walk faster, ignoring what was around me. Finally I arrived at the rotary and, as I had done on previous days, I walked across it, headed up the external ramp of the main entrance, went past the beggars, the peddlers, and again the gate, the sign of the cross, the path, the circles around the first churchyard, those around the second, and, finally, Abba Chereka's tree.

I sat down, letting myself drop onto the stone slab, and did not take off my sweater. I caught my breath and tried to shake off the last residue of city noises. I put my elbows on my thighs, rested my face in my cupped hands, and lost myself in the comings and goings of the churchgoers. It must have been a special day, the feast of a saint. Perhaps St. George's monthly celebration. In the first courtyard there was a series of monks and nuns, both young and old. With their yellow shemma and their black caps, they stood out among the churchgoers in their white clothes. They walked slowly, tapping the ground before them with their monks' staffs. They prayed and knelt down. There were even a few priests. A tall, stately priest went by, carrying some books under his arm. With a long, quick stride he arrived at the entrance, knelt once in front of the Tabot door, and went out through the other.

A little later the turtle lady passed by. She was holding some lettuce leaves. She greeted me: "Good morning, dear child, did you sleep well?"

"Yes, thank God, and you, Mother?"

"Yes, I did, thank God. I'm going to see the turtle to bring her food, otherwise, to spite me, she eats the flowers in the garden. And you?" she asked. "Are you waiting for Abba Chereka?"

"Yes, Mother!"

"Ah, then enjoy your wait!" She smiled and left. I looked at her while she was leaving; she held her hand at hip level and was waving the lettuce leaves. "Eliye! Eliye!" she called out in a low voice, so as not to bother those who were praying. With each step her enormous behind swayed back and forth, left and right. I laughed quietly, remembering one of my few Ethiopian friends in Bologna who, swaying his hips and sticking out his behind, imitated the walk of some rather plump old Ethiopian woman and repeated, *Tussu, tuss; tussu, tuss.* I let my gaze wander again. I would have liked to pray, following the directions that Abba Chereka had given me the previous day, but I was afraid to close my eyes. So I let the quiet of the church fill them up until my mind was sedated.

I do not know how much time went by before a warm voice shook me out of that hypnotic state: "Dear child, will you buy something?"

I turned around, still in a daze. In front of me was a little old man. Skinny, wearing a brown outfit, a smiling face, his short beard and his hair were both gray. . . . It took me some time to recognize him. "Abbaba Igirsa Salo!" I called out, startled. He was the narrator on TV. The old storyteller who had brightened the Saturday mornings of countless numbers of Ethiopian children. The old man smiled. In my ears echoed the theme song of his program and his usual greeting: "Good morning, children. How are you, children? Did you sleep well, children? You, our flowers of today, our fruits of tomorrow."

"Abbaba Igirsa Salo, is that really you?"

"Certainly, my dear child!" he confirmed with a smile, then offered me storybooks, videocassettes, tee shirts, and audiocassettes. "Dear child, since I brightened your childhood with my stories, now it is your turn to brighten the life of this old storyteller. Buy something."

I inquired about the price of the various articles. "Abbaba Igirsa Salo, I only have a little money with me. I can only buy the storybooks."

"So be it." I fumbled in my bra, took out the money, removed ten birr that I put back in the bra, and gave the rest to the old storyteller. He gave me the books and then said, "Dear child, if we meet again another time you'll buy the rest. Even if you keep your money in your bra like our mothers and grandmothers do, I can tell from your clothes that you come from abroad, and those who live abroad have more money than we do." I smiled—how many more times was I to hear that sentence? "Where are you coming from, dear child?" he asked.

"From Italy, from Bologna."

He made the sign of the cross. "May God keep the men of that country far from us." I looked at him—he was the second person in two days who talked to me about the past, about the Italians. He sat down next to me on the stone slab, and slowly, as if he were talking to himself and not to me, said, "They killed my whole family, in Harar, during the invasion. My father died, shattered to pieces by their weapons on the battlefield, and my mother, who had followed him as our women used to do in those days, was machine-gunned down. My two uncles were hanged in the public square of Harar, following Graziani's orders. At the time he was the commander of the army troops coming from Somalia. When I think about it, sorrow still fills my eyes with tears."

"I'm sorry, Abbaba Igirsa Salo," I said.

"What can you do, dear child! Just think, during the five years of occupation, I learned Italian. I could still speak it now, but I refuse to speak the language of those who killed my parents."

I didn't know what to say, and so I muttered the usual phrases: "May God repay them according to the work of their hands. Good with good, evil with evil."

"Amen, dear child, amen!" Abbaba Igirsa Salo remained silent for a few minutes and then said, "If you want, I can tell you a part of my story, of those days. Perhaps one day it might be useful for you." Again I felt that strange, curious urge. I nodded and he immediately began telling me his story.

The Story of Abbaba Igirsa Salo

A couple of years before the invasion I was already living in Addis Ababa with an aunt. My parents had sent me to the capital to study at the French School.

At that time, following an ancient tradition that later was suppressed by our Mengistu, on the day of Meskel there was a military parade. In the capital, the imperial armies and the troops of the noble families of the region marched in front of the Negus. In the main cities of the various principalities, the armies and the regional troops of the noble families marched in front of all the Ras. As a child I had seen the armies march in front of the Ras of Harar. "But the parade for the Negus is much more impressive," my father had often repeated on those occasions. He had seen the armies parade in front of our Negus Menelik. Every night of the feast of Meskel he told me about the magnificence of that event in Addis Ababa. For me it had become legendary. So, that year, the year of the invasion, I went to the parade along with my aunt and, for the first time in my life, I saw Haile Selassie's Royal Guard march by, the Great Imperial Army led by Ras Mulugheta, who at the time was the minister for war. Then came the troops of all the noblemen, and the officers and military cadets of the Holeta Academy, participating in their first parade. This was a military academy, founded by Haile Selassie. He had hired some Belgians and Swedes to train the young men, modeled on the European armies. For a few hours, thousands of warriors in full regalia paraded past. Some groups rode on beautifully bedecked horses, others walked with spears, swords, shields. There were young soldiers in different uniforms: the uniforms of the Honor Guard, those of the Ababa police led by their chief, Ras Abebe Aregay. . . . Some groups only wore traditional clothes, and carried traditional weapons; among them, their leaders were wrapped in black capes embroidered with golden thread. Other groups wore modern khaki-colored uniforms with cavalry pants, rifles, and cartridge belts.

That day, as ecstatic as a child witnessing magic, I feasted my eyes for several hours on that show of military grandeur. I had never seen so many warriors; if the truth be told, I had never imagined so many existed. And these were only the warriors of the Shewa Province. Other armies, although smaller, were present in the northern and southern regions, the armies of the many Ras, all ready to fight in the name of Ethiopia.

In the afternoon, after their men had finished parading, the leaders knelt in front of Haile Selassie to swear their oath of allegiance. With the tips of their swords pointed toward the ground, shouting and chanting, they pledged their eternal allegiance to him, to our country, and to the God of Ethiopia.

A few days after the feast of Meskel, five days to be exact, the Italians crossed the River Mereb and occupied some villages in the northeastern Tigray, thus making their intentions clear.

Addis Ababa was small then, very small, and it was easy to live close to Haile Selassie's palace, the Gebi. The morning following the start of the invasion, I was awakened by the sound of the horns and the escalating rhythm of the great imperial negarit drums. My aunt, who was sleeping next to me, woke up abruptly when she realized what those sounds meant, and began to say again and again, "Oh my God, the war is starting, the war is starting!" Instinctively, we got up, got dressed, and left the house to go to the imperial Gebi. In the streets many people were heading the same way. When we arrived at the Gebi we found half of Addis Ababa walking around the surrounding fortified wall like a swarm of angry bees protecting their beehive. In the middle of that swarm were the warriors who had paraded on the feast of Meskel.

In those days each leader had a horse that had been given a battle name. For instance, the great chief Wubneh, nicknamed Amoraw, the Falcon, had a horse named Abba Nefas, Father Wind. Haile Selassie had a horse too: his name was Teklil, the Chosen One, blessed by heaven. And when the warriors chanted the fukera, describing their future acts of bravery, they did so vowing that they were ready to launch themselves into battle in the name of their leader's horse. So great was the respect they felt for their leader that they would not even pronounce his name. That day, in front of the Gebi, I heard the warriors chanting and vowing, in the name of their leader's horse, that they would return with ten, fifteen slain talian sollato, with the cut-off genitals of at least five, ten men. . . . They were chanting and dancing, wielding their long spears and curved swords in the air.

At the time I was young and ignorant; I knew nothing about international politics and did not even know how wars in Europe were fought. I was convinced that everywhere people fought like we did in Ethiopia, face to face, man against man. I knew nothing of tanks, of hand grenades, of the air force, and, looking at our warriors, I was certain that soon we would celebrate another victory against the white men, a new Adwa.

A few days later, the men of the Great Imperial Army, with their commander in chief, Ras Mulugheta, headed northeast to join the armies of Ras Kassa and Ras Seyoum. The people of Addis Ababa went to bid farewell to them and so did I, along with my aunt. Thousands of soldiers and barefoot warriors marched out of the city heading north. They were divided into groups: the Oromo warriors with their headdresses made from baboon skins, the Amara warriors dressed in white with black capes around their shoulders, the foot soldiers with studded spears and shields, the cavalry with their beautifully bedecked horses, the modern battalions in their khaki uniforms carrying their weapons on their shoulders. . . . Many warriors and enlisted men had their wives and mules accompanying them, some carried tent poles on their shoulders, others sacks of dirkosh, quanta, and shiro. Behind every group there were mules laden with tents and food; flanking the long column were men on horseback carrying the imperial standards. Leading them all was the commander in chief, Ras Mulugheta.

It took two months for the Great Imperial Army to reach their destination. Sometime after their departure, the Negus with his Honor Guard also headed north to Dessie, where he was to establish his headquarters. A fortnight before Ras Mulugheta and the Great Imperial Army arrived at their destination, the troops of Ras Imiru, in the northwest, engaged in the first clashes with the Italian army.

In those days there were only a few phones and hardly any telegraph lines, and yet every day in Addis Ababa we received news about the front and the movement of our troops. It was as if the wind carried the news to the capital and then, passing from mouth to mouth, it spread all over the city.

The news about the early clashes seemed good. Ras Imiru's men had crossed the Tekeze River and had won, they had reached Dembeguina and had won, they had also won at Enda Selassie . . . and they were about to cross the border and enter the Italian territory in the Eritrean Colony. The northeastern armies had attacked and fought off the Italians on the Tembien River. Soon that war would be over and the Italians would return to where they had come from.

Then, suddenly, the wind changed direction and tragic news began to arrive. The Italians had begun to use a weapon unknown to us. Not even our leaders knew what it was. Perhaps someone who had been to Europe, like Ras Imiru, had heard of it. It was a poisonous, light fog inside large containers that were dropped from the planes. Once they made contact with the ground, the containers would break open, releasing the poisonous fog. This mist was almost invisible and settled in the valleys, in the crevices, in the gorges, and killed our men, burning them from the inside, from their lungs.

Terrified by this weapon, many deserted, and those who didn't scurried away like mice as soon as they saw the planes. Our armies began to lose ground.

Then our men found out they could escape the poisonous mist by running up the hills or climbing onto the higher rocks as soon as the planes dropped the containers. Our men recovered lost ground, and the wind, once again, changed direction. In Addis Ababa we began to receive good news again. Again, we thought we would make it, but at that point the Italians stopped using the containers and began spreading the poisonous mist with dusters attached under the wings of the planes. They would pass overhead in ten, fifteen planes at a time and spread poison and death, death and poison.

Their hearts seemed to be possessed by the devil. Who else, if not the devil, is willing to spread poison, killing men, women, children, cattle, poisoning crops, water . . . sparing nothing? Not even the womb of the earth itself that nourishes us? What dreadful times we endured! Addis Ababa began to fill with lamentation, *woy woy*. The list of the dead was endless. Dead soldiers, dead leaders, the population of entire villages dead. . . . Ras Imiru's troops began to retreat and so did Ras Kassa's and Ras Seyou's in the Tigray, and the Great Imperial Army, even the troops from Dessie, where Haile Selassie had his headquarters, and in the Ogaden the troops of Deggiac Nasibou. . . . There was no way to fight against the diabolical weapons of our enemies.

At that point it became clear that we were about to lose. We would lose our country, our freedom. We would fall into the hands of a people that would crush us under their heels, exactly as the hermits had been predicting for a long time: "Five years—for five years Ethiopia will be under foreign domination." The patriarch of Addis Ababa asked the people to fast and pray for three days, to plead for God's mercy.

And during those three days, like the thunder and lightning at the end of the world, my aunt and I received news from Harar: our family had been massacred.

I do not even know who brought us the news. My aunt tried to tell me in the gentlest possible way, but she was so shaken that while talking she burst into tears and could no longer contain herself. That is how I found out that my mother had been mowed down by a machine gun, that my father had died in battle, before my mother, in front of her very eyes, that my uncles had been hanged, that our home, the home where I was born, had been destroyed because my family had not agreed to extend their hands to Graziani's army. We were now alone, my aunt and I. Our neighbors tried their best to erect the mourning tent, but we were so devastated that not even once, during the three days of weeping, did a lament, a *woy woy* of sorrow, come out of our mouths. From that moment on I lived as if I were immersed in a dense fog, and I only remember what happened after as a sequence of faded images. I remember the long discussion regarding the Negus that involved the entire city: there were those who said that times had changed, it was right for him to leave the country to go and ask for help abroad, from the British, and then there were those who said the Negus should remain in the country and die with his men, like the Negus before him had done. Then I remembered the arrival of the Italians at Debre Brehan and that terrible inscription, "Long Live the Duce," that they carved on a rock face, and then the flight of Haile Selassie, and finally the arrival of the Italians in our capital—a sea of white men dressed in black and an endless line of trucks.

After that, I descended into total darkness.

I spent a few months in a sleep that was close to death. There was no way of bringing me out of it. I coughed, ate something forced on me by my aunt, threw up part of the food I had ingested, and slept. I spent all the rest of the time sleeping.

My aunt consulted several traditional doctors, kallicha, and hermits, but all in vain. Everyone said I had gotten sick with the "cough of sorrow," but no one was able to find a remedy. Then, one day, a kallicha suggested taking me to the Italian doctors. Perhaps they were able to cast not only bad spells but good ones, too. . . . In desperation, my aunt took me to Menelik Hospital, the first Ethiopian hospital that Menelik himself had built. During the occupation it was renamed after the Duke of Abruzzi. I spent two months there, being treated by the hospital's chief of staff, Dr. Quiniti, a relative of Graziani's by marriage—I cannot remember whether he was his father-in-law or brother-in-law—and finally, after those two months, I woke up.

A few days after I woke up, my aunt asked Dr. Quiniti if she could take me home, but he explained that I had suffered from a serious lung infection and had to stay in the hospital for a few more months to recover. She did not insist; she could never have done so. That Italian doctor had saved my life. . . . During my months of recovery I got to know the hospital. In the mornings Dr. Quiniti examined me and then I spent the rest of the day wandering around the corridors. You know how it is, our people like to socialize, and I do too. In a short time I got to know everyone in the hospital—nurses, doctors, and patients—and I became very close to a nurse, Nurse Worknesh. I followed her everywhere, like a shadow, even during her rounds and in the morning when she dressed the patients' wounds. The patients in the hospital were almost all Italian soldiers and some of our women who had turned to prostitution after the arrival of the Italians. The most common disease among the patients was syphilis. A disease that soldiers and prostitutes passed on to each other.

After some time, Nurse Worknesh taught me the procedures and I became her assistant. When the time came for me to be discharged, she asked Dr. Quiniti to give me a job. My aunt was not against it—after the killing of my parents and the confiscation of our goods, we had been reduced to poverty, and the offer of a job was certainly not something we could turn down. So I was hired: I was to help Woizero Worknesh during the daily dressing of the wounds and I had to hold the lamp up in the operating room during Dr. Quiniti's surgeries.

I had been working for about a year when, one day, a blackshirt arrived at the hospital. He was to work with us.

At the end of the hospital corridor there was a statue of Menelik. The blackshirt entered the hospital as if he were in charge, so full of himself! Like his big boss, the one who was in Italy.

He immediately noticed the statue at the end of the corridor and he began to shout: "Why is the statue of this black here?"

I happened to be there and impulsively said, "He is not just any black—he is Menelik, our Negus."

And the blackshirt: "Exactly. A black, and you are a black too."

And I: "He isn't black, and neither am I. You are black. Your heart is so black that even your shirt is black."

"How dare you," said the blackshirt, and he began hitting and kicking me. Rage had overcome him like a sudden storm. He was so furious that I think he would have killed me had it not been for Dr. Quiniti who rushed to my defense. He pulled me away from the hands of the blackshirt and reprimanded him: "Let go immediately of this young man! He is a great worker. He holds the lamp up in the operating room for hours. A heavy job that needs a steady hand that few people have. He has, though, and therefore he is very valuable." The blackshirt let me go, but from that day on, every time that he saw me in the corridor he gave me a kick in the ass with his black boots and said to me, "Comma," meaning that his speech had been interrupted and was not finished.

In time, the whole hospital began to call me Comma. Nurses, patients, doctors, even Nurse Worknesh. And I went along with it. With my head down, I accepted the kicks in my ass and the nickname. Unfortunately, even though I had recovered from my physical ailments, I still suffered from a sickness resulting from a soul broken by historical and personal events that were too intense for a young man like me. This sickness had put down roots among the broken pieces of my soul and had made me weak, without a strong will. So I gave in to the Italians, I accepted their occupation and I learned to live with them, between the kindness of Dr. Quiniti and the blackshirt's kicks in the ass. My days were filled with *ishi getoch,* "Yes, boss."

Then one day, a young monk was admitted to the hospital; he was about ten years older than I was. He was a friend of Nurse Worknesh. It was unusual to have a monk among the patients—first, because it was rare for a monk to accept being treated, and second, because it was rare for the Italians to treat a monk. The monks were accused of being the silent flame that fed the revolt. They made dire predictions that the Italians could not tolerate: "Five years—their rule will last only five years." But for that monk there was the assurance that Nurse Worknesh had given to Dr. Quiniti: "He is on the Italian side." A Submission Paper in his possession, stamped and signed by the governor of Jimma, confirmed it. Never once did Dr. Quiniti question if the infected wound on his right thigh had really been caused by an accidental fall. Never once did he linger to observe the margins of the wound that showed marks very similar to those left by a grazing bullet. After all, between the pus and that rotting flesh, it wasn't easy to be sure of the origin of those marks. But those marks were there. . . .

The monk remained in the hospital for a few weeks and I was put in charge of cleaning his wound and applying compresses of water and salt to the margins. He was in a big room with many beds and many patients. That's the way hospitals were in those days. He was a quiet type; he never spoke to anyone, except to Nurse Worknesh. But he observed everything. His eyes were constantly looking around. They flashed from one side of the room to the other, catching every movement. I felt them on me while I was treating him or taking care of other patients, when I followed Nurse Worknesh and Dr. Quiniti on their morning rounds, when the blackshirt arrived with his usual "Comma."

One day, while I was medicating his wound, he gave me an order: "Put your ear near my mouth." I did so. "Remember," he said, "Ethiopia belongs to us. To us alone. Don't give them your soul like you are doing. You can pretend to accept their rule, but your heart must remain free. You cannot become their property." I moved away quickly and stared at him, my eyes wide open. He motioned for me to get close again. "I am not a monk," he whispered. "I am a warrior." He was an arbegna, a patriot! In a slight state of frenzy caused by my surprise I started looking around to find Nurse Worknesh. The fake monk understood, and when I looked back at his face, he nodded. Nurse Worknesh was an arbegna as well. "She is a *wst arbegna*," he whispered again.

My God, I couldn't believe it! I felt lightness in my heart, as if someone had lit a lamp on a dark, starless, moonless night. He was an arbegna, Nurse Worknesh was a wst arbegna. And that was not all. I had never realized it because my mind was clouded by my sickness, but, looking carefully, one could sense an underground swarming. Our country was like an enormous anthill, almost invisible above ground, with only a few small holes on the surface, but populated by a whole universe below. Warriors, informers, organizers . . . they moved around unnoticed all over the country and the capital. I understood all of this a few days after that revelation, and when the fake monk was discharged, as I said goodbye to him, I whispered, "I want to fight for our freedom too." He motioned to Nurse Worknesh and from that moment on, apart from being her helper in the hospital, I also became her collaborator in the Resistance movement. A wst arbegna like her.

At night, when the city was enveloped in sleep, she and I went to meet the messengers and we delivered medications and information to them. Up to the very end of the occupation we delivered medication and information without ever being discovered. And my name became, for our people, "Arbegna Comma."

CHAPTER FIVE

ABBABA IGIRSA SALO HAD FINISHED TELLING HIS STORY. After a short pause, he got up to leave. Saying goodbye to me he added, "Dear child, if you use my story in the future, make sure to word it so that no one can ever find it offensive. You know, talking about people is like turning them into guests. Guests of their own words. And for us, guests are sacred." He started walking away, then he turned to add one last thing: "I forgot. I forgot an important thing, the name of the fake monk. His name was Haile Teklai." And after saying that he left definitively.

As if they were taking turns, as soon as he disappeared from sight the turtle lady appeared from the opposite direction. "Dear child, are you still here waiting?"

"Yes, Mother."

"Are you weary of waiting?"

"No, Mother."

"Good! Abba Chereka says that patience is the first great virtue. If you have patience the rest will come." She lingered a few seconds, lost in thought, and then started talking again. "I noticed that, now and then, people sit down next to you and entertain you with their stories. Do you like stories?"

"Yes, Mother, I like stories," I answered. I don't know why; my words tumbled out without me thinking. It was unusual for me, but I felt like sharing a secret with her: "I have always liked them, ever since I was a little girl."

"Good, my child!" Once again she paused for a few seconds, lost in thought, and then she asked me, "Dear child, but where do you live abroad?"

How could it be so obvious, even if I tried to blend in? I was even wearing a netela—what else could I do? "In Italy," I answered.

"Ah! Italy! Good! Good," she remarked, and off she went, disappearing in the same direction as the old storyteller.

Again, my eyes started wandering slowly around, only to make me fall once more into that hypnotic state created by the slow circling of monks and worshipers.

Suddenly, the usual clanking of metal announced the arrival of Abba Chereka, who sat down next to me. I turned and met his seraphic expression. A shiver of pleasure went down my back. We greeted each other.

"How did you sleep, child?"

"Well, thank God, and you, Abba, did you sleep well?"

"Yes, I did, dear child, thank God." The old hermit stared at me for a few moments. In silence. Then he began talking again. "So, dear child? The turtle lady told me that while you were waiting for me, both yesterday and today, someone stopped by to keep you company."

"That's right!"

"She said that they chatter on and you are happy to listen."

"Yes."

"Can I ask you what they talk about?"

"They talk about the old days, of the Italian occupation."

"Ah!" he exclaimed without commenting further. After a few minutes he said, "Let's pray now, my child." He took my hand. "Close your eyes and pray the way I taught you yesterday: 'Bless the Lord, O my soul, and all that is within me; bless His holy name. Bless the Lord, O my soul, and forget not all His many benefits.'" I closed my eyes and I felt as if I were falling backward into the usual abyss. I instinctively squeezed his hand tightly. "Don't be afraid, child," he reassured me. "If you fall, God will catch you. Let yourself go."

I began to repeat the prayer. At first my heart was throbbing in my temples, my breath was caught in my throat, it would go neither up nor down, and then things became more normal; my heart began to beat less fast until it slowed down. Like the day before, images tied to my childhood and adolescence flashed through my mind. I saw again the flight of steps leading to our kitchen, the small courtyard, the vegetable garden. I saw old Yacob, bending down to pull the weeds; I saw the mango tree, the old wooden bench, and old Yacob sitting together with old Yohanes and old Selemon. Silent tears started rolling down my cheeks. It was no longer the paralyzing grief that, until two days before, made me feel as if I were drowning. It was a calm grief that allowed me to look back on my memories without feeling overwhelmed by them. I cried until I felt empty. I cried and prayed without ever opening my eyes. When Abba Chereka told me that it was enough, I opened them again; around me was St. George's garden with monks and worshipers still praying, above me a clear sky with the black kites etched against it, showing off their prowess.

That day, at the gate, Abba Chereka told me, "The psalm I taught you is balm for the soul, it soothes you. We are so accustomed to asking without ever thanking, but it is in thanking that we can let ourselves go. It is in thanking that we open the hands of our soul that is clasped around our grief, and we allow ourselves to share it with the rest of the world, to distribute it among the many who will help us carry it. . . . From now on, you'll feel better, my child!" Before leaving he asked me for the usual offering. I gave him the ten birr I had saved in my bra. "Child, you won't be sorry you gave it to me," he added as he had the previous days. He went back in, and I entered the chaos of the city, holding Abbaba Igirsa Salo's books tightly in my hands.

That night my father came to bring me a lit candle and two new packages of candles. He put everything down on the little metal table, in front of the icon of the Virgin Mary, and sat down on the bed. "My child, why aren't you having dinner with us?"

"Father, I need to be by myself."

"I worry about you. You didn't pick up strange habits in Italy, did you? Because those people like solitude instead of company." Suddenly, I remembered a letter he had written to me soon after my departure: "Daughter, I was holding you in the palm of my hand, a tender bird learning to fly, I opened my hand and let you fly away, far away. I hope you are well and that you can fly in the direction you need to." I embraced him, and he pretended to smile, but he was worried.

"Father, 'those people' are like us. Perhaps they do not share our same communal way of living, and their culture is very different, but they are the same species as us, you know? They are human beings," I told him, teasingly. His fake smile turned into a grimace. "Anyway, I did not pick up strange habits. I need to be by myself to pray. As if I were on a retreat in preparation for one of our feasts."

He was reassured and finally gave me a real smile. "If that is the case...," he said, and he embraced me too. At the door he asked me, "Do you want me to turn off the light?"

"Go ahead, anyway the candle is lit."

Once alone, I slipped into bed, trying to find the position that would best lull me into sleep. My eyes turned to Abbaba Igirsa Salo's books of fairy tales that were lying on the shelf, to their covers: one was red, one yellow, and one green, the colors of Ethiopia. I remembered his last words: "If you use my story in the future, make sure to word it so that no one can ever find it offensive." I thought that if I were ever to use it, I would not change anything. There was nothing offensive in his story. Then again, I thought his had been a pointless request. When would I ever use his story?

The next morning my mother came to wake me up at seven, with the genfo and the dense aroma of butter and berbere. "How did you sleep, child?"

I took her hands and pulled them toward me. "Mother, I dreamed of Abba Yacob."

"Good for you, child! And what did he tell you?"

"Nothing—he was smiling at me with his solitary tooth." She held me tight. Some tears rolled down my cheeks.

"How are you feeling, child?"

"Better, Mother! I feel much better."

After the usual breakfast, I left. I walked along the path and at the end I turned left, toward the bridge. I decided I would avoid walking in traffic. Once at the stop, I got on a van headed to St. George's. During the ride I tried to shut out the noise. At St. George's rotary I got off. I crossed it, walking with a decisive step; I quickly passed through the hustle and bustle of the ramp and entered the path. I touched the ground with my fingers, made the sign of the cross, and continued on my way. I reached the courtyard, went all the way around the first courtyard, then the second. I stopped in front of the icons. I knelt down. "What if I started praying!" I asked myself. I immediately felt a pang of fear. "Tomorrow, I will pray tomorrow," I thought as I went toward the tree and sat down in the shade on the stone slab.

A gust of wind made the leaves of the old tree rustle, as if welcoming me. I smiled. I still did not dare to pray by myself, but I felt better, definitely better.

The turtle lady came by shortly after. "How did you sleep, child?"

"Well, thank God, and you, Mother?"

"Well, thank God. So? Are you feeling more at home in your country?"

"Yes, Mother! Thank you!" She gestured with her hand and went on her way, swaying with her *tussu tuss* gait.

A few minutes later a strange lady came toward me. She was not wearing the netela. She was dressed in bright colors and her head was wrapped in a purple scarf. "Hello, dear child," she said, sitting down next to me. "The turtle lady sent me. She told me to come and keep you company. She told me you like stories, the ones about the talian. So she told me to come here and tell you about my master . . . and the talian." She pushed me over with her behind. "Dear, move over a bit further. When you tell a story, you must be sitting comfortably, not just on half a behind. One of my butt cheeks is up in the air." I moved over. "Yes! That's good. All of my flesh is resting on the slab so I can begin. Here we go." She fixed her scarf. "Now I can start. My name is Docho, but ever since I was a child everyone calls me Dinke, short for Dinknesh, meaning 'You are a marvel,' because when I was little, everyone used to marvel at the mischievous things I would get up to. Well then, are you interested in my story or do you want me to leave?"

"You are welcome to stay, Mother, make yourself comfortable."

"Don't call me Mother, call me Dinke. Good. Here I go. I was born a slave. Yes! Don't look at me with that face. I was a slave. My children tell me I was born when Ethiopia was a feudal society and today, thanks be to God and to Mengistu Haile Mariam, who only did this one good thing and nothing else—abolish feudal society—slavery does not exist any longer. But I say: that isn't true. Slavery still exists. It took on different forms. It disguised itself as a 'need.' Everything is indispensable, and yet, when I was little we survived all the same, without all these needs. We still met even without the indispensable phone, and there were people who lived to be over one hundred years old, more than today. That is why I tell my children that they are dumb and blind. Therefore I don't want to hear any of those sympathetic comments like, 'Oh, poor woman!'. . . I will continue. I'll start from the beginning. I will tell you about my master: Commander Farisa Alula. The Great.

Farisa Alula the Great

When Farisa Alula was born, his mother had already given birth to eleven children. She had lost all of them a few months after delivering them. She desperately wanted at least this one child to survive. Farisa Alula's mother had heard about Deggiac Yilma, a half brother to the reigning Ras, Teferi Mekonnen, who was later to become our Haile Selassie.

Deggiac Yilma had been officially acknowledged by his father, Ras Mekonnen, only after the Adwa War. In that war Deggiac had shown his bravery by heroically saving his father's life. He was a true hero. His actions had impressed the country and someone began referring to him with an epithet that everyone ended up using, the only name ever used to refer to Deggiac: *Ie Hiwot Tebaki,* "The Guardian of Life." And of course, you know what Ethiopians are like, amazing stories began to circulate about him. There were those who swore they had seen the apparition of a Tabot next to him. Those who had seen the Tabot of St. George that had been carried into battle, stretching out a hand to bless him while he was saving his father. Just think of it. His story traveled far and wide around the country. Each time the story was elaborated upon, it traveled farther and farther around the country, reaching cities and villages that had not heard even the slightest mention of it before.

That's how Farisa Alula's mother found out about Deggic Yilma and thought of entrusting her son to his care. She took him to Gondar and in the courtyard of the gebi where she was received, she entrusted her son to Deggiac Yilma, begging him, "*Ersow iasadegut,* raise him as your own." She left the newborn there and went away.

And so the child grew up. He became an adult. He grew not only in years, but also in courage and manliness. A true warrior, the pride of Deggiac. Believe me! He sat on Deggiac's right during official functions. Farisa Alula had taken part in the hunting expeditions to kill the lions and leopards that were attacking Deggiac Yilma's herds. He had killed them with his own bare hands, armed only with a spear. Deggiac Yilma had given him the earring bestowed only upon heroes. Ah! What an honor! He had not bestowed that gift on any of his own children. Not even to Mengesha Yilma, his real son, his own flesh and blood, who died fighting against the talian in Wollo Province. Anyway, let me go on. When Farisa Alula got married, Deggiac Yilma had lands in Arussi Province granted to him and gave him the title of commander. And when he left with his bride to go to his home in Arussi Province, the two slaves whom Deggiac Yilma had given him after the first hunting expedition went along with him. A woman, Assebellet le Farisa degenet, "The Keeper of the Integrity of Farisa," more commonly known as Assebellet; and a man, Setegn Meriko, "He Gave Him to Me with His Blessing," more commonly known as Setegn.

In those days when they left on a hunting expedition, they were gone for months and they departed with their entire entourage. There were servants, cooks, and slaves. There were donkeys carrying tents, pots of tej, sacks of dirkosh and quanta. Farisa also had his own entourage, and his two slaves had an unusual task. Setegn carried his rifle. Farisa Alula killed his prey with his spear, but in the event that he missed his target, he had to be ready to defend himself from the beast, so Setegn always stayed by his side with the rifle. Let's be clear, he never needed to use it.

Assebellet, on the other hand, followed him with two buffalo horns around her neck. They were filled with tej, in case Farisa Alula got thirsty.

"You are following me so far, right? Shall I go on?"
I nodded.

I was born in his home, in Arussi Province. My mother, one of his slaves, died when I was little. Before dying, she put me on Farisa Alula's knees and begged him to raise me *inde lijiot,* as if I were one of his daughters. And since when did people in our land not grant the last wish of a dying person? If you ask the people of that house what I was like, they will tell you that I scorched more than fire. I enjoyed playing pranks, coming up with new mischief and putting it into practice. But Farisa Alula never raised his hand against me, not even once.

In those days it was customary to keep reserves of everything. They used to make big holes in the ground known as *gibe,* where people placed baskets taller than a man and about five feet wide. Inside they stored wheat, barley, and teff to use during the rainy season, the longest period without crops. It wasn't like today when farmers feast after the crop, sell everything, eat and drink, and then plead hunger during the long rainy season. Back then people planned ahead! Anyway, in those days honey was used for medicinal purposes. The storeroom for honey was in our house. Honey aged for one, two, three, five, or seven years was kept in different clay pots. The seven-year-old honey was considered a miraculous remedy. Well, I convinced Farisa Alula's little daughter Seble, who was about six like me, and two other little girls in the household to go and steal the honey. Just as a prank. Had we asked for some, no one would have refused us. But I wanted to steal it. We entered the storeroom and I grabbed the seven-year pot. I was not aware I had picked precisely that one. Had I realized it, perhaps I would have had even more reason to choose it, to satisfy my mischievousness. We ate the honey, taking it out of the pots with our hands. After all those years it had become almost solid; it felt like gritty sand under my teeth.

Some time later, the daughter of the great Farisa Alula became ill. She was his daughter from his first wife; she was already married and lived in Addis Ababa. Well, Farisa ordered his servants to go and get the seven-year-old honey and take it to Addis Ababa, to his daughter. You can imagine the faces of the servants when they opened the pot and found only a scant two bull's horns' worth of honey. Their eyes widened and became as big as eggs.

They took the pot to the master, crying, "*Woine,* thief! *Woine,* thief!" He examined the remaining honey and noticed that there were small fingerprints in some spots.

He had the four of us brought before him. I was shaking. He was sitting with a whip in his hands and said, "If you tell the truth, I won't touch you." The other girls remained silent, out of solidarity, thinking that their silence would exonerate them. I, being afraid of the whip, spoke up. They were whipped, and I was spared. Gosh! What a devil I was! I got up to all sorts of pranks. Another time . . . there was a large ram, a large ram that they were fattening up to kill for a celebration that his daughters from Addis Ababa were also going to attend. The ram was so fat that I could not even lift up his tail. One day I told one of the servants that I was curious to see what the ram's fat was like without the skin, and he explained that in order to see the fat under the skin it had to be killed. So I started planning what I could do. The servant . . .

You see, that's what I'm like. I always talk about myself, of what I used to do. Instead you are interested in hearing about the story of my master with the talian. Sorry, sorry. So, let me tell you about it. The story you will hear came directly from the lips of Assebellet, his favorite slave. When she told me this story, she was already an old, toothless woman.

All right, now I'll begin. It was the beginning of the long-expected invasion. Everyone knew that the talian would try to occupy our land. People had been talking about nothing else for a year. In our home everything was ready. Some *gibe* had been prepared for what was expected to happen: some were filled with rifles and ammunitions, others with food: quanta, dirkosh. . . .

Well, one morning, Farisa Alula had a proclamation read out: everyone had to start marching to join Deggiac Sebhat who was the ruler of Agame, in the Tigray. The household was packed up just as it was and in just one day they set off on their journey. The only people left in Farisa Alula's house were the old people, very small children, pregnant women, and a few warriors. About forty of them. The remaining people, about 450 warriors, wives, servants, slaves, began walking.

Dinke stopped and looked at me. "What should I do? Should I go on, or have you had enough of my story? I'm about to get to the good part."

"Go on, go ahead!"

"Do you like it?" I nodded in agreement. "Believe me, it's all true. Every single word. Don't think it is one of the fairy tales that Abbaba Igirsa Salo tells on television."

"Don't you worry, my dear. Go on," I replied, keeping in check my natural tendency to speak to her formally and to address her as Mother.

"Okay, I'll go on."

Now, the caravan reached its destination after a journey that lasted about fifteen days. Perhaps longer, I can't remember, but it doesn't matter. Let's say it took fifteen days. They reached Deggiac Sebhat's house. To celebrate their arrival Deggiac Sebhat gave a great feast. Mind you, they were not the first to arrive. Outside the gebi courtyard, other chiefs and warriors had already set up camp. Their many tents formed a circle. In the middle of it, every night, the warriors got pumped up with war chants and dances.

Ah! Assebellet also sang us the fukera when she used to tell us the story. I can't remember them right now, but you just go ahead, close your eyes, and imagine the mounting rhythm of the drums and the roar of the warriors.

A few days after, a messenger arrived. You see, in those days they had special messengers; there were not many phones, perhaps a total of twenty. Or two hundred, or perhaps two thousand. But not more than that. So news was carried by messengers. Handpicked people. Men who could run over forty miles a day up and down our mountains.

Eh! Men in those days were real men. When I was born they no longer existed. I ended up with a lazy one! So lazy! Very lazy! Just picture this: not even his hand could run from his plate to his mouth, not even when he was famished.

Anyway, I'll go on. A messenger comes and announces that a column of talian with 2,500 men and thirty dromedaries loaded with weapons has entered Italian Somalia in Afar Province, and is heading toward the wells of a place called Elfan or Efan. Deggiac Sebhat gives the order to start moving.

Picture this! The dust raised by our warriors and by their entourage could be seen from the distant mountains! Who would ever think of challenging them?

According to our Afar informers who pretended to be siding with the talian but then came to report to us, they were heading toward the River Enda. In that season the river was dry and it could be used as a road. Deggiac Sebhat said he would wait for them in the little gorges along the river. They would attack them there. The warriors cheered.

Well, a few days before reaching the gorges, the leader of the talian finds out that our men are preparing this ambush. You see, some Afar were not just pretending to be on their side; they really sided with them. Just a few, though. About two hundred. The others, thousands of them, were on our side. I know all this because Assebellet was always by Farisa Alula's side. Like his shadow, along with Setegn, who carried Farisa Alula's rifle on his shoulder, but Setegn never told me anything. Well, the Italian leader, informed by his Afar supporters, sends a message to Deggiac Sebhat. He tells him that Deggiac Sebhat's honorable father, Ras Sebhat, had been a friend of the Italians and that he should let the Italians pass through, to honor Ras Sebhat's memory. Deggiac Sebhat answers that his father had been their friend only until the Battle of Adwa. When he had realized what the Italians wanted to do with his country, he had apologized to Menelik for having believed in the Italians and from then on had fought against them. It was this second part that he would honor, in memory of his father.

So, here we are at the gorges of the Enda River.

Our army set up camp on a hill not far from the gorges. Deggiac organized the ambush. Farisa Alula, with his men, was to lead the attack.

What I am going to tell you now is something that Assebellet did not see from up close, but from the hill, sitting on the ground, next to Deggiac Sebhat who was standing with a kind of lens that lets you see far away. An eyeglass, they call it.

Farisa Alula did not want Assebellet to go with him. "This is not a hunting expedition, and not even a simple skirmish. I do not want anything to happen to you. You stay here," he ordered.

She pleaded with him, "In the name of Yilma who raised you."

He silenced her: "Stop! Do not evoke his name in this matter." And he departed with Setegn by his side, who had been allowed to go. He was a man and he carried his rifle. But he never told me anything, as I already have mentioned.

At this point the column of Italians enters the gorge. It was midday; the sun was blazing down mercilessly. There was a column of men in the bed of the river and two lines of Ascari on the banks, above the gorges.

Ah! So dumb! Just imagine, they never realized that there was a strange bird singing in the bushes on their left. The monotonous

tweeting of a bird that is not scared away! When does a bird not fly
away when so many men are passing by? The tweeting was coming
from another of Farisa's slaves. Hidden between the column and the
line of Ascari above the gorge. Behind him, all of Farisa's men. What
useless warriors those talian were! They marched in line without
anyone carrying their weapons next to them. The talian had no one
in charge of carrying their weapons. And neither did their leaders.
While most of their column was in the middle of the gorge, their
weapons were still behind it, on the backs of the last dromedaries.
At that point their leader must have suspected something. He sent a
man to stop the front of the line and another one to the back of the
line to give the order to distribute the weapons.

A nervous dance ensued. The white soldiers and their Ascari began
to pass out the weapons and assemble the machine guns. But it was
too late. My Farisa gave the signal. Our troops, hidden behind the
bushes, jumped out on the column.

*Engrossed in her storytelling, Dinke began to sing: "Ah, such warriors,
such great warriors, great warriors . . . those were real men." Her hand
was up in the air, mimicking the gestures of someone wielding a spear.
All of a sudden the worshipers shot angry looks in her direction to shush
her, so she began telling her story again in a tone that was only slightly
lower than her singing voice.*

Not all of our men had guns, but it did not matter. They threw
themselves into the fray. The talian looked like confused little birds.
They did not know what to do. They were so confused that at some
point, one of ours began to scoff at them by making rude farting
noises with his trumpet made from a bull's horn. The battle, if we
can use this term to describe that chaotic scene in which our men
charged ahead and the others acted like dogs running in circles chasing their tails, lasted all day long. That evening our troops left with all
the weapons that were on the dromedaries belonging to the column.

They left behind twenty-three dromedaries and a few dead soldiers, in addition to two wounded Italian leaders.

That's it! This is the story of the ambush in the Enda gorges. Later, unfortunately, things did not go so well. Farisa Alula with his men headed to the north, to Wag Province where most of the Ethiopian Army was located ... and there ... we lost. Shall I tell you the names of the sites of major battles? There were Sekota, Adegi, Woleh Mariam, Amba Gabriel, Amba Work, Amba Alagi. On the Amba Alagi Mountain eight thousand people were burned to death. *Woine,* the smell of burnt flesh! Assebellet said it penetrated everything. Even the leaves on the trees smelled like burnt flesh. Really. I'm not exaggerating! For years, roasted meat in those parts was called Amba Alagi–style meat. Just imagine, eight thousand people burnt to death, and those, almost all Ethiopians. That's how the talian conquered our country. Then our troops took up the Resistance. Hidden in the bush, they fought for five years, until the talian finally left. And do you know what our Farisa did in all those years? He was a great arbegna. He hid in Wag Province and fought alongside Deggiac Taffere Tesemma and Commander Moges Tesemma. Shall I sing the song of the warriors going into battle?

> On the battlefield
> When shooting begins
> Taffere, our priest
> Moges, our deacon.

And Assebellet? She was a wst arbegna. Just imagine, her, a slave! She belonged to a great band of women who took care of supplies and who also carried information to Deggiac Taffere's group. And there was a woman warrior among them. A woman who had fought near Holeta for two years, but then had to move north. A woman who, until a few years ago, used to come here to St. George's. She had become a nun and would come here to pray; she's dead now. In those days she was a great warrior. Assebellet was with her. So, that's how it went. Just as I told you, believe me.

CHAPTER SIX

AT THIS POINT, SHE SUDDENLY INTERRUPTED HER STORY
and asked me if I knew the time, but I was not in the habit
of wearing a watch. She proceeded to stop the worshipers, asking
everyone for the time, until she found someone who was wearing a
watch. It was past ten o'clock. "Woine! I've been here a really long
time. Well! *Ciao*. I'm off. Italians say *ciao*, right? *Ciao* when they meet
and *ciao* when they leave. I'm off. We'll meet again." She got up and
walked away with her purple scarf half untied, flapping in the wind.
Passing close to the hedge, she saw the turtle lady and called out to
her, "I've done it! I did what you wanted, I kept her entertained."

Half an hour later, preceded by the usual clanging, Abba Chereka
appeared. This time I perceived the noise as he was approaching.
There was just a faint sound of metal clinking, but I was able to make
it out. I turned around and saw him. We greeted each other with a
slight nod.

He sat down by my side and, remaining silent, we both turned to
look at the church courtyards. A little later, slapping my knee, he
said, "Let's pray." He took my hand, and I closed my eyes and began
to recite the psalm. I immediately had the sensation of plummeting
into an abyss, but this time I was able to control it. I prayed, and as
had happened on the two previous days, the tension gradually dissipated, overtaken by images from my past. I cried. But this time
they were just tears of tenderness for my deep longing for what no
longer existed.

I do not know how long I continued to pray. Unlike the two previous days, Abba Chereka did not interrupt me. When I opened my eyes again, he was looking at me. "Good, my child, good," he remarked. "I can see you are feeling better." I smiled and dried the final tears with the back of my hand. "Dear child," he said, bringing me back to the present. "Listen! We are allowed three days to mourn for our dead. The same number of days the Virgin Mary wept when Christ died. After the third day, belief in the resurrection must take the place of that inconsolable grief. In these three days I have helped you to pray, to deliver yourself from that excruciating pain. Now you are feeling better, and if you want to continue, you can pray on your own. You do not need me any longer."

These were such unexpected words that I immediately felt abandoned. "So?" I asked, frightened.

"So what?" he replied, making me feel even worse.

"So, starting from tomorrow, what should I do?"

"Start living your life again, child. Over these past few days, we have addressed your grief—now it's time for you to continue on your way."

Continue on my way? Which way? Was I headed somewhere? What was I supposed to do? "Abba Chereka," I said in a faltering voice, "but I don't know what to do. I don't know which way to go."

"What, you don't know where you are headed? How old are you?"

"Twenty-three."

"At twenty-three a person has known how to walk on her own for a long time."

At this point I felt not only lost, but also embarrassed. I took a deep breath and screwed up my courage. I had to find a way to make him understand. "I don't know what to do without my elder. Without him I can only see darkness ahead of me. As if someone had erected a tall black wall, an insurmountable wall. Something that is pushing me backward."

He raised an eyebrow and stared at me for what felt like an interminable length of time, and then he told me he had to pray. He closed his eyes and went into deep meditation. I was on pins and needles the whole time he kept his eyes closed. When he opened them again he asked me, "Is there perhaps a promise you made to your elder that you have not kept?"

I looked at him, surprised by the question. "Why?"

"Answer, and I will explain."

I searched anxiously through the depths of my memory, but could not find anything, only a useless pile of odds and ends. "I don't think so," I answered.

"And yet," he insisted, "there must be something. My child, sometimes we feel paralyzed after the death of a relative, exactly the way you did. Normally this feeling of paralysis springs from words said in the past that we have forgotten or that we no longer consider important. Let me think." Once again he sank into a meditative silence, from which he emerged with these words: "My child, I will allow you three more days of prayer. This time we will pray to loosen the knot that is holding you back. While we pray you must always remember: there is something binding your feet, made up of words that you and your elder exchanged. Words that you must carry to conclusion." I was in a daze and said nothing. "So?" he asked. It wasn't as if I had much of a choice. I agreed. "Good," he remarked. "Now you must go home." He got up and I followed him to the main gate and, as usual, he asked me for an offering. I slipped my hand into my bra and gave him ten birr. "You won't regret this," he said, and we parted. He went back in, and I merged into the chaos of the city.

I do not remember how I got back home. My feet moved one after the other, leading me like a guide dog with blind person. I realized I had arrived back home only after I had closed the gate behind me. I went across the main courtyard and through the house, looked into the smaller courtyard to quickly greet the women, and then retired to my room.

My mother immediately sensed something was wrong. I had just stretched out on my bed when I heard her voice behind the door: "What's wrong, Mahlet?" I did not know what to answer, whether

I should tell her everything or keep quiet and make some excuse. Before I could make up my mind, she opened the door and sat down on the edge of my bed. Her face betrayed her worry. She stretched out a hand to caress my cheek. "What's the matter, my child, what happened? This morning, when you left, you were fine ..."

I would have liked to bury myself in her arms. "It's true, I was fine, but with just a few words Abba Chereka made everything crumble."

"What happened?" I remained silent. "Go on," she encouraged me gently. I screwed up my courage and told her everything. "So," she remarked, having regained her calm expression, "what's the problem? You will go and see him three mornings in a row, as he asked you to, and you will find a way to loosen that knot."

"What if I cannot find a way to do so? What if I remain forever stuck, immobile, unable to make out the way ahead of me?"

"I don't think that will be the case. Remember! Abba Chereka is a great hermit. An extraordinary hermit. They come from as far away as America to ask his advice, you know?" I mumbled something. "You'll see, my daughter, you will loosen the knot. Have faith!"

I remained in my room for the rest of the day. My mother brought me lunch, and my father, dinner. "What's up, my little chick?" he asked me. Unlike my mother, his eyes betrayed his troubled spirit. He was still partly convinced that my strange behavior could be traced to my stay in Italy, and he felt guilty about it. He thought he should never have agreed to let me go, notwithstanding Abba Yacob's insistence. "So, my little chick?" he repeated. My mother must have told him everything and he was trying to find the right words to comfort me, but couldn't. Words he had already tried to find to console himself, but to no avail. In the place where these words had always resided, he had only found an empty space. Then I thought, "I am the one who should do something for him." I stretched out my hand, held his in mine, and said, "Tomorrow night I am having dinner with all of you. Just for today, I am staying in my room to pray to the Virgin Mary, but tomorrow we'll have dinner all together. I promise."

"Really?" he asked.

"Wait and see. Tomorrow will soon be here." He kissed me with a more serene expression in his eyes and left the room.

After dinner, I took a candle from the box, lit it, put it in front of the icon of the Virgin Mary, and slipped into bed. I tossed and turned for a long time, unable to fall asleep, with that one obsessive thought in my mind: "Three days—I have only three days. Will I make it?" The candle was more than half burned-down when a thought flashed through my mind: "Pray. I could pray by myself." I closed my eyes and began reciting Abba Chereka's prayer: "Bless the Lord, O my soul . . ." For a second, just a split second, I felt that terrible emptiness. I resisted, and it immediately dissipated. I continued to recite my prayer. All of a sudden, I was aware of a voice inside of me: "And on my lips, the name of God was born again." I abruptly opened my eyes, repeating the sentence: "And on my lips, the name of God was born again." Where had I already heard it? I tried to remember, but my memory failed me. In the meantime, the candle was down to the last bit of wick. I searched for that sentence again. Then the candle went out. I was tired and the wings of sleep were already enveloping me. "It will come back to me," I thought. Once again I began praying, this time addressing the Virgin Mary, and without realizing it, I was carried away on the wings of sleep.

The following morning my mother came to wake me up at seven o'clock. In her hands was the usual container of genfo that she put down on the little table with the icon of the Virgin Mary. "Good morning, dear child, how did you sleep?" she asked me, searching my eyes inquisitively.

I lowered my head—I did not want her to notice my inner turmoil. "Well, thanks be to God. And you, how did you sleep?"

She did not answer. She lifted my chin with her hand. "Why aren't you looking at me? What's wrong, my child?"

"I dreamed of Abba Yacob again."

A ripple of emotion ran through her body. "And what did you dream about?"

"I dreamed that he was in front of the door of a room, he was facing me, and the door was behind him. It looked as if he wanted to lead me inside, but then I woke up . . . right in the middle of the night!"

"Abba Yacob is trying to tell you something, my child."

"Too bad I woke up too soon," I remarked with a hint of regret in my voice.

"Don't do that. Don't be afraid. You will be able to loosen your knot. And as far as Abba Yacob is concerned, I am sure he will return in your dreams. Now go wash and then have breakfast before the butter for the genfo gets cold."

I got up, put on a track suit, put my bathrobe on over it, and, shivering, crossed the smaller courtyard. I quickly greeted the watchman and entered the bathroom. After washing, I ate breakfast and left. My mother accompanied me to the gate, said goodbye, and blessed me. I felt her eyes on my back until I reached the paved road. I turned around, before turning left, and I saw our gate close.

I went to the bridge, boarded the usual van, and got off at St. George's rotary.

That morning, immediately inside the gate to St. George's, I stopped, and, gaining strength from gently touching the ground, I made the sign of the cross several times, repeating, "Lord help me." I felt somewhat concerned about my precious dream having been interrupted the night before, and feared that three days would not be enough to find myself again. But in that inner turmoil of mine there was also a stirring of lightness, like a gentle breeze in the midday heat: at last I was able to pray by myself.

I walked down the entrance path, reached the first courtyard, and circled it. I walked up to the second one and did the same thing once, and then again. I knelt down in front of the sacred images and I prayed, marveling at that inner feeling that for so long I had looked for, then suffered through, and finally found again. I prayed with ease; I was ready to receive like an empty chalice about to be filled at the source. The wave of grief was gone. Gone forever.

I prayed, kneeling here and there until the pain in my knees turned into a mass of sharp pins. Only then did I go and sit down on the stone slab under the tree. I cast a glance at the slow procession of worshipers to make sure that I no longer needed to be hypnotized by their movement. Along with the pain, that inner noise had also disappeared, as did even that feeling of losing consciousness. I could close my eyes and look inside myself.

I was lost in my thoughts when the turtle lady passed by. "Good morning, dear child, how did you sleep?" she said, startling me.

I raised half an eyelid. "Well, thanks be to God, and you?"

She didn't answer. "Were you praying? I also saw you praying earlier, in front of the images of our saints. It is the first time I see you praying by yourself," she added, flashing a half-conspiratorial smile. I tried to mask my embarrassment with an unsuccessful smile. She proceeded: "Well! What can I say? I hope you can continue. In fact, I do not want to interrupt you. Pray, go ahead and pray, dear child," she said, and she left, only to return a few moments later. "My child!" she called out to me, startling me again. "My child," she repeated in a lower, hesitant voice, "there is something I would like to tell you."

"Tell me, Mother," I urged her.

"I had come with a precise intention in mind, but then I saw you so concentrated in prayer . . ." She did not continue.

"Go ahead, tell me," I egged her on again. She stared right at my face, as if to ask if I was really sure. I invited her to come near me. "Come, sit down here."

That was all she needed. Her face lit up with excitement. "If you are collecting stories from the Italian period," she said, whispering in my ear, "I would like for you to listen to my mother's story as well."

"But I am not collecting anything," I said firmly.

"What do you mean? Even Abba Chereka told me so."

"What?" I exclaimed, raising my voice.

"Listen, my child, do you or don't you like stories?"

"Sure, I like them. I already told you so the day before yesterday."

"Well, in the meantime just listen, then—when the moment comes you will remember them and you will use them." I wanted to contradict her, but I kept quiet and she began to talk.

The Turtle Lady's Story

I have always been very slow, as slow as a turtle—that's why I get along so well with the turtle at this church. We share the same rhythm. We share the same speed, the same way of examining things before we make a move.

I have been this way since I was a child, and since I was a child it has always taken me a long time to become aware of something.

In the courtyard of the home where I was born, in the countryside near Fiche, there was a large sycamore tree. Throughout my childhood, after the cotton harvest was over, my mother and I spent whole days in the shade of the great tree, spinning cotton, and during those long days she nurtured my femininity by telling me the stories of great Ethiopian women. Among the many stories there was one that she told me every day. The first story, the one from which all other stories unfolded, the story of the great Empress Taytu.

Sitting in the shade with the pile of raw cotton by our side and the spindle in our hands, she would ask me, "Are you ready?" And as soon as I nodded, she would start telling her story.

"Empress Taytu was great, Empress Taytu was strong.

"In the past, the life of a woman was different from today, and empresses had their own armies. Empress Taytu was the last to have one. Her army was made up of five thousand foot soldiers and six hundred horsemen. With her army, on the front line, along with her husband Menelik, she fought the Italians at Adwa.

"Empress Taytu was great. Empress Taytu was strong..."

As I told you at the very beginning, I am very slow, as slow as a turtle. Throughout my childhood, until my adolescent years, I lis-

tened to the stories my mother told me without ever wondering if
she had a story of her own. From her storytelling I had definitely
understood one thing: everyone has a story.

It isn't that I had no questions for her, but these questions were
buried in the darkness of the earth, like seeds waiting to sprout.
Seeds need water, rain falling on the soil, in order to be transformed
and come out of the ground.

Then, one year, I must have been about eleven, my mother took
me along with her to Addis Ababa. Every year I had seen her leave at
the same time. She used to go to the city to visit my Aunt Saba, her
younger sister. She would spend a couple of weeks there, and then
she would come back. In the days before her departure she would be
busy getting everything ready. She used to bring with her spun cotton spools, teff, honey, butter . . . presents for her women friends, she
would say. I never asked any questions and she, the morning of her
departure, before leaving, would look into my eyes and say, "When
it's the right moment, you will come with me."

That year, she began the usual preparations, then she called me
aside and said, "The time has come. Prepare your things."

That trip was for me like water for seeds.

In Addis Ababa, at my Aunt Saba's home, I met my mother's
women friends. She had so many of them. They kept coming, and
each time they rejoiced, embracing, kissing, and exchanging presents. There was a constant stream of food coming out of the kitchens,
while the hands of the guests were being washed with the water that
Aunt Saba poured out of silver pitchers. There was a constant stream
of incense smoke, hot embers, coffee, prayers, laughter, and memories. So many memories.

One morning, toward the end of our stay, my mother and I, along
with all of her friends, went to Arat Kilo to see a parade marching
past Emperor Haile Selassie and the Ethiopian patriarch. Halfway
through the parade, my mother said, "Stay here," and entrusted me
to the eyes of a woman that she picked randomly out of the crowd.
My mother and her friends got closer to the stage where Haile Selassie was sitting, he got up and greeted them, one by one, then the

imperial guards presented arms. The woman I had been entrusted to turned toward me. "So, dear child! Your mother is an arbegna?" she asked me. I nodded proudly, although I was not sure of the exact meaning of the word used in reference to my mother.

When we returned home, to our land, I took my mother under the big sycamore tree and told her, "Today, Mama, I want to hear your story, the story of your days as an arbegna," and so she began to recount it.

Kebedech Seyoum

Every event has a story, every story a beginning. Today I am going to tell you about me and the old days, when our country was in the hands of the Italians.

At the time, we were simple farmers working the land, the same land that we own today. In those days we were one of the many families of farmers working for the Kassas, the noble family of Fiche. The men of my family did not take part in the war against the Italian invasion, but the income from our land, including part of the food reserved for us, along with many animals, were given as a contribution to sustain the Ethiopian Army and the troops of two of Ras Kassa's sons: Wondwossen and Aberra. The war was a marginal affair for us, something that never came too close. Sure, we were frightened at the idea of falling into the hands of foreign invaders, especially because of what people said about them—that they were savages that did not respect the laws of our Christian God—but you know, if falling into their hands was what God had planned for us, nothing could prevent it. We tried to support our soldiers with fasting and prayers, but to no avail—we lost, and a few months after the beginning of the war, the soldiers who were withdrawing began to pass through our lands: men, women, pack animals . . . and only a few weeks after them came the Italians, preceded by all sorts of rumors. "The Italians are coming." "They travel on iron birds." "They are as numerous as the population of a whole anthill." "They are powerful, allies of the devil." "Some of our soldiers have already switched sides." "Among them there are whole companies of Tigrinya people from Eritrea.". . .

They first appeared on what we called their iron birds. Who knew about planes then? After a long time I discovered that, at the beginning of the war, we had some planes too. Twelve, to be precise, and since there were not enough of them to be used for fighting they were used to transport the emperor and the other leaders from one side of the country to the other. . . . Anyway, the Italians' arrival was announced by the roar of their iron monsters.

I remember that day. Saba and I were in the forest gathering wood. The noise started as a soft humming, similar to that of certain bumblebees, but then it got louder; it became deafening, and in the end, through the treetops, I saw one in the sky. Terror surged up inside of me like a rearing wild horse. I instinctively felt like fleeing. Saba took my hand and dragged me under a tree: "Fleeing is no use, it's better to hide under a tree." Following her example I flattened my back against the bark of the tree. She was on one side of the tree and I on the other. I put my arms backward, wrapping them around the trunk, until I touched the tips of her hands. "Shut your eyes, don't look!" she told me, and I followed her order.

The iron birds flew back and forth over our heads several times, but did not see us. We waited until dark to return home. It was better to brave the forest and its wild animals at night. They were less unfamiliar and frightening than those men who in my imagination embodied the most horrible monsters. Those described by the priest when he talked about the Apocalypse of St. John.

We returned home and together with our family and our few animals we sought refuge in a cave in the forest.

The greater part of the Italian Army arrived a few days after the appearance of their iron birds. They took possession of Fiche, turning the great gebi of Ras Kassa into a fort. A few weeks later they sent the Ascari, the ones from Eritrea as well as those from Ethiopia who had switched sides. They were in charge of combing the countryside to encourage people to come out of hiding, to return home without fear. The Ascari roamed around in groups of ten or fifteen, shouting, "Come out, the Italians won't hurt you. Come out!"

We moved back into our home. We never left it for over a month. Until some supplies we had always bought at the Fiche market ran out: salt, wool, incense.... Less than a month later the rainy season would start, and goodbye market for the next two months. We needed to get all necessary supplies while the weather permitted it. So my parents decided that my mother, my father, my sisters, and I would go to the Saturday market, leaving my brothers at home. We were afraid for them. Being young males, they ran the risk of being killed.

As we went from our house to Fiche I burned inside with the deepest fear of meeting some Italian soldiers. Ever since that day in the forest, I had been frightened of them. What could these men traveling on firebirds look like? What were their souls like? Why had they left such a distant country to come and conquer our land, our people? I was relieved when we reached Fiche without meeting any Italians and we found ourselves in the usual market. It looked as if nothing had changed. The division of the various stalls was the same: grains on the right, inside rows of jute sacks, vegetables in front of the grains, blocks of salt near the vegetables.... Even the people were the same. Both the sellers and the buyers. Someone asked us why we had not been around for a month. My father answered, "The talian ..." One of the women selling vegetables said, "They are better than we expected!" A man asked if we had come to sell. He wanted to buy our dried chickpeas. My father said we had only come to buy. People started chatting. A small group gathered around my parents. While they were talking, I stepped a little to one side and noticed a long line of men. Following my gaze Saba said, "At the end of the line there is a table. Behind the table there is a talian." My heart skipped a beat. "Come," she said. "Let's go look!"

"Are you crazy? No, I'm not coming!"

She has always been less fearful than me. "Come on, come with me! We'll just have a quick look, from a distance," she insisted, pulling me by the hand. We got a bit closer, moving sideways to the line. I managed to catch sight of the table, then him. The talian sollato. I struggled to overcome my fear and peeked out at him. He was a man with short hair and a short mustache, the color of dark honey. He moved his head as he looked first at each man at the front of the line, and then at the table where a large open book was resting. One of his hands moved quickly over the book while holding a pen that he was repeatedly dipping in ink. By his sides were some Ascari. He would address one of the Ascari, who in turn addressed the man who was first in line. Then the Ascari talked to the Italian again, and another Ascari would take the finger of the man in line, dip it in a box, and press it onto the open book. Yet another Ascari gave the man some money and pointed to a place behind the Italian, and the man headed that way, looking satisfied.

I went back to where my parents were, still surrounded by people. I pulled my father by the arm: "There is a talian sollato," I told him, turning my head toward the line of men.

Someone overheard my whisper, and said, "They are signing up Ascari and workers. Many are shifting sides or working for them. Rumor has it that they get paid, and well, too."

Before the rainy season came we went to the market another time. Once again, my father, my mother, my sisters, and I. This time the sign-up table was not there, but some Italian soldiers were wandering around the market. I was bargaining for a block of salt when two passed behind me. I tensed up. The salt seller noticed it: "Child, relax. They are not really the devils we imagined," he told me. I turned slightly to look at them. A small group of children followed them: "Sollato! Sollato!" they were shouting. The two soldiers turned, and the children saluted them and stretched out their right hands. The two soldiers laughed, one of the two slipped his hand into his pocket and pulled out something that he gave to the children, and the children ran away happily. "See?" the salt seller pointed out.

"What did he give them?"

"Some candy or some small change."

That day, on the way home, I found myself looking at some nettles that had sprouted up along the side of the path. The Italians had forced their way into our midst like those stinging nettles. Just one storm followed by a sunny and peaceful day had been enough for their roots to take hold. And our people, treating them like nettles, had learned to walk in between them.

The rainy season came and went and then my father and my mother decided it was time to take up our places at the market again. My father announced his decision, but warned us not to trust what we had heard at the market during our previous visit, that is, that the Italians were better than we had imagined. It was too early to form a realistic opinion. It was better to continue to have doubts, to keep our eyes open.

We returned to the market. This time my brothers came along, and as we used to do before the arrival of the Italians, we scattered to various parts of the market: Saba and I sold vegetables, my mother with my other sisters sold chickpeas and dried peas, and my father sold grains with my brothers.

I cannot say that it seemed normal to me, after several Saturdays and Sundays at the market, to see Italian soldiers among us, but I did get accustomed to their presence, and I overcame my irrational fear of them. I learned some Italian words, the necessary vocabulary for bargaining with them. Following the example of other women at the market, spurred on by Saba's sense of enterprise, the two of us, on the other weekdays, began to go to their fort to sell there. One thing was certain: they bought and paid, and quite well, too.

I don't know who among the fort's soldiers realized that Italian came easily to me. It was enough for someone to tell me a word one day and then it was part of my vocabulary on the following one. So when the major said he wanted a girl to take care of his quarters and his things, they suggested my name. I was hired against my will and that of my family. My father was only able to secure one condition: since Saba and I were not accustomed to being by ourselves, the major should at least take on her as well. The major did so and the two of us went to live at the fort. During the day we stayed in his quarters, and at night we slept in a small shack.

I have always been a bit of a scaredy-cat, but I have always adapted easily. As I had with the market, I soon got accustomed to living at the fort, learning to follow the rhythm of their lives. An Eritrean Ascari working in the kitchens taught us to cook pasta and some sauces: tomato sauce, meat sauce, pasta with vegetables or with tuna. . . . We learned how to cook a roast and other dishes. While we were in the kitchen with him, the Ascari talked to us about the Italians. Captivating stories that he told us while we were chopping onions and peeling potatoes. "They are good fathers," he said in his broken Amharic. Who knows if he was right? I would have liked to believe him, but Saba, turning up her nose, reminded me of our father's warning.

About a month and a half after we had been hired, the Italians killed Ras Kassa's sons, Wondwossen and Aberra. My father came to visit us the following market day, a Wednesday. He was shocked by the news. Not so much because Wondwossen and Aberra had been killed, but because of how the events had unfolded. When we had lost the war, Ras Kassa's sons, their men, and their wives had hidden in the mountains between Fiche and Debre Libanos and had begun the Resistance movement.

My father told us that the Italian general who had set up camp in the area in order to defeat the bands of our arbegna had managed to have a message delivered to the two brothers: they were to turn themselves in, otherwise there would be serious retaliations against their people, the population of the town of Selale. If they turned themselves in, their lives would be spared. Then he sent Ras Hailu, one of the Ras who had shifted sides because of old disagreements with the emperor, asking him to negotiate. Ras Hailu went and confirmed the Italian offer: "If you surrender, the Italians will not touch you—they will either exile or imprison you. I will intercede for you." If they surrendered, Ras Hailu added, their lives and those of their men would be spared.

The two Kassa brothers came down the mountain and turned themselves in. The Italian general welcomed them in his tent along with Ras Hailu, then he sent the Ras away with the excuse that he had to go and get someone. Betraying the word he had given to the Kassa brothers and even to his ally, he called two Italian military police and had the brothers led outside the tent and shot. When Ras Hailu came back, the two Kassa brothers were already dead. "Woine!" the Ras screamed, covering his face with his cloak at the sight of the two corpses. The Italian general laughed, and patting Ras Hailu's back, said, "Don't worry, I'll be the only one going to hell. You have nothing to do with this." Luckily, my father pointed out, the two Kassa brothers came without their men, otherwise the Italians would have killed them as well. He then added, "The Italians are starting to show their true colors. They cannot be trusted. They do not keep their word."

About ten days after that ugly incident, the morning before the Italian Christmas, the major informed us that he had been transferred to Addis Ababa and we were to go along with him. The following day was a market day. I could not sleep all night. In the morning I ran to the market to look for my father. "I don't want to leave!" I said, crying. My father tried to send the priest to talk to the major, to intercede on our behalf. Saba and I had spent our whole lives between the market and Fiche, the priest told the major; we knew no other life. We did not want to leave and, furthermore, we did not want to be separated from our family. The major would not budge. He pointed out that we had already left our family the moment we had gone to live at the fort. If we did not know anything apart from the land we farmed and Fiche, going to the capital was a chance to get to know other places.

That night I cried for a long time. Saba scolded me: "Why are you crying?"

"I'm sad. I don't want to leave."

"But we'll be back home soon."

"How is that possible?"

"When the right moment comes, we will run away. Now stop crying. You've been weeping for hours. You've soaked the blanket with tears."

I stopped crying and she hugged me. "I had started to believe the words of the kitchen Eritrean Ascari," I said in between sighs.

"I never did," was her reply. "When he told us that both his father and grandfather were Ascari I thought that with such a family history it must have felt normal for him to keep his head down, like a pack mule . . ." That night, any possible feeling of acceptance I might have begun to have toward the Italians vanished. I shut them out completely.

About two weeks later, before the Ethiopian Christmas, we left for Addis Ababa. Partly because my mind was busy fighting the sadness of the impending separation, partly because I had never left Fiche before, I could not imagine what our big city would be like. The capital of our Ethiopia.

When I arrived I was wide-eyed with wonder. There were large homes, even two-story homes, made with bricks. There were cars, and the roads were paved or flagged in stone. There were former gebi, some that had belonged to the emperor and others that had been the dwellings of the many Ras. There was the town hall, the market . . . and then, there were them: the Italians. So many Italians. Not like in Fiche where they only ventured out near the fort. They were everywhere, so many that our city looked like the capital of their country, not of ours.

Unlike Fiche, here there was no fort. There were barracks, several of them. Surrounded by tall walls, and with gates guarded by soldiers.

We ended up in the barracks near the Ras Mekonnen Bridge. A large building with lodgings for enlisted men and for the Ascari. There were mess halls and, in a separate area, the lodgings for the officers. Our major was assigned one of these. Inside there was a room for us as well, with two beds, mattresses, pillows, and blankets . . . but I longed for the mud and straw *medeb* of our home, where Saba and I slept close to each other, wrapping ourselves in a single gabi.

This time, in contrast with what I had done in Fiche, I made no attempt to make my surroundings more familiar. I did not want to shake off my longing for home, as if it could keep me company.

Our major did not like the food served at the mess hall. He wanted to eat in his quarters, food that had been cooked only for him. That was why he had brought us along. Every day, after taking care of a few household chores, Saba and I went to the market to buy vegetables, or meat or eggs. We were always accompanied by an Ascari, each time a new one selected by the major. The Ascari would escort us and then sit and wait in some tej house. I did the shopping while Saba socialized with the locals. She would chat with the vendors, she made friends with people, learned about everything. She was young, she had a fresh mind, and she was able to react effortlessly to every stimulus. She was like virgin soil in which any crop grows easily. I was the same, but my fearful personality limited me.

At night, in my bed, I cried. I tried to cry in silence so that Saba would not hear me. But she could tell from my breathing. She would come into my bed and scold me: "Stop crying. We must concentrate on how to escape, and crying sure does not help us to think things through." Then, one evening, she told me that the Italians would soon leave our country. Her words irritated me. It did not even seem conceivable to dream of such a possibility, let alone have it really happen.

"How could that be possible? Who would chase them away?" I asked angrily.

"Don't you listen to what people are saying at the market?"

"I don't listen—I never listened to idle gossip, you know that. When I am at the market I concentrate on bargaining, not listening," I answered, still angry.

"That's a mistake. There are many things to learn. If you listened, like I do, you would know about the Resistance . . . ," she said, pausing to see my reaction. I remained silent, all wrapped up in my sadness. "Listen," she said, starting to talk again, "there are many armed groups fighting against the Italians. They might have conquered our capital and made our Negus and Ras flee, but people are still fighting them everywhere."

I did not feel like giving in right away, giving hope a chance. "And why did we never hear anything about the Resistance in Fiche?"

"Excuse me? What about the Kassa brothers?"

"They were the children of Ras Kassa, it was normal for them to fight the Italians. They were fighting to protect their wealth."

"Sister, what would you say if I told you that the Kassa brothers' men continue to fight in the name of their leaders and that many men and women from the rural areas around Fiche are joining in their fight?"

"And how do you know?" I asked, while a small ray of light was already making it through, reaching all the way to the center of my heart.

"From the market, from Etie Elsa, the woman who sells vegetables. She knows everything. Tomorrow we'll switch—I will do the bargaining and you will listen to her." I surrendered to her words completely and spent the night in eager anticipation.

The following day my sister introduced me to Etie Elsa. Then, while the Ascari was drinking his tej at the tej house and Saba was bargaining at the food stalls instead of me, I took her place in front of Etie Elsa, my ears wide open and my feet firmly planted on the ground. Before heading toward the area where they sold chickens and eggs, Saba urged Etie Elsa to tell me the whole story of our Resistance fighters. It took over an hour, but Etie Elsa gave me a detailed account of all the groups that were fighting in the Showa, Minjar, Menz, and Bagemader Provinces. She told me the names of the leaders of each group, and at the end of the long list she pronounced the name of Kebedech Seyoum.

"A woman? How come there is a woman leader?" I asked, surprised.

"She was the wife of Aberra Kassa. After the Italians killed her husband, she hid in the mountains and took over the command of his troops. Believe me," she said in a low voice veiled in secrecy and wonder, "they say she is a better leader than a man. A fighter with no equal. Her men idolize her. Every ambush set by her troops ends in victory. After every victory more peasants and people from Selale leave their homes to join her. The Italians look for her, they keep

looking for her, but they haven't yet managed to capture her. Not her
and not even a single one of her men. They say that the soul of her
husband and the patron saint of the Kassa family are at the side of her
army. And it's easy to believe it," she concluded solemnly.

That day I returned home inebriated. With that feeling of euphoria
that I felt each time I stirred up the fire, blowing on the hot coals, the
lack of oxygen making me lightheaded. On the way back home from
the market I kept asking Saba, "But is it all true?"

"Sure, sure it's true," she whispered to prevent the Ascari, walking
a few steps behind us, from hearing.

"But is the story of Kebedech Seyoum also true?"

"Why on earth shouldn't it be? Actually, you know what? One day
we'll run away and we will join her."

After that first meeting with Etie Elsa I stopped crying at night,
and if I woke up abruptly, feeling anguished, I turned my thoughts
to Kebedech Seyoum. "One day," I used to tell her silently, "we will
come to you and join your army." Just thinking about it had the
power to calm me down. It gave me courage, it gave me the strength
to conduct my life in the city, at the service of an Italian. A talian
sollato.

We had already been in the city for a month and a half when one
morning some Ascari went all around the city crying out, "Announcement, announcement! To the workers and the people, so that
you'll be able to say that you have a generous government, so that
you'll be able to say that our government treats you even better than
your previous one. The heir to the Italian throne has been born. To
celebrate this happy event, the viceroy of Italy in Ethiopia, Marshal
Graziani, on Yekatit 12, will distribute money to the poor in front of
the small gebi."

People immediately started saying that it had been Ras Hilu who
suggested to Graziani the idea of the celebration, with the specific intent to outdo Emperor Halie Selassie's custom of handing out money
to the beggars on the feast of St. Michael. When we arrived at the
market to do our daily shopping, the news had already given rise to

the most poisonous and malicious comments. The one that struck me the most was Etie Elsa's. While she was handing me a bunch of her carrots, she quickly lifted her eyes and, looking at me, said, "They think they can substitute an archangel's feast with one for the birth of their Negus's son! They are godless!"

"You're right," I commented, and couldn't find anything else to say. With a few words she had said it all.

Yekatit 12 arrived. That morning the major went out in full dress uniform, everything brand new. In the yard, an army car with a driver had been waiting for him for at least half an hour. "Aren't you coming?" he asked, casting a quick glance at us on his way out.

"No, Major," Saba answered. "We prefer to stay at home. It's going to be too chaotic. We are not used to it."

"All right, I'll see you later," he said, and then added, "Ah! Today I am having dinner with the other officers." And he left, leaving the door open. We heard the car door slam shut and the noise of the engine getting fainter as it went down the gravel driveway.

The wall surrounding the barracks was about thirty feet from our place. We could hear the voices of the people headed for the small gebi, walking on the other side of the wall. "That sounds like a lot of people," Saba remarked. "They are going for the money. They should not go, even if they are giving out money. I don't like the fact that people are so eager to accept their money."

Part of the morning went by. The sound of the voices on the other side of the wall died down. We had almost forgotten about the celebration when we were startled by a series of explosions, like deafening thunder. Saba went outside to ask what was happening. "We don't know," answered one of the Ascari who was guarding the courtyard. Half an hour after the explosions we began to hear people screaming and fleeing. From that moment on, all hell broke loose.

Two hours later the major returned to the barracks, breathing heavily. He had walked back. After he arrived the news of what had happened began to circulate all over the barracks. Two young men had thrown two bombs to try and kill Marshal Graziani. The major, along with two captains, gathered together most of the soldiers and they all left the barracks. Before leaving he ordered us not to go out, for any reason, until his return.

For the next three days Addis Ababa went through hell. There was never a moment of silence. No break, during the day or the night. A continuous barrage of machine-gun fire and explosions. Everything accompanied by agonizing screams of women, of men and children. Screams like those of animals being slaughtered. A dense smoke cloud covered the whole city. Everywhere there were flames and spirals of black smoke that mixed with the smoke already lingering in midair, and a tension similar to that on a hunting expedition.

After those three days the major, along with the two captains and the rest of the Italian soldiers, came back to the barracks. On the fifth day he gave us permission to go out. We went through the gate, convinced we were fully aware of what we would find on the outside. Two days after the beginning of that hell, vultures had appeared in the sky and the falcons had multiplied in number. At night the ghostly laughter of hyenas mixed with the growling of stray dogs fighting over scraps of flesh from the corpses. As if these warning signs were not enough, the stench of the decomposing bodies was carried by a ghostly air coming from the restless souls waiting for their bodies to be buried. The corpses had been deliberately left rotting in the streets—"It will serve as a warning for those still clamoring for the Negus," the Italian officers said. But although we were mentally prepared, what was outside the barracks, in the streets, was so horrendous that I had nightmares about it for many years to come. It was not the corpses of men, women, children, or the elderly that shocked me. Not even the genital mutilations and the organs scattered on the ground. What stabbed my soul like a sharp hook was the sight of pregnant women with their bellies ripped open and the fetuses in plain sight. Something indescribable, an image that to this day I find unbearable.

That day Saba and I took just a few steps outside the barracks, then our stomachs rebelled and we were overcome by retching. We went back inside.

We did not go out the following days, not until the city was cleaned up by the men and by the wind, a generous wind blowing from the north. Not until the ghostly air stopped spreading the stench. And when we went through the gate again, Saba and I had clearly made up our minds: we would flee, join the Resistance, join Kebedech Seyoum. With the excuse of returning to our daily routines, we told the major that we were going to the market. As usual we were stuck with an Ascari following us. In fact, what we wanted to do was talk to Etie Elsa, to ask for her help. She, who knew everything, would certainly know how we could reach Kebedech Seyoum. But that first day she wasn't there. Many people were missing from the market and we still did not know who had died and who simply did not have the courage to leave their houses. A week later we finally heard the comforting news that Etie Elsa was still alive. Two days later she returned to the market.

She was still frightened by the violent turn of events. Half her neighborhood had been set on fire. She still found it hard to believe that she had escaped alive. We asked her to help us. Almost trembling, she told us this was not the right moment. "This is not the right moment to talk or to flee. Hold on. Wait a few weeks and we'll see what happens! . . ."

We waited, feeling tense and impatient. We wanted to leave, to stop living among them. Especially me. Those who get near the fire always get burned more. Saba had known how to keep the right distance, but I, on the other hand, had gotten too close and now I was even more eager than she was to go far away.

A month went by, then Etie Elsa told us about a certain Belai Bogola, owner of the Abay Coffee Shop near St. George's: he was a wst arbegna and could help us.

We had to wait another three days, then we finally ran away, accompanied by one of Belai Bogola's men. We went to the market with the basket and the money for the shopping and while the Ascari on duty was drinking at the tej house, we fled through the stalls, heading for the Entoto Mountains, toward Sululta.

It took us ten days to reach Kebedech Seyoum's army. After cresting the Entoto Mountains, we crossed a series of long, cultivated valleys and forests. At night the farmers offered us food and hospitality. There were many of them who supported the Resistance. The massacre, carried out as a reprisal for the attack on Yekatit 12, had convinced those who had put their faith in the Italians to side with their own people, their own leaders and warriors.

On the last day of our journey we walked down a valley. It was the first time that we were descending after climbing up the Entoto Mountains. Halfway along the valley our guide began ascending the right side, toward a rock face whose peak rose up against the clear sky, free and bare, while the base was hidden behind an impenetrable forest, a tangle of centuries-old trees, their thick crowns intertwined. The dark green leaves of one tree blended with the lighter green foliage of another.

The path became very challenging over the next few hours. For the final stretch we had to use our hands as well as our feet. We held onto enormous rocks, our fingers tightly gripping every possible hold, and finally we entered the forest. A strip of land a few hundred yards wide and a couple of miles long. Our guide, without any hesitation, headed toward the thickest part of the trees, toward the rock face, until, getting close to it, we were able to make out a series of cave openings. Only then did I realize we were in an encampment. Traces of campfires could be seen everywhere. Our guide began whistling—two long whistles followed by a short one, repeated three times.

Some men came out of the caves. "That's them," he said, and he introduced us. The men took us to a cave. We could hear the low murmur of many voices. The cave opening let very little light in, but it was enough to make out the silhouettes of men, women, children, objects, blankets. . . . The cave branched out in different directions. Following a series of tunnels, the men took us to another room in the cave. That's where Kebedech Seyoum was to be found. They introduced us. Saba told her our story, and then asked her to let us join her. Kebedech Seyoum asked no questions; she simply said, "Welcome."

There is something unique in women who are born to be warriors, something that cannot be explained, that is mysterious and that erupts from the depths of the earth with unparalleled force, mixed with the essence and sweetness of a mother. This is what I thought when I heard her voice.

Our fighters attacked mainly at night. Under cover of darkness, it was then that we moved around to prepare ambushes, that we received messengers or the farmers with food supplies. Kebedech Seyoum went out at night to meet the other leaders of the Resistance. During the day we prepared food, when the sunlight dispersed the smoke rising from our encampments, hiding it from the eyes of our enemies. During the day was also when the warriors waited in silence, and our great leader rested. As a result, it was only a few days after our arrival that we realized that Kebedech Seyoum was pregnant. One of the older women, Mama Martha, explained that she was eight months pregnant. "Poor woman. She was four months pregnant when her husband, Aberra Kassa, was killed," she told us. "I was with her when she heard the news. He had gone to turn himself in without telling her anything. All he had told her was that he and his brother, Wondwossen Kassa, had to meet some other leaders. He had entrusted her and the whole army to his cousin Shileshy, and had gone down from our hideout. A few days later, along with the news of her husband's death, Kebedech Seyoum received some of his belongings and a letter. She read it: 'Dear, respected, beloved wife. . . . I am turning myself in to protect our people. . . .' Without shedding a tear, she folded the letter and went to Shileshy: 'I am taking over the command of my husband's men,' she said. Then she gathered us all together: 'We will continue our fight,' she said. Believe me, not even for a day . . . what am I saying, not even for a moment did the men see her simply as a pregnant woman. She is our chief, she herself leads every ambush brandishing her Mauser rifle."

Almost two months after our arrival Kebedech Seyoum gave birth to a baby boy and named him Tariku, which means "History." When she went into labor she left the encampment accompanied by Mama Martha. They were gone for two days. When they came back, Kebedech Seyoum carried a bundle tied to her back: her son.

During the two months before Tariku's birth, Kebedech Seyoum supervised Saba's and my training. Right away, admitting to my fearful nature, I said that, unlike Saba, I was not willing to shoot. I was willing to take care of the camp, the food, the wounded . . . but I would not shoot. I would never shoot anyone. Kebedech Seyoum laughed. "Your fearful soul clouds your vision. Haven't you noticed that the fighters are almost all men? Apart from me and a few others, the rest of the women take care of the camp." Because of what I had said, up until Tariku's birth, every day she told me, "No one is asking you to fight, but this does not mean that you can allow your fearful nature to lead you around like a dog on a leash. You must learn how to keep it under the sole of your foot, otherwise your fear will control you and this could be dangerous for you, and not only for you, but for us all." Then she would ask me, "If a devil showed up, what would you do?"

"I would pray," I answered.

"Well, remember, the talian sollato are devils and in order to stop them, prayers must be accompanied by the pulling of the trigger. You must learn to use a rifle. Even if you never fight, you must learn to take aim, to load it. . . . One day you might need it. Everyone in the camp, except small children, knows how to use a gun." Then she would send me away with an arbegna who taught me how to load and take aim, without ever shooting. We could not waste ammunition and we could not make our presence known through the sound of shooting.

In those two months there was only the occasional attack or ambush, but two weeks after Tariku's birth the army started to set night ambushes again and from that moment on we began to move camp.

There were groups of our men scattered all over the area and they kept on the move, monitoring the paths leading to our hiding places. Their job was essential, especially after particularly successful ambushes, when the Italians sent whole military units out searching for us. So, when one of our men spotted Italian soldiers, he would play a horn to signal their presence. The sound of those horns could be heard from far away. Using a code based on the length of the sounds, the lookout on duty would communicate how many hours away from the hiding place the Italians were, as well as the direction they were marching in. If our man was too far from the hiding place for us to hear the sound of the horn, he would pass the information on to other men spread out in the nearby valleys and on mountaintops. They would pass it on to others until the information reached us in our hideouts. We were always prepared to move on at a moment's notice.

As soon as we got the signal, we would bury half of our supplies of food and weapons, and leaving no trace of our presence, we would take off. Women, the elderly, and children were in front, while the arbegna stayed a few miles behind us to guard our backs. Along the way, if they saw good places to set up an ambush they would lie in wait and attack the talian sollato.

For over a year we moved around continuously in the same area, moving from one hiding place to the next. Always in a circle, going back to the places where we had buried our food and weapon supplies.

During all that time, Kebedech Seyoum participated in every attack. Every time we moved, she stayed in the back with the arbegna, while her son Tariku, entrusted to Mama Martha, stayed with us. That year, for the first time since the arrival of the Italians, Saba and I had different tasks. While I, along with the other women, took care of the wood, the water, the food, and the tej for the arbegna, she fought alongside the men. I moved during the day, she at night.

She would leave with Kebedech Seyoum and the other few women. Side by side, in military uniform, with cartridge belts, guns, ammunition, and their hair hidden under black scarves. Around them, hundreds of fighters.

By the command of Kebedech Seyoum, when I left the camp to get firewood or water, I carried a rifle. Everyone, even those who did not take part in the attacks, when leaving the camp had to carry a rifle on their shoulder, just in case. I obeyed that order because it came from our leader, but each time I picked up the rifle I felt a shudder of revulsion. I slung the rifle across my shoulder convinced I would never use it, not even if I needed to, and I tended to keep that metal barrel, as cold as the chill of death, away from my body. I considered it a useless burden. I did not want it to become something familiar, and to this very day, I cannot believe I ended up using it.

In those days the Italians seemed to be more determined than usual to try to find us. They searched the area like rabid dogs. They sent units on foot in one direction and airplanes in the other, hoping to force us in one direction, the way one does with herds of animals. But we were not simple cattle, and besides, we were in our own mountains. We came from that very earth. We knew every inch of it; we could recognize the depth of every cleft, the evidence of small and large caves, the streams, the hidden water springs. . . . Moreover, our system of protection was an invisible and very effective network. We had escaped all of their searches, sometimes walking a few hundred yards above them. We would be on the ridges, and they in the gorges. We in the forests, and they in the valleys at the edge of the forests. We almost passed in between their ranks. We knew their exact location while they kept looking for us, moving around like the blind do in a new home. Their rage toward Kebedech Seyoum and her army kept growing.

That day we had changed our hiding place. At sunset the previous day, one of our men had warned us, blowing on his horn. Some Italians and a few Ascari units had set up camp half a day's walk from us. From their movements it was not clear whether they would spend the whole night at the camp or if some of them would set off to look for us. It was almost dark when we broke camp and, taking advantage of the moonlight, we left in the middle of the night, all together. At dawn, in a gorge, we split up. Kebedech Seyoum and the fighters stayed behind—it was a favorite spot to set an ambush. I continued with my group. Before we parted, I went to embrace Saba. Unlike me, she felt serene. Kebedech Seyoum came close to us and, almost scolding me, said, "You haven't tamed your fear yet?" Saba spurred me on: "Be brave! See you later."

A few hours after we had split up we heard gunshots and machine-gun fire. The Italians had arrived in the gorge. We continued our march while behind us the attack went on for a long time. Then, as usual, all of a sudden, silence. The attack was over. We walked a few more hours, toward an old hideout, at the foot of some waterfalls, on a plain covered by a forest.

When we arrived we started our usual tasks: digging up the supplies we had left the previous time, setting up camp, gathering the firewood. I, along with other women, went to fetch water. I was about to leave the camp when one of the elders called me back: "Child, you forgot your rifle!" he yelled from far away.

"Gosh, I was forgetting that damn piece of iron," I mumbled.

I went back, took one, slung it over my shoulder, and was about to go when the elder called me again: "Child, did you make sure it is loaded?" Without answering I took a cartridge belt, put down the clay pot I was carrying on my back, wrapped the belt around my waist, and retied the pot to my back. I checked that the rifle was loaded, then I hastened to catch up with the other women on the path to get water.

Mama Martha, who took care of Tariku, was also with us. I was surprised when I saw that the child was on her back. "I want him to get some sun," she said, noticing my reaction. "This child does not know the warmth of the sun. He is always in the caves or among the trees of the forest. I want him to spend some time in the sun in the meadow near the river."

Once we reached the river we scattered. Basically, we were almost above our hiding place, at the spot where the tall, vertical cascades began creating the waterfall that ended in the plain, where our camp was situated. It was one of our best hideouts. Nearby there was an old Portuguese bridge and a few miles away the Debre Libanos Monastery.

I went toward the water, to a spot where some large, flat rocks surfaced from a deep hole. I put the rifle down on one side, the clay pot on the other, and began to wash myself. First my feet and my legs, without taking my clothes off, then higher up, lowering my clothes to my waist. Baring my chest I began to splash water on my neck, my face, my breasts. More and more water, like a blessing. I washed off the sweat and the dust of the long march, splashing myself with abundant water. I cupped my hands to collect it and threw it on my body. It was cold, refreshing, transparent, sweet in my mouth that was dry from exhaustion. I wanted to go on forever; I was mesmerized by the sheer pleasure of it.

At some point I was startled by a scream. I raised my head. On the other side of the stream Tariku was walking on all fours, and behind him, just a few feet away, close, too close, was a talian sollato. I heard another scream: "Shoot him! Shoot him!" It was Mama Martha. "Shoot him! Shoot him!" she kept screaming, her face terrified. The talian sollato and I looked each other in the eye for a split second, but so many things went through my mind! Did that talian sollato know that the baby was Kebedech Seyoum's son? He could certainly figure it out. The Italians knew that she had given birth to a son. They too, like us, had spies and informers. "Shoot him, for God's sake!" the older woman screamed again. I took aim, and the eyes of the talian sollato expressed confusion. He was not armed. I hesitated. His eyes focused and found their direction again; he took a few steps and got closer to the child. At that point an impulse totally foreign to me took hold of my being. I thought of Kebedech Seyoum's words: "Prayers against them must be accompanied by the pulling of the trigger." I thought of our dead on Yekatit 12. Something inside of me screamed, "Out of our land!" I took aim as they had taught me, closed my eyes, and shot. The ricochet made me lose my balance. I fell backward, opened my eyes, and got up, ready to shoot again. The talian sollato was on the ground. I had hit him. Another soldier appeared on the hill. I shot him too. I fell backward, got back up, took the cartridge belt, and reloaded my rifle, but no others showed up. The two I shot had died. Who knows where they had come from—perhaps they belonged to the unit that our men had attacked. We never found out.

That night, Kebedech Seyoum came to thank me. I began to cry: "I have killed two men. Two of God's creatures. Whatever they might have done, they were children of God, like me. I will never go to fetch water again. I never want to shoot anyone else."

"Sister," she told me, putting a hand on my shoulder, "right now you are distraught, but it will go away, and you will go back, with the rifle, and if needed, you will do again what you did today. You will shoot. Unfortunately we live in such times. We must fight."

Thank God, it didn't happen a second time. A few months after that event, Kebedech Seyoum told us that she had received permission from Haile Selassie to leave, permission that the messengers had brought. She would lead us to exile in Sudan. We would remain there, in a British camp, while she would continue on to the Holy Land, where she would join her father-in-law.

It took us several months to reach the border, fighting all the way. Once in Sudan, as planned, we parted. She came back to Ethiopia at the end of World War II, while I, with Saba and Kebedech Seyoum's army, returned to Ethiopia two years later, along with Orde Wingate and Haile Selassie. The Italians had lost and were leaving while we were returning home with our Negus.

CHAPTER SEVEN

"SO? DID YOU LIKE THE STORY ABOUT MY MOTHER?"
Did I like it? "Like" was not the right word. I was struck by it. The correct word was "struck." But I did not feel like spending time explaining. "It is very beautiful," I said.

"Beautiful, true, important," she added. "When you use it," she continued, "don't forget any of the details. Every detail is essential to the understanding of those times."

"Sure, Mother," I reassured her, without trying to dispute that bizarre suggestion. Me, a collector of stories? And when was I ever going to use her mother's story? To be honest, it was not the first time I had been called a collector of stories. Abbaba Igirsa Salo had used those same words. Who knows where in the courtyard of the church this rumor had started. With Abba Chereka? I really could not believe that he could have substantiated such an extravagant rumor. I would check it out anyway, I thought. But then he arrived with the usual clanging of metal, and I forgot to ask him.

I was concentrating on my prayer when his clanging startled me. I opened my eyes and there he was, next to me. This time I had been unaware of his arrival. But in contrast with my first days there, what was absorbing me was not what I was seeing around me, but rather what I was seeing inside of me. Notwithstanding the turmoil he caused in me, I had to admit that the credit for my regaining the ability to see both inside and outside of me went to him. I cast a half-thankful glance in his direction. He pretended not to notice. He turned his head, concentrating on what was going on in front of us, and I did the same.

The usual worshipers dressed in white were walking around the two courtyards. Many were habitual churchgoers. I had seen them pass back and forth in front of me, as if the first courtyard were a merry-go-round and they were insatiable children clinging onto it. I recognized their features, even those of some women although their faces were almost completely covered by their netela. I recognized some by their feet: bare or wearing thin plastic flip-flops. Others I recognized by their shoes.

By now, they recognized me too. Passing near us they would greet Abba Chereka, and then me. An older woman wrapped in a large gabi bowed her head in greeting as a sign of respect toward Abba Chereka, then she greeted me as well, addressing me by name. When the older lady left, Abba Chereka remarked, "Everyone already knows you. They know where you come from and even your name." Then he turned his gaze in front of him again, and I, abandoning all thought except for my reason for being next to him, did the same.

A little while later he turned to me. "Today," he told me, "I will teach you another prayer, one that is useful to chase away the clouds that are darkening your inner eye. Repeat after me. This prayer must be recited in a low voice: 'Blessed be the Lord, my rock, who trains my hands for war, and my fingers for battle. He is my loving God and my fortress, my stronghold and my deliverer, my shield, in whom I take refuge.'" I began to repeat it, and we chanted it quietly over and over again for a very long time. Little by little I felt something similar to an electric charge running through my veins and something inside of me pushing to claim space. Just as the feeling became clear and defined, Abba Chereka stopped. "My child," he said, "this morning I caught a glimpse of you praying, kneeling down in the second courtyard, and here too, when I was coming toward you, I saw you praying. Is that true?"

"True."

"So you are able to pray by yourself."

"Yes, I can!" I replied with satisfaction.

"Then go home and repeat this prayer until it becomes a part of you. Repeat it over and over again, endlessly." Then he got up and I followed him. We headed toward the main exit. At the gate he asked me for the usual offering. I gave him the usual ten birr, taking it out of my bra. He repeated the usual phrase—"You won't regret this, my child"—and we parted. He went back in, and I entered the chaos of the city.

I went down the access ramps passing in between the beggars. I crossed the rotary and went toward the Ras Cinema. It was almost noon and the street was teeming with people, even more so than in the morning. Waiters carrying trays full of food and spiced tea were coming out of the cafes, and kept crossing the road to take food to the shopkeepers. They zigzagged in between cars while the drivers sounded their horns full blast. Along the wide strip dividing the road, young boys of all ages snoozed and chatted under the trees. Lazybones hiding from the blazing midday sun. Their many activities—including some pilfering—would start up again after three, when the sun became less hot. At the bus and van stops, women held their netela up against their faces to shield themselves from the sun.

I was trying to decide whether I should take a bus or walk when a taxi pulled up to the curb. "Where are you headed?" the driver asked me.

"No, thank you," I answered. "Today I'm using my feet."

"Under this hot sun?" he insisted.

He had a friendly face. I decided to accept his offer. "I'm going near Enrico's Pastry Shop. Between the pastry shop and the bridge. How much will that be?"

"Ten birr," he answered, smiling.

"Are you crazy? It's just nearby. Forget about it. I'm walking," I said, and I headed off.

He let go of the clutch and the car inched forward until it drew parallel with me. "All right! All right. Five birr," he yelled from inside the car.

"Okay," I replied. I opened the car door and got in. Then I pulled the door, but it would not close.

"Shut the door well," the driver urged me. I pulled harder, but the door stayed open. "Harder!" he insisted, putting more emphasis in his voice to make me pull more forcefully. I pulled hard, but again the door would not close. "No, no," he said, raising his voice, "not that way, more forcefully I said." I pulled the door with all my might, but the stubborn door did not close. The taxi driver gave me a dirty look. "Move over," he ordered. I flattened myself against the car seat. He leaned over, grabbed the door, and pulled so hard that the whole car shook. But the door did not close. He glared at it and then said to me, "Oh well. Hold the door with your hand." I grabbed the door handle and the taxi moved off.

Our cars, our cabs were all twenty-five, thirty years old, if not more, like certain Fiat 1100s that were still in circulation. With improvised parts, used and reused—not just parts for the engine, but also for the body of the car, like the inside of a car door I had seen patched up with a piece of plywood covered in contact paper with a flower pattern against a blue background. Cars that needed to be treated roughly in order to shut the doors or start the engine. It had taken me a long time in Italy to get accustomed to their cars: new, noiseless, and with doors that did not need to be slammed shut but simply pulled gently.

It reminded me of my first year at the university in Bologna. I had a friend, Claudio. His parents had given him a brand new Lancia Epsilon for his high school graduation. Sometimes we went off somewhere together, and each time, while I was getting out, he would say, "Mahlet, don't slam the door, Mahlet don't slam the door, Mahlet don't slam the door!" But then I would slam it . . . and he would get mad. "What do you think you're doing?" he would mutter. "Do you think my door is the crooked gate of your African home?" It took me a year to learn how to do it. In the end it became automatic for me to close the door without slamming it, and now I had to relearn to slam it instead of pulling gently. I chuckled to myself. The taxi driver noticed it. "So," he remarked, "you are used to the cars in your country and you're making fun of mine?"

I was tired of being viewed almost as if I were a foreigner because my clothes revealed that I lived abroad. I got angry. "Listen, wise guy! I have no other country but this one. I am Ethiopian, got it? And what I chuckle about is none of your business!"

"All right, sorry, sorry," he said, almost backing off. "I was just teasing."

I shut him up: "I don't appreciate your teasing." And for the rest of the trip we remained silent.

Once home, after going through the gate, I stopped to look around. I really liked our home in Arada Sefer. There was something magical about it. It resonated with the past, reminding me of our old roots. Perhaps because the placentas of our ancestors were buried under the old tree. I was truly happy that old Yacob had asked us to spend the first eighty days following his death in this house. No place could have been more fitting for my return.

I crossed the front courtyard, then the house, and entered the inner courtyard. It was filled with women, busy with different chores in the shade of the old tree. In addition to the women of our family, our neighbors were also there. An older woman was spinning cotton, teaching Alemitu and Mulu. "Ah! Young women today," she would remark, keeping her eyes on their clumsy fingers. "They are no longer able to undertake women's work. They are only interested in office work." Alemitu and Mulu were laughing while their threads of cotton, not being thick enough, kept breaking off. "Not like that," the older woman said. "You must make it thicker. Thicker!" Then, addressing the other women, she added, "It's hopeless, you have to learn this as a child . . ."

When the women realized I had arrived, the older woman spoke again: "Here is our foreigner!"

Again! I thought, irritated, but I smiled to be polite. "Mother, I am not a foreigner. I am Ethiopian, my mother and my father are Ethiopian, my grandparents were Ethiopian . . ."

"Then," she continued, still not convinced, "if you are Ethiopian show me how to spin cotton."

"I am a modern Ethiopian, like my cousins," I quipped.

All the women in the courtyard laughed, but the older woman refused to give in. "Then come over here, I will teach you."

"No, thank you, Mother," I answered. Strangely enough, she stopped insisting.

I went up to the heap of raw cotton and dipped a hand in it. I squeezed some cotton lint in between my fingers and turned my thoughts to the turtle lady and to her mother's story. "Mother," I said.

"Tell me, child," my mother replied.

"Do you know who Kebedech Seyoum was?"

"Of course, child. Everyone knows who the great Kebedech Seyoum was."

The older woman started talking again: "Ah! Those were women!" The courtyard filled again with laughter. I took advantage of that moment of gaiety and left. I went to the kitchen, and Aunt Fanus's voice penetrated the semidarkness of the room. From the courtyard, she shouted out to me, "There is some shiro in the pot if you want to have something to eat."

"Would you all like some too? Shall I prepare a *tri* for everyone?" I asked.

"No, thank you, we've already had lunch," my mother answered. I ate and retired to my room to pray. I took a candle from the box, lit it, placed it in front of the icon of the Virgin Mary, and began to repeat the new prayer: "Blessed be the Lord, my rock . . ." When the candle burned out, I lit another and continued until that one also burned out. Meanwhile my body had begun to feel that strange electric charge, just like in the morning. Inside of me something had started exerting pressure again to claim a space. It was a strange turmoil, a strange pressure. I stopped praying and lay down on the bed, waiting for it to ease up. My thoughts wandered in no precise direction, then they lingered on my meetings at St. George's: the old bishop, Abbaba Igirsa Salo,

Dinke, and the turtle lady. I thought about their stories. How much their words contradicted what I had heard people in Italy say so many times: "We built roads, schools, homes for you . . ." Each time, I had smiled, and it was a bitter pill to swallow, but now it would be different. Once I was back in Italy, the first person who dared make those stupid comments would get an earful.

As night fell, the room began to grow dark. I did not turn on the light and remained lying on the bed, my mind dwelling on the stories I had heard at St. George's. At a certain point, someone knocked on my door. It was my father. "Mahlet, are you sleeping?"

"No, Father."

"What are you doing in the dark?" he asked, walking into the room. He turned on the light and sat down on my bed. "My child, you make me worried," he said.

I did not attempt to reassure him. Instead, I shared my thoughts with him. "At St. George's, all this time, while I waited for Abba Chereka, every morning someone came to tell me a story about the Italian occupation."

"And so . . . ?" he said, urging me to continue.

"And so . . . in Italy they are all convinced that the Italians came here on a sightseeing trip to Ethiopia and that they beautified and modernized our lousy country with roads, homes, schools. You can't imagine how many times I had to listen to this version."

"And what do you think about it?" he asked.

"What do you expect me to think! I never answered because I did not know how to object, but today I know what I would say. Everything they built, we paid for. Actually, we have already paid for all the buildings of the next three centuries. Considering the great number of Ethiopians they killed, they owe us a lot of war reparations!" While I was talking I could feel a raging fire burning inside of me. I had a hard time recognizing myself.

"You are right, those were horrendous times, but what can you do, it's over now."

"If you heard what they say about it in Italy, perhaps you would think differently! It is over, but not so over that we should stop talking about it. We should give them our version of the story," I answered more calmly.

He made no comment. "Child, why don't you simply come back home instead of thinking of how to answer them?" That was his fixation. He was terrified that I might remain in Italy.

I began to laugh. "Father, stop worrying. This year I'll graduate and then I will be back."

He hugged me, then told me something that I never would have expected to hear from him: "Perhaps, in order to tell our story, so that no one in Italy can just give their version, during your last year in Bologna you could use the stories you heard at St. George's."

Unbelievable. Here was another person repeating that crazy idea. "And in your opinion, how could I use them?"

"What do I know? The stories chose you, not me," he joked.

That evening, for the first time since my return, I had dinner with the whole family.

After dinner, my parents accompanied me to my room. "I would like to remind you two," I said, "that I am an adult now and that you did not accompany me to my room even when I was small."

"Child, let our eyes be filled with your presence," my father pleaded. They left me in front of my door.

It was late. I took a candle from the box, lit it, and placed it in front of the icon of the Virgin Mary. I slipped into bed and began to repeat the new prayer, but almost immediately I fell asleep.

The following morning my mother came to wake me up at the usual time—around seven, with the genfo container in her hands. "Good morning, child, how did you sleep?" she asked me while she placed the container on the table where the icon was.

I did not answer. "Mother, I dreamed again of Abba Yacob last night," I said.

She turned suddenly toward me. "What did I tell you yesterday? You see, he came back! Come on, tell me," she urged me, coming to sit on the edge of my bed.

"I was in the same room as yesterday, but this time we were inside and not outside. It was a strange square room with a long corridor, open on one side to the right of the door. At the end of the corridor was a pile of stuff. Abba Yacob was at the top of the corridor, his gaze directing my attention to the pile."

"And then what?" she insisted.

"I woke up, like I did yesterday." I answered sadly. I hugged her. "Mother, he's trying to tell me something, but I always wake up too soon."

"Don't worry, child. You'll see, he will come back in your dreams tonight. Now, go wash before the butter of the genfo gets cold."

Just as on the other mornings, I walked down the path and once on the road I turned left and continued toward the bridge. Even before I reached it, a few yards from the bridge, a little van stopped quickly, the side door opened, and the ticket collector, tapping his fingers on the van to attract my attention, yelled, "Hey! Which way are you headed?"

"St. George's," I replied.

"Then get on. There's one seat left." I got on, paid for my ticket, and went to sit in the back. At St. George's rotary I got off and, repeating the steps and movements from the previous days, I reached the first courtyard. I had changed nothing. My steps were the same—perhaps I even put my feet in the same invisible tracks I had left on the previous days—but that morning, for the very first time, I walked among the worshipers, feeling I was part of them. I turned my gaze left and right to look for myself in other people's eyes, and recognize myself as one of the many women who had gone there to pray. I too, like all the other women, was wrapped in a white netela with embroidered edges; I, too, was walking in step while softly repeating the psalm.

Walking in the middle of the surging crowd of the faithful, I repeated the prayer I had learned the day before. When I got tired of walking I went to sit on the stone slab under the old tree. I closed my eyes, and with my back resting against the tree trunk, I continued to pray. That strange frenzy was swelling up inside of me again when someone sat down by my side. It was not Abba Chereka. I knew it wasn't him because there was no metal clanging, but also because of the softness of the body that touched mine. I opened my eyes and the owner of that soft body smiled at me. I greeted her and she introduced herself. "Nice meeting you—my name is Bekelech."

I introduced myself as well. "Nice meeting you—my name is Mahlet."

"Ah!" she exclaimed. "Then I'm in the right place."

"Excuse me?" I responded in surprise.

"I said I'm in the right place. Mahlet! Aren't you the one who is collecting stories about the Italian occupation?"

Not again! But where had this rumor started? "Yes, I am Mahlet, but I am not collecting any stories. Especially not those of the Italian occupation."

She wrinkled up her nose. "But the turtle lady told me she even heard it from Abba Chereka."

This time I will ask him for an explanation, I thought. "There must be a mistake," I insisted.

She looked at me sideways. "Maybe! But it is not like Abba Chereka to go around making up rumors." I did not know what to answer. "Where have you come from?" she insisted.

"From Italy," I answered.

"That much I knew already. I wanted to know from which city in Italy."

"Bologna," I answered, dryly.

She got excited. "Bologna? Bologna? What a coincidence. I lived in Bologna for over twenty years. First in Vidiciatico for two years, then in Bologna, on Via Saragozza. Do you know Via Saragozza?"

I was caught by surprise and opened my eyes wide. "Sure I know it. The street that leads to San Luca. Did you really live there?"

"Yes, child, right there. Right outside the city walls, a few yards from the Meloncello Portico."

"Really?" I asked, even more surprised.

"Sure. I returned to Ethiopia for good two years ago. I could not take living there any longer. They live a life that is not for me. And then, I did not want to die of 'mal d'Afrique.'" I could hardly contain my laughter. "Listen, I am not joking. 'Mal d'Afrique' really exists. I met a man who suffered from it. He is over ninety years old. He lived here during the Italian occupation and when he returned to Italy he realized he had left half of his heart in Ethiopia. No, no! I don't want to live with my heart split in two. That is why I came back. I want to live the rest of my life here and die here."

At that point her story was piquing my curiosity. "Listen," I said, "I am not collecting stories, but if you want to tell me yours, I would be happy to hear it."

She began laughing, throwing her head back. "I've done it. Exactly what I wanted to do: make you burn with curiosity. So, take heart, my child, and listen to my story."

The Story of Woizero Bekelech and Signor Antonio

Everything began in Addis Ababa, almost twenty years ago. At the time, I was about thirty years old and I worked in the homes of two Italian families. Two couples of teachers in the Italian secondary schools in Addis Ababa. They lived next door to each other. I cooked for both families, alternating between one and the other. Half a day at one house, half at the other. One week I began the day at one house, the following week at the other. I got along well with both families, with both wives, but I had a closer relationship with the Mandrioli family. This was because of Signora Franca's personality: so open, so sunny, always ready to laugh. We understood each other from the very beginning and we were very close, like sisters. At least, so I thought.

I worked for both families for more than two years, then the Mandrioli family returned to Italy. Signora Franca's elderly mother needed her daughter around. She couldn't live on her own anymore. Therefore, they had no choice but to return home.

The day of their departure I wept, clutching onto Signora Franca. That morning she repeated again what she had told me on several occasions: that she would return to get me with a work permit. For over two more years I remained with the other family, the Barbieris. I had almost forgotten all about Signora Franca's promise when one day a letter arrived from her containing a contract.

Two months later she came to get me. I took my leave of the Barbieri family in tears. In those last two years the ties with Signora Laura Barbieri had become equally strong. You know, you don't feel an immediate connection with everybody. Some people need a little time to open up. They're like flowers that blossom slowly. They take a long time but when they finally open, they reveal their soft, fleshy petals and they give off an unforgettable perfume. Signora Laura belonged to that category. My relationship with her had grown like a shemma of many colors on the loom of a gifted weaver. Carefully so as to be precise in the geometric design, slowly so as not to tangle the threads. With a tight weave and a warp that lasts a long time.

When the letter from the Mandrioli family arrived, for a few days I kept telling myself that I would not go. I would ask the Barbieri family to write the letter for me. But then . . . I just could not do it. Who knows what hoops they had jumped through to get that contract . . . ? What's more, I had given my word, and a promise made between people is not something that can be reneged on so lightly, even more so if its roots had been put down over two long years. So, I decided to leave, even though I did so with a heavy heart.

For her part, Signora Laura did her best to reassure me: "The Mandriolis live in a small village where we have our summer home. We will meet every summer. Don't worry."

The Mandriolis came to Addis Ababa, and within two weeks we departed. It was the month of Meskerem. Everyone leaves in the month of Meskerem, and so it was for me. We reached Rome and then we took another plane. Signora Franca explained that it was to go to a city near their village. A city called Bologna. I was astonished. How could I have ever imagined that Italy was more than just Rome and the area around it? Once we reached Bologna, we got into a jeep and we continued our journey. The journey from the airport to the Mandriolis' house seemed endless. How much ground we covered! In the dark, along a road lined with the shadows of unfamiliar vegetation, with bends that made my stomach turn upside down, my mother's words came to mind: "Forget about it! Don't go. The talian are all sollato. They will sell you." At the time, I had laughed, but in that moment I felt a strange shiver of fear rise up inside me: what if she was right? Finally, after a journey that never seemed to end, we arrived. As they later explained to me, the Mandriolis lived in a small village in the mountains, about an hour and a half from Bologna. And as I came to understand in the following months, they lived in a small village full of older people whose eyes popped open in surprise whenever I went out and happened to meet one of them. I think that, around there, no one had ever seen a black person except on television.

Even Signora Anna, Signora Franca's elderly mother, must never have met one in the flesh. The morning after my arrival, she went up to her daughter and asked her in a low voice, but not low enough to prevent me from hearing, "She won't bite me, will she?"

Signora Franca laughed heartily, but I didn't. "Woi gud! Where have I ended up?" I thought to myself.

My life in that village soon took on the appearance of a woolen sweater that has shrunk after being washed in hot water, and that, when you put it on, not only makes you look silly but also leaves much of your flesh exposed to the elements. The Mandriolis left each morning to go and work in a larger village where there was a high school, and they came home in the early afternoon. I stayed home to look after Signora Anna. I have to admit that for most of the time my hardest task was keeping my nerves under control. That old lady drove me crazy with her absurd questions. Every morning I went out to do the food shopping and when I got back, she came up to me with that ghostly face of hers. She was thin, her skin like a wrinkled piece of newspaper, her bluish veins like the inside of a gecko's stomach, one of those geckos whose skin is so thin that you can see its insides. And then she would begin: "Listen, . . . but . . . are there cannibals where you live?" "Listen, . . . but . . . do you have houses or only huts?" "Listen, . . . but . . ."

Fortunately, after lunch she would take a nap. It was then that my mind became lost in thought. What a strange village that was. It was a village muffled in silence, and during my first months there, also by a gray autumn sky. I was used to a country where you can hear the sounds of life at all hours of the day. Even at night, when sounds penetrate the thin walls that separate the houses, you can hear the whimpering of children unable to fall asleep. And when, the following morning, you greet your neighbors at the beginning of the day, you can say to them, "Selemon just couldn't fall asleep last night, could he? I heard him," and you can feel comfortable offering all sorts of advice. Not like in that village, where the only sound was that of the occasional car passing through, of the wheels skidding on the wet asphalt. Even that was a special treat for me since our house was far from the main road.

I just couldn't understand what made that village tick. There was something terribly wrong. It was like a tree that had sprouted in the wrong direction, with its branches in the earth and its roots up in the air. That silence seemed heavy with ominous foreboding. With death rather than with life. Anything could happen from one moment to the next. Just thinking about it troubled my soul. "Oh God of Ethiopia, protect me. God of Ethiopia, may I return home safe and sound when You decide that the time is right. Don't let me go crazy in this silence." With this my daily prayer, the fall, the winter went by and then at last spring arrived, and life as I knew it seemed to suddenly come out of sleep and burst forth with the leaves on the trees. In the morning I would open the windows and spend half an hour listening to the birds. Some chirped like crazy, as if they wanted to be the center of attention. "*Adamtugn! Adamtugn!* Listen to me, everybody, listen to me!" was the message of their chirping. "They're blackbirds," Signora Franca told me.

With the arrival of spring, the village began to come alive. Even though there were still only older people around, they began to go out, to the market on Wednesdays and Saturdays and to church on Sundays.

May went by, then June. July came around and the village began
to fill with vacationers, with people who lived in Bologna and who
had a holiday home in our small village. Then one morning, on my
way to the market, I saw Signor Barbieri in front of me. I recognized
him immediately from afar—relaxed, tanned from the sun of the
high plains in Ethiopia. My heart leapt. "Signor Barbieri!" I shouted
out, still some distance away.

He turned and saw me. "Bekelech!" he shouted in reply. He came
up to me, running. We embraced.

"But what are you doing here?" I asked him.

"What do you mean, what am I doing here? We told you that we
have our holiday home here." That was true, they had told me about
it, but the low clouds of the Italian fall had blotted out everything.
"The school year in Addis is over," continued Signor Barbieri, "and
we are on vacation. We just arrived last night." Then he said, "Go on,
come on over. Laura is dying to see you. She was going to come over
to see you straight after lunch."

"I don't know whether I can, Signor Barbieri. I have to go back
home with the shopping."

"Go on, Bekelech, just for a coffee."

I had such a strong urge to see Signora Laura. "Why not? Just for
a coffee then," I answered happily. We began to walk toward their
house, which in fact was only a few yards from the Mandriolis'.

"See?" said Signor Barbieri. "We're neighbors here, too." Even
before we walked through the garden gate, he began to shout out,
"Laura! Laura!"

Signora Laura leaned out of a window. "Bekelech!" she exclaimed.
She ran toward me and we embraced. How happy I was to see her.
"So, Bekelech, how are you?"

"Well, well! And you both?"

"We too," replied Signora Laura, holding tightly onto my arm.

"And my Ethiopia?" I asked her.

"Your Ethiopia, too, is well. You miss her, right?"

"Heavens, how I miss her! You never told me that this country of
yours is so strange!"

She laughed again. "What good would it have done? The few times I tried to tell some of you, nobody believed me!"

"You're absolutely right," I said. "We all think that Italy, that Europe is a paradise . . . but now that I have seen it, I think it is a country of crazy people, no offense to anybody."

She laughed again. "Bekelech, I'm not offended, no, I'm not offended. I think the same thing."

We went into the house. They offered me a coffee and we began to chat. After half an hour, the talk turned to my job. "Bekelech," asked Signor Barbieri abruptly, "how much do they pay you?"

"Carlo, leave it, let it drop!" said Signora Laura, trying to stop him.

"Do you want to bet that it is just like I said?" She threw him a dirty look. "Bekelech," Signor Barbieri went on, "I don't want to interfere in your business, but . . . I'll explain later. Tell me how much they pay you."

"Four hundred thousand lire, plus my expenses, which they take care of, and a couple of phone calls a month to my family."

"See, see! Those Christian Democrats, what did I tell you?" he said to his wife. She looked at him aghast. "Bekelech," he continued, turning to me, "we are Communists—we would never have done what they're doing to you. They're ripping you off, Bekelech. They're paying you half of what they should."

Communists, Christian Democrats. At the time I was clueless about what he was saying, but then, in the coming years, I came to understand. Ah. The Italians! Divided between Communists and Christian Democrats . . . Juventus fans, Inter fans . . . supporters of the South, of the North . . . of Modena, of Bologna. . . . If you were to listen to half of them, there should be a separate nation for every three people.

However, that day, thanks to Signor Barbieri I understood that the Mandriolis were ripping me off. Once again my thoughts turned to my mother, to her words: "They will sell you!". . . Dammit, in some way it was true. If they hadn't exactly sold me, they had sacrificed our friendship for a paltry sum. But perhaps that friendship had never existed. I had invented it myself, exaggerating the meaning of Signora Franca's easy laughter.

"Bekelech," said Signora Laura when she had calmed down again, "if you want, we can find you work in a family as soon as tomorrow. The right kind of family, and not here. In the city, in Bologna." I was too confused and stunned by Signor Barbieri's revelation to make a decision. "I'll think about it, Signora Laura, I'll think about it," I answered, and then I left.

The summer went by, August came and went, and the Barbieris departed once more for Addis Ababa. All summer long they repeated the words they had spoken on that first day: if only I wanted to, at the slightest nod they would take me away from the Mandrioli family. I always answered with the same words: "I'll think about it." When they left I was still thinking about it and I thought about it all fall and all winter long, enveloped in the loneliness which was interrupted only by Signora Anna's ludicrous questions.

Toward the end of March, Signora Franca told me that during the school Easter holidays, two weeks later, we were going to Rome to renew certain papers of mine at the Ethiopian embassy. Perhaps dazed by the rain and snow that had fallen abundantly all those months, I didn't immediately realize the significance of that trip and so my surprise was even greater.

Rome, the wide streets, the light, the historic buildings, and then . . . our embassy. It didn't strike me till then that I had not seen anybody of our color for over a year and a half. To see your reflection in the eyes of someone who sees you as the same—what a feeling of warmth, what a feeling of infinite well-being! How long had it been since I had felt like a normal person and not like someone who had just arrived from the moon? How long had it been since the sweet sound of my language had delighted my ears and my spirit?

The lady in the Passport and Permit Renewal Office, a certain Woizero Helen, called me "Immebet Bekelech," making my mouth feel as sweet as if I had just drunk a sip of milk and honey. While she prepared my papers she asked me in Amharic what the village where I lived was like, how the family was treating me. When our chat had reached a more confidential level, she asked me how much they paid me. After hearing my reply, without changing her expression, so as not to arouse Signora Franca's suspicions, she said to me, "They are thieves. They should be paying you at least double that. When you get back to the house, give them to understand that you know how much your pay should really be . . ."

Three days later we returned to our village. I waited a couple of weeks, then one evening I asked Signora Franca if they could increase my pay. I asked her almost timidly, my voice a whisper. "Are you joking?" she answered, almost offended.

A month later, I asked her again. "Listen, the people at the embassy haven't given you any ideas, have they? What more do you want than what we give you?" was all she said in reply. I swallowed the bitter pill of that reply without saying anything more. But I'm not someone who gives up easily. I returned to the attack a month later. Again the same no.

"But you . . ." I answered, raising my voice, "you don't pay me a fair wage. The embassy told me so and so did Signor Barbieri."

An offended expression flashed across her face. "What gratitude! With everything we have done for you, this is the way you thank us. Do you believe them or us? Tell me, what has your embassy done for you? And the Barbieris? We're the ones who took you out of that African hole of yours!" Woi gud, just think what I had to hear. I did not reply. In any case, in a few days the Barbieris would arrive and I would leave without looking back.

That same evening, as I was washing the dishes in the kitchen, I heard Signora Franca tell her husband what had happened. "Those Communist busybodies!" he exclaimed.

My rage stayed with me, rumbling inside for many days after. One afternoon, while I was ironing, Signora Anna came up to me. I had already promised myself that at her first ludicrous question, I would explode, announcing that I was going to leave.

She came up close with her usual lopsided walk. "Listen," she said. Here it comes, I thought. "Listen, but do you all have hair down there too?"

I pretended not to understand. "There where?" I asked.

"There," she answered, fixing her eyes between my legs.

"I don't understand," I replied.

She took a few steps closer, as if someone could hear, and whispered, "There, on your pussy!"

It was the end of June, it was already hot, and I was only wearing a green shift dress with snaps and underneath it a light top and underwear. Suddenly I tore open the shift and pulled down my underwear. "Look!" I said to her, almost shouting.

She ran off, waving those skeletal arms of hers in the air, like a ghost. "She's gone mad, she's gone mad!" she shouted.

That evening Signora Franca came into my room to scold me. "She is old," she emphasized. "You should use better judgment. Here they say, 'If you have a head, use it'—it's up to you to be understanding."

"Listen," I butted in. "Do you think I am an object, something you own? As if it weren't enough that you pay me half of what you should, you also want me to bow my head when your mother asks me offensive questions? You know what? Find another maid. I am leaving."

At first she was speechless, but she recovered quickly enough. "You can't," she said. "Your contract expires in September."

"I can! I can! Just try and stop me!" I repeated without adding another word, and she left, slamming the door.

Fortunately, two days later the Barbieris arrived and I left the Mandrioli household. I stayed with the Barbieris till the end of August, when I went to work in Bologna, on Via Saragozza, for their friends' family, the Busis. A family with a husband, a wife, Signora Busi's parents, and Claudio, the Busis' small son. A six-year-old sweetie pie of a boy. As sweet as honey, the color of his hair, with eyes as black as burnt coal.

In that family I once again found the warmth that had been missing from my life for those two long years. What's more, the Busis had given me a regular contract, with a high wage, as well as two afternoons off a week, Thursday and Saturday, and forty-five days' vacation time in the summer so I could go to Ethiopia. And then there was Claudio. My little sweetheart. Honestly, I loved him as if he were my own son, and he loved me too. I'm certain of it. At least you can trust children. They don't pretend.

One day my little Claudio came to me and said, "Bekelech, do you know that my friend Marco's granddad"—referring to the son of the family that lived on the same floor as us—"speaks your language?"

"What language, sweetie?" I asked, expecting to hear the usual reply, "African." Since I had come to Italy, half the people I had met referred to me as "African," that I spoke "African," that I ate "African style.". . . I had stopped being Ethiopian and I had become part of a gigantic continent, even though in the minds of the Italians it was infinitely small, since for them we all spoke the same language, we ate the same food. . . .

"Which? Like yours," he replied, looking at me in amazement. "Yours in Ethiopia." Right, the Ethiopian language. If for half the people I had met I was "African," for those who had some idea of what I was talking about, I was someone from the ex-Italian colonies, where there was little difference between the various countries. Therefore, lots of people mixed up Ethiopia, Eritrea, Somalia, and even Libya, which was much closer to them than to us.

I looked at Claudio hesitantly. "Come on, I'll introduce you to him," he insisted.

"Sweetie, are you sure he speaks my language?"

"Bekelech, I tell you he speaks your language. Marco tells me that he's always speaking about Ethiopia. Always, always. Go on, please, just for a moment," he begged, tugging on my hand.

"All right, let's go," I agreed, more to make him happy than anything else. I couldn't refuse that cute face anything, but as we went along, I said to myself, "Even if he speaks an Ethiopian language, who knows if he speaks Amharic, Tigrinya, Gurage . . . we have so many languages."

Once in front of the door, Claudio rang the bell of the other apartment and Marco, his little friend, came to open it. "I've brought her
along," said Claudio. "Is your granddad here?"

Marco nodded and, cracking a big smile, he rushed inside.
"Grandma, Grandma, Claudio's nanny is here. The one from Ethiopia." His grandma didn't reply. I couldn't hear any talking from
inside the apartment, but after a few minutes, Claudio reappeared,
pulling an older man by the sleeve. A tall, thin, old man with white
hair, as white as cotton, and slightly cloudy blue eyes. The older man
extended his hand in the Ethiopian manner. "*Tenastellen*. Antonio
ebalalehu."[1]

Heavens, he really did speak my language; he spoke Amharic. I
was speechless with surprise. He repeated his greeting. Little Claudio shook me: "Bekelech, answer him."

"*Tenastellen*. Bekelech *ebalalehu*." Two tears of nostalgia appeared
in the eyes of the old man, who continued, still in Amharic: "It's been
so long since I spoke your language. At the time of the Italian colonization I was a junior officer in your country for four years. For the
last two I was a translator from Amharic into Italian." While he was
speaking to me, little Marco began to shout, "Grandma! Grandma!
Come and see the nanny from Ethiopia."

From somewhere inside came a scratchy voice: "Say hello to her
for me. Tell her I will meet her another time."

Signor Antonio and I spoke for several minutes, only in Amharic,
then we said goodbye, promising to meet again soon. The two children said goodbye to each other, satisfied smiles on their faces. I
returned home with my little Claudio holding onto my hand, and
after a few minutes, when I regained my composure, my mind began
to whirl.

From the time I had arrived in Italy I had never been able to communicate with my family in Ethiopian the way I wanted to. On the
telephone we could not go beyond the usual greetings. It cost too
much and international calling cards did not exist yet. As for letters,
I did not know how to read or write. But if Signor Antonio had been

---

1. "May the Lord grant us good health. My name is Antonio."

a translator, he most certainly must know how to read and write. I could ask him to write to my family. Finally, I would be able to tell them everything that I had not been able to tell them for those two long years. But then I asked myself, what would Signor Antonio say about my reflections? There were certain things I wanted to tell them about this country . . . what if he were to take offense? Or what if he wrote something different from what I dictated to him? I knew of certain "scribes" in Ethiopia who wrote, modifying things the way they wanted to. I reflected on this for several days and then I came to a decision: I would ask him to write a first letter, just to test the waters. And I would check it out. . . . I called Claudio and I sent him to Signor Antonio with my request: "If he is free on Thursday afternoon, I will stop by his house to have him write a letter for me."

Claudio disappeared, only to return a few minutes later. "He agreed," he answered, his eyes shining. I kissed him. That child! . . . I was certain he had been sent to me from heaven.

The following Thursday afternoon, at three o'clock on the dot, I rang the bell of the apartment opposite ours. Signor Antonio himself opened the door. I was nervous. He greeted me in Amharic and invited me in. I almost didn't register going down the corridor. I felt very uncomfortable. Apart from the Barbieri family, who didn't really count in this context, this was the first time that I had entered an Italian house as a guest and not for the purpose of accompanying someone from the family I worked for. Before going into Signor Antonio's study he wanted to introduce me to his wife, Signora Pina. A graceful woman, as tall as him and with elegant gestures that belied her scratchy voice. Signora Pina looked hard at me, scrutinizing me from head to toe, and then she apologized. "Please do not consider me rude, but this is the first time that I've seen an Ethiopian woman up close. My husband often speaks of your people and of your land. Actually, to say he speaks about it often is an understatement. Ethiopia is an obsession with him, and for a while it was with me too . . ." Then, dropping the subject, she said, "Go ahead, go ahead—I think that we shall have the chance to see each other again."

Signor Antonio led the way toward his study, a small room whose walls were hidden behind wooden bookcases overflowing with books. I sat down. He stretched up to a shelf and took down a book in Amharic and offered it to me. "It's a grammar book," he said. The shelf he had taken it from was full of books in Amharic. "Amharic is easy. You can learn it quickly. If you want, I can teach it to you. Can I use the familiar 'you' form of address with you?"

"Certainly, Signor Antonio, you may use the familiar form of 'you' with me," I replied, all the while still using the formal 'you' in our language with him.

"In any case, I could be your father, right, almost your grandfather. So," he asked a second time, "what do you say, would you like to learn Amharic?"

"No, thanks," I replied.

"You know, I learned it very quickly."

His eyes were so brimming with nostalgia they wanted to speak. I decided to ask him a few questions to give him the pleasure of sharing his memories. "How did you learn it?"

He certainly didn't need to be asked a second time—that single question removed the barrier, releasing a flood of words. "I sailed for Ethiopia in January 1938. From Naples. The voyage lasted fifteen days and in that brief span of time, while my companions took advantage of every possible form of entertainment, I studied all the Amharic grammar books that I had been able to bring with me: the one by Guidi, by Afraworki, by Beateman. . . . Beateman's was the best. If you wanted to learn, I have it." And, saying this, he started to get up as if to get it.

"Don't bother, Signor Antonio," I stopped him.

He sat down again and continued his story. "When I arrived in Massawa, I was already able to speak a few words of Amharic. From Massawa we went by truck in the direction of Debre Markos. Once again, I took advantage of the traveling time. At night, in my tent, by the light of a candle I continued to study. Once we reached Debre Markos, we continued our journey on foot. My battalion and I were stationed in the back country at Kera Kolla. When I arrived I could already speak a little: greetings, general expressions, some simple questions. Just think, a few days after reaching Kera Kolla, a woman came up to me one morning. 'Woine! Woine!' she was shouting, her hands in her hair. I asked her why she was shouting and she replied that a talian sollato had entered into her hut and stolen her money that she kept in an earthenware pot. I was astonished that I could understand her words, and even more so when I was able to tell her, in some way or other, to come with me, that we would go around the military compound and if she recognized the thief, she was to point him out to me and I would take care of the rest. We had only been walking around the compound for a few minutes when she pointed out a young soldier to me. 'That's him,' she said.

"I sent her away and I went up to the soldier. 'Give me the money that you stole from the native woman,' I told him. At first he swore that he knew nothing about the matter. 'I saw you with my own eyes,' I insisted. He gave up and returned the stolen money to me, a few Maria Theresa thalers. I gave them back to the woman, who began to utter trills of joy. Thanks to the little Amharic I had learned, I was able to understand that woman and do her a good turn, which won me the respect and goodwill of all the Ethiopians in the village. Guess what happened afterward! For every single problem from the smallest to the biggest, they would come to me."

Once he had finished his story, he again suggested teaching me to read and write. "I'm no longer a young chicken, with the ability to absorb things," I said to him. "I wouldn't be capable of learning anything." He didn't say a word, his eyes lowered, his brow creased, his fingers pressing against it as if he wanted to squeeze something out. Before he could begin to speak, I slipped in the reason for my visit. "So, Signor Antonio, will you write a letter for me? To my family. Since I arrived in Italy, I have never been able to tell them much. . . . Calling costs too much."

He lowered his hand, smoothed his brow, and lifted his eyes. "Certainly!" he answered. He pushed his chair back, opened the desk drawer, took out a sheet of paper, and put on his glasses. "I'm ready," he said, taking hold of a pen. "I am at your complete service."

Before I began to dictate my letter, I said a prayer to God: "Lord, may my lips not utter anything offensive." I began to dictate:

በስመአብ በወልድ በመንፈስ ቅዱስ በጌታችን በመድሀኒታችን በእየሱስ ክርስቶስ ስም ለምወዳችሁ ዉድ እናቴ ዉድ አባቴ ወንድሞቼ አንዲሁም አሀቶቼ ለጤናችሁ እንደምን አላችሁልኝ? እኔ ከቡር አምላከ ይመስገነዉ ለጤናየ በጣም ደህና ነኝ፡፡ ...

He began writing, without saying a word. Every now and then his slightly pendulous bottom lip tightened, rose, and then extended in a slight smile, his only comment on my words. Once I had finished dictating, he folded the letter and gave it to me. At the front door, before I went out, he said to me, "Bekelech, the mere thought of your presence warms my old heart. Come and see me whenever you want. My door will always be open for you." I gave a sigh of relief; I had not offended him. Now all that remained was to find out if Signor Antonio had accurately transcribed what I had dictated to him, without removing, adding, or modifying anything. I posted the letter and fifteen days later I went to the Sip telephone center, in the middle of Bologna, from where you could make international phone calls though an operator, like we do through our telephone office on Churchill Road. I called home. My younger brother, Tesfaye, answered. After we had exchanged the usual greetings, he said to me, "Two days ago your letter arrived. I still have it in my pocket." He stopped for a moment and then began again. "Every so often I reread it. Is Italy really like that?"

I didn't answer. "Read it to me," I ordered him.

"But it's long, it will take a long time!" he said, referring to the cost of the telephone call.

"It doesn't matter. Tesfaye, don't waste time. Read it to me."

From the telephone came the sound of rustling fabric and paper. "Here it is," he said.

"Read it!"

"'In the name of the Father, the Son, and the Holy Ghost. In the name of Jesus Christ, our only savior, dear Mother, dear Father, dear brothers and sisters, how are you? Thanks be to God, I am well. Dear all, I am doing well now, but until a few months ago that wasn't the case. Life with the Mandriolis turned out differently from what I had experienced with them in Addis Ababa. Once I arrived here, they began to act like bosses, or should I say, like masters, almost as if I were an object instead of a person.'"

At that moment I could hear my mother's voice butting in: "Daughter, I told you not to go with the talian."

"Hurry up, carry on," I told Tesfaye.

He started reading again. "'But now I'm fine. Thanks to the Barbieris I have found work in a good family, and also a surprise, a lovely surprise: an Italian gentleman by the name of Antonio who knows how to read and write our language. He's the one who is writing this letter. Thanks to him I can describe this country in more detail. Dear everyone, Italy is not what I imagined it to be. It is a strange country. You might say it is the home of solitude. People live shut up in their own homes. Neighbors are not in the habit of having a coffee together, neighborhood associations do not exist. Elderly people are alone, children do not go in and out of each other's houses, calling out to each other to come play. Adults live like small birds—they leave the nest at dawn and return late in the evening. Everything is done in a hurry, always running. It seems that they like hurrying very much. The most common phrase is, "I don't have the time, I'm in a hurry." But all this rushing about of theirs has no purpose. In this country there is wealth, roads are lit up at night with rows and rows of streetlights, there are hospitals that heal you, trains, buses. There is so much food, so much that you can throw some away without thinking about it. There are no beggars to whom you can give the leftovers from your meal, but in spite of all this, in spite of their well-being, they are not happy. They don't make use of their wealth to gladden their lives, and I still haven't worked out what they really use it for. . . . Dear all, I ask you to pray for Signor Antonio and his family, I ask you to pray for my new family, the Busis, for the Barbieris, and also for the Mandriolis—perhaps they need your prayers more than everyone else. So now, goodbye to you all and may God's light illuminate your path as the streetlights do here in the evening.'"

The letter came to an end and I was satisfied: every single word I had dictated was in the letter, nothing had been modified. Therefore, Signor Antonio was a trustworthy person, just as he appeared to be!

I paid for the call and went outside. It was mid-November, and the overcast sky was taking on the darkness of evening. It was cold but for the first time I did not feel the coldness flowing in my veins.

Two weeks later I went back to Signor Antonio for another letter. It was the first Thursday in December. I rang the bell and Signor Antonio came to open the door. Behind him I could make out the dark corridor, barely distinguishable in the pale autumn light. A voice came out of the darkness—it was Signora Pina's voice. "Who is it?"

"It's Bekelech!" shouted Signor Antonio.

"Good afternoon, good afternoon, my dear!" she shouted back, without coming out of the room where she was.

"Good afternoon," I answered in turn. Then Signor Antonio moved aside from the doorway to let me in.

The smell of the house hit my nostrils. Perhaps it was because I had been nervous, but the preceding time I hadn't noticed it, even though it was a familiar smell. It was the smell that the houses in and around Bologna had, houses in which older people lived. The smell of meat sauce that had been cooked for a long time, mixed with the stale odor of old sofas and armchairs. Of things placed on the furniture and left there, taking on the smell of time. I had already noticed that smell in Signora Anna's room, even in the Busis' house, and I had worked really hard to get rid of it. Perhaps that smell was the most stubborn occupant of the house, almost as if it had a greater right than the Busis to be there.

It was a smell that made me nauseous. In Ethiopia, breezes blow through our houses, taking away the smells, and only during the rainy season does any smell linger, but it is a young odor, very short-lived, one that is born, that exists, and then dies in the span of two months. At its heart, the odor of spices, of roasted coffee and incense. Not of anything that has built up over years.

Signor Antonio led me toward his study. We settled down as we did the previous time.

That day, yet again, he tried to convince me to learn to read and write Amharic. "Bekelech, it's easy. You already know how to speak it, and reading and writing it would be a breeze," he insisted. And he began to explain the structure of our alphabet. I said nothing, but through my body language I tried to express my feelings. I lowered my eyes to my interlaced fingers. "You really aren't interested, are you?" he asked me at a certain point.

"Signor Antonio, I would be interested, but—"

He interrupted me: "So let me teach you. Look, while I was a prisoner in Kenya, it used to take me nine minutes to explain your alphabet. I made bets with whoever wanted to learn. If they got it in nine minutes, I won three cigarettes. I was able to keep myself in cigarettes during my entire imprisonment thanks to this scheme. You know, I had even written an Amharic grammar book. Then I threw it away. When I found out that we had lost the Second World War and that we had therefore definitively lost Ethiopia, I threw it in the trash." He stopped and then spoke again. "So! Do you want to learn?"

"Signor Antonio," I replied, this time looking him straight in the eye, "I would like to learn, but you must understand! All the energy I have is divided between my work and my attempts to live according to your culture that, as you know, is very different from ours." He understood and did not attempt to teach me again. In silence he opened the drawer, took out a sheet of paper, put on his glasses, and glanced at me to let me know he was ready. I dictated my letter:

በራ አፊላላገዉ እንድ መልካም ቤተሰብ ዉስጥ በቤት ስራተኛነት እስቀጠሩኝ፡፡ የሚገርመዉ ነገር ቢኖር አሰሪዮ ስኞር እንቶንዮ የኛን ቋንቋ ማንበብና መጻፍ እሳምሮ ይችላል፡፡ አሁንም ይህንን ደብዳቤ የጻፈልኝ እሱ ነዉ፡፡፡...

Just like the previous time, Signor Antonio made no comment, apart from the movement of his pendulous lower lip. When he had finished writing, he took off his glasses, put them down on the desk, and said, "Bekelech, the Busis are very good people, but if they should ever treat you badly, even just once, let me know. I would never want you to be treated with disrespect. I want to think that here you receive the same treatment that I received from your people. You know, once I lived in one of your villages! I had caused such a ruckus, such a pandemonium, that I had to leave the military, and I rented a *tukul* in a village near Addis Ababa. A few miles from the station at Legahar. I stayed there for almost six months. I came and went, in and out of all the houses, just as I wished. I chatted with everyone to improve my Amharic. Then I returned to the army, but to the regular army this time.

"The day I left the village, when the car sent by the commander came to get me, the village headman had everyone line up to say goodbye, and as I was getting into the car he said, 'You were a good person.' But it's easy to be a good person when you are treated with so much courtesy."

Once he had finished his story, he repeated his invitation to return whenever I wanted to, and went with me to the front door.

I posted the letter and fifteen days later I called home. I was already convinced of Signor Antonio's good faith, but something, a tiny doubt, had begun to buzz around in my head, like a moth flying around a lighted lamp at night in a room. Was Signor Antonio truly as he seemed to be? Truly somebody whom I could trust wholeheartedly? What if he had modified something this time? I had already been burned by my trust in the Mandriolis. Better to make sure, one last time. Only this one time. If everything was as I had dictated it, I would not check up on him anymore, I swore I wouldn't, but just for this last time, I was going to do it.

Once again Tesfaye answered the phone. I asked him if the letter had arrived.

"Yes, it arrived."

"Read it to me," I ordered him.

"I don't have it here, I must go and get it," he said, and so he passed the phone to my mother, who began to say, "My daughter, come home. What don't you have here on the banks of your river? We may not have great wealth but we aren't dying of hunger. My daughter, come home!" Fortunately, Tesfaye came back with the letter. My mother's words were like torture for me. I, too, asked myself every morning what I was doing here and why I didn't just leave. Perhaps it was a challenge. I wanted to feel I was up to living here. Or perhaps by doing so I would not have to admit my failure to my people. Who would have believed me if I had said that after all, life was not all that great in Italy? Who would not have thought that it was because of a weakness on my part? I don't know! I could not fathom the stubbornness that had come over me. A sick stubbornness, sick like that of the lifestyle of the people among whom I lived.

Tesfaye began reading: "'In the name of the Father . . . Dear Mother, dear Father, dear all . . . how are you? I am well, thanks be to God. As I told you the last time, the Mandrioli family was a big disappointment. And to think of how much I had believed in my friendship with Signora Franca. I spent two years in an arid desert, with no human warmth. Alone every evening in my room, I spoke to God out loud. "*Getaye,*" I used to say to him. "Here I am, speaking with You just like mad Ato Selemon, our neighbor. And to think of how much I used to laugh when I heard him talking. Today I'm saying the same things. Why did You put me in this hole? Where did You put the exit? There must be an exit. Don't they say that when You put a person in a hole, You put the exit nearby? If I am unable to see it, help me, before I go completely mad. And, I beg You, show me some sunshine, make my days a little lighter."

"'Dear all, like the last time, I ask you to pray for Signor Antonio, for his family, and also for the Busi family.

"'May the God of Ethiopia and Bet Israel protect us all.'"

Tesfaye's reading of the letter confirmed Signor Antonio's trustworthiness. "I'm lucky," I said to myself. "I am truly lucky to have met him. Finally, God, you have allowed me to come out of that hole that I had fallen into. Thank you."

Ten days after that phone call came the Catholic Christmas, and two weeks after that came ours. In those twenty-five days I spent little time with Signor Antonio—the occasional chat and warm

greetings when we would meet on the landing, and my best wishes
for the Italian Christmas and New Year. I certainly did not expect to
see him for our Christmas. Especially because even I hardly remembered it. How could I, with all the work I had ... and then remember
it for what? With whom would I have shared the holiday?

That morning I was finishing cleaning up the house before I began getting lunch ready. The day before had been the Three Kings
holiday and in the afternoon Claudio and his school friends had
had a party at our house. Consequently, the floor in the front parlor
seemed to be covered in glue because of all the sweet drinks that had
been spilled on it. I was washing the floor when the doorbell rang.
"Claudio, please, can you answer it?" I shouted from the parlor. He
rushed to open the door and then came running to me.

"It's for you," he said, then disappeared with lightning speed. I put
down the mop and went to the door, asking myself who it could be. I
looked out and was struck dumb. In front of me was Signor Antonio
with two traditional Christmas cakes, a *panettone* in one hand and
a *pandoro* in the other.

"*Melkam Lidet,*"[2] he said, smiling at me. Deep emotions shot
through me from head to toe. I did not know which feeling should
have the upper hand: I was surprised, moved, and overjoyed. He
stood there in his blue and green plaid robe, with slippers on his
feet and his two outstretched hands which were holding the two
cakes. "So?"

"Signor Antonio, I had forgotten!" I exclaimed.

"Me," he said proudly, "I never forget. Every year on this day, I go
into the kitchen and I eat a slice of pandoro. I don't like panettone
with all that candied fruit. . . . I eat a slice of pandoro, and do you
know what my wife says to me each time? 'Antonio, you didn't by
chance have a woman over there, did you?' And I answer, 'Pina, you
know I am an honorable man. If you had not been my wife, I might
have done so. But we were already married and I have never betrayed
you.' 'If you say so!' she says. She doesn't believe me, and I don't try
to persuade her otherwise. . . . I don't try to explain anything to her.

2. "Merry Christmas."

She wouldn't understand. No one who has not been there can understand the passion that rises up within you. Little by little, without you even noticing it. No one can understand the nostalgia that grips you when you leave. And not for a woman that you have left behind. No. Only for that magical something that is in the air, that not even you can explain." For a moment in his cloudy blue eyes, there were flashes of distant fires; his mind had gone back in time to dig up memories. I remained suspended, waiting for him to return. "Well then," he asked me after a while, "aren't you going to take my cakes?"

"Thank you. Thank you so much, Signor Antonio." I did not know what else to say—I was so surprised that I was speechless.

"Bekelech, it's just a small gift to remember your Christmas." Still dumbfounded, I stretched out my hands to take the two boxes. He gave them to me and then turned around to go back into his apartment.

"Signor Antonio," I called him back.

"Tell me," he said.

"This afternoon is my day off. What do you say to eating a slice of pandoro with me, in your kitchen?"

He beamed with pleasure and began to gesticulate with his arms, as if an electric shock had suddenly jolted him to life. "Maybe . . . maybe we can even go to the Church of San Luca on foot, to pay our respects to the Virgin Mary."

"That would be great!" I replied, and a wave of tenderness for that old man with a soul as pure and as white as his hair swept over my heart.

"Well then," he added before he left, "well then, it's a deal."

"It's a deal," I replied in turn.

How welcoming was Signor Antonio's heart, and how pleasant it was to warm myself in his gaze! That afternoon, in his kitchen, as we ate the pandoro, I shared these thoughts with him: "Thank you, thank you for your friendship. It makes me feel alive. During the two years I spent with the Mandriolis I felt invisible. A person without a past, with nothing interesting to say, coming from a country without history."

"Are you joking?" he said. "You come from the country of the Queen of Sheba. You are the descendants of King Solomon."

"For the Mandriolis I was only someone who came from 'that African hole,' as Signora Franca told me one day."

"Bekelech, while you live here, you mustn't forget that we are a pack of idiots. If you agree to see yourself through our eyes, you will feel that you are nothing more than a savage," he told me, munching on a piece of pandoro.

After we had eaten a slice of pandoro and drunk a glass of tea, we left to go to San Luca. Our apartment building was at the end of Via Saragozza, a few yards from the Meloncello Arch. In the ten or so yards that separated us from it, and all the way up to the church and again all the way down, with only one stop to pray in front of the Virgin Mary, Signor Antonio spoke only of Ethiopia and of the Amharic language. As his wife, Signora Pina, had told me, it was a real obsession with him.

"Language," he said, waving his hand in the air, "language is the soul of the culture. The skeleton of a civilization. If you have the skeleton you can make hypotheses about how the flesh was or will be draped over it. Language tells us about the people who speak it. And Amharic! Ah! Amharic, Bekelech. Certain words fill your mouth like the pulp of the papaya, of the avocado. You know what I mean. And then, the way you all have of expressing yourselves. The poetry, the double meanings, your qene," he went on, accompanying his words with his hand, which continued to make circles in the air, attracting the attention of the pilgrims who were going to the sanctuary. "Just think, the first year I spent in Kera Kolla, a priest gave me lessons of qene, for an hour, every day. In the first months, I wasn't able to solve even one. He wrote some couplets. . . . I read them, then I looked at him, totally lost. 'Well, then?' he would ask me. 'Where's the gold?'

"'Who knows?' I would reply, reading and rereading it. 'I can't find it.'

"'It's in the second sentence!' he hinted to me, but I was still totally in the dark. He would shake his head and say to me, 'You don't speak Amharic, you just babble in it. As long as you are unable to understand qene your Amharic will resemble the footsteps of someone who has a limp—you will never be able to run along a road at the pace you wish.' But then I learned, and how! And the priest arrived one day with a large earthenware pot, with some freshly prepared doro wot. He opened it, releasing the aroma into the room, and said, 'Today we shall celebrate.'

"'Celebrate what?' I asked him.

"'We shall celebrate the fact that you have learned real Amharic and I have finished my work with you.' And from that day on I never saw him again."

Signor Antonio talked and talked. He continued to talk, to gesticulate, to stop when he wanted to give his words more emphasis. I listened . . . , listened, and sometimes when I could no longer bear standing still, under the covered arches, with him gesticulating and me feeling embarrassed by the people staring at us, that strange couple composed of an old Italian man and a young black woman who were speaking a strange language made up of dry, guttural sounds, I took a few steps, went on ahead so he would follow me, just like a mother with her small child. Then he would start walking again, only to stop a few hundred feet ahead . . . and again I would stop and then take a few more steps. . . .

Two and a half hours after we had gone out, we finally returned to the landing outside our apartments. I thought we would say goodbye to each other, but instead he began again, with the words, "Listen to this one, Bekelech, listen to this: at Kera Kolla, after the priest no longer came to teach me, a famous journalist arrived from Italy. A big shot from the newspaper *Corriere della Sera*. He had been sent to Ethiopia to write about life in the military forts. One day, during lunch in the officers' mess, I found him sitting next to me. He was with our major. For the entire meal, the two discussed the origins of the Queen of Sheba, repeating the theory of the historians, some of whom said she was Ethiopian, others Yemenite. At the end of the meal, the major walked away from the table, leaving the journalist alone. I immediately took advantage of the opportunity. 'She was Ethiopian,' I told him all of a sudden, opening the conversation.

"'What, excuse me?' he asked, surprised.

"'Please forgive me for butting in. I overheard your conversation with the major. The Queen of Sheba was Ethiopian,' I repeated.

"'And you, sir, how do you know that?'

"'From her name,' I replied, and, quoting a lesson that the priest had taught me about the significance of names in the Amharic, Tigriny, and Ga'ez languages, I carefully explained the origins of the name Saba. He was impressed and wanted to talk to me about Ethiopian culture for the entire afternoon. In the ensuing days, he wanted to spend more time with me. At that point, we spoke not only about Ethiopian culture, but also about politics and other things. At the end of his short stay, before he left, he gave me his contact information, saying to me, 'Antonio, I have contacts with higher-ups in our government. When you encounter problems—because there is no doubt that you will have some problems because of your personality and your ideas—come to see me. I will be able to help you.' And in fact, less than two months after his departure, I caused the ruckus and I ended up in trouble. But I didn't ask anyone for help—I got out of it on my own, by myself, with nothing but the help of my men."

For the entire recounting of his story we had been standing on the landing. I had clicked on the time-activated light switch countless times and I had begun to get impatient. The landing was certainly not the best place for a conversation, but Signor Antonio, intently chasing after his memories, was oblivious to everything. He continued to speak, to gesticulate, and I continued to activate the light switch. At a certain point, close to my limit, I interrupted him: "Signor Antonio, my afternoon off is over. I have to go in now." Like water that suddenly finds a wall blocking its way, I could sense his emotions rushing together, gurgling within the walls of his chest. For a moment or two, he was disoriented, trying to find his balance, still bowled over by the abrupt blocking of his words.

"You're right, Bekelech," he said to me once he had regained his composure. Then we said goodbye to each other and went our separate ways.

Poor Signor Antonio. Some might say he was a *lib aderk,* someone who could sap your heart, but that wasn't the case. He talked so much because he had been silent for so long, convinced that nobody could understand him. Now that he had met me, an Ethiopian, a torrent of words had burst from his lips.

No, poor Signor Antonio, he most certainly was not a lib aderk— believe me, I can recognize them very easily. I have met so many.... I have to say that there are more of them in Italy than in our country. Perhaps that's because there people spend so much time alone, or because they lead with the head and not with the heart. I have met some who talk and talk without even noticing you who should be listening to them. They don't notice if you are participating in the conversation, if you're interested in it or if you are tired of listening or not. They don't notice if your body language speaks of boredom or of being in a hurry. Some, even after you tell them you have to go, that you have things to do, continue to talk. Just as if you had said, "Go ahead, today my time is all yours, my ears are all yours. Go for it!" I have had certain lib aderk Italian women friends . . . very nice people, with hearts of gold, always ready to run to the help of others, but when they start to talk . . . that's it! There was a friend of mine, Dorina, well, she . . . was like a river between mountains where it's always raining. A constant flow. Just think, sometimes, when she called me on the phone, I would listen for ten minutes, I would put down the phone and go and take care of a small chore or other, then I would come back and she would still be talking. I would listen for a few more minutes, and again I would go to do another small chore.... I went on like that for the entire call. On average, at least an hour. Do you think she ever noticed anything? Never. And her babbling?

A long story like *The Bold and the Beautiful*, in which someone had died, but then he wasn't really dead, he had just disappeared and suddenly had come back, causing someone's relationship to go to pieces.... It was just like that with her. She had a boyfriend—no, a lover, a married man. They would break up, start over, then he would get to the point of leaving his wife, but then he changed his mind. Oh my God! And that wasn't all. I was so familiar with her way of babbling on that even though I only heard part of it, I could figure it all out. Just like *The Bold and the Beautiful*, which you only have to see once every two months and you will still be able to figure it all out. Argh! Dorina's babbling was a torment for me. And yet, she was the kindest person.

Whatever, let's go back to Signor Antonio. After that afternoon on our Christmas Day, we got into the habit of walking to San Luca about every two weeks. First, he wrote a letter for my family, letters that I never checked up on again, as I had promised myself. He would read the letters that eventually arrived for me. Then we would go out. After that first afternoon, his conversation quieted down. Perhaps the pressure caused by that infinitely long silence had abated, a silence that had lasted almost fifty years. Between us there sprang up that harmonious balance that exists between two dancers. He talked a bit, then I talked a bit. Obviously, everything centered on Ethiopia, but that wasn't the only subject we discussed. He very much liked to talk about God, gesticulating with his hands in the air, and I liked to lay out my ideas about the strangeness of Italy. "I get the impression of a great emptiness. An emptiness that is sealed in containers of various shapes, that knock against each other and make noise, a noise that serves no purpose especially since there is nothing inside them," I said to him.

And he: "Once it was not like that. Once we were full.... It's just that the world is getting worse—consumerism empties you out like a tube of toothpaste."

"Maybe you're right," I commented.

"It's true, Bekelech, you should have seen this city even just ten years ago. Piazza Maggiore was always full of people. You could go out at any hour of the day, without a worry. And if you shouted out for help in the street, the whole city would come to their windows. Bologna was a paradise of humanity! Just think, you didn't even have to pay on the buses."

During those long months of walks under the sanctuary portico, he referred several times to the "ruckus" he had created in Ethiopia, two months after the departure of that famous journalist. He referred to it but never spoke about it. Only the occasional half sentence, casually tossed out. Eventually it piqued my curiosity. What could he have ever done? Emboldened by the easy familiarity that now existed between us, one day I said to him, "Signor Antonio, I'm weary of hearing you speak of this! What was this 'ruckus' that you caused? Either you should tell me about it or you should stop referring to it."

We were almost at the end of the covered portico on Via Saragozza. Just before the traffic light, in front of the Billy pastry shop. Three times Signor Antonio took a deep breath. Three times he opened his mouth slightly, as if in suspense, but then shut it, saying, "No, no, no! I can't." The fourth time he turned to me: "Let's go up the first flight of steps and sit on the little wall. I will tell you the whole story, but I have to sit down." Without saying a word I followed him. We climbed the steps, we reached the little wall, and we sat down. He and I both in silence. He bent his head, and as he usually did, he ran his fingers over his brow as if he wanted to squeeze it. After a few minutes, he began to tell me the story.

"I left Italy as a junior officer in the militia. I left as a volunteer, even though in reality I didn't believe in the war. I didn't think much of Mussolini, but it was impossible to live and work in Italy if you didn't belong to a Fascist group—if you hadn't committed acts of bravado in the name of Il Duce, Mussolini, it was difficult to get in anywhere. So my father asked a childhood friend of his, a big shot in the army, to get me in as a volunteer, emphasizing that I was a junior officer. During my military service I had been a captain. My father's friend had me posted as an officer in the militia. I agreed to my father's scheme, thinking that once I arrived in Ethiopia, I would leave the army and look for a job, maybe as a translator. With this plan in mind, I departed, taking all the Amharic grammar books I could find with me. I was not the only one who had the idea of quitting the army once in Ethiopia. Many had already resorted to the same strategy and many left Italy with the idea of putting it into practice. Even in the company that I led, several young men, simple soldiers, wanted to quit the army once they arrived.

"Unfortunately, once we arrived the plan proved to be much more complicated, not because of bureaucratic hurdles or anything else, but because of those damn officers who demanded a five-hundred-lire bribe from every soldier who wanted to demobilize. Five hundred lire! Do you understand? It was a lot at that time. A specialized worker barely made three hundred lire, so imagine a simple soldier.... Every evening some young men would come to see me to complain and ask for advice. I didn't know what to say to them. Until the number of young men who were complaining reached such proportions that an idea began to form in my mind....

"A few weeks later we had a visit from the governor of Gondar. He arrived accompanied by two officers, one from the air force, the other from the supply corps. In the courtyard they sounded the assembly call and we all gathered there. After our salute, the governor took the stand. He greeted us briefly, almost annoyed, and then began to speak. He had come to give us a telling-off. 'Since when have real men, real Fascists, written anonymous letters? I have received more than a hundred anonymous letters. I must say that cowardice does not do any of you honor. Instead, seek to be worthy of the uniform you wear. A uniform of courage. You hold an important role— try to be worthy of it.' He ended his speech, saluted us again, still annoyed, and after he had received our salute, he left the courtyard to go to the major's office.

"I ran after him. Just picture it—along the short gravel path, a captain was running and shouting, 'Governor! Governor, stop! Just a moment.' The two officers looked at me as if I were mad. 'Just a moment,' I continued to shout. 'I must speak to you.' He stopped and I reached him.

"'Speak up,' he said, his voice polite, but his face drawn.

"'You expressed your opinions and without waiting for any possible responses, you left. When certain accusations are made, one must give the accused the opportunity to respond, and I wish to make use of that opportunity.'

"'Go ahead,' he replied, his face still more drawn.

"'Not so fast!' I answered. 'You spoke in front of the entire fort, therefore I intend to answer you in front of everybody.'

"'But that is not possible,' he brayed, his voice going from polite to cutting.

"'If it's not possible to do so in front of everybody, then at least in front of the officers. All the officers of this fort.' Even though he was decidedly annoyed, he agreed and gave orders to the major to assemble all the officers. We went into the major's office and when they were all present, I began my accusations: 'Governor, sir, it's not the soldiers who are unworthy of wearing the military uniform, but you, sirs,' and I emphasized my point by indicating each of the officers. 'These rogues make people pay them to fill out the demobilization orders. Five hundred lire for each order.' One of the officers tried to interrupt, ordering me to keep quiet. 'You,' I said, 'have the right to speak on the battlefield, and in that case I have to obey, but not here. You are one of the accused. Therefore, it's my turn to speak. After, if you have something to say in your defense, you can speak up.'

"'Continue,' said the governor to me.

"'I was the one who advised the men to write the letters, anonymous letters, to avoid possible repercussions. With this scum you can never be sure. You said the men are not worthy of wearing the uniform since they are cowards. Tell me, Governor, sir, does this mean that under this empire you can't be cowards, but you can be thieves?'

"This was the ruckus that I unleashed. When the governor left, there was chaos in the fort. The officers seemed to have been bitten by a tarantula, and the men were rejoicing. . . . They thought that everything had been resolved. But I, who knew the higher-ups and their ways much better than they did, I advised them not to celebrate too soon. It was premature.

"And so it was. In fact a few days later, instead of punishment or anything for the officers, there arrived an order for me: immediate repatriation for behavior unbecoming to an officer. You understand, Bekelech, don't you? They were repatriating me immediately because it was simpler to get rid of one honest man than many thieves. After a few days they sent me from Kera Kolla to Bechene, and from there, after a few weeks, they sent me back with a column to Addis Ababa.

"I thought that they would really repatriate me, but then the men at Kera Kolla wrote some letters, this time signed letters. They sent them to the governor of Gondar, to Addis Ababa, and even to Italy, to several newspapers. Accusations which could not be ignored. In the end, they repatriated the officers from the fort of Kera Kolla; I stayed behind at Addis Ababa. I resigned from the militia and I rented the tukul that I have already told you about. After six months I re-enlisted, but this time in the regular army. This, then, in brief, is the story of my ruckus."

I was stunned. I did not think that such dishonesty existed at that time. Signor Mandrioli often used to say that, even though it wasn't perfect, during the Fascist period the Mafia did not exist, that there were no thieves. Everything was orderly. Like a recently tidied room. Signor Antonio grimaced. "Orderly, my foot! . . . Bekelech, some Italians like to hear the strong bark of the *Maremma* sheepdog, just like the sheep do. If they hear that certain kind of barking, everything seems to be more orderly and they feel that someone is in charge."

Since that afternoon when he told me about the "ruckus," many years have gone by. Meanwhile, our friendship continued to grow stronger. He told me every detail about his time in Ethiopia. He told me about the war against the British, of the brigades from South Africa and Rhodesia, even about his imprisonment in Kenya and of his silver medal for military valor. . . . For some of his stories he swore me to silence, confessing to me that his wife and son knew nothing about them. Signor Antonio was just like an onion that you peel back, layer after layer in order to finally get to the soft heart of his incredible tie to our land. He was truly "sick for Ethiopia." However, there was one subject he never wanted to discuss: when I asked him about our Resistance, about our arbegna. Then his Ethiopian sickness was cured. Suddenly he turned into a true Italian patriot. "Bekelech," he used to say emphatically, "what could a few thousand poor souls do against our army? A well-equipped army. A European army of the twentieth century. Small skirmishes to little effect?"

"Maybe," I replied, convinced that things had been quite different.

Throughout those years, each time I returned to Ethiopia, I asked him to come with me. "If it were still a colony of ours, I would come," he replied. "But as things are . . . I'm not really interested." I would get irritated. How could he wish that our country were still in Italian hands? But I did not answer; he was too old for me not to respect him. Then, before my definitive return, one day, in the kitchen of his house, he asked me to make a promise: "Take some flowers on my behalf to the tomb of Ras Abebe Aregay."

"What?" I exclaimed, somewhat surprised.

"Yes! Yes! You heard me correctly. Some flowers on my behalf to Ras Abebe Aregay!"

"And why should I ever do that?"

"As a sign of my respect. He was a great man. A great fighter."

"But you have always said that our Resistance amounted to very little."

"Bekelech, sit down," he ordered me. "Today your ears will hear the last story from my lips." He took hold of a chair, brought it over to me, and gestured for me to sit down. "So, I have always told you that we only ever engaged in skirmishes with your Resistance. I didn't tell you the truth. Listen: I was in the regular army, close to the gorges of the Blue Nile, in a fort near the Church of Kocho Mariam. Among the Italian conscripts, there was a young man from Palermo, with a first name and family name almost the same as mine. I was Antonio Biondo and he was Antonio Biondi. One day he called me over to show me a photo of his fiancée. The previous evening the post had arrived with a column and he had received a letter. I looked at the photo: a beautiful, dark-haired girl. We chatted for a few minutes and then I went off. Almost a whole day went by. Around four o'clock in the afternoon, beyond the walls of the fort, all hell broke loose. Ras Abebe Aregay with his men were attacking us.

"I ran to the major and I asked his permission to go out with a company of Italians. He denied me permission. 'Only the Ascari can go out.'

"'Why?' I insisted. Do you know why, Bekelech? In Italy they thought that Ethiopia was entirely in our hands. Nobody knew that more than two-thirds of the country was in the hands of your Resistance. Therefore, there was no way they could justify the deaths of Italians without revealing the lie. The Ascari could die, as many as there were, but not Italians. Not even one.

"However . . . Ras Abebe Aregay knew everything—he even knew of that fact, and he had adopted certain tactics to draw us out of the fort, among which were insults in Italian. Insults of the kind that are like pins that get under your skin and give you no relief. From beyond the walls his men tossed out insults. Our men could not stand it and after a while they would go out. That's what happened that day, too.

"The major kept me in his office till the attack was over. Only then did he let me leave with the order to bring him a report of the dead and injured.

"I went out and one of the Ascari called out to me: 'Captain, come here.' I went up to him. At his feet there was a sheet. He lifted it up. Under the sheet was the dead body of Antonio Biondi. In his pocket he still had the photo of his fiancée.

"Poor man," Signor Antonio sighed, lost in thought.

"Signor Antonio, Signor Antonio," I called out to him. "Listen, I will ask you just once more, one last time: come to Ethiopia with me. A short trip. I will take you to my home."

"Bekelech, I won't come. I would never be able to come."

"And why?" I asked in a testy voice. "Because we are no longer a colony of yours?" I added.

"No, Bekelech. I lied to you about this too. I won't come because I could not look anyone in the eye. In all these years, reflecting on many things, on many events that occurred while I was there, there began to rise up inside of me a deep shame. Bekelech, I am ashamed. I am ashamed of what my country did to yours."

CHAPTER EIGHT

"So, my child, that's the end of the story of me and Signor Antonio. When you make use of it, let me know through the turtle lady. Well, my child! May God bless you for what you will do!"

And with that she went off.

I was stunned. Warriors, galloping horses, troops camped on the plains, groups of soldiers moving rapidly behind rock faces, lions, monkeys, Signor Antonio . . . the stories I had heard over those five days were beginning to run together, overlapping and blending like water on the crest of a wave. They were tossing me here and there, depriving me of my equilibrium. My mind, saturated with images, continuously spewed forth new ones, disjointed ones that faded, then blended again and suddenly resurfaced. Sharply defined and tangible. "Woi gud!" I exclaimed under my breath. "I'm going crazy."

Fortunately, Abba Chereka arrived almost immediately, with that metal clanging of his. After a brief greeting, he sat down next to me. I didn't give him time for his usual interval of silence. He was about to turn his gaze on the worshipers, with his customary serafic calm, when I began to speak. "There are rumors about me going around this courtyard," I began.

"That doesn't surprise me," he commented, keeping his eyes fixed ahead of him.

"I'm not happy about them."

"Oh, yes?" And what might these rumors be?" he asked, turning toward me.

"That I collect stories about the Italian occupation."

"And are these rumors true?" he asked, his face completely expressionless.

I did not reply. Instead I said, "The turtle lady says that confirmation of these rumors has come from your own lips."

"Child, no confirmation of such rumors has come from my lips. I only pointed out to the turtle lady the strange coincidence that so many people come to you to tell you stories about that time."

I would have liked to point out to him that it was not by pure chance that some—no, the majority of them—had come to sit next to me. Two had been sent by the turtle lady and one was the turtle lady herself. Only two had happened to come to me by chance. But who knows? Maybe even they had not come by pure chance! I was about to open my mouth—in fact it was already open—but he raised his hand to silence me. He had guessed what I was going to say to him. "Our people do not like recounting stories about the Italian occupation, even when asked to do so. They toss out a few sentences and manage to talk without revealing anything. If they opened up to you, there must have been a reason."

"Maybe there was," I said, trying to end the conversation. I was irritated that I couldn't come up with any rejoinder.

"Let's pray," he commanded. I closed my eyes and began to quietly recite the new prayer, but soon after I opened them again. That new prayer aroused in me an unpleasant feeling of agitation. Inside of me I could hear the stomping of nervous, fenced-in horses. I stopped reciting the prayer and Abba Chereka opened his eyes. "Well, that's enough for today," he said, looking at me, and he said nothing more. We stood up and we started going toward the main gate. It wasn't far. Then, from behind a hedge, the turtle lady popped out. "Mahlet, before you go home, stop by Shi Selemon's place to have some baklava. What you need is the honey and syrup of a piece of good baklava to dissipate the bitterness of our stories," she advised. I thanked her for her suggestion.

At the gate Abba Chereka asked me for my usual offering. Taking it out of my bra, I gave him the usual ten birr and he repeated the by-now-familiar phrase: "You won't regret it, my child." We went our separate ways. He went back in and I entered into the chaos of the city.

I went down the ramp that led up to the church, my ears filling with the deafening noise of the car horns. I crossed the maze of cars in transit around the rotary and I headed down the avenue. Halfway down the avenue, just past some dress shops, was the pastry shop. When was the last time I had gone in? Alemitu, Mulu, and I used to go there often, around the time of the liberation. That pastry shop had existed forever. It had always stayed open. Even during the troubling period of transition from the Derg government to the present one. The entire city would go there to sweeten their palates, as a way of relieving the fear of that uncertain future. A piece of Shi Selemon's baklava and everything seemed better.

I went in. It was just the same as the last time I had seen it: the same spacious room with its unadorned walls, the counter with the glass case full of pastries and the odd fly, the old cash register, the old espresso machine. In the center of the room, the round tables, their metal surfaces full of scratches. There were still booths around the sides of the room that, at that hour, were filled with groups of students. Even the waiters seemed the same, perhaps because of their outfits, the colors unchanged: bottle-green jackets and black pants.

I went to sit at one of the round tables and without delay, a waiter came up with a brisk step. He cleaned the table with a damp cloth and asked me what I wanted. "A piece of baklava and a glass of spiced tea," I replied. He went off and, as quickly as he had arrived, he returned to the table. In the palm of his right hand, held up high, was a tray. He lowered his hand and I was able to see the tray and the glass of tea. It was half-full of sugar. Darn it! I had forgotten to ask for tea without sugar. It was another one of those habits I had picked up in Italy. Besides learning to close a car door without slamming it, I had learned to drink tea without sugar. "In your country, do you use a shovel to add sugar?" Claudio, my university friend, used to ask. "How can you taste the tea with all that sugar? Tea is for washing out the mouth, not to make it all gooey." I had started out by reducing the amount of sugar in order to forestall his comments. In the end, I had stopped using it altogether, agreeing that he was right. It was much better in its natural form.

The waiter put down the plate with the baklava and the glass of tea on the table. "Shall I stir the sugar for you?" he asked me.

"No! No! Thanks!" I attacked the baklava with the teaspoon. The honey, mixed with syrup, was dripping from all sides, and with each mouthful it spread over my tongue. I didn't recall its being so sweet. I took a sip of tea to wash out my mouth, but even that, in spite of my not having stirred it, was too sweet. The hot liquid had melted some of the sugar. I asked for a glass of water. The attentive waiter brought me one. I ate the baklava, diluting the excessive sweetness with the water, then I paid the bill, left a tip, and went on my way.

The sweetness of the baklava should have dissipated the bitterness of the stories, so the turtle lady had said. Instead it had done nothing. My mind continued to spew out unpleasant images that kept surfacing thanks to the many stories, too many stories. They tormented me as I walked all the way home.

Once I reached home, I sat down in the inner courtyard, in a corner off to one side. Wrapped up in my own world, I ate some injera with *sigawot* in silence. I was so lost in thought that not even the ongoing chatter of all the women gathered in that courtyard reached me. That evening I had dinner with everyone, to prevent that worried look from returning to my father's eyes, but I was still immersed in my thoughts. Once dinner was over, my father and mother accompanied me to my room and we said good night at the door. I barely heard their words of blessing for the night, for dreams rich in portents for the future. I went into my room and without turning on the light, I closed the door behind me. Feeling my way, I reached the small table with the icon of the Virgin Mary, took out a candle from the box, lit it, and went to sit down on my bed. The dancing flame from the candle created shadows on the wall. Shadows that then recalled other shadows, of bodies twisted in battle, of night ambushes, of men

on the march, of chance encounters for the exchange of messages....
It was becoming an obsession with me. I knelt in front of the icon of
the Virgin Mary and begged her: "I did find the path to inner peace,
but I immediately lost it. I beg you: remove or at least diminish these
images that continue to pile up in my head." Then I got up, I slipped
into bed, and I began to repeat the new prayer. Immediately that
disturbing inner turmoil returned and the images that I was trying
to banish grew in intensity. I immediately stopped and began instead
to recite some other prayers to the Virgin Mary. I finally fell asleep
after having twisted and turned countless times.

At seven o'clock the following morning, my mother came to wake
me up, carrying the usual genfo. I had dreamed again about Abba Yacob that night. The eloquent look in my mother's eyes silently asked
the question. I replied affirmatively by nodding my head.

"I told you so, my child! He came back. Just like I said!" she answered contentedly. I lowered my head, disheartened. Yet again the
dream had been interrupted by an abrupt awakening in the middle
of the night. I told her about it but it did not seem to bother her at all.
"Describe the dream to me," she continued, a serene look on her face.

"There was that same room. This time he was at the end of the corridor, seated on a chair, next to a green trunk with two locks. There
was a strange wind, and this time the knickknacks piled up at the end
of the corridor from the previous night's dream were flying around
in the air. That's it. Then I woke up." She laughed heartily and I got
upset. "And what's so funny?"

She immediately pulled herself together, and looking down at her
hands in her lap, she tried to find an excuse. "What made me laugh
was the image of the knickknacks flying around and Abba Yacob
sitting at the end of the corridor."

I took hold of her hands and shook her. "Mother, words exchanged
years ago between Abba Yacob and me are holding me back from my
future. He is trying to explain them to me in a dream, but I always
wake up before he can speak to me! And you find this funny?"

"My daughter, you must remain calm, have patience! You mustn't
upset yourself like this."

"What are you saying? Today is the third day. Abba Chereka gave me three days. I have not found any clue, any key to free myself. And you tell me to stay calm?"

Anger was mounting inside me and she, as calm as ever, said, "It's seven o'clock—the day has just begun. You still have a lot of time ahead of you."

My anger was increasing; I tried to hold it back, but a small part of it carried over into my voice. "What good are the daytime hours to me? When I am awake I cannot stop seeing the images from the time of the Italian occupation. With all those stories they have told me . . . the prayer that Abba Chereka taught me is of no use whatsoever. All it does is create a powerful tension inside of me, as if I were about to explode. And you tell me I have plenty of time ahead of me? I have no more time. It ended when I woke up this morning."

She scolded me: "Mahlet, don't speak to me like that. I told you that Abba Chereka is a great hermit. He knows what he's talking about. He will help you to find your way, but you, for your part, must help him by having faith. Do you understand? Faith and patience! Now, that's enough. Go and wash." And then she left, almost slamming the door.

After I washed I went into the kitchen to look for my mother. "Please forgive me for speaking like that," I said to her.

She hugged me. "It doesn't matter, my child. I do understand your tension, but it's out of line. You'll see, today when you come home you will have your answer."

"Maybe . . ."

"You'll see," she repeated. "Now let's go to your room so you can eat and then go to St. George's."

Before I went out, together we lit a candle in front of the icon of the Virgin Mary. At the gate, she gave me a look of encouragement. I walked along the path. Once I reached the paved road I turned left toward the bridge. My body was as drenched in agitation as a soaked mop when it is pulled out of the water. At the bridge I boarded the first bus, only to find out that it was going in another direction. I got off at the first stop and then caught another, this time checking the destination that the ticket collector called out. All the way to St. George's I sat with my fists tightly clenched. "St. George's!" the ticket collector called out just before the rotary. I got off, crossed the rotary, went past the beggars on the outside ramp, and entered the churchyard. I did not make the sign of the cross. I did not walk around the courtyards. I did not kneel before the sacred images. I did not pray. I was too agitated.

I thought of going to sit on the stone slab under the tree and wait for Abba Chereka. That was all I was capable of doing: waiting. But then I was terrified that someone would come and offer me another story about the Italian occupation. No, I just couldn't do it. I could not wait and I would not wait. I would look for Abba Chereka.

I began to look behind the bushes until I found the turtle lady. "Good morning, my child," she exclaimed delightedly. "Did you sleep well?"

"Yes, Mother, thank God," I replied, and instead of repeating the same question to her, I asked, "Where can I find Abba Chereka?"

"At this time," she whispered, so that the worshipers nearby would not hear, "he's behind the museum. Over there." She pointed to a small building at the right edge of the garden.

He was behind the trees, behind the museum wall. He was reading his prayer book. "My child!" he exclaimed in surprise when he saw me.

Without even greeting him, I said to him, "Abba, I would like to speak to you!"

"Very good, my child, go and wait for me under the old tree. I'll be right there."

"If you wish to finish your prayers, please go ahead, but I shall wait here. I will stay next to you in silence." He raised a perplexed eyebrow, looked at me for a while, then snapped his prayer book shut and began to walk off. I remained standing there, unsure of what to do next.

"Well, my child?" he said, turning around. "Didn't you say you wanted to speak to me?" And, turning around again, he began walking in the direction of the courtyard. I followed him. He reached the old tree, sat down, and, patting his palm repeatedly on the slab, he invited me to follow suit. I accepted his invitation and then, in silence, we both turned our gaze on the slow passage of the worshipers moving around the courtyards.

Inside of me the volcano of restlessness was boiling up, just like the tension on the battlefield as everyone awaits the firing of the first shot. I stared in front of me, seeking a measure of tranquility, but that which, only a few days previously, had cast a spell on me, numbing my pain, now seemed unable to make even a dent in that unbearable tension. I was completely incapable of controlling my emotions by directing my gaze either outside of me or even inside of me. I was suspended, flying around on the wings of a strange, irritating wind.

Suddenly, almost brusquely, Abba Chereka turned to me. "Let's pray," he said, "the new prayer I taught you." I had learned from an early age that there is a time and a way to speak, to listen, and to keep quiet. Certain situations exist in which it is permissible to cry, and in others it is not. Older people exist and they are to be respected and so are hermits like Abba Chereka who are sacred to men and to God. I had learned to dance the different steps: I knew when to wait and when to move forward. With a gentle and subtle firmness I had created within myself different spaces. But in that moment, none of that existed anymore, erased like footprints in the sand when the wind blows.

Without observing the customary manners, I turned toward him. "No! No! Not that one! I won't say it. Your prayer doesn't work. It doesn't work at all," I exploded.

Without showing any disapproval of my inappropriate tone of voice, he asked me, "And why, according to you, doesn't it work?"

"Ever since I started reciting it that little bit of peace that I was able to find has been shattered. Entirely shattered. Like a glass broken into a thousand pieces."

"What do you mean?" What did I mean? I wanted to scream, but I remained silent. "My child, if you want me to help you, you must explain to me how you feel," he said.

We remained silent for a few minutes. Only a few seconds before, I had wanted to scream, and now I wanted to remain silent forever, but I spoke up. I had no choice if I wanted to get out of the hole that I was in. "At the beginning, on the first day, I felt a certain, almost pleasurable exhilaration, but then it became so strong as to be annoying, and finally it transformed itself into agitation. An agitation that doesn't allow me to think and that shakes me like women when they slap down the milk in the goatskin bag to turn it into butter. It roams around my body like a rabid dog."

Something flashed in his eyes, something almost amused, taunting. "Child, the prayer I taught you awakens in us the divine wind. That's what is agitating you inside so much. It serves to get rid of the dusty sediment that conceals us from ourselves. Something in you is buried deep somewhere and that prayer is helping to make it resurface."

"But nothing is resurfacing in me. I don't even know if there is space for it to resurface," I commented tersely.

"Child, either you trust me and explain everything to me, or we're both wasting our time here. What do you mean?" he asked me brusquely.

"I mean that I cannot get all those stories out of my head, the stories about the Italians that were told to me."

"Woi gud! Wait for me here. I'm coming right back," he said, and he went off, only to return soon after with the turtle lady. They were talking quietly. "It's hidden, embedded in some part of her or other," he was saying to her. They stopped a few feet from me.

"What should I do?" she asked.

"Go and call him."

Abba Chereka came and sat down next to me again, while the turtle lady disappeared behind a hedge. Soon after, she reappeared with a man. An old man with white hair, small and thin, wearing brand new, sparkling white clothes and holding an old masinko with signs of wear on the leather strap around his shoulder and on the side pocket that served to hold incense. The man came up and spoke to me: "If I were young, I would bow, but being old I shall greet you as best I can. Pleased to meet you, I am Aron the azmari." I stood up to offer him my hand. "Sit, sit, my child," he said to me while the turtle lady pulled up two chairs that she placed in front of me and Abba Chereka. She and Aron the azmari took their seats.

"Sing it to her the way I told you," ordered Abba Chereka. The old azmari lifted up the violin and began to turn the piece of wood to which the violin string was attached. Every so often he moved the bow to check that it was in tune. When he seemed satisfied, he put the body of the violin between his legs, took hold of the bow with one hand, positioned the fingers of the other on the string, and began to play and recite verses:

Dinner is over
The table is cleared.
Now the grown-ups
Begin to talk.

"That's enough, child,
Leave the room,"
They say over and over
To little Mahlet.

But pretending to have fallen asleep,
The little one of the household
Steals from every word
The soul of the stories.

Tella to wet the mouth,
Kolo to munch on.
The adults all together
With the elders of the household.
Of the days of his youth
And of his adulthood,
Of his fighting days
And of those that came after,

> Mixing up the events
> They tell of Abba Yacob.
>
> And when sleep finally
> Does overcome her,
> Slipping into her dreams
> What reveals itself to her
> Is a message entrusted to her
> By the elder of her heart.
> "I'm counting on you, child.
> Don't lose the story.
> Carry it to the final resting place
> Of Saints Peter and Paul."

The old azmari broke off. All three of them turned their eyes on me. "But it tells of me!" I commented in surprise.

"And so?" asked Abba Chereka.

"And so what?" I asked disconcertedly.

Abba Chereka turned to the old azmari. "We're not there yet. Go on, but don't drag it out. Go straight to the point." The old azmari repositioned his masinko and began to play and recite verses once again:

> One day from afar
> We see a tank.
> Hidden among the trees,
> We prepare ourselves to set
> The ambush as arbegna.
>
> Oh Alemtsehay,
> Brave warrior woman!
> You are the one who creates the opening.
> With deceit in your smile,
> You are the one who stops the tank.
>
> Behold, a *nech* sollato
> Pops out of the tank:
> I raised my Mauser
> And I shot him!

But when I saw the head
Of the second one appear,
With my still-smoking Mauser
I shot that one too.

But still those soldiers
Did not all fall down dead!

From the tank again they appeared.
Their hands grasped their weapons,
Their eyes fixed in our direction,
Their feet steady. They are ready to shoot.

"Protect us, help us, God the Creator."
So shout the people around us.

And behold, to our help comes the great Yacob!
He waves his sword and springs up onto them,
Swirling his weapon proudly in the air.
And then, lower down, he throws himself onto heads.
With my eyes, in these very eyes, I say,
I saw the reflection of two heads rolling down.

All together we run to the tank,
Full of weapons to the brim, so it seems to us.

There is great joy, as if a prayer had been answered.
The weapons are numerous and will suffice for many
of our warriors

Yet again Aron the azmari broke off. I was even more stunned. The song spoke of Abba Yacob, of the time when he was an arbegna. Yet again the three of them turned their eyes on me, but no words came out of my mouth. "So?" asked Abba Chereka.

I couldn't understand what they expected of me. "So what?" I asked with a note of nervousness in my voice.

"It must be embedded very deeply," he commented to the other two. "Start again, Aron. Sing the last part," he ordered. The old azmari took up the masinko and began singing again:

> All this occurred in those times of sadness,
> And when, through fighting, we conquered the oppressor,
> When the country was restored to our hands,
> The arbegna walked in procession with the flag
> That, high in the sky, had returned to sing of celebration.

> And those who, in the times of the Resistance,
> Had turned to the heavens—
> "Free our land, O Lord!
> And I shall not ask for bride,
> or betrothed, or wife"—
> Said goodbye to the world,
> Goodbye to the desires of men on earth,
> And in prayer were content to live
> To the end of their days.

> Among these great men
> We only need to recall one name:
> Haile Teklai, the leader from Holeta!

> Dear child, thus ends my song.
> Wherever you might go, do not forget
> Your elders, who fought back then.
> Like a star let them guide your pride
> Now and forever till the end of the days to come.

The song had come to an end but I was just as devoid of ideas as I was at the beginning. They looked at me. I lowered my face. "I don't understand, I just don't understand," I lamented.

"All right then," said Abba Chereka. He slid a hand into the side pocket of his tunic and pulled out some money. "Here is sixty birr. All the money from your offerings."

I trembled, thinking that he was returning the money to me because I was a lost cause. "Don't you want it?"

"I never asked you for it for myself, you know. It was money that I was saving for you. Now you will need it and I'm giving it back to you."

This man had the power to confuse me. "And what should I do with it?"

"Buy some notebooks and write. Mahlet, you must write down all the stories that you have heard over the course of these days, and not only those."

There it was again, that fixation with using the stories from the Italian occupation. This time I was really going to get angry. "Listen, all of you, I'm not going to write down a thing."

In reply, he slipped the other hand under his tunic, passing it through the opening at his neck, and took out a notebook with a rough, aquamarine cover. "Take this, it's yours," he said.

Something in me burst wide open. I knew that notebook. I took hold of it with a trembling hand. "The notebook of the battles," I said in a tiny voice. "I had totally forgotten about it." I slowly caressed the cover, all the way down to the lower edge, then I opened it. Inside, in tiny handwriting, were listed some names: Tekeze, Dembaguina, Enda Selassie, Tembien.... I began to weep, tears of liberation. "The promise. I had forgotten it. This is what I must do. Keep my promise." On Abba Chereka's solemn face, for a single instant, for the shortest of instants, flashed the vague hint of a smile.

"I have to go," I suddenly said, clutching the aquamarine notebook tightly in my hand. The turtle lady laughed and, turning to Abba Chereka and to Aron the azmari, observed, "Boy, it was certainly very well concealed!"

I got up and went toward the exit. As I walked away I could hear Abba Chereka's blessing—"May the light follow you"—and the turtle lady's suggestion: "There's a good stationery store at the corner. Just past Shi Selemon's pastry shop."

With wings on my feet, I reached the stationery store. "How many notebooks can I buy for sixty birr?" I asked. "The big notebooks."

The shop assistant opened her eyes wide in amazement. "For sixty birr?"

"Yes, for sixty birr."

"Many. Thirty," she replied in surprise.

"Please let me have them."

"Thirty?" she asked, again in surprise.

"Yes, thirty."

"Let me go and get you a box," she said, and disappeared in the back room, only to return with a box full of notebooks. I picked up the box, slipped in the aquamarine notebook, paid, and left.

A taxi pulled up alongside the curb. "Hi, sister! Can I take you home?" It was the taxi driver with the broken car door. I got in. "Don't slam the door," he said to me. "I've just had it repaired." I began to laugh and so did he.

The taxi driver let me off right in front of the path to our house. I paid for the ride, got out, and went down the path. The front gate was closed. I knocked hard so they could hear. The box was heavy and I wanted to wait there as little as possible. My father came to open the gate for me, out of breath. "What are you doing here at home at this time of day?" I asked in surprise.

"Child, have you forgotten that today is Saturday? I don't work on Saturdays." His eyes fell on the box. "And you? What are you doing with that box of notebooks?" he asked in turn.

"I have to write," I answered.

He didn't give me time to add another word. "Sellas! Sellas! Come here fast!" he began to shout. "Come and see. She's remembered! She's remembered."

I saw one of the doors of the house open and my mother came running out. She hugged me and began to laugh, her same laugh from that morning, and everything became clear.

"But you knew all along?" I asked.

"Sure," replied my father proudly.

"And you let me stew all this time?" I asked, offended.

"Not here, daughter," said my mother gently. "Come, let's go and sit under the ancestors' tree."

I followed them, holding the box tightly in my hands, not wanting to give it to my father. "She has remembered everything," he said to the women in the inner courtyard. Our neighbors got up. "You'll have lots to do," they said, and they all disappeared together.

We sat down in the shade of the ancestors' tree. Aunt Fanus was there, Aunt Abeba, Mulu, Alemitu, Uncle Mesfin . . . all of them. My mother began to explain. "We knew the whole story, but we couldn't tell you anything. You had to figure it out for yourself. That was what had been decided by Abba Chereka and Abba Yacob. They were sure that, because of the bond that existed between you and Abba Yacob, you would follow every clue that he would leave you. You could have remembered your promise at any point in time. If that had happened, the stories you had not heard would eventually be told to you. As you must have guessed, those people were all sent to you. But instead, you got to the very end without figuring it out!"

"If only you knew how concerned I was for you," said my father, intervening in the conversation.

Aunt Fanus and my mother laughed. "Every evening," continued my mother, "he wanted to come and tell you everything. I had to hold him back by force. Every evening I would say to him, 'What kind of elders will we become if we don't master the art of waiting? Wait and have faith.'"

Now I felt better, but I badly wanted to be hugged. My mother noticed it and put her arm around my shoulders. "Take heart! The biggest hurdle has been overcome. Now all you have to do is write."

I savored the warmth of her hug for a few minutes, then I got up. "I'm going. I will start immediately."

"Would you like me to bring you lunch and a thermos of tea to your room?" she asked. I nodded.

With the box of notebooks in my hands, I went through the house. Once I reached the veranda, I turned right and went on down to my room. I opened the door and went in. How strange. Apart from the addition of a desk on which I put down the box of notebooks, and a chair, I hadn't noticed that the room was laid out exactly like old Yacob's room in Debre Zeit, and yet my mother had told me it was so. In one corner there was a small table with the icon of the Virgin Mary, and behind it, half-hidden, other icons of the saints. The bed frame with the mattress, the shelves on the wall next to the bed, the spiders in the corners, and the green trunk with the locks. I went up to it, opened it, and put my hand inside. My fingers touched the soft material of a shemma. I ran them over the wavy folds, then I thrust my hand down into the next layer and I explored every inch. I went deeper—there was another shemma. Once again, wavy folds of cotton cloth woven by the Dorze people in Chencha. I went carefully through every layer, even of the second shemma, and then I moved on to the third. I continued, slipping my hand under the third shemma. I found a rougher material, cotton used for shirts. I fingered collars, pockets, buttons, the fine thread of the seams, and darned patches. I pushed my hand further down and found some pants, two with a belt, others without, and still more side pockets, back pockets with buttons, seams, darned patches . . . and under the pants in a corner was a small rectangular cardboard box. The candle box. I went back to the middle of the trunk and I began to finger the small shirt pockets until I found what I was looking for. I thrust my hand into a small pocket and took out a rolled-up envelope. I unrolled it. I opened it. Inside was that sheet full of stamps, the beginning of old Yacob's story on that morning so many years before. I laid it out on the desk, next to the cardboard box. Tears of nostalgia and emotion were pricking my eyes.

At that moment my mother came in with a tray. She smiled when she saw my hand resting on the Submission Paper. An understanding smile. She put down the tray on the small table where the icon of the Virgin Mary was and came over to hug me. "That paper," I said through my tears, "was the beginning of everything."

"The paper for Rosa. Your Abba Yacob was a great man. A man capable of great love. He was like a giant sycamore tree in the yard of a farmer's house. He gave shelter and shade to us all. Now, he is no more, and now it's our turn, us, your father, me, your uncles and aunts, to begin our journey toward becoming wise elders. Who knows if we will live up to his memory."

"True, a great man," I repeated.

"Well, now I must be off. You have work to do." We took our arms away from each other. She was about to leave the room when she remembered something. "There are still two things I have to tell you. The first is not important. This morning I was laughing because of the trunk in your dreams. I was surprised that you weren't able to make the connection to this trunk at the foot of your bed. That promise of yours was really buried deep down! The second is important, though. Now that you know everything, have you asked yourself who Abba Chereka is?"

"Mama, I have had enough surprises for today. Don't make me figure it out. Just tell me."

"He's Haile Teklai. Yacob's commander during the Resistance, the one who became a monk after the liberation."

I pushed her out the door. "Well, all I can say is that you really fooled me." I took a candle out of the box, lit it, and put it in front of the icon of the Virgin Mary and went back to the desk. I placed the cardboard box on the floor. I took out the aquamarine notebook and a big notebook and I placed them next to the Submission Paper. I opened the window and sat down. In a corner of the desk there was a box full of pens. They had thought of absolutely everything. I took one, opened the big notebook, and began to write.

CHAPTER NINE

I WAS BORN IN THE TOWN OF DEBRE ZEIT, THIRTY MILES from Addis Ababa. There are five lakes within the city limits and the outlying areas—some are surrounded by houses and some are at the edge of town. At sunset flamingos fly across the sky, going from one lake to the other, and the deep pink of their wings blends with the colors of the setting sun. They fly at the end of the day, in the hours when the sky turns the color of amber, along with flocks of other birds. But you can always recognize them because, when they are flying, their legs stick out from their bodies like two parallel reeds etched against the sky. You can also recognize them by the noise they make: that ridiculous screeching sound that goes on throughout the night, thus letting the jackal know their exact location.

Debre Zeit is the city of lakes and of the great sycamore tree on Lake Hora where, in Meskerem, the kallicha celebrate the end and the beginning of the year by giving thanks and taking offerings to the god of the lake. As a child, I used to go there often with my cousins to see our images reflected in the waters inhabited by the spirit. The priests said that the spirit was none other than the devil and that we should not go near the water. But we used to go there secretly, to poke among the reeds, to follow the flight of the kingfishers in order to figure out where to cast our fishing rods made out of twine and small salvaged nails. At night, when everything was cloaked in darkness, we were gripped by fear. Each one of us, at some point, was convinced she had seen the devil with his black wings take to the sky from Lake Hora, and fly above us in a menacing way.

Debre Zeit is the city of dust, of flowers that, once faded, fall from the plants and swirl around, carried by whirlwinds.

Dust, flowers, spices from the market, pink pepper trees, a pungent smell of urine at the street corners, and a sign, painted on the wall of a house near the bus station: "Only dogs piss in the streets." Our home is right there, near the one with the sign, near the bus station. It is light blue with dark blue doors and windows.

It is on a slope. It is a two-story home in the front, where the main courtyard is, along with the old mango tree, the bougainvilleas with their purple flowers climbing up the main wall of the front of the house, coffee trees, and other flowers and trees whose names I do not know. There is only one floor in the back, where there is the kitchen and the inner courtyard with the vegetable patch and the chickens.

I grew up in a big family that lived spread out over half the neighborhood. During the day when the men were out working, the women called each other from their courtyards to get together and drink coffee. And the three elders of our home were always there. They sat in a corner to one side, wrapped in their cocoon-like shemma, looking distinctly like protective birds. They took note of everything around them and blessed the three cups of coffee for the women.

The three elders . . . I remember them always being there. As if they had existed since the beginning of time.

There was old Selemon, my father's uncle, my grandfather's brother. In his younger days he had been a farmer. His hands, the palms all rough, still smelled of earth. They were big hands, belonging to a body that exuded strength, even in his old age. He had a round head with a cloud of short, white hair. Under his shemma he wore military clothes: a sweater, a shirt, pants, and boots. "They last forever," he used to say.

Then there was old Yohanes, old Selemon and my grandfather's brother and my father's uncle. He was tall and thin, and his face was oval in shape with a long nose, curved at the tip, and two small eyes. To my child's eyes, he looked like a parrot, and when he spread out his thin arms, I expected him to fly off and glide over our roof. When he was younger he had been a teacher. The first teacher from his village. He liked to tell stories to make people laugh. And he made people laugh so hard that they had to clutch their stomachs.

And lastly, him, my favorite. Old Yacob. Brother to my great-grandmother Helen, my mother's grandmother.

One big tooth in a triangular face wrinkled up and weathered by time. There was a font of precious knowledge nestling in between those wrinkles. He had sweet eyes, a gentle gaze, with no sharp angles, softened by all the many things he had seen.

And the three of them, the venerable elders of our household, used to tell me over and over again, all through my childhood, while the women were drinking coffee, "When you grow up you will be the one to tell our stories." Then, one day old Yacob called me into his room, and I made a promise. A solemn oath in front of his icon of the Virgin Mary. And so, that is why today I am telling you his story. Which is also my story. But now, yours as well.

The Ethiopian-Italian writer and performer **Gabriella Ghermandi** was born in Addis Ababa in 1965 and moved to Italy in 1979. For many years she has lived in Bologna, Italy, her father's native city. She has published short stories in a wide variety of journals and magazines, and is also a playwright. In recent years, she has focused on oral storytelling and performance in Italy and abroad, and has also presented at several major universities in the United States.

She was chosen to be part of the jury panel for the 2014 Neustadt Prize for Literature, the most prestigious international literary award given in the United States. Ghermandi is a founding member of the editorial board of *El-Ghibli,* an online journal of migration literature.

Her debut novel, *Queen of Flowers and Pearls,* based on the stories of Ethiopian patriots fighting against the Italian occupation and of Italians involved in the history of that period, was originally published in Italian in 2007 and has won several prizes in Italy.

She is also the creator of the Atse Tewodros Project, which fuses traditional Ethiopian music with jazz and other Western musical expressions to open up dialogue and exchange.

Giovanna Bellesia-Contuzzi is Professor of Italian Language and Literature at Smith College. She is translator, with Victoria Offredi Poletto, of *Little Mother* (IUP, 2011).

Victoria Offredi Poletto is Senior Lecturer in Italian Emerita at Smith College.